The Maiden of Mayfair

THE GRESHAM CHRONICLES

The Widow of Larkspur Inn
The Courtship of the Vicar's Daughter
The Dowry of Miss Lydia Clark

TALES OF LONDON

The Maiden of Mayfair

Lawana Blackwell

The Maiden of Mayfair

BOOKSPAN LARGE PRINT EDITION

⬧BETHANYHOUSE
Minneapolis, Minnesota

This Large Print Book carries the
Seal of Approval of N.A.V.H.

LAWANA BLACKWELL is a full-time writer with eight published books, including the bestselling GRESHAM CHRONICLES. She and her husband live in Baton Rouge, Louisiana and have three sons.

This book is lovingly dedicated to
my mother-in-law and father-in-law,

Zita and Edwin Blackwell,

whose devotion to each other
is a precious thing to witness.

Part One

August 4 , 1869

London

❧ One ❧

The privilege of joining Mrs. Abbot's weekly forays to the greengrocer's was granted with the understanding that two rules be obeyed without exception. First, there would be no "sampling" of any fruit or vegetable, no matter how meager the breakfast porridge ration happened to have been.

Secondly, talking to strangers was strictly forbidden. Such a rule would not be necessary were the Saint Matthew Methodist Foundling Home for Girls located in fair Kensington or even bustling Charing Cross. But in the shadowy northern part of Drury Lane, with its crumbling tenements, gin shops, and abandoned factories, more than one girl had been approached by a seedy character offering "good wages" in exchange for her virtue, youth, and health.

Sarah Matthews was sorting out the best potatoes—which, considering the state of

Mr. Brody's merchandise, meant those not quite so soft or covered with gnarly eyes—when a voice interrupted her concentration.

"Got a penny, Miss?"

She looked to her right, her left hand automatically hiding in a fold of her gray linsey-woolsey gown. The boy seemed not much older than herself, though rotted teeth and an accumulation of grime made it impossible to tell. Sarah shook her head and went back to sorting. Thankfully, Mrs. Abbot was still conversing with Mr. Brody over last week's bill. "Please go away!" she urged under her breath. "You'll have me in trouble!"

"A farthing?"

With a sigh, she turned to him again and froze. Beggars were as plentiful as coughs in Drury Lane, but what captured her attention was the knot tied at the end of the ragged sleeve. He raised his arm for her closer inspection, obviously in the hopes of gaining her pity and the coin she did not possess.

"Got it caught in a cutter at th' match factory on Bow," he said with a shrug.

Tears stung Sarah's eyes. She tried to follow all rules to the best of her ability but could not stop herself from whispering, "I'm sorry. But I've no—"

"Sarah!"

Guiltily she looked up at Mrs. Abbot, who stood with Mr. Brody near the turnip crates. She could hear scurrying footsteps behind her. "I'm sorry, Mrs.—"

"You get outer here!" Mr. Brody shook his fist in the direction of the fleeing boy. "I'll have the police on you!"

"Oh, please don't, sir," Sarah pleaded. "He was just asking for a farthing."

Ignoring her, the greengrocer turned again to Mrs. Abbot and muttered, "This were a decent place to live when I were a boy. Now the thieves is thick as flies."

"There is more than one kind of thief, Mr. Brody," Mrs. Abbot said in a quiet voice.

In the dead silence that followed, Sarah cringed inwardly at the implied accusation. It wasn't that she feared injury to Mr. Brody's feelings, for it was well-known even among the girls of Saint Matthew's that the Irishman overcharged for his stale produce. But he towered over Mrs. Abbot's middle-aged form, and the rage mottling his beefy face made Sarah fear that he would do her physical harm or, at the very least, refuse their patronage.

"What is that you're sayin', Mrs. Abbot?" he demanded.

Sarah hastened to the cook's side. Not that she had the brawn to defend anyone, but at least she could pull her away if necessary.

Fortunately, Mrs. Abbot backed down. "I meant nothing," she said, then turned to Sarah while Mr. Brody glowered over her shoulder. "Have you finished with the potatoes?"

"Almost . . ."

"Well, I'll help you. I've got to get back to my kitchen." Five minutes later Mrs. Abbot was dropping coins into Mr. Brody's hand and reminding him meekly to place the greens on top in the delivery wagon this time instead of allowing the potatoes to crush them.

"Will you tell Mrs. Forsyth?" Sarah asked, lagging at the cook's elbow because walking side by side was hindered by the congestion on the narrow pavement.

"That you spoke to the boy?" Mrs. Abbot slowed her steps and turned her face to the

side as much as possible. "You know better, Sarah. Why did you do it?"

His hand, Sarah wanted to say, while her
own left one stayed burrowed in the coarse
folds of her gown.

"Well . . . ?"

Before she could reply she caught sight
of the boy, sitting at the base of a broken
streetlamp. He raised his head to catch
Mrs. Abbot's eye while lifting his knotted
sleeve. "A penny, kind lady?"

Mrs. Abbot's steps resumed their brisk
pace, for a penny in a beggar's pocket
meant one less for the food needed to feed
over sixty orphans and workers at Saint
Matthew's. Sarah averted her eyes from the
grime-covered face. But a curious thing
happened when they were some six feet
past him. The cook halted abruptly and
turned to Sarah.

"Watch where yer goin', old woman!"
sneered an old man in worn sailor's garb
who had to sidestep to keep from colliding
with the two of them.

Mrs. Abbot paid him no mind. Anyone
who became unnerved at every angry voice
in Drury Lane was a prime candidate for
Bedlam. "His hand?"

"An accident at the match factory," Sarah whispered.

With a sigh Mrs. Abbot withdrew her purse from her apron pocket, both hands holding it protectively close. "You may give him a farthing. It's all we can spare."

"Yes, Mrs. Abbot. Thank you."

It was the first time Sarah had held even so meager a coin, yet she was more than willing to surrender it to the boy, who gave her a smile and tipped the bill of his worn cap. "God'll bless you fer it!" were the words that accompanied her back to Mrs. Abbot's side.

He has already, she thought, for she could have easily shared the poor lad's fate.

———

She had not sailed far on the deep,
Before a king's ship she chanced to
  meet.

Naomi Doyle kept her voice soft and low on the staircase of the Berkeley Square town house. She was fond of singing but only did so when no one was in earshot, for a schoolmistress had told her when she was nine that the only way she could hope to stay on key would be to keep a brass one in her pocket.

Oh all you sailors, come tell me true,
Is my sweet William on board with
*   you?*

She paused at the ground-floor landing and looked down the corridor. Marie Prewitt had stationed herself outside the sitting room in an armchair. As she drew closer, Naomi realized she was asleep, with needlework lying idle upon her lap. Delicately she cleared her throat. The lady's maid let out a snort and jerked up her head.

"*Qui est la!*" Marie exclaimed, blinking, then narrowed her eyes. "Why must you slip about so! Like a ghost you pop up from nowhere and startle me!"

Your snoring may have something to do with it, Naomi thought but restrained herself from saying. Not out of intimidation, for skilled cooks were in high demand in Mayfair, London's most prestigious residential district. But after having been reared in a household where disharmony was as thick and pervasive as London fog, she did all she could to keep her temper in check and avoid confrontation. So instead she lifted the hem of her skirt just high enough to reveal a pair of laced brown leather shoes.

"These are why you didn't hear me."

"*Men's* shoes?"

"Actually . . . boy's." Naomi's feet were as small as her body was slender. "They're for playing cricket, the shop assistant said, but they make the kitchen floor feel like a cloud."

"They are hideous."

"No one but Trudy sees them when I'm cooking."

Marie wrinkled her nose primly. "If I were the last person on earth, even then I would never wear anything so *gauche*."

Naomi had no difficulty believing that. They were both in their early thirties, but while her own toilette had shortened over the years to a twisting of her strawberry-blond hair into a comb, Marie still plastered meticulous spit curls across her forehead and fastened hairpieces among her looped braids. Were the gulf between them not so wide, Naomi would have advised her that a pleasant expression would do more for her appearance—and consume far less time.

"Will you please stand aside?" she said with a glance up at the door. "Mrs. Blake asked me to look in on her after lunch."

"Later. Madame wishes to see no one at present."

"With all due respect, I would rather hear that from her."

Marie's dark ringlets quivered with the shake of her head. She waved a hand in the direction of the staircase. "I forbid it. Go back to your kitchen and I shall send for you."

This was too much. In the hierarchy of service, a lady's maid commanded higher status than a cook. But Naomi had little patience for priggery. "Miss Prewitt, you will kindly remove yourself," she said with controlled calmness, "or you'll be fetching your own trays from now on."

Panic filled the amber gold eyes, for Marie could not bring herself to condescend to dining in the servants' hall with the others. Naomi obliged her with trays delivered up the dumbwaiter—not because Mrs. Blake required it, but for selfish reasons. Mealtimes were simply more pleasant without her.

She had to step back as Marie rose to her feet and pulled the chair aside by the arm with shrill scraping along the lustrous oak floor. "Thank you," Naomi told her, wincing out of pity for the parlormaid who would have to wax the area again.

Marie only folded her arms under her generous bosom and looked away.

The voice that answered Naomi's knock was so soft that she wasn't sure if her ears were hearing *Who is there?* or *Go away!*

"It's Naomi, Madam. You wished to see me about the dinner party menu."

Again, an unintelligible reply. She had no choice but to turn the knob and slip inside. The curtains were drawn and the lamp extinguished. Mrs. Blake sat on the divan, a figure in black, looking very out of place against the cheerful honeysuckle-patterned upholstery.

"I said I did not wish to be disturbed," her employer said in a fragile voice.

"Why, Mrs. Blake . . . what's wrong? Is it your rheumatism? I could get some—"

"Nothing is wrong. Leave me now."

But Naomi could not obey in good conscience. She reached back to close the door, ignoring Marie's protests from the corridor. "It's not good to sit alone in the dark with your troubles, Madam. Won't you allow me to open the drapes?"

"No."

"Is there nothing I can do for you?"

After a space of silence, the woman asked, "Can you turn back time and give me my life to live over?"

Naomi crossed the carpet in her silent shoes, and without being invited to do so, she perched herself on the edge of the divan next to her mistress. It was the first time she had taken such a liberty in her fourteen years of employment. "Would that we all could have a second go-around. Regret is a hard burden to bear."

Mrs. Blake clutched a black-bordered handkerchief so tightly in one hand that the blue veins stood out starkly against the spotted skin. Black lace covered her gray chignon, and fine wrinkles now webbed the cheeks that were once as clear and smooth as porcelain. Her eyes, like chips of pale blue ice, were rimmed in red. "How would *you* know?"

The face of a young man entered

Naomi's mind from so many years ago. She was as flighty as a goose at seventeen and unable to bear the mockery her family made of the severe lisp in his voice. The last she had heard he owned a bakery up in Leicester and was happily married with several children. And only one man had attempted to court her since—a loud, boorish factory bailiff. "I'm not unfamiliar with regret, Madam."

Sighing, the older woman rubbed her brow. "I just came from the churchyard. It's been nine years. Nine years today."

How could I have forgotten? Naomi glanced at a portrait on the east wall of a young man dressed in a scarlet hunting coat and cord breeches, with a hound lounging serenely at his feet. "I'm so sorry."

"He would have been thirty-two on Christmas past, you know. I used to tell him that only the most special people were born on Christmas Day." There was pleading in the liquid eyes fastened upon Naomi's face, as if they begged her to understand the depth of her loss.

"Yes, Madam," was all Naomi could say. Even for kindness' sake she could not offer the usual comfort—that her son was safe and happy in heaven. It would be akin to blasphemy after the way Master Jeremy lived his life.

"He was such a good boy at heart," Mrs. Blake murmured, wiping her nose with her handkerchief. "So trusting. So easily led by his friends. If not for them, he would never have been there that night."

The *there* to which she referred was Haymarket, where Jeremy Blake was attacked by robbers after leaving a brothel. Naomi touched the blue-veined hand. "You mustn't torment yourself. He wouldn't have wanted that." That seemed not quite so disingenuous, for perhaps there had been some fragment of affection in his heart toward the mother who doted upon him.

Pathetically Mrs. Blake seized upon that condolence and nodded, a wistful smile at her lips. "No, he never wanted me to be sad."

"See? So why don't you—"

The smile faded. "But you don't know how it is, being all alone with no family."

That was so, for Naomi did have sisters and cousins in various stages of distemper with one another all over England. And, of course, sixteen-year-old William, who would be leaving to study science at Lincoln College at Oxford in two months. She had fetched her nephew from Leicester seven years ago after a scarlet fever epidemic claimed the lives of his parents and infant brother. And he had been under Naomi's guardianship ever since.

Mrs. Blake, on the other hand, had no remaining siblings nor had her late husband, Arthur, who passed away of apoplexy two years ago. The love they must have shared in the beginning found other outlets over the years—his in an immensely successful shipping line, and hers was lavished upon their son.

"You have your friends," Naomi reminded her. "And you'll have such a fine time with them next Tuesday. I've just come across a recipe for *Salmon a la Genevese*—"

"My friends." The sorrow in Mrs. Blake's voice turned to bitterness. "Augusta Stafford decided to leave for Sussex early with her brood. It wouldn't occur to her that I might care to winter away from London as well."

You would never leave this house for that long. It was her only remaining link to her son. The self-pity was beginning to grate upon Naomi's nerves. "But that still leaves Mrs. Gill and—"

"And were it not for my money, I daresay they would not grant me a nod in the park! Besides, they prattle on incessantly about their children and grandchildren."

Not to mention Mrs. Fowler trying to hire away your cook, Naomi added silently. And for almost a third again over her present wages. The woman had even offered a position to William. Naomi felt there was nothing wrong with taking advantage of such opportunities and might have been interested were she not aware of the long procession of cooks through the Fowler kitchen over the years.

"Now, now, Madam. It's the day that has made you sad. Why don't you sit in the garden? It's quite pleasant in the shade. And I'll bring you a cup of tea."

For a second Mrs. Blake seemed to consider this. But then her shoulders rose and fell with another sigh. "No. Leave me."

"Very well, Madam." Naomi stood. She was halfway across the room when an unsettling thought gave her pause just long enough to alter the rhythm of her steps. Just as quickly she dismissed it and continued. But her hand was no sooner on the doorknob when the thought returned, more insistently. *Is this from you, Father?*

"Naomi?" The voice from behind had an irritated tone.

Releasing the knob, Naomi turned. The subject had been a forbidden one for over thirteen years. By bringing it up she could be sacked on the spot. Even though positions in other households—besides the Fowlers'—were out there, she rather liked working for Mrs. Blake, who never interfered with the way she ran the kitchen and generously allowed William time off for schooling.

If you don't speak about it, who will? asked the voice inside her, becoming impossible to ignore. She crossed the carpet again.

"What is it, Naomi?" Mrs. Blake asked, frowning. "I thought I made it clear that I've changed my mind about that dinner party."

"May I sit again?"

Mrs. Blake gestured with her hand, and Naomi perched herself in the same spot. "Forgive me for speaking bluntly, but it is very possible that you do have family."

"I beg your pardon?"

"I'm referring to Mary Tomkin, Madam."

The lined cheeks turned ashen. "What has she to do with me?"

More than you care to admit, Naomi thought. True, Master Jeremy had been the one to take advantage of the scullery maid, but it was Mrs. Blake who dismissed her when it became obvious she was carrying a child.

"She was a strumpet," Mrs. Blake said. "I'll not have women like that in my employ."

"She was barely fifteen." Mary Tomkin might have been silly and flirtatious around Master Jeremy, but in Naomi's opinion he bore the greater responsibility, being five years older at the time. "And if her child is still living, it would be your grandchild."

"That's simply not true. Jeremy promised me he had nothing to do with her."

In for a penny, in for a pound, Naomi thought. She might very well find herself packing her trunk tonight, but the pump had been primed. She would speak her piece now after so many years. "Begging your pardon, Madam, but would you expect him to say anything else? Don't forget, Mary and I shared a room."

Naomi was a brand-new kitchen maid back then. When her warnings to the girl about Master Jeremy's flatteries and little gifts had no effect, she even dared to approach Mrs. Blake with her worries.

"My son was reared to be courteous to the servants" had been the woman's frosty reply. *"And he's certainly above amorous entanglements with scullery maids."*

It had been difficult enough to speak on Mary's behalf in those days. What Naomi had not been able to tell Mrs. Blake, because she so desperately needed her position, was that she, too, had been the object of her son's attempted "amorous entanglements" to the point that she would not walk out in the garden alone at night for fear of meeting up with him.

"Fifteen years old," Naomi pressed. "Still a child herself."

This time Mrs. Blake did not deny her probable relationship to Mary Tomkin's offspring. "Don't forget. Mr. Blake was just as adamant as I was about it," she said defensively. "Besides, I only did what would have been done in any other home."

True, Naomi thought. The surest way an unmarried female servant could be dismissed would be to turn up in a family way. Only God knew how many of those situations involved the sons of the household. "It was a difficult situation," she admitted.

"Then why do you bring it up? It's very cruel of you, Naomi, to torment an old woman so."

"Cruel?" Naomi shook her head. *At least I've a bit of money saved to tide William and me over.* "Foolhardy, perhaps, considering you can sack me on the spot. It just seemed the right thing to say, with your sitting here grieving."

"Well, you've only made matters worse."

Stifling a sigh, Naomi rose to her feet. "Then I do beg your pardon."

"I'll have that tea now," Mrs. Blake said in a peevish tone.

"Very well, Madam."

When Naomi reached the door this time, Mrs. Blake added, "And you might as well have Marie go down with you for it. She has nothing better to do."

Any small satisfaction Naomi would have gotten from that order was overshadowed by a wearying sense of failure. She was so certain that God had directed her to speak. But she wondered now if she had been

guided instead by her own guilt over not informing Mrs. Blake of her son's advances
toward her back when that information
could have possibly helped Mary.

By the time she had reached the kitchen
and dispatched a sulking Marie with a tray
and teapot, she was feeling a measure of
comfort. *God's ways are not our ways*, she
reminded herself. And, knowing how people generally balked at anything that threatened to lure them from the routine of their
lives, what had she expected? Mrs. Blake
to clasp her heart and gush with gratitude
over the reminder that she could have a
grandchild somewhere in the slums of London?

A seed had been planted. Whether Mrs.
Blake chose to nurture it or allow it to die
for lack of interest was in her own hands.
God was the One who planted the seeds,
but He generally left the tending of them to
people.

❧ *Two* ❧

"As you can see, Miss Doyle . . ." Cookware peddler Mr. Sutton said almost two months later, the curled ends of his mustache quivering with every accolade, "Perkins Patented Stock Pot's unique strained tap allows you to collect the broth after the fat has settled at the top of your gravies, thus saving the tedium and inefficiency of skimming with a spoon."

"A clever idea," Naomi agreed, her slender fingers turning the handle above the tap of the cast-iron pot on the kitchen worktable.

"Solid brass that is, Miss Doyle." His hazel eyes glinted with anticipated victory, just as his oiled hair glinted in the lamplight above. "And you have the famous Perkins Patented Cookware guarantee. Full replacement up to five years and free mending for life."

"That sounds like something we could

use, Naomi," Trudy said from the other end of the table, where she sat peeling beetroot. The scullery maid was a medium-framed young woman of twenty-three with coarse blond hair, several moles dotting otherwise clear cheeks, and round brown eyes as moist looking as a spaniel's.

"Hmm." Naomi lifted the lid and peered inside. "And whose life would you be referring to, Mr. Sutton? Mrs. Blake's, mine, or the pot's?"

He chuckled. "Why, the life of the pot."

I like the handles on the sides, she thought, replacing the lid. "And how long would that be?"

"Until it's no longer usable, of course."

"But then you would mend it and make it usable again, yes?"

Mr. Sutton stroked his chin contemplatively. "Well . . . yes."

"So that means the guarantee should never expire?" Naomi asked.

Making a gesture of surrender with his hands, he said, "I've forgotten what an astute customer you are, Miss Doyle. The Perkins Patented Cookware guarantee will apply for as long as you wish it to. I shall personally make note of our agreement on the certificate in the event that the question arises in the future."

"That would be very good of you, Mr. Sutton."

"Does that mean you're ready to put this remarkable innovation to use at once?"

Naomi gave him an apologetic smile. "I'm afraid Mrs. Bacon is away for the morning."

His face fell. "Away?"

"She's seeing one o' them oculists about a new pair of spectacles," Trudy offered unnecessarily, for no matter where the housekeeper happened to be, "away" was still "away."

"So you'll have to bring it back on your next rounds," Naomi told him. "With the signed certificate, please."

"A whole month without the convenience of the patented tap and strainer." Mr. Sutton blew out his cheeks. "And I cannot promise I'll have it in stock next time. No doubt you're familiar with the saying, 'He who hesitates is lost'?"

"There is a saying here, too, Mr. Sutton, that household expenditures over the costs of food and small utensils must be approved by Mrs. Bacon."

He sighed heavily and closed his eyes as if hearing of the loss of a dear friend. But when they shot open again, hope had replaced the despair. "What if I left it here for her inspection? If Mrs. Bacon approves, I'll collect the money next month. If not, you can just set the pot aside in a cupboard until then."

Naomi considered that. As she did not often pressure the housekeeper for extra expenditures, she was almost positive she would agree.

"It would save us a lot o' work, Naomi." Trudy's tone was hopeful.

"Write out your certificate, Mr. Sutton," Naomi said.

The peddler smiled and produced a pen and tablet from his coat pocket with a flourish. As he wrote, Naomi went to her spice cupboard and measured out a few cloves into a square of brown paper. When she had inspected the certificate to her satisfaction, she accompanied him to the tradesmen's door, leading to a flight of steps up to Berkeley Street.

"It is always a pleasure doing business with you, Miss Doyle," he said as she handed him his felt bowler hat from the wall rack.

"For me as well, Mr. Sutton." First sending a glance back over her shoulder, Naomi took a half-step closer and raised herself on her toes to whisper. "Have you many more calls to make today?"

He looked surprised. Then a smile spread under his waxed mustache. "Not any that can't wait, Miss Doyle," he whispered. "And I must say, I've always admired your fine blue eyes and trim little figure."

Heat rushed through Naomi's cheeks. She considered striking him or at least abandoning the courtesy she had intended to pay him. But rather than have him leave with an incorrect assumption, she pulled the folded paper from her apron pocket and handed it over. "I thought you might care to have some cloves, Mr. Sutton." His expression went blank, so she was compelled to explain as succinctly as possible. "Your breath."

"Oh!" Now it was his cheeks that flushed. "Yes, th-thank you."

"You're welcome," she said while reaching beyond him to open the door.

"I . . . I had pickled tongue for lunch," he stammered. "With onions."

"That will do it every time, Mr. Sutton. Do pay my regards to Mrs. Sutton."

She was just guessing about the wife, but his expression told all. "Yes . . . well . . ." He put on his hat and started through the doorway, only to turn again. "That was what I assumed you meant all along, Miss Doyle," he said, not quite meeting her eyes. "The breath, I mean."

"Just chew on a clove now and again, Mr. Sutton."

When the door closed, she walked back toward the table from which Trudy gave her a knowing little smile. "I heard you whispering up there."

"Peel your beetroot, Trudy," Naomi told her.

The bell from the parlor tinkled just as chambermaid Hester Campbell stepped inside the room. Trudy's cousin was a pretty girl of nineteen, with holly green eyes and corkscrews of carrot-red hair escaping here and there from her lace cap. Her teeth were small and white, and her gums showed whenever she laughed. But laughter did not appear imminent. "It's you the

Missus wants to see," she said to Naomi in her high-pitched girlish voice. "And she's in a foul mood. I thought she would snap my head off."

"Yes?" Naomi sighed under her breath. An amorous peddler and a disgruntled employer were a lot to bear in the same morning. "Very well."

She started across the flagstone floor toward the corridor door. Hester pulled out a chair to steal a chat with Trudy. Naomi ignored their whispering until she caught the sound of her own name. Swiveling around to face them, she declared, "The man is *married*! And I was simply advising him he had foul breath."

The two gaped at her for a fraction of a second before bursting into guilty laughter. Naomi narrowed her eyes but could not stay angry and sent them a wry smile. "Don't visit for too long—you both have work to do."

The Georgian four-storey town house, No. 14 Berkeley Square, was built to a formula almost standard in upper-class Mayfair. A staircase rose from the back of the hall with bathrooms off the landings. The kitchen, servants' hall, and coal bin were in the cellar, as well as the bedroom shared by the gardener, Mr. Duffy, and his wife, Claire, a parlormaid. There were smaller rooms, such as the pantry and larder, and a closet where laundry was collected to be sent out every Monday. The entrance hall, dining room, sitting room, and library occupied the ground floor. Above that were the late Mr. Blake's study, a never-used breakfast room, and the parlor where Mrs. Blake entertained callers. On the third story were the principal bedrooms, with small bedrooms for the servants in the attic or garret.

Music met Naomi's ears as she neared the second-storey landing. Mrs. Blake had not played the piano since her son's death. Were it a more cheerful arrangement, she would have taken it to mean her mistress's melancholia had lifted. But the notes drifting from the parlor were as somber as a funeral dirge. *Schubert*, Naomi guessed. Even though she could not sing well, she did know a little about music, for there were often concerts in Hyde Park just five short blocks to the west. She reached the door and knocked. The music stopped and her mistress's voice bade her enter.

If the sitting room was spring with its

pastel walls and floral upholstery, the parlor was autumn. An Oriental rug of burgundy, gold, peacock blue, and olive dominated the oak floor, and the serpentine-backed furniture was upholstered with plush mauve velvet. Covering almost every inch of the muted green walls were portraits—mostly of Master Jeremy, a huge gilt-framed mirror, a tapestry of King Arthur and his knights, framed landscapes and still-life, and shelves of bric-a-brac collected from all over the world. From each side of the massive black marble fireplace, two carved lions held up a mantel crowded with more bric-a-brac. Marble-topped tables displayed still more bric-a-brac, which took parlormaid Claire Duffy all of every Tuesday just to dust.

If I ever have my own cottage, it won't be filled with clutter crossed her mind as she approached the piano. There was scant chance of that, but even a thirty-two-year-old spinster cook could dream.

Mrs. Blake looked up at her and the piano fell silent. "Naomi."

"Yes, Madam?"

The torchère lamp painted Mrs. Blake's skin a jaundiced hue, with shadows lurking in the hollows of her face. Yet her voice was pleasant enough. "I instructed Marie to ring for you on her way out."

"And here I am."

"So you are." Her long hands dropped to her sides to rest upon the bench. Self-consciously she nodded toward the open score.

Naomi was gratified to see *Gretchen am Spinnrade by Franz Schubert* written at the top of the page.

"I wasn't sure if I would remember how to play."

"You've always played beautifully."

She acknowledged the compliment with a shrug. "Has William begun packing?"

"Days ago." Naomi had to smile at his eagerness to set out for University, though she would miss him terribly.

"He's a bright young man. You should be proud."

"Thank you. I am."

"I've instructed Mrs. Bacon to give him five pounds from the household account before he leaves."

"Why, that's very generous of you, Madam." Even though William would earn his way as a servitor—making beds, polishing shoes, and waiting tables for sons of rank and privilege, a young man needed spare pocket money.

"Just warn him not to stray into bad company." Mrs. Blake moved a hand to her high black lace collar. "If only I had warned Jeremy!"

"Please don't torment yourself, Madam," Naomi pleaded, aware that it was just as futile as asking the River Thames not to flow.

The elderly woman made an abrupt change of subject again. "I spoke with Doctor Raine yesterday about my sleeplessness. He left a bottle of laudanum. Only I dislike the way it makes me feel during the day. As if I'm walking about in a fog."

"Then please don't take it. I've heard it can be just as habit-forming as opium."

The pale blue eyes clouded. "What does it matter at my age?"

But it did matter, Naomi thought, or she wouldn't have mentioned it. Mrs. Blake clearly wished to dance around the subject upon both of their minds instead of approaching it directly. Well, Naomi knew how to dance. "Could it be that something is troubling you, Madam? Robbing you of sleep?"

"Such as?"

"What we spoke about in the sitting room some weeks ago?"

"Sitting room . . ." Mrs. Blake murmured unconvincingly.

"Mary Tomkin's child?"

Discomfort flickered across the older woman's shadowed face. "I just don't see what you expect me to do, Naomi. Invite the girl and her child to live here? Treat them like respectable family? After she seduced my Jeremy?"

She was fifteen rose to Naomi's lips, but she did not give it voice. Mrs. Blake would lie to herself about her son's true nature until her dying day. But at least she seemed to have accepted that the child was related to her.

"Mary came from a poor family, Madam," Naomi said. "Perhaps the child has needs?"

And that was the conclusion Mrs. Blake had required her assistance in reaching, for she pursed her lips only for a brief moment before replying, "I contribute to several charities. It would be no different, would it?"

"Not if you don't wish it to be."

Another space of silence passed. "And if I'm going to provide some financial assistance, I suppose I should *see* the child. Only once, mind you. Just to be certain that my money is being used properly."

Reserving her smile for later, Naomi replied, "You'll always wonder if you don't."

❧ *Three* ❧

On the eleventh of April of the following year, solicitor Jules Swann held his hat clamped to his head against a bullying wind and approached a little red-brick terrace house. But for the number eight on the door, it was identical to its neighbors on both sides of the lane, built for the workers of the Grand Junction Locomotive Works.

His search had taken him one hundred fifty miles to Crewe in the county of Cheshire, but at least it no longer involved London's notorious Saint Giles slum known as The Rookery. For six months he had walked those filthy lanes, knocking upon doors of decaying tenements, fearing he would be murdered for the shillings in his pocket and hoping that the Bob Hogarth family had not relocated still another time.

As he knocked, his ears caught the sound of distress above the wind's howl. The door opened, and he stood facing a woman carrying a wailing tot astride one hip. Jules began to doubt the information he had paid half-a-crown for in the Rookery. This woman seemed far older than Mary Tomkin was supposed to be. Combed rows of oily brown hair flowed from her square face into a topknot so much off-center that it appeared in danger of sliding down past her right ear. Creases curved from the corners of her lips to her jawline, as if she had packed eighty years' worth of frowns into her twenty-nine years.

She's had a difficult life, he reminded himself. He removed his hat, aware that he presented just as sorry a sight, with hair whipped to disorder like a madman's. "Good morning, Madam. Please permit me to introduce my—"

"Beg yer pardon?" she yelled, frowning as she jiggled the tot on her hip. The child wore only a little linen shirt and napkin and had apparently been in such a state for some time, judging by the sheen glistening on the lower part of his face.

"My name is Jules—"

The child wailed still louder, this time stretching both arms toward Jules.

"Stop all that squallin', Georgie!" the

woman ordered, which only caused an increase in volume. She turned again to Jules and shouted, "He wants his papa! He's been workin' up to Goostrey for days and days!"

A rosy-cheeked girl of possibly seven or eight years appeared at the woman's other side. With relief Jules assumed the weeping tot would be handed to the care of the older sister. But the woman thrust the infant out toward him. "You're gonter have to hold 'im if you want 'im to stop!"

"Yes, of course!" Jules grimaced inside as the small face pressed into the lapel of his coat. The napkin covering Georgie's bottom was more than a little damp. But at least the weeping ceased after a series of convulsive liquid-sounding inhalations.

"Now, you see?" the woman said, the frown lines fading with her smile. "He thinks every man's his pa. It's a good thing you happened by when you did, Mister."

"Swann," Jules supplied.

"Eh?"

"Jules Swann!" He looked past her shoulder at what he could see of a surprisingly tidy parlor. "May I . . ."

Soon he was seated in a brown horsehair

chair, his hat hanging from the rack at the door. The woman and girl sat on a green sofa across a table from him. Wind whistled through the chimney and caused the coal flame to dance and sputter in the brick fireplace. On the hearth a small boy turned from the tower of wooden blocks he was building only long enough to send Jules a curious glance. If only Georgie had paid him so little interest, Jules told himself. A wide doorway led into the rest of the house. He wondered if Mrs. Blake's grandchild was inside. But surely he or she would have peeked into the parlor by now to see what was going on.

"May I assume that you're Mrs. Hogarth?" he asked, smoothing his hair with his free hand.

"He took to you right away, didn't he?"

Jules patted the little fellow's back. "Would your maiden name happen to be Tomkin?"

"Why do you want to know?" she asked with a resumed frown. Clearly reconsidering having trusted her child to Jules' tending, she moved to the edge of her seat as if she might spring any minute. "You ain't police, are you? Because we paid up our arrears before we left London. My husband makes decent—"

"I assure you I'm not from the police. I'm a solicitor in private practice." He glanced at the girl, whose wide eyes were fastened upon him. "And I wonder if it would be possible for us to speak privately?"

"You're a what?"

"A lawyer." *More detective than lawyer, lately*.

After a moment's hesitation, Mrs. Hogarth ordered the girl to take her brother and play in the kitchen. When she eyed the tot in Jules' arms, he gave her a benign smile. "Why don't we let him sleep? I'm not here to cause you any trouble, Mrs. Hogarth. I intend to be out of your way as soon as possible."

"Well, what is it you want?" she asked, easing back from the springing position.

"You are the former Mary Tomkin?"

She shrugged. "Aye."

"Very good." This would be the most difficult part, Jules thought, because the woman would justifiably have bitter feelings about the way she was abused and dismissed. With as gentle a manner as possible, he said, "I represent Mrs. Arthur Blake.

You were once in her employ in a residence on Berkeley Square, were you not?" He was not surprised when her cheeks flushed crimson and eyes narrowed.

"Aye," she fairly spat. "So the old witch ain't dead yet?"

"Mrs. Blake is still very much alive. But her son has passed away." He thought it important that she know that. Perhaps it would dilute some of her bitterness enough so that she would be agreeable to what he would request of her.

"I hope it was painful."

"It was." And it was time to move on. "Mrs. Blake regrets her part in the injustice you suffered."

"She does, eh?" Mrs. Hogarth said with a scornful little laugh. "Well, don't my heart bleed for her!"

"She commissioned me to inquire about the child you bore, Mrs. Hogarth."

"The baby?" Several seconds lapsed. "My pa took it away the night it was born. Made me stay inside for weeks beforehand and wouldn't even fetch a doctor. He said he didn't want folks lookin' down on us. I weren't even allowed to give her a name."

It was the first he had heard the child

was a girl. Mrs. Blake would be disappointed, for Jules assumed she was hoping for a boy, and one who would be the image of her revered son. "What do you mean . . . away?"

"He left her in a lard pail on the porch of some church. In January! I fretted that a dog or rat would get her even if the cold didn't, but he said it would serve the little brat right if one did."

"I'm sorry." He meant it.

She shrugged but gave him an appreciative look.

When an appropriate half minute had passed, Jules said, "Would you happen to know the name of this particular church?" There were hundreds in London, of all denominations.

"He wouldn't tell me or even my mum on account of bein' afraid we would try to get her back."

"I see." This was not good news, but Jules was still hopeful. Just because the man would not tell his daughter those thirteen years ago didn't mean he couldn't be tempted by money—courtesy of Mrs. Blake. "Does your father still reside in London?"

Bitterness again drew up the square face. "You might say that."

Jules eased himself up a bit to fish in his coat pocket for his notebook and pencil. "May I trouble you for his address?"

"He's over to Kensal Green."

Kensal Green, he scribbled, then looked up again. "You mean he's a gravedigger?"

She made a mirthless chuckle. "No . . ."

———

Late that same evening Naomi and William, who shared half-Mondays off, hired a hansom cab from the dozens queued with private carriages along the Strand to collect theatregoers from the Adelphi. Naomi had Wednesday mornings off as well, which she spent sewing blankets for the Dorcas Society and visiting the lending library, but Mondays were for William. To make up for the boy having no other family in London, she always managed to find activities that amused them both. That wasn't so difficult, as the park, museums, and galleries were free or inexpensive, and theatre seats could be had for sixpence if one didn't mind staring down from their lofty heights for three hours.

Their outings were even more meaningful to her now that he had started Oxford. Having completed Michaelmas term last fall and the Hilary term earlier this year, he would be leaving again in less than two weeks to begin the Trinity term.

She watched him squint at his pocket watch as the pair of horses carried them beneath a sliver of moon, which was no match for the Strand's hissing gaslights. He was a handsome lad, with the medium frame, square jaw, and unruly brown hair of his deceased father, Naomi's brother Preston. The smoked-glass color of his eyes was from his mother, Orabel, whose quiet, withdrawn ways must have at least harbored a calm soul, for William had not the volatile temper of the other Doyle men. Naomi wasn't sure from where the dimpled cheeks came—perhaps a gift from some long-forgotten ancestor.

"Half past eleven," he said, repocketing the watch.

She drew her wool wrap closer about her shoulders. "Well, what did you think?" They had seen *The Prompter's Box*, of which last week's *Observer* had lauded, *"Original, has a clearly told story, is amusing, moreover in style and treatment it hits the taste of the present day."*

The shadow of the carriage's hood could not conceal the hesitancy in William's expression. She realized his reluctance came from not wishing to disappoint her because she had splurged and purchased three-shilling seats.

"I thought it wore on a bit," Naomi prompted.

"A bit," he agreed, then hastened to reassure her, "But our seats were outstanding, weren't they?"

"Outstanding."

"It was thoughtful of you to do this. I enjoyed every minute of it."

"Worth every penny," she told him. "I enjoyed it as well. Even though it did drag on."

"Just a bit." Another hesitancy, and then he turned to her. "Would you care to know what it reminded me of?"

"Yes, of course."

He gave her an apologetic smile. "An important essay on 'The Alkali Act' I was once assigned at the Wesleyan School."

"The Alkali Act?"

"It imposed limits on noxious emissions

in the air from chemical works. But Mr. Duffy and I were painting shutters at the time, and it slipped my mind to go to the library. So I took the only information I could find in one small newspaper article and stretched it into the five required pages."

"Meaning, the author of the play did some stretching himself," Naomi said, returning his smile. "Perhaps he was painting shutters as well? But seriously, I can't recall your making a poor mark."

"Mr. Stillman called me aside after school and asked me to rewrite it. He said it was obvious my time had been preoccupied."

"How kind—and perceptive—of him."

"I was very grateful." He smiled again. "But I believe it was the paint stains on my hands that gave me away."

They laughed together, and Naomi said, "Had you but worn gloves when you were painting, you might not be at Oxford today."

The hansom stopped in front of 14 Berkeley Square, and before Naomi could reach into her reticule for the eight-pence fare, William was handing coins up to the driver. "I have it, Aunt Naomi," he insisted.

She started to argue, for he needed

money now more than ever. But she had to remind herself of a principle that had somehow occurred to her in the earliest years of her guardianship. A child never allowed to give would surely become a self-indulgent adult, his happiness dependent upon whatever was put into his outstretched palm. So she thanked him instead. They bade each other whispered goodnights inside the hall, and he slipped through the house for the stable while she crept up the stairs.

"That you, Naomi?" came Trudy's sleep-thickened voice as Naomi felt for the nightgown folded upon the foot of her own bed.

"It's me, dear."

"Dreaming about boiled carrot pudding . . . may we make some tomorrow?"

Naomi smiled in the darkness. It was not the proper time to remind her that the carrots in Mr. Duffy's garden had yet another month to go. "Soon, Trudy. Now go back to sleep."

The room was small but cozy with a colorful woven rug stretched out between the two narrow beds. They each had a chest of drawers and shared a dressing table and wide wardrobe. Upon the wall hung two watercolors in simple wooden frames—

gifts from Christmas past painted by parlormaid Avis Seaton. Naomi's painting was
of a stone garden bench overrun with purple clematis, and Trudy's, a scene of
marigolds growing from an iron washtub.

There was also a brick fireplace, rare in
servants' quarters. She had heard tales of
attics so frigid that the unfortunate occupants had to sleep with wash flannels over
their faces and would awaken later to find
them frozen stiff. And a long garret window
more than compensated for the lack of
space. It looked out through the leafy tree-
tops of Berkeley Square's thirty-three plane
trees.

She crept down the corridor to the bathroom to sponge bathe and get into her
nightgown. No sooner had she settled herself between the sheets when the squeak
of the doorknob caused her to sit up in
bed. The door opened slowly, and Marie
walked into the room, hair wrapped in papers and eyes blinking in the flickering light
of the candle she carried.

"Marie?"

She moved closer to the bed and whispered, "Madame wishes to see you."

"Now?"

"Would I be waking you now if it were any other time?"

"We'll need currants," Trudy murmured. "And raisins."

"Raisins?" Marie said with a perplexed glance toward the other bed.

Naomi threw back her covers and felt for the wrapper hanging from her bedpost. "She has a yearning for carrot pudding."

The candlelight was all they shared on the staircase, for Marie offered no explanation. "Do you know what this is about?" Naomi finally asked in the bedroom corridor on the next floor.

"All I am allowed to know is that Mr. Swann called this evening." Marie turned and headed for her own room, leaving Naomi standing in the dark.

Naomi looked at the retreating figure and sighed. There was nothing she could do about Marie's jealousy, though she understood it. How could she explain, without betraying a confidence, that the only reason Mrs. Blake chose to confide in her was because she had been the one to bring up the subject of a missing grandchild?

Though she had been summoned, she raised her hand to knock softly. A strained voice bade her enter. Lamplight flowed into the corridor as Naomi opened the door. Mrs. Blake sat propped upon pillows, her nightgown-clad figure overwhelmed by the massive proportions of the four-poster bed.

"Forgive me for waking you, Naomi," the elderly woman said. It was obvious from the anxiety in the lines of her face that she had not slept.

"I wasn't asleep, Madam. We've only just returned from the theatre."

"And how was the play?"

"It could have been trimmed a bit, but it had its fine moments."

"I see. Would you care to sit?"

"No, thank you," Naomi replied after a glance at the nearest chair. With Mrs. Blake's mattresses so high from the floor, it would be like trying to chat with someone atop a ladder.

"Mr. Swann paid a call while you were away."

"Has he come any closer to finding out anything?"

"Yes." A pause, and then, "Mary Tomkin's father put the infant on a church porch immediately after she was born."

Naomi's breath caught in her throat. "No."

"According to Mary Tomkin, whom I suppose has no reason to lie about it now."

"Did she survive?" It dawned upon Naomi that they were speaking of a girl.

"We don't know." Mrs. Blake sighed, looking much older and very weary. Her bony fingers worried the lace at the edge of her satin coverlet. "I fear I did something very impulsive and foolish."

"What is that, Madam?"

"It grieved me so much, the thought of dear Jeremy's . . . daughter being put out like a pail of rubbish that I ordered Mr. Swann to find her and bring her here to live. *If* she's still living."

"But of course you did. Why would that be foolish?"

"Because I know nothing about her. What if she's a brat?"

Like her father? Naomi doubted that was so, for surely no child was allowed to rule the roost in an orphanage as Jeremy Blake had been allowed at home. Fearing her mistress on the verge of changing her mind, she suggested, "If you found her company less than agreeable, you could always send her away to school."

It was what many of the upper class did anyway, for in England it seemed children were an encumbrance to a household. But surely even a boarding school would be preferable to the child's present situation.

Naomi became aware that her palms were pressed together as if clasping her last penny. She could not help but remember how nine-year-old William had wept on the train journey back from Leicester, his little head buried in his arms in her lap while she helplessly patted his shoulder. Somewhere out there was a girl, if she was still living, who had never had a home and family. Was she suffering? "But it may be that the child will be a comfort to you, Mrs. Blake. Have you ever thought of that?"

Longing came to the aged face, but she shrugged it away. "But what will people say? Vicar Sharp? My friends? I don't want them to know what Jeremy . . ."

Grateful that she was not herself burdened by a social class with such rigid conventions, Naomi reasoned, "The vicar won't judge you, good soul that he is. And is it worth clinging to unhappiness just because your friends *might* raise eyebrows?"

"But how would I explain taking the child in?"

"You owe no one an explanation, Madam. You could just say you're performing an act of Christian charity . . . which you would be."

"But if I say she's my grandchild . . ."

Naomi thought for a minute. "You could say she's your ward."

"Even to her?"

"Perhaps at first." That would actually be best, Naomi realized, for the less this child knew about her parentage, the better. Better to think that she was brought here out of the goodness of Mrs. Blake's heart than to learn she had such a scoundrel for a father.

Mrs. Blake angled her head musingly, but then shook it. "The servants would know better. And they would gossip. I knew this was a ridiculous notion all along."

"But there are only three of us left from those days," Naomi said, grasping at straws. "And we would carry this to our graves if you asked us."

"Three?"

"Mrs. Bacon and Mr. Duffy, besides myself." The housekeeper and gardener, both of reliable character. "Of course you might have to include Claire."

Claire, a parlormaid, was Mr. Duffy's wife. Even as she spoke, Naomi knew that this would not be enough. Tales of Jeremy Blake's misdeeds had weathered the years, being passed from former to present servants who had not even known him and even to other households bordering the square. Anyone with half a mind could figure out who the girl was, especially if she resembled portraits of her father. But no servant would be foolish enough to speak of such things in Mrs. Blake's hearing, so hopefully she would be insulated enough to believe no one capable of putting two and two together.

"I'm so afraid, Naomi," her mistress said.

Moving closer, Naomi coaxed her to lie down so that she could tuck the covers around her narrow shoulders. "It's the things I neglected to do that cause me the most pain, Madam," she said softly. "Five years from now, when the girl is grown and probably impossible to locate, will you look back on this moment with regret, or the assurance that you followed your con-science?"

Mrs. Blake took in a shaky breath. "More regret would kill me."

"Then you acted wisely. Why don't you put your doubts to rest now?"

"I will." Closing her eyes, she said, "You'll pray for me, Naomi?"

"Always, Mrs. Blake."

❧ *Four* ❧

A hansom stopped on Drury Lane on the eighteenth of April in front of an aged, narrow three-storey building. Jules Swann climbed out of the cab and called above the traffic noises to the driver in the box behind him. "Are you positive there's an orphanage here?"

Twisting the lid from a tin of snuff, the man called back, "Aye. Saint Matthew's."

Jules' confusion was caused by the stenciled letters in the top panel of the aged oak door. Even through the ubiquitous fog, he could read:

MACDONALD LTD.
ARTIFICIAL TEETH

Even the meanest of orphanages he had visited during the past week had managed to display at least a scrap of wood for a signboard. What if he owned his own carriage and was not dependent upon the driver's competence? He looked past the horses. A wagon was piled high with sacks that seemed to be the object of a heated discussion taking place between a man and woman facing each other on the pavement. Across the lane, two lowbrow men scowled at him from the doorway of a public house. The air stank of gin, courtyard privies, and the heaps of refuse below open windows.

"Want me ter wait again?" the driver called.

"Yes!" Jules exclaimed, slipping his fingers down over the purse in his coat pocket. The building he approached was oppressively dark, its red brick stained sooty by decades of coal fires. On either side shabbily dressed people lounged in the open doorways of what appeared to be tenements converted from businesses that had either gone out of business or moved to safer locations. On the east, an aged signboard for J. BENSON'S INDIA RUBBER TRUNK AND PORTMANTEAU WORKS dangled from rusty chains, and on the west, FORE'S PRINT-SELLERS, PUBLISHERS AND FRAME MAKERS was stenciled in faded gilt across a cracked window.

"Spare a penny fer a honest fellow?"

It was the advanced age of the ragged man that caused Jules to respond, even though he had learned from painful experience in The Rookery that giving to one beggar encouraged others to swarm about like pigeons when one of their lot had been given a crust. After placing tuppence into the trembling palm, he hurried to the door in front of him. His ring was answered by a young woman wearing a white apron over a gown of serviceable gray. Had she not been so clothed, Jules would have mistaken her for a boy, for her brown hair was barely past her earlobes. Removing his hat, Jules said, "Good afternoon. I'm looking for—"

"Sorry, we don't sell teeth, sir. We're an orphanage—Saint Matthew's Methodist Home for Foundling Girls. Our old signboard fell from its chain and broke in half, so the Ladies' Mission Society is having another—"

"I am not here to purchase teeth," Jules was finally forced to cut in.

"Oh." Her cheeks flushed pink. "Beggin' your pardon."

"No offense taken," Jules said in spite of mild embarrassment. Though he had fairly decent teeth, there was one chipped at an angle almost in half—the result of a fall from the roof of a chicken coop when he was a boy—which he usually managed to cover with his top lip whenever he spoke or smiled. "I'm looking for a girl who was brought here over thirteen years—"

"Then would you care to wait in the parlor, sir?"

As she opened the door wider, Jules stepped into a tiny windowless room that probably once served as a vestibule for the teeth factory. On one paneled wall hung a cheap landscape print—he knew it was so because an identical one hung in his own office. Three mismatched chairs and a small table were arranged upon a faded rug of indeterminable color.

"Mrs. Forsyth will be back inside shortly," the young woman said, taking his hat and hanging it on the rack just inside the door.

"Thank you." Jules waited until she had walked through an arched doorway before settling into one of the chairs. He supposed Mrs. Forsyth was the woman who was speaking to the delivery man. Through the doorway he could hear signs of life in the building, a fussy infant being soothed by a woman's song, and several childish voices reciting the multiplication tables.

He was well aware why someone of Mrs. Blake's social standing and wealth would hire him, a solicitor with a dingy hatbox of an office below his flat on Cheapside. And it was not because he commanded far lower fees than the legal experts who advised her on matters of business and finance. Such a matter as this required the assistance of someone who was not likely to rub elbows with the woman's peers at social gatherings.

She need not have worried. Discretion was a necessary part of the vocation. But he was glad for the money that would tide his family over the times between clients who could afford to pay no more than pittance.

———

Though passersby sent stares in her direction, Olivia Forsyth did not wish to bring the altercation inside. The children were well enough aware of their lowly positions in the scheme of life. They did not need to overhear that there were people who would purposely feed them rubbish.

"And I'm telling you, Mr. Brody, there was mold again in that last delivery," she insisted to the man standing before her. Her fury rose at his mask of disbelief, for his eyes could not conceal his guilt. "You assume because they're orphans you can sell us your old merchandise with a clear conscience—if you even have one!"

The man already loomed a head taller than she but seemed to grow even more so. "I'm a God-fearin' man, I'll have ye know! And ye can't go blamin' me if ye let them oats sit too long in a damp cellar!"

Her righteous indignation was only producing unrighteous anger on his part, so she forced herself to calm down. "Mr. Brody, is it reasonable to believe that we have the luxury of allowing food to sit about until it spoils? All I'm asking is that we open up one of those sacks out here in the sun—"

"I haven't time. Ye ain't my only customers. So do ye want them unloaded or not?"

Olivia sighed. Anger and reason had not worked, so she had no choice but to pull a third arrow from her quiver. She drew in a deep breath and forced a smile. "Very well. You may bring them inside."

His mouth gaped, exposing teeth as gray and crooked as old headstones. "Yes?"

"We can't very well cook them out here in your wagon, can we?" she quipped.

Mr. Brody actually threw back his head and chortled. "The horses wouldn't take too kindly to that, now, would they, Mrs. Forsyth?"

"Indeed they wouldn't." But before he could turn, Olivia said as if an afterthought, "Oh, I should mention that I discussed the recent troubles we've had with mold with Father Malone."

His eyes darted a glance down Drury Lane in the direction of Saint Theresa's rectory a half block away. "Father Malone?"

"He said I should send for him anytime I question the quality of one of your deliveries so he can inspect it with me." Sending a glance in the same direction, Olivia said, "Why don't you go ahead and unload, since you're in a hurry? I'll just have one of my workers nip over to—"

Wariness crept into his expression. "But you're Methodists."

"Quite true, but our families were neighbors on Moorgate. My sister and I played many a game of *Whist* with Father Malone and his siblings. Of course that was back in the days when he was just 'Tom.' He stops by occasionally for tea and to argue religion." She smiled again. "Good-naturedly, of course. As you know, Father Malone is a gentle soul. But I've heard he can be a bear when it comes to handing out penance."

Now it was Mr. Brody who sighed, rubbing a hand over his beefy face. "I expect I should take this load back and look through it myself," he said, not quite meeting her eyes.

"That seems a great inconvenience, when you can do that right—"

He was already striding toward the wagon seat. "Too much noise here. I'll be back before nightfall."

Relief accompanied Olivia back to the door of the home. It would have been a pity to ask Father Malone, who suffered from lumbago, to hurry up the street on a mission of mercy.

Thank you for the good people you've put on this earth, Father, she prayed. Such as Mr. McDonald, who had donated the building when his factory relocated. That was twenty years ago, when Saint Matthew's was founded by her late husband, Samuel Forsyth, a minister.

She and Samuel had no way of knowing in those early years of their marriage that they would not be blessed with their own children. But there was little time to feel any loss, and Olivia's arms were seldom empty.

Nor were the sixty-two beds and cradles, which was why she worked hard to find positions and apprenticeships for the older girls. She could recall still playing with dolls at fifteen, and it never ceased to grieve her to send a girl that age out into the world to earn her keep in domestic service. Still more terrible would be having to turn helpless infants and younger ones away. It was like having a choice between typhus and cholera.

She turned the knob with a work-roughened hand and opened the door. A dark-haired man rose to his feet. On his medium frame hung a frock coat that had gone out of style sometime during the last decade. Oddly, he looked at her as if they were acquainted.

"Mrs. Forsyth, I presume?"

"Forgive me," Olivia said, closing the door behind her. "Have we met?"

"The young lady who allowed me in gave me your name. But I noticed you out on the pavement just a moment ago."

She grimaced. "Oh. I wish you hadn't."

"Is there something wrong?"

"Not anymore. Just a delivery man who needed a wee dose of conscience."

"And did you get him to take it?" the man asked with a smile.

"He did. With the enthusiasm of a child taking cod-liver oil, Mr.—"

Stepping around the tea table, he hurried over to her. "Do forgive me. My name is Jules Swann."

"Olivia Forsyth, Mr. Swann," she said, offering her hand. After the introduction, she untied the strings of her bonnet and hung it next to the bowler hat on the rack. The surprise in his expression was no surprise to her. It had dawned upon her long ago that the lice epidemics that plagued the home two or three times yearly would be more effectively fought if *everyone's* hair was kept short. And as lice did not confine themselves to the orphans, she and her staff followed the same rule.

She thought of the myriad of duties awaiting her. As cordial as her visitor was, they had devoted enough time to pleasantries. "How may I assist you?"

He glanced toward the inner doorway through which drifted young voices in unison:

Bring me my spear: O clouds unfold!
Bring me my chariot of fire!

"William Blake?" he asked, leaning his head to listen.

"We strive to instill an appreciation for literature, Mr. Swann." Olivia felt equally as passionate about teaching proper grammar, penmanship, and manners. There would be those who looked down upon the girls from Saint Matthew's simply because they were orphans, but if Olivia had anything to do with it, none would be able to fault their way of speaking and conducting themselves.

"Very admirable." Mr. Swann cleared his throat. "This is a matter of some delicacy, Mrs. Forsyth. Perhaps it would be better discussed in an office?"

Olivia shook her head. Most of the children in her keep were the results of "delicate matters." "This is the only available room, I'm afraid. My late husband and I gave up our office for a nursery years ago."

The desk and filing cabinet in the corner of her bedchamber sufficed as a makeshift office, but it was unsuitable for conferring with callers. She moved to close the inner door, abruptly cutting off the sound, then turned to him again. "The walls are thick, so you will not be overheard. Do have a seat, please."

"Thank you."

But he waited until she was seated before resuming his chair. Olivia could not help but notice some fraying at the ends of his sleeves and caught glimpses of a chipped tooth when he spoke. Yet he was well groomed and composed and did not seem to be a victim of dire poverty. She thought again about those duties awaiting her attention. "Now, what is the purpose of your visit, Mr. Swann?"

Jules nodded, understanding her need to be abrupt. Time was surely a precious commodity here. He felt uncomfortable with what he would have to ask her before stating his business. But he was bound to the directives of his client and so cleared his throat and said, "May I rely upon your discretion, Mrs. Forsyth?"

"You may," she replied with no sign of offense.

"Thank you. Several months ago I was commissioned by Mrs. Arthur Blake to find her granddaughter," he said, and when no recognition entered her expression, he added, "I trust you've heard of the Blake Shipping Line?"

"The name sounds familiar," she replied. "And you believe her granddaughter to be here?"

Jules nodded. "Mary Tomkin was the child's mother, a servant in the Blake household. She's married and living up north now, which is why it took me so long to find her."

"Mary Tomkin . . ." Mrs. Forsyth said thoughtfully and shook her head. "I don't recall the name."

"You wouldn't have met Miss Tomkin. Her father left the newborn in a lard pail outside a church on the night of January twenty-ninth in 1857."

"Over thirteen years ago. We have a half-dozen girls that age, Mr. Swann."

"But how many were left in church doorways, Mrs. Forsyth?"

"You would be surprised."

Jules opened his mouth to respond but closed it upon realizing silence was the more prudent course. Something seemed to be weighing at her. He stared with no fear of being rude, for her hazel eyes stared blankly past him. She appeared older than he by at least a decade, as her short auburn hair was dulled with gray. At first glance her face had seemed unremarkable in its ordinary arrangement of features, but he now realized she had once been quite striking. No doubt the years of trying to meet the needs of the children in her charge had eroded the beauty. He rather admired the character that had settled in its place, the mixture of compassion and strength and even humor, as she had demonstrated with her remark about the delivery man and cod-liver oil.

Finally she came out of her reverie and looked again at him. "We were brought a newborn from Saint Mark's thirteen years ago. She was left in the doorway in the dead of winter, curled up in the bottom of a lard pail with only an old pillowcase for covering."

Jules' pulse jumped a notch. "Yes?"

"It was a miracle that an animal did not find her first or that she did not freeze."

Everything Jules found out about the case made him more and more relieved that it was almost over. "The circumstances surrounding the birth were . . . painful." *And disgusting*, he thought. While Mrs. Blake had not admitted her son had taken advantage of Miss Tomkin, it was obvious that was what had happened. He thought of his oldest daughter Margaret, who had just turned fifteen last week. How terrible it would be to have to send her—or any of his children—into domestic service. His wages did not allow for luxuries such as fashionable clothing and holidays to Brighton, but he was grateful that he was able to at least provide a home and some education for his family.

Mrs. Forsyth's voice broke into his thoughts. "I'm curious," she said, her hazel eyes studying his. "You said Mrs. Blake hired you several months ago?"

"That is correct."

"Why has it taken her so long to seek out her grandchild?"

Jules had expected the question. "She did not confide the reason to me. But the girl's father was an only child and passed away leaving no other children, so I gather she has no other family."

So that she could not see the distaste in his expression he looked down at the two slips of paper he was withdrawing from his waistcoat pocket. He leaned forward and stretched out his arm to hand over the first, a legal document.

"Mary Tomkin, now Mrs. Hogarth, relinquishes the right to any future claim on the child," Jules explained unnecessarily, for she was reading the words herself. Fearful that she would ask if Mrs. Hogarth had been paid for her childish scrawl—which *had* earned her fifty pounds—he stretched out the second paper toward her. "And Mrs. Blake has commissioned me to present you with this. All we have to do is sign your name."

Mrs. Forsyth took it from him and stared at it. "One hundred pounds?"

Jules could appreciate the wonder in her voice. It was a small fortune, representing at least two years of his own wages. "As an expression of gratitude for caring for her granddaughter."

"An expression of gratitude?" Over the slip of paper her eyes met his. "Or an appeasement of conscience?"

She was voicing something Jules had wondered himself. He glanced around at the shabby furnishings. "Surely the money could be put to good use, no matter what the motive."

"Obviously it could."

"Very well," Jules said with a nod. "I suppose there are other papers to sign. . . ."

"Mrs. Blake intends to become legal guardian, then?"

"But of course." He had to look away from her scrutinizing eyes for a second. "But she asks that the girl not be told of the kinship they share."

"And why is that?"

"She fears that knowledge will cause the child to harbor some bitterness against her." He could not voice his suspicion that Mrs. Blake also wished to maintain some distance at first, just in case the girl did not meet with her approval. *And she's probably off to boarding school in that case.* One institution for another. *But that's none of your affair*, he reminded himself.

Mrs. Forsyth nodded. And then she did a curious thing. Rising to her feet, which prompted Jules to do the same, she held out the check. "I'm afraid I must give this some thought."

He stared in disbelief at her outstretched hand. "Some thought?"

"I shall have to peruse my records to see if this is indeed the right child."

"I don't mind waiting. In fact, I would be more than willing to assist you."

She shook her head. "*And*, I must confess some misgivings at the care a child would receive after being allowed to languish in an orphanage for over thirteen years."

"But Mrs. Blake was unaware that the mother no longer—"

"Surely she could have found out. You may return tomorrow, Mr. Swann. And I will give you my decision then."

"Your *decision*?"

"The girls in my charge are not a litter of kittens, sir. They are not handed out to just anyone who stops by."

Jules did not consider himself a volatile

man, but a vein in his temple began to throb. "I would hardly call Mrs. Arthur Blake just *anyone*."

"Your loyalty to your client is commendable. But my decision is firm."

While her tone remained calm, the hazel eyes told him it was useless to argue any further. He had no legal maneuvers at his disposal, for the home was a private institution, and as Mrs. Blake's son had not married Mary Tomkin, the child was not a legitimate heir. "Very well," he sighed, taking the check and pushing it into his pocket. "I'll return tomorrow."

She did not reply but turned toward the door. Jules followed. He did not anticipate telling his client she would have to wait a little longer. As he took his hat from the rack, he remembered the question Mrs. Blake asked the day he had informed her that he had located Mary Tomkin. At least he could give her a reply to that.

"The child," he said to Mrs. Forsyth. "What is her name?"

The door opened with a *click*. "Tomorrow, Mr. Swann. We will discuss everything tomorrow."

❧ *Five* ❧

When her visitor was gone, Olivia held the doorknob and wondered if he had noticed the tension in her voice. She suffered an inner battle over whether to fling open the door and go after him, but then she turned to walk through the parlor. Lily Jacobs limped down the corridor toward her. Raised in the home since the age of six, she worked in the kitchen—and industriously so, not expecting preferential treatment because of a club foot.

"Gertrude says Mr. Brody is here?"

"He had some concern over the quality of his merchandise," Olivia told her. "He'll return before nightfall."

"Mercy!" Lily's eyes widened. "How did that happen?"

"I'll explain later." Had Mr. Swann not paid a call, Olivia would have lingered long enough to share the story. But she walked on up the corridor, past the classroom, and up a flight of stairs. From the open door to the nursery she could see Beth Woodward tending five infants, including the newborn recently left in the comfort room of Paddington Station in a basket. When she reached her chamber she closed the door, went over to her bed, and lay across the quilt.

Why didn't you tell him? she asked herself, drained by the tumult of her thoughts. There was no need to look at her records, even after so long a time span. The child in question had been woefully underweight and exposed to the cold for too long to thrive under even Beth's tender ministrations. Her two-day-old body was buried in Saint Matthew's churchyard under a small wooden cross.

While she had not *said* that the child still lived under her roof, lies of omission were just as sinful as those spoken. The urge to pray was strong, but she couldn't bring herself to do so. Not when she was still considering going through with the plan she had impulsively set into motion in the parlor.

If only Samuel were here! Her dear husband would not be wrestling with this temptation. It was not enough that he walked the straight and narrow—Samuel had kept himself in the middle of that path so as not even to place a foot near the edge.

Mrs. Blake's money could help the children in so many ways, but it wasn't the primary reason she had not been forthright with Mr. Swann. Olivia was used to squeezing pennies—in fact, she halfway expected to look down at her thumb one day and see the image of Queen Victoria. She had another, more compelling reason for her duplicity. But could she carry through with it?

A gentle knocking sounded at the door. "Mrs. Forsyth?"

"Yes?" Olivia raised her head.

"Lily says you look peaked," said Mrs. Abbot, the cook. "Shall I bring you some broth?"

"No, thank you." With a sigh she got out of bed and brushed the wrinkles from her gown made of the same coarse fabric as the girls'. Her staff had enough to do without having to look after her, and she could struggle with her conscience just as well with busy hands.

That evening when the house was quiet,

Olivia took a candle and went up another flight of stairs to where the oldest girls were housed. The topmost storey was divided into two rooms. What had once been a supply closet now served as a bedchamber for Mrs. Kettner, the school-mistress, and, like Olivia, the widow of a minister. The long room was almost too narrow for the twenty beds arranged toe to toe along the plastered brick walls. According to Mr. McDonald, this was where porcelain teeth and gums were painted before being fired downstairs in what served now as the kitchen.

Olivia moved between the rows listening to the sounds of steady breathing. Sometimes before retiring in the wee hours of morning, she would pass through one or another of the dormitories. Never did she feel more maternal than when looking upon sleeping children, from the infants in their iron cribs to the oldest girls here. A child in peaceful slumber indicated one who was well tended and that she and her dedicated colaborers were "doing for the least of these as unto Jesus."

She turned into the narrow space between two beds, shielding her candle with her hand so as not to wake Sarah Matthews, lying on her left side with her blanket tucked up around her shoulder. The cap of blond hair reflected a bit of the light that escaped through Olivia's fingers. Typically, the girl's left elbow was bent before her, her hand under her thin pillow, as if hiding it even in her sleep.

A fisherman had brought her to the orphanage almost eleven years ago, when she could not have been older than three. He said he had "pulled her from the Thames when she was an infant," and his family could no longer afford to tend her. Olivia had had misgivings over his story, but the fact that the child was undernourished and filthy and that the man reeked of alcohol had hastened her decision to make a place for her.

Little Sarah was bright enough to know her given name and to be aware that her deformity attracted looks of pity and even disgust. Even at that early age she kept the fingerless hand with its nub of a thumb down at her side in a fold of her ragged little gown.

No one came to claim her. Sarah was given the surname that all the foundlings

without known family were given—
Matthews, for Saint Matthew, who wrote
the account of Jesus Christ admonishing
His disciples to suffer little children to come
unto Him. And she was loved by Olivia and
the staff with as much love as could be divided over sixty ways. The other children
loved her, too, for her quiet, helpful manner.
Why, when surrounded by so much acceptance, she would still be ashamed of
her hand was a puzzle.

Olivia blinked away tears. She seldom
reminisced, knowing that for every sleeping
child there was a tragic past. But it was
Sarah's *future* that concerned her. While
she capably performed chores such as
making her bed, washing clothes, and
helping tend the younger children, she naturally took longer than did the other girls
her age. In an overcrowded labor market,
who would care to hire someone who could
not keep up with the other servants? The
workhouse was the only possibility, but
Olivia felt she would rather die than send a
child there.

And so she had resigned herself that
Sarah, like Lily, would spend the rest of her
years at the home. It was not a bad life.

She was bright enough to become a teacher to the younger girls one day. But her world would be so narrow, composed of the four walls and a tiny walled garden. Even Sunday chapel was conducted in the schoolroom by three local ministers on a rotating schedule. Because the workload was so great, advanced schooling would be impossible. Opportunities to meet decent, eligible young men were nonexistent in Drury Lane, and so, again like Lily, she would probably never marry.

Unless this is a way out.

If Mrs. Blake wished to atone for past injustices, shouldn't she be allowed to do so? Mr. Swann had mentioned that she had no other family. Surely it would be kinder to substitute another child instead of telling her that her actions probably contributed to her infant granddaughter's death.

Olivia frowned at her rationalizations. *Mrs. Blake's angst means nothing to you*, she thought. *You wouldn't consider committing such a sin for someone you've not even met*. It was for Sarah's sake that such a plan had formed in her mind.

Something troubled her. Just because Mrs. Blake did not wish to tell her she was her granddaughter now did not mean she wouldn't change her mind in the future. Miss Tomkin's poor little infant was brought in shortly after birth; therefore, this plan would only work if Sarah believed she had also been here her whole life. How much of her early childhood did she remember? She would have to find out before proceeding further.

And if Sarah had no memory of anything but the orphanage, she would have to lead the girl to believe that she was but thirteen years of age, not the fourteen she was most likely to be. That should be relatively easy, for birthdays and approximate ages were acknowledged only in Olivia's records—not from a lack of sentiment, but from lack of time and funds for celebrations, and because at least half of the children had no idea of the specific dates of their births. Being as slight of build as she was, Sarah could easily pass for one year younger.

There would be even more deception necessary concerning her staff, especially Beth, Mrs. Kettner, and Mrs. Abbot, who were employed when little Sarah was brought in. She could make them believe that Mrs. Blake wished to take in an orphan simply out of kindness, but Sarah could not be told of her fictitious past until the last minute.

Oh what a tangled web we weave, Olivia thought.

"They look like angels when they sleep . . . don't they?" came a whisper from her right.

Olivia turned to see Mrs. Kettner standing there with a wrapper over her nightgown and a nightcap over her short white hair. "Yes, they do," she whispered back. "Did I wake you?"

"You didn't, Olivia. I often finish my prayers by passing through and whispering them to the Lord by name." Her face glowed in the light of her own candle. "It's the only way I can be certain I've not left anyone out."

The girl in the bed stirred, causing Olivia to move back into the aisle. Mrs. Kettner stepped aside to give room. "I should go before I wake them all," Olivia whispered.

"Good night to you, then. May you have pleasant dreams."

They won't be pleasant, Olivia was certain. She touched the older woman's sleeve. "While you're praying for them . . . pray for me as well?"

Mrs. Kettner studied her face in the candlelight. "Is there something wrong, Olivia?"

"A decision I have to make." She wished she could pour out the whole story. But the good woman would only tell her what she already knew, that deception was wrong even for the purest of motives.

"Ah, then," Mrs. Kettner said. "I'll be praying God grants you an extra dose of wisdom."

After thanking her, Olivia went back downstairs to her room, took a drink of water from the chipped glass carafe at her table, and knelt down by her bed.

"Father," she murmured at length. "Dear Mrs. Kettner promised to pray that I would have wisdom. I ask you instead that the punishment for the sin I intend to commit not be more than I'm able to bear."

———

Sarah was halfway through her bowl of porridge on Tuesday morning when she felt a hand upon her shoulder. She twisted in her seat to look up at Miss Jacobs.

"Mrs. Forsyth wants to see you in the dormitory when you've finished," Miss Jacobs leaned down to say in a low voice. Though she wore a smile, her face was oddly splotched and the whites of her eyes stained pink.

"Yes, Miss Jacobs," Sarah whispered, wishing she could ask if she was ill. But because the dining hall was only large enough to seat half the girls at once, silence was strictly enforced during meals in the interest of saving time. She watched the worker limp toward the open doorway.

Turning back to her bowl, she discovered her appetite had forsaken her. She could only shrug at the wide-eyed looks sent to her from the other seven girls at the table. Mrs. Forsyth was a kind woman, but a busy one. A summons from her usually meant one of two things. Some serious breech of the rules had been committed, or someone would soon be leaving to take on a position. Sarah tried to recollect any of the former of which she may have been guilty of lately and was disappointed when none came to mind. *But why would anyone want to hire you?* she asked herself, shifting the fingerless hand in her lap.

Wasting food wasn't allowed, so she lifted her bowl a bit and raised her brows questioningly. Lucille waved from the foot of the table.

"You're not leaving, are you?" Mary whispered on her right when Sarah handed her the bowl to pass.

She glanced at Mrs. Kettner at the next table. "I don't think so," she whispered back, then pushed out her chair.

Mrs. Forsyth stood at the far end of Sarah's dormitory room in the stream of light slanting in from the lone window facing Drury Lane. She turned to smile, which should have reassured Sarah but instead swept away all doubt that she was here for the second reason.

It was not that she was lazy. But Saint Matthew's was her home, and the staff and girls were her family. And she felt safe inside these walls. From what, she wasn't certain.

"I like to look out over the fog and grime," Mrs. Forsyth said when Sarah reached her. She nodded toward the glass. "It reminds me that there are things which extend far beyond our limited vision."

Sarah didn't think the headmistress was

referring only to rooftops. And she thought she understood a little. After all, she fervently believed in God, whom no one but Moses had seen, and then only from the back.

"You've finished your breakfast?"

"Half of it," Sarah confessed.

"Very good," Mrs. Forsyth said as if she had not really heard her reply. There was a space of silence, and then, "Do you recall anything about your life before you were brought here?"

"Brought here?" She had not expected that question.

"Yes. Think hard, Sarah."

After a second of concentration, all that came to Sarah's recollection was a pungent and yet musty odor, like rotting apples. But no images or faces other than those already familiar. "I must have been very young."

The woman turned to the window again. Through the glass Sarah could see the clay roof of the public house across the lane. "It was thirteen years ago on January thirtieth. And you were only a few hours old."

"I was? But I'm fourteen."

Mrs. Forsyth shook her head. "I looked

through my records last night and discovered we've somehow accidentally added a year onto your life."

"I see." The disappointment at suddenly being a year younger lasted only long enough for it to dawn upon Sarah that she wasn't in trouble. And even better, she was too young to be sent away. "But who brought me here?" she asked. While she took for granted that her parents had died, it had never occurred to her to wonder about other people in her life. Had she aunts or uncles somewhere?

"You were left in the doorway of Saint Mark's. That's a chapel on Chancery Lane."

A scene sparked in her mind. She was very young, perhaps four or five, and an older girl was helping her write her alphabet on a slate by guiding her right hand. She could not recall the girl's name or even face—so many had grown up and left over the years—but she was saying, *"I was out sweeping the pavement when a filthy-looking man appeared, carrying you on his shoulder. You stared at my broom as if you'd never seen one before. All I could see of your face was dirt and those wide green eyes."*

How could that have happened if she came here as an infant? Had Mrs. Forsyth confused her with another girl? That didn't seem possible. More likely, the older girl had made the mistake. *Or you dreamed the whole conversation*, Sarah told herself.

"Come with me, Sarah."

They walked down the row of beds. Mrs. Forsyth's familiar black-bound Bible lay open upon Sarah's mattress. The headmistress picked it up and then sat, motioning her to sit beside her. "Do you remember the story of Naaman's servant girl?"

"Yes, Mrs. Forsyth." Thanks to daily chapel before the start of school, the girls of Saint Matthew's were well grounded in Scripture.

The headmistress smiled. "Very good. Allow me to read it to you again. 'Now Naaman, captain of the host of the king of Syria, was a great man with his master, and honourable, because by him the Lord had given deliverance unto Syria: he was also a mighty man in valour, but he was a leper. And the Syrians had gone out by companies, and had brought away captive out of the land of Israel a little maid; and she waited on Naaman's wife. And she said unto her mistress, "Would God my lord were with the prophet that is in Samaria! For he would recover him of his leprosy." ' "

"What happened next, Sarah?" she asked.

"Naaman went to Elisha," Sarah began, noticing that her voice was beginning to sound squeaky, like the privy door. "He sent a message for him to wash in the River Jordan seven times."

"And Naaman was healed." Mrs. Forsyth smiled again, though the hazel eyes were sad. "The little maid was torn from her family, having every right to sulk and despise the people in that household, and yet she became a blessing to them."

Sarah's skin began to prickle.

"We don't know what ever happened to the girl. But it's written here that Naaman attempted, unsuccessfully, to reward Elisha with silver and fine clothing. So we can be certain he rewarded the little servant girl in some way as well."

She paused as if expecting some comment, but Sarah could only nod.

Mrs. Forsyth closed the Bible in her lap. "When we seek to become blessings to others, Sarah, we find ourselves blessed.

Perhaps not right away, and not always in material things, but just the same we reap what we sow eventually. Even though we don't know the little maid's name, she teaches us to find a way to make the best of any situation in which we find ourselves."

Thirteen is too young to be sent away, Sarah reminded herself. She realized that Mrs. Forsyth had started speaking again and guiltily focused her attention on her.

". . . by an attorney yesterday, who represents a Mrs. Arthur Blake. She would like you to come and live with her."

The prickles in her skin made her shudder. "Me?"

"Yes."

"In a house?"

"Of course." Mrs. Forsyth smiled. "A very nice one, actually."

"But why? She's never even met me."

"She's without family and lonely, according to her solicitor, and has asked for a girl to be a companion to her."

It was against the rules to argue, but Sarah couldn't help but feel this was a mistake. There were plenty of girls who spoke of their longings to live in a real house. "But wouldn't it be better to send someone else?" She thought of Helen, who slept two beds over and played piano in chapel. Anyone would be charmed to have such a girl for a companion. "Helen would be—"

"This is something you must do, Sarah," Mrs. Forsyth cut in with a little edge to her voice, yet she did not seem angry. "One day you'll understand. I want you to gather your things and come down to the parlor."

"Yes, Mrs. Forsyth." Sarah's eyes clouded. "May I tell everyone good-bye?"

"Yes, of course." But then she reconsidered and shook her head. "Wait until after Mrs. Blake's attorney comes for you."

Mrs. Forsyth did not explain, but Sarah understood and pressed her hand in closer to her left side. For once she was glad for her deformity. Surely the attorney would take one look at her and change his mind. Or this Mrs. Blake would.

"I'll see you downstairs."

"Yes, Mrs. Forsyth."

The headmistress rose, and Sarah did so as well. Before she could step aside to allow Mrs. Forsyth into the aisle, Sarah felt the touch of her hand upon her shoulder.

"When I realized I could bear no children," Mrs. Forsyth said with hazel eyes somber, "I thought the disappointment would kill me. But out of that pain came a life so fulfilling that I thank God for every day of it. You must build a faith so strong that it will see beyond the pain."

"I'll try," Sarah whispered. But she couldn't imagine never hearing from her friends again—if this Mrs. Blake did not send her back. "May I write?"

Sadly, the woman shook her head. "I don't think that would be wise, Sarah. Again, it's very important that you direct your energies toward making the most of your new situation." She drew Sarah into her arms. As Mrs. Forsyth's embraces were usually reserved for the smaller girls, Sarah choked back tears and wished they could stay like that forever.

"But remember you have someone who is a Father to the fatherless, Sarah," the headmistress said over her head.

"Yes. Thank you."

After watching the woman's blurred image walk down the corridor of beds, Sarah pulled the apple crate from beneath her bed and began spreading her treasures upon her mattress. Most were gifts from the charity ladies from Christmases past. A wooden-handled toothbrush. A worn copy of Jane Austen's *Emma*. A slightly chipped china mug with a serene young Queen Victoria on the side. A stone from the tiny garden, imprinted with what appeared to be the backbone of a fossilized little animal. From the nails over her headboard she took her extra clothing—a pair of wool stockings, linens, her nightgown, extra gown, and green crochet wrap, fuzzy from years of being handed down.

Mrs. Forsyth had not told her how to pack, so she spread the spare gown and arranged everything else to be rolled inside. The wrap she folded in case she should need it outside. Straightening again, she tucked the bundle and wrap under her left arm.

She looked longingly at her feather pillow. The other girls teased her, telling her she could rest her head just as comfortably on a handkerchief. Since no one else seemed to appreciate a thin pillow, she considered bringing it downstairs and asking Mrs. Forsyth if she might take it with her. But the impulse passed. She had seen beds emptied and filled on the same day.

Someone from downstairs would move up to take her place, making room for the inevitable younger one. She leaned down to give the patched, yellowed case a loving pat, saying to the empty room, "You'll like the pillow once you're used to it."

❦ Six ❧

"I thought you might be here early," Mrs. Forsyth told Jules Swann from the parlor chair facing his.

She had served him a cup of tea that was comfortingly hot on such a brisk April morning but weaker than even his frugal wife, Anne, brewed. Still, it was better than no tea at all, which was what he had had at home, for he had just been sitting down to breakfast when Mrs. Blake's coachman, a good-natured fellow by the name of Stanley Russell, had knocked at his door.

"Not too early, I trust?" Jules replied.

"She's gathering her belongings now."

"Very good." After another sip from his cup, he said, "I do thank you for deciding in Mrs. Blake's favor." And she had announced such before he could point out that his client had doubled the amount of the bank check lying upon her chair arm. He was almost glad she had given him such a fright yesterday, for now the good woman would be able to buy even more provisions for the orphans. *And hopefully some fresh tea*.

"Please thank her for her generosity," Mrs. Forsyth said. There was a click as she leaned forward to replace her cup and saucer on the tray. "And while Sarah is still upstairs, there is something I should tell you."

The gravity in her voice made him a little anxious. "Yes?"

"She has a deformed hand."

"A deformed . . ." Jules found himself echoing stupidly.

"A defect of birth. Did Miss Tomkin not tell you?"

He shook his head and wondered if he should take leave to inform Mrs. Blake. Putting himself in her place, he would not be deterred from taking the girl in. Family was family. But his client's frame of mind was still a mystery to him. She had paid a small fortune to find and take custody of her grandchild, yes, but did that mean she expected perfection for that money?

"Is this a problem, Mr. Swann?"

He sighed and set his own half-finished

cup on the tray. "I'm just uncertain of what she'll think. Mrs. Blake, that is."

"Then perhaps you should go and tell her. I wouldn't want Sarah to suffer the humiliation of being rejected and sent back."

Again Jules sighed, pulling himself to his feet. "It wouldn't matter to me, you understand."

"I understand."

"Thank you." Unnecessarily, for she had not risen from her chair, he said, "I'll show myself out." He took his hat from the stand and opened the door. Through the fog he could see Stanley leaning against Mrs. Blake's handsome brougham coach, hands hooked under armpits while he chatted with a young woman wearing the garb of a factory worker.

He'll be disappointed to leave, Jules thought wryly. But that wasn't what compelled him to glance back over his shoulder. It was an odd feeling that the situation had somehow changed. And sure enough, a very thin girl stood in the arched doorway.

He turned the rest of his body around. Large green eyes—which locked with his for just a fraction of a second before lowering—were set in a face almost transparent for its paleness. Her nose was straight, her features delicate beneath a cap of hair the color of corn silk. Compared to his daughters, who loved the out-of-doors and had to be reminded constantly by their mother to shield their faces from the sun, the girl looked sickly.

Mrs. Forsyth was staring up at him from her chair. Suddenly Jules felt very silly and more than a little ashamed. What had Mrs. Blake hired him to do, find her a purebred pup? He replaced his hat on the stand. "Yes, I see the coach is still there."

The headmistress gave him a knowing smile and motioned the girl to come into the room. She carried a bundle of gray cloth the same color as the dress she wore and a folded bit of hideous green wool. "Mr. Swann, this is Sarah," Mrs. Forsyth said.

Jules gave a little bow. "I'm very pleased to meet you, Sarah."

"Thank you, sir," the girl said in a strained voice as she dipped into a bob.

He tried not to stare at the misshapen hand at the end of the arm curled around the bundle. Yet he could not help but dart another glance. Surely Mrs. Blake would feel the same pity that touched his heart. It occurred to him to wonder why Mrs. Hogarth had not mentioned her daughter's deformity, but then, why would she feel it necessary?

"Are you ready to leave?" he asked gently and caught sight of the panic in her eyes before she turned again to the headmistress.

"Sarah would like to say her farewells to everyone," Mrs. Forsyth told him. "Would you mind waiting a bit longer?"

"But of course not. Take all the time you need."

"Thank you," the girl murmured with a feeble attempt at a smile.

"You may leave your things here," Mrs. Forsyth said. She turned again to Jules after Sarah had put her belongings in the second empty chair and left the room. "It's very kind of you to wait."

"I don't mind." Jules sat down and picked up his cup again. "It will give me time to finish this excellent tea."

Reaching for the teapot, she gave him an amused little smile. "You are quite the diplomat, aren't you, Mr. Swann?"

She had seen right through him, and he

laughed appreciatively. "One learns to be when he lives in a household of women."

If Sarah did not want to leave before, her reluctance intensified when she stood at the center of a circle of weeping girls in the schoolroom. Even Mrs. Kettner sobbed profusely into a handkerchief.

"But didn't he see your hand?" Becky, who shared a desk with her, asked as tears streamed down her freckled face.

"I made sure of that," Sarah replied. She wouldn't allow herself to weep for fear that she would not be able to stop, but the lump in her throat had welled to a raw ache. After embracing and trading endearments with everyone in the room, she went to the nursery to bid farewell to Miss Woodward and the babies, and then down to the kitchen, where Miss Jacobs wept and planted kisses upon her forehead, and Mrs. Abbot stopped kneading bread to catch her up in a floury squeeze.

She had not even left yet, and the homesickness lay so heavy upon her heart she considered finding a place to hide until Mr. Swann grew weary of waiting and chose a more willing girl. But that would anger and embarrass Mrs. Forsyth. *You'll have to make the best of this*, she told herself as her leaden feet carried her back to the parlor.

"I'm ready, sir," she told Mr. Swann.

I should have found her a sack. Olivia stood in the doorway and watched Mr. Swann carry Sarah's little bundle out to a waiting coach. In the cellar were several tin trunks provided by the Methodist Ladies' Home Mission Society for those girls going into domestic service, with enough storage room for two alpaca uniforms, some undergarments, and a nightgown. But a tin trunk was the customary baggage of a servant, which Sarah was not to be.

At the door to the coach, which a handsome man in full livery held open, the girl turned to wave. Olivia returned the wave and watched her step inside. The sight of the fine brougham and team of two horses had been a little reassuring, for she recalled Mr. Swann had arrived in a hired hansom yesterday. Hopefully it meant that Mrs. Blake was willing to go to some pains to make Sarah feel important.

She has no knowledge of what I've done,

Father, Olivia prayed. *So please don't lay any of my punishment to her account.*

Olivia nodded at Mr. Swann, who also looked back at her before climbing inside. The coachman was climbing up to his box and taking up the reins. A white face stared at her from the window. Olivia waved again, smiling reassuringly. She watched them move down Drury Lane and disappear into the fog, then she closed the door. There were sixty-one other girls who needed her.

Sarah's heart ached as if a fist held it in an iron grip. She pulled her green wrap around herself and stared out the window. All that was visible through the morning fog were ghostly facades of buildings and houses.

"You can see more on this side," Mr. Swann said from the rear-facing seat with a nod toward her right.

"Thank you." She turned her face to look simply out of politeness. In the opposite direction headed an endless parade of dray wagons and carriages, riders on horseback, and coaches. She was surrounded by sounds—wheels humming, hoofbeats against cobbled stones, and human voices.

A hackney cab driver peered down at the window and tipped his hat. Sarah turned her face away. Mr. Swann gave her an uneven-toothed smile.

"It's a big city, isn't it?"

"Yes, sir," she replied, lowering her eyes to stare at the worn felt hat balanced upon his knees so she wouldn't have to look at his face. Not because she blamed him, because as Mrs. Forsyth had said, he had been employed by the woman whose companion she was to become, whatever that entailed. But she hardly knew the man, and the farther they traveled, the less secure she felt. What Mrs. Forsyth had said about Naaman's servant girl returned to her mind. *At least you aren't in chains*, she told herself.

"I have daughters too."

He said this after clearing his throat, which led Sarah to wonder if he felt as awkward as she did. Surely not, with his being an adult.

"Four of them, actually."

She glanced at his face and then down at the hat again. "How old are they?"

"Let's see," he said, folding his arms. "Margaret is fifteen, Kathy, fourteen, Elaine, nine, and Lucy, six—no, she's seven now. She asked for a set of watercolors for her birthday, and now all she cares to do is paint."

With effort Sarah mustered a polite smile. Actually, the warmth in his voice put her a little more at ease. Surely a father who loved his children would not bring another child to a situation that would be intolerable.

"Flowers, birds, houses . . ." The man went on. "She even attempted my portrait. I didn't say this to Lucy, mind you, but if only there would have been a hoop in my ear, I would have made a fearsome pirate."

This time the smile wasn't such an effort. Sarah had never given much thought to what it would be like to have a flesh-and-blood father, but she found herself wondering if Mr. Swann's daughters knew how fortunate they were.

"We're on Piccadilly, by the way," he said with a nod toward a window. "Berkeley Square is to the west."

"Will we cross London Bridge?" she asked impulsively.

"*The* London Bridge?"

"Yes, sir." There were others she had

learned about in school such as Blackfrier's and Waterloo, but their names were not attached to the game she had played in the tiny courtyard with her friends at least a thousand times.

"I'm afraid not. It's in the opposite direction."

They had traveled for some time and through fog as thick as treacle. But she could not resist turning to peek out of the small oblong back window, just in case. All she could see were the pair of draft horses and the wagon moving behind them.

"Have you never seen the bridge?" Mr. Swann asked.

She turned back around in her seat. "No, sir. I've not even seen the Thames."

"Never? But Saint Matthew's is but a half mile away, if that far."

"We should probably have seen it if not for the buildings," Sarah explained.

He gave her a sad little smile. "But you might as well have been on the moon, eh? I don't suppose there were too many outings."

"We took turns going with Mrs. Abbot to the greengrocer's," Sarah told him lest he should pity her too much.

Mr. Swann stared at her for a moment, then reached for a cord above his left arm. Presently the coach slowed to a stop, and he opened the door and stuck out his head. "My good man," he called, "would you mind letting us have a look at London Bridge?"

"Oh, please don't," Sarah said to his back. Already she had inconvenienced him and the coachman by taking time for farewells. And what if their Mrs. Blake didn't approve?

"You'd scarce be able to see it for the fog, sir," reached her ears.

"We would be happy for any sight of it," Mr. Swann persisted in a cordial voice.

"Please, sir . . ." Sarah attempted.

"As long as you're willin' to explain to the Missus," the coachman called back. "I've all the time in the world!"

"Very good of you!"

The solicitor settled back into his seat and smiled as the wheels started turning again. "You've been more than gracious about being uprooted at such short notice, Miss Matthews. I think if you have a desire to see the bridge, you should see it."

"But Mrs. Blake . . ."

"Was once a girl herself. She'll understand."

She would have been more reassured had there been more confidence in his voice. But then the anticipation of seeing the bridge pierced just a little of the despondency wrapped around her. "Thank you," she told him shyly.

His smile widened. "You're very welcome."

Sarah gave him a smile before timidity moved her back to the window on the left. For some three quarters of an hour she read the signboards on the upper storeys of buildings rising out of the mist, such as HILDYARD'S DOG CAKE, GOOD'S PATENT BOTTLES, and several PREMISES TO BE LET ON LEASE. And then the buildings ceased abruptly, leaving nothing but blank gray space.

"London Bridge," said Mr. Swann.

Sarah squinted out at the distance. "But I don't see it, sir."

"That's because you're on it," he said with a little chuckle.

Sure enough, when she lowered her eyes, she could see stone roadway extending out to a wall about the height of a man's waist. People, mostly men wearing top hats or bowlers, moved alongside it. Beyond loomed nothing but fog. She turned to the other window. Traffic moved in the opposite direction, then pedestrians and another wall. They could have been crossing the Sahara for all she could see of the Thames. But it was still London Bridge.

"I wish you could see the river," Mr. Swann said. He moved closer and motioned her aside. "But it might be possible to open this window at least." He pushed the glass up easily, then moved a little hook on each side to keep it in place. The street noises intensified, and she could hear bits of pedestrian conversations. When he raised the window on the opposite side, cool damp air breezed through the coach.

Sarah stuck her head out the left window and drew in a deep breath. The fog-shrouded river smelled of Drury Lane after a rain, though not quite as foul, and with the faint odor of fish. She was pulling in another breath when from somewhere came an unsettling memory. Tight arms held her close, that same odor all about her. Quickly she sat back in the seat and tried to shake the thought from her head. But it persisted, bringing with it the recollection of water all around her and through her, clogging her nose and mouth. And most terrifying of all, the arms letting go.

"Are you all right?"

Mr. Swann's voice. She had forgotten he was even there, but he stared across at her with concern in his eyes. She pulled her wrap closer. "I'm fine, sir."

"You know the bridge is perfectly safe," he reassured with a smile. "No danger of falling down. Some of those old nursery rhymes aren't fit for children's ears."

"Yes, sir. Thank you." Because he had gone to all the trouble of asking the coachman to bring her here, Sarah told herself she should resume looking out the window. But first she asked, "Would you mind lowering the glass again?"

✿ Seven ✿

"It'll be good to stretch our limbs again," William said to Naomi as the Great Northern Railway engine slowed for the approach into King's Cross Station. They had spent Easter in Leicester, visiting extended family members William had not seen since he was nine. Naomi had thought it important that he do so before setting out again for Oxford on Saturday to begin the two-month Trinity term.

But they might have been approaching Paris, Naomi told herself, for all they could see from the windows of their second-class coach. "Yes, it will be good," she replied.

Still, she would have had the train turn around and start them on the trip all over again if it were possible. She loved the boy as if he were her own and missed him sorely when he was at University. Yet she wouldn't take any of it away from him. He had worked hard since first arriving at Mrs.

Blake's, balancing duties in the stables and garden with classes at a Wesleyan grammar school on Charing Cross Road. And though he never complained, his duties at Oxford were taxing.

"What are you thinking?" William asked her.

She could not tell him without sounding clinging and overly sentimental, so she ignored the question and said, "I suppose the young ladies of Leicester will be inconsolable."

"Inconsolable?" he asked, then narrowed his smoke-colored eyes. "They were little girls, Aunt Naomi. And annoying ones at that. I couldn't even take a stroll without them following."

Casually she smoothed a fold from the serge skirt of her peacock-blue-and-black-checked gown. She felt no guilt for teasing him, for he was not above a little teasing himself. "What about Arietta? She's your age."

"You refer to my *first cousin* Arietta?"

"Queen Victoria married her first cousin. They were very happy." In fact, the Queen still wore widow's weeds, though nine

years had passed since the Prince Con-
sort's death.

"No, thank you." He feigned a shudder. "I
can appreciate what the fox feels like at the
hunt."

Finally Naomi allowed herself to smile.
"She did seem a little aggressive."

The tall gentleman seated in the bench in
front of them groaned, causing the wife and
small daughter at his right to turn to him.
The wife asked, "Have you a headache,
Huntley?"

"Try saying that three times quickly,"
William leaned close to whisper, and Naomi
gave him a warning look.

"No, it's my legs," the gentleman replied,
groaning again as he swayed from side to
side like the needle in a metronome.
"They've gone numb."

His wife's sympathy evaporated. "Well,
it's no wonder, with the scant padding on
these seats. I shall be black and blue for
weeks!" She went on to upbraid him for his
cheapness, her voice becoming more and
more nasal in tone, while the little girl resumed staring out the window.

That explains it, Naomi thought, for she
had wondered why a family so finely

dressed—his well cut Chesterfield coat, her traveling outfit of rich buff-colored silk trimmed in velvet, and the child's red poplin dress with matching coat and little cap— would travel second class. Perhaps he was a miser like Ebenezer Scrooge.

"And what if the Penningtons catch sight of us leaving this coach?" the wife went on. "He won't be so willing to sell if he thinks you can't afford—"

"Would that he give the whole kit and caboodle away to someone else!" her husband cut in, ceasing his swaying. "You're the one who wants to live in the country, not me!"

Before Naomi knew what was happening, William was tapping the man's shoulder. "I beg your pardon, sir."

She touched his arm. "William . . ."

But it was too late, for the gentleman twisted in his seat and snapped, "Well, what is it?"

"That expression, sir," William said in an apologetic tone. " 'Kit and caboodle.' Would you be so kind as to explain its meaning?"

"*What?*"

"Our coachman collects unusual words

and expressions. And I'll wager he's never heard that one. Has it to do with a country estate?"

"*You* have a coachman?" Disbelief dripped from his tone.

Curling her fingers around the reticule in her lap, Naomi thought, *Gentleman or not, if you hurt that boy, I'll tell you what I think of your arrogance.*

William only grinned. "Oh, no, sir. Mrs. Blake's coachman. I clean the stables for him when I'm not helping Mr. Duffy the gardener."

The man's eyes bulged, and Naomi braced herself for the sounding out that would surely follow. But then his face relaxed. "I'm not quite certain, to be honest," he said, pursing his lips. "But one hears it all the time in that context."

"Pray tell . . . what context?"

The wife and daughter had turned in their seats by then, the wife giving Naomi a curious glance before settling her gaze upon William. "It doesn't necessarily have to refer to an *estate*," she explained. "But if you used it in that context, it would mean everything to do with the estate—the houses, lands, and such."

"Everything to do with the estate . . ." William echoed doubtfully.

The gentleman nodded and, above the squealing of brakes, said, "For example, suppose your trunk were to turn up missing at King's Cross. You might say to the stationmaster in a fit of pique, 'You've misplaced the whole kit and caboodle,' meaning not only the trunk but its contents as well."

Awareness flooded William's expression. "Yes, I understand perfectly!"

"Very good!" the gentleman said with a chuckle, though ignoring the hand William thrust out at him, for they were not of the same social ranking. But he did wish them a subdued good-day before exiting the coach with his family five minutes later.

"I don't see Stanley," William said above the hum of the crowd on the platform as they stepped to the side to make way for other departing passengers.

"Why don't you let him find his own words?" Naomi asked him, still smarting from the tone of the man's "coachman" re- mark. "And you should have mentioned you're at Oxford."

He gave her a puzzled look. "Why?"

"So he would know you're more than just a servant."

William's dark eyes were affectionate upon her. "I failed to mention it because a very wise person once taught me that maintaining one's integrity is more important than trying to impress others."

Tears stung her eyes and she looked away, pretending to search the crowd. He was right, of course. And she could have easily borne the man's judgment of herself. But she felt so vulnerable when it came to William.

"Aunt Naomi?"

At the touch of his hand upon her shoulder, she blinked and turned to smile at him. *You can't shield him from all pain*, she had to remind herself. That was how Jeremy Blakes were created. "Well, I still don't understand Stanley's fascination with words," she said with lingering irritation. "It's not as if he reads."

"He says they impress women," he said before waving into the distance. "It's Mr. Duffy."

Stunned speechless, Naomi followed as he threaded his way around groups of people. She was at first disappointed but then relieved that it was indeed Roger Duffy moving toward them, for she would have had to fight a strong impulse to show Stanley Russell the rough side of her tongue. *What is he telling that boy?*

"It's good to have you both back!" the gardener's deep voice boomed while his great paw pumped William's hand. From under the bill of his felt cap, thick joining brows made him appear angry and fierce. The gray-flecked beard sprouting wildly from his face, and that he was built as big as a draught horse added to that illusion. But he was quite pleasant and his smile all the more endearing because of its unlikely source.

"My uncle sent some gladioli bulbs," the boy told him.

"Very fine." After exchanging greetings with Naomi, he lifted his dark brows meaningfully. "Stanley took the coach on a errand. So Mrs. Bacon said I should hire a hackney so's you won't be lookin' for him to come for you all day."

There was clearly more to the story, which prompted Naomi to send William to find a porter. When he was out of earshot, the gardener glanced at the faces in the immediate vicinity and said in an undertone, "That lawyer found the girl yesterday."

"Yes?" Naomi breathed.

He nodded. "But the woman over to the orphanage said he should come back today. So mayhap she'll be there, mayhap she won't."

"Oh, I do hope so."

"Aye."

"But has Mrs. Blake said anything to the others?"

"Last night after supper Mrs. Bacon called us together in the sitting room. The Missus said she was considerin' taking in an orphan girl in the morning." His eyes, brown as the soil he tended, were bitter. "Made it sound like she was bein' charitable, after all this time."

Naomi put a hand upon his sleeve. "She is, Mr. Duffy. Better late than not at all."

———

Jules did not attempt to engage the girl in conversation as the coach moved down Piccadilly. She seemed content to sit and stare out the window, though for a minute on the bridge he had wondered if she was taking ill. And he had his own thoughts to mull over, such as how good it would be to spend more time at his desk, even though his clientele would be decidedly less well-heeled than Mrs. Blake.

When the coach turned north onto Berkeley Street, Jules cleared his throat. "We're almost to Berkeley Square."

She turned to give him a smile that did not travel up to her somber green eyes.

"It's so called because it's situated around a square—or rather rectangle," he said. "It's one of the loveliest spots in London. I brought my daughters there once to have ices at GUNTER'S. They set up tables in the square . . ."

This time she nodded in the middle of his words. Her expression was pinched, as if her mind was so filled with foreboding that she could not concentrate on what he was saying. He decided to spare her the description of the plane trees. She would have years to make their acquaintance.

They stopped midway up Berkeley Row, a continuation of Berkeley Street on the east side of the square. No. 14 was a four-storey stone Georgian, standing cheek by jowl with other houses just as old and magnificent. Spotless windows shone above boxes filled with early blooming flowers. There were ornate lamp holders and spear-headed iron railings running the length of each side from the arched portico. To the right of the four white entrance steps, another set of steps descended to the trades-man's entrance.

"I'll wait here for you, sir," the affable Stanley said after opening the coach's door.

"Thank you." Jules allowed Sarah to be assisted to the pavement before he stepped out himself, scooping up her for-gotten bundle under his arms. The girl stood staring up at the top floors, her head so inclined that he feared she might lose her balance.

"Your new home, Miss Matthews."

When their eyes met, hers were filled with fright instead of the awe he expected. "This is it?" she asked in a voice between a croak and whisper.

"Yes, it is. Shall we?"

She nodded resignedly. "Yes, sir."

Mrs. Bacon answered his ring at the arched oak door. Framed by the coolness of the hall, the housekeeper peered at them through wire spectacles perched upon the tip of her nose. "Good morning, Mr. Swann," she said, stepping back so they could enter. She was perhaps fifty, with graying brown hair drawn up into a top-knot. Her status as the highest-ranking female servant allowed her to clothe her tall figure with gowns of her own choosing—in this instance, a rose calico. She wore an apron, however, from which dangled a chain with several keys.

"Good morning." Jules handed over his hat and entered, figuring the girl would rather follow than be pushed right away into her new circumstance. He turned and was relieved that she had indeed stepped across the threshold. "This is Sarah Matthews, Mrs. Bacon."

Sarah had the look of an animal cornered, but she dipped into a curtsey. The housekeeper's smile widened. "It's a pleasure to meet you, Miss Matthews. But you mustn't go bowing to me. Now, may I relieve you of that shawl?"

"Yes, Madam," Sarah said, causing the housekeeper to send Jules an amused look.

The girl clearly had no idea that being a ward meant she did not address servants with courtesy titles. Jules wondered what she would think about being the grand-daughter of the owner of the house. *It would probably overwhelm her.*

To Jules, Mrs. Bacon said, "Mrs. Blake is expecting you in the parlor, sir."

"Shall we?" he asked Sarah for the second time.

But Mrs. Bacon shook her head. "Begging your pardon, Mr. Swann, but she wishes to see you first. I'll wait here with Miss Matthews."

"Very well." Jules set her bundle on a brightly polished rosewood settle, and after sending Sarah another smile, he walked down the corridor. He knew his way well, having met with Mrs. Blake several times over the past six months. At the staircase he paused to glance behind him. Sarah sat next to her bundle on the settle while Mrs. Bacon asked her questions about the ride over. As he climbed the stairs, Jules thought it was good that the servants he had met here proved to be sociable. The only exception was a lady's maid, who glowered at him every time she was sent away so Mrs. Blake could meet with him in private.

"Come in," a familiar voice responded to his knock.

He opened the parlor door and walked inside. Mrs. Blake sat alone on the sofa, long hands folded upon her lap. There was a degree of anxiousness in her expression. He was certain it was because he was not able to assure her yesterday that he would turn up today with her granddaughter.

That assumption proved correct when she said before inviting him to take a seat, "Is she here?"

"Yes. Her name is Sarah Matthews."

Mrs. Blake closed her eyes briefly and seemed to sigh with relief. When she opened them it was to give him a puzzled look. "Matthews?"

"The name given to all the children without known surnames, according to the headmistress."

"It certainly took you long enough to get here."

With a nod, Jules explained about the bridge. "I didn't know when she would have another opportunity to see it."

He was relieved when she allowed that to pass without complaint. "And you're positive she's my granddaughter."

"Positive," Jules replied. "Mrs. Forsyth—the headmistress—is of sterling character and assures me it is so."

"I see."

He shifted upon his feet. "Wouldn't you care to meet her now?"

"Soon. Do have a seat. Shall I ring for tea?"

While her words were sociable, Jules had the strong impression that she was willing to be rid of him as soon as possible. He took a chair, or at least perched himself on the end of it, but declined the tea.

"I will have delivered to you this afternoon a draft for the remainder of your fee," she told him, "with the addition of a bonus of twenty-five pounds."

"That's very generous of you, Mrs. Blake."

She nodded in the manner of an aristocrat bestowing favor upon a peasant. "In return, I expect you to continue with your discretion, even though our acquaintance will be severed shortly."

That chafed him more than a little, for she had reminded him of his responsibility to keep the matter secret every time they met. Did she assume that now that the assignment was over he would take out an advertisement in *The Times*? Politely though, he replied, "But of course."

"Very good. Then you may take your leave now and send the girl in."

He rose, made a little bow, and went to the door. Miss Prewitt, the lady's maid, was standing just to the left when he walked out into the corridor. She did not raise her hands from studying her fingernails to speak to him, and Jules wondered if she had even given a word of welcome to the newcomer downstairs. When he reached the ground floor, the girl stood and watched him approach. "Mrs. Blake is eager to meet you," Jules told her.

"Thank you, Mr. Swann," she said in a weak voice.

"I'll take her on in, sir," Mrs. Bacon said, handing him his hat. She shook her head at Sarah, who was picking up her bundle. "You may leave that out here, dear."

"Thank you," Jules told the housekeeper, more for the "dear" than for the hat.

He met the girl's eyes, wanting to say something in the order of, "I wish you a good life here," but as she appeared to be teetering on the edge of control, he feared any expression of sentiment might cause her distress. Besides, whether or not she had a good life was beyond his hopes now and in the hands of the people who resided under this roof.

"I'll let myself out," he said to Mrs. Bacon.

"Very good, sir. Good morning to you."

Watching Sarah follow the housekeeper, Jules noticed that she held her left arm rigidly to her side, the hand tucked between the folds of her skirt. *You thickwit!* he chided himself. In his pique at Mrs. Blake, he had forgotten all about it. And surely it would have been better if she had had some time to get used to the idea before summoning her granddaughter.

The temptation came and went—to pass the two on the staircase and dash back into the parlor. *It's none of your affair now*, he reminded himself. But he could not make himself step outside. *What can she do . . . dismiss you?* He replaced his hat and folded his limbs next to her humble little bundle on the settle. If the girl was to be rejected, he should be the one to escort her back to the orphanage, not someone who was even more of a stranger to her than he was. He owed Sarah that much.

❧ *Eight* ❧

The parlor was a mixture of *Arabian Nights* and Christmas, all crimson and gilt, with more bric-a-brac and ornament than Sarah's eyes could take in at once. A low fire snapped in a marble fireplace veined with gold. There was even a stuffed peacock with his plumage cascading down over a wall shelf. The carpet was so intricately woven, the colors so rich, that she feared soiling it with her scuffed leather slippers. But she was nudged gently forward by Mrs. Bacon toward a woman seated on a velvet sofa and dressed all in black. She looked older than Mrs. Kettner, with gray hair pulled back into netting and fine lines webbing cheeks the color of whey. In a chair to the woman's right sat a younger woman with dark braids and curls.

No one spoke for what seemed like hours. The woman's pale blue eyes studied her face intently, as if she were trying to recollect where she had seen her before. But of course that couldn't be.

It was Mrs. Bacon who finally broke the ice. "Mrs. Blake, this is Sarah."

"Good morning, Sarah," the woman said, then added curiously, "I didn't expect your coloring to be so fair."

The light pressure of Mrs. Bacon's hand upon Sarah's shoulder gave her just enough fortitude to dip into a curtsey and reply, "Good morning, Madam." She found herself too intimidated to follow the plan to display her hand. Surely Mr. Swann or Mrs. Forsyth would have told her about it anyway. That she was still wanted here was a mystery she could not fathom.

The woman smiled, the blue eyes still appraising. "I'm pleased to see that you're well-mannered. But tell me, were you not fed at Saint Matthew's?"

"Yes, Madam. I've just been thin since I can remember." Sarah could not bring herself to add that she was almost always hungry after rising from her breakfast porridge or her supper of tea and toast. Mrs. Forsyth did what she could. And lunch was almost always filling enough, usually brown bread and a hearty soup.

"And why is your hair so short?"

Because it's short, jumped into Sarah's mind, though she kept her expression ironed of any insubordination. She felt like a bug under a looking glass, and even *she* knew that it was rude to find fault with a person's looks. But then, she was only a child, and perhaps outside the walls of Saint Matthew's it was the accepted thing to do.

"It's in case we get lice, Madam," she replied.

Horror flooded both women's faces. "And have you them now?" Mrs. Blake asked.

"Oh no, Madam. I'm quite sure I haven't. You can usually tell."

There had been lice infestations over the years, which Mrs. Forsyth and the workers got rid of by applying kerosene to heads and boiling all the clothing and linens. The implication that she *might* have some of the creatures crawling about caused Sarah's head to itch in a dozen spots. She didn't dare scratch.

"Do you know who I am?" the woman asked.

"You're Mrs. Blake, Madam."

"Indeed." She motioned with a long slender hand toward her left. "And this is Marie, my lady's maid."

The maid merely favored her with an almost imperceptible nod, as if she begrudged her even that much activity of her face.

"And do you know why you're here?"

Sarah thought about what Mrs. Forsyth had told her. "To be your companion?"

"You're to be my ward," Mrs. Blake corrected.

"Yes, Madam."

An eyebrow raised in the regal face. "You wish to ask a question, Sarah?"

"I just . . ." She dipped into another curtsey, since it had pleased the woman so much the first time. "I beg your pardon, Madam, but what does a ward do?"

Mrs. Blake smiled again, and it seemed a little more warmly. "We will decide that in the days to come. In the meantime, you are to conduct yourself with the manners with which I see you are capable."

"Yes, Madam." She thought she was about to be dismissed, and even Mrs. Bacon shifted her weight beside her as if preparing to turn. But then the lady's maid rose to her feet, walked over to the sofa, and whispered into Mrs. Blake's ear. As the maid moved back to her chair, the older woman fixed Sarah with an odd look.

"Are you hiding something, Sarah?"

Sarah's toes curled in her slippers. "H-hiding?"

"In your hand. Surely you wouldn't take advantage of my hospitality by stealing from me?"

"No, Madam. Never." She realized she was scratching her head and dropped her right hand to her side. Even though Mrs. Blake and her maid were essentially strangers to her, it stung that *anyone* would accuse her of theft. She had only stolen once in her life, a rose-shaped button from the jar in Mrs. Kettner's room. She was but seven then and had confessed the crime and returned the button days later when her conscience would allow her no peace.

She had no choice but to raise her left hand from the folds of her skirt. The lady's maid let out a gasp, and Mrs. Blake's face paled even more so. For a second the grip of the hand upon Sarah's shoulder tightened.

"How did that happen, child?" Mrs. Bacon asked in a kindly tone.

"I was born this way."

And because the sight disturbed them, she hid her hand again. She was surprised to see Mrs. Blake's pale eyes glistening. "I had no idea," the woman said in a voice barely above a whisper. Even the maid's expression had softened somewhat.

"It doesn't hurt." Sarah felt compelled to assure them.

Mrs. Blake didn't answer but took a handkerchief from her lap and dabbed at her eyes. Presently she looked up. Her voice became formal again. "Mrs. Bacon, we must make some plans. Sarah, Marie will give you a bath now."

"Me, Madame?" the lady's maid asked with stunned voice.

"You have excellent eyesight, so you can inspect her for lice. And I suppose we should burn those clothes for the sake of caution."

If being suspected of thievery and having to display her hand shamed Sarah, this was doubly humiliating. It was all too obvious that she didn't belong here. Couldn't Mrs. Forsyth have seen this? Why, someone like Helen would be at the piano now, charming Mrs. Blake and even her vinegar-faced lady's maid with beautiful songs.

You have to tell her now, she urged herself. Once they burned her clothes—and heaven only knew what they would expect her to wear after that—she had a feeling it would be impossible to leave. She drew in a deep breath just as the maid was getting to her feet and Mrs. Bacon had moved the hand from her shoulder. "I beg your pardon, Madam?"

The woman raised a pale eyebrow. "Yes?"

"Please . . . may I go back to Saint Matthew's?"

"Why? Do you not find my house to your liking?"

"Oh no, Madam. Your house is beautiful." She swallowed and lowered her eyes to the black lace collar. "But there are other girls there you would like much more."

"Indeed?"

"Yes, Madam." Fearing interruption, she spoke faster. "I'm not very quick with chores, and I can't play the piano like Helen—she plays in chapel and lost her mother when she was ten and would very much like to live in a—"

"That is enough nonsense talk," Mrs. Blake cut in with a frown and wave of a long hand. "Now, on to your bath."

Sarah looked up at Mrs. Bacon, who patted her shoulder. "Marie will tend to you, Miss Matthews."

Chin raised, the lady's maid led her through the doorway and to the staircase. Sarah looked longingly at the stairs leading to the ground floor. She had traveled a long way to get here, but mostly because of turning to see the bridge. Perhaps she could find her way back. Surely Mrs. Forsyth could be made to understand that she had made a mistake.

As the maid took hold of the bannister and began climbing, Sarah took a deep breath, then veered off to the left. Her foot touched the first step tentatively—she fairly flew down the others with heart racing. Incredibly, Mr. Swann was in the corridor, rising from the settle. They looked at each other across the distance, and every apprehension Sarah had suffered since breakfast fell upon her. Eyes brimming, she called out, "Mr. Swann?"

He frowned, but it seemed not out of anger. "Sarah . . ."

Sarah hastened down the corridor, stopping just in front of him. Were she bolder, she would have thrown her arms around him. "Please, Mr. Swann . . . will you take me back to the Home?"

"I'm afraid I can't do that, Sarah," he told her, his face filled with sadness.

"Come, Miss Matthews!" an out-of-breath and peevish voice said from behind her. "A lady does not make a scene."

She sniffed hard, ignoring the maid. "But I don't *belong* here, sir. Mrs. Forsyth—she'll understand. There are other girls—"

"Mrs. Forsyth would have no choice but to send you back. But you'll have greater opportunities for your future here."

"I don't *care* about my future."

"Miss Matthews! Your bath!"

First sending a quick pleading look over her head, Mr. Swann patted her shoulder lightly. "It will be better with time, Sarah. You must remind yourself of that every day." He turned away from her, but in the doorway turned again. "Every day. You'll see."

The click of the door behind him had a sad note of finality to it.

Woodenly Sarah followed the lady's maid up two flights of stairs. The bathroom was just as elegantly appointed as Mrs. Blake's parlor, with wallpapering of green, gold, and pink stripes, framed mirrors and pictures, thick Oriental rugs, and a potted fern curving gracefully from one corner. She had only known the wooden hip bath in front of the kitchen fire at Saint Matthew's that held only a scant six inches of water without overflowing whenever someone eased down into it. This bathing tub was huge, gleaming richly like piano ivories and resting upon magnificent claw feet. At one end a copper tank gurgled and sent up wisps of steam like a teapot. But her surroundings were all just reminders that she was not home, their unfamiliarity making her almost queasy.

The maid pulled a stool from a table filled with bottles of assorted shapes and sizes. "Sit here," she ordered.

Sarah was unable to articulate even the most perfunctory response. But she moved to obey, and the woman began parting sections of her hair with her fingers. "I do not know how she expects me to see anything, with hair so fair," she grumbled.

"Miss Jacobs brushes our hair over a handkerchief," Sarah offered meekly.

"And why would she do that?"

"They're gray . . . the lice are." Right away she added, "But I'm almost sure I haven't any. My head only itched in the parlor because I thought about them."

"Hmph!"

Sarah wasn't sure if the low snort of derision was for Miss Jacob's method or skepticism over her not having any lice. But the maid stepped over to a wooden cupboard and took out a white linen cloth. "A towel will do?"

"I think so, Madam."

"You do not address me as Madam," she said on her way back. "We put this on your lap, yes?"

"Yes." Without the added courtesy title, Sarah felt as guilty as if she had sworn. She smoothed the fabric in her lap while from a drawer beneath the table the maid pulled out a silver-handled brush. Sarah winced. If she actually did have *lice*, she would feel wretched about sullying something so fine.

But she lowered her head, and after at

least five minutes of brushing, the maid said, "Is that enough to tell?"

"I'm quite sure." Lowering her head even farther, Sarah inspected the towel for any signs of life. All that lay there were four or five blonde hairs. "I don't see any, Miss."

"You are not to say 'Miss' to me either," the maid reproved, then took the towel by the four corners and lifted it from her lap. There was relief in her expression, though she had not ceased frowning since Sarah first set eyes upon her. "Your bath now."

She went over to the copper tank and twisted a flat handle on the side. Water began gushing out of a spigot extending over the bathing tub. Sarah surveyed the rising steam and wondered if she were to be poached like an egg, but presently the flow stopped, and the woman twisted a round handle over another spigot from which more water flowed. Then she turned to Sarah. "The hot first, then the cold."

"Thank you," Sarah said. And as the maid was still staring sullenly at her, she said by way of attempting polite conversation—not that her heart was in it, but in the hopes of the woman not being so angry at her—"You have hot water all the time?"

"No," was the unsmiling reply. "Mrs. Blake ordered the water heated earlier so it would be ready. You must undress now."

It made Sarah feel a little better that her bath had been planned in advance and not because she looked dirty. But after reaching back to unfasten the button behind her neck, she could not bring herself to pull off her gown. Bathing in Saint Matthew's bustling kitchen was one thing, but in the presence of this glowering stranger was quite another.

"Well?"

Sarah bit her lip. "Would you mind?"

The maid rolled her eyes and turned her back, muttering something having to do with the English being taught prudishness from the cradle. "Leave your clothes on the floor," she ordered seconds later, as if she could see Sarah looking for a place to put her folded gown.

"Yes, Madam."

"And you do not say that to me. Do you know nothing?"

"No, Ma—" Sarah began, then silenced herself. She stepped over to the bathtub and lowered herself inside. The warm water was soothing against her raw nerves.

Turning toward her again, the maid wore a no-nonsense expression, as if she had made all of the allowances she intended to make for Sarah's modesty. "I cannot assist you if I cannot see you. Do you know how to use a soap and flannel?"

Sarah merely nodded so that her speech wouldn't betray her again. Into her right hand was pressed a honey-colored oval cake with Pears etched into the side. It smelled like lavender, not like the coal tar soap at the home. But she thought she would gladly bathe in coal-tar for the rest of her life if she could only go back there.

"Well?"

The irritated voice startled Sarah back into action. Unhooking two fingers from the soap, she took the flannel from the maid, draped it over her left hand, and anchored it with her bit of thumb. She dipped it in the water and rubbed it against the soap before scrubbing at her face.

Apparently satisfied, the maid rose and pulled a gold braided cord that hung from the wall near the dressing table. The door opened a minute later, breezing cooler air into the room along with a woman wearing the same black gown with white apron. Under her lace cap, carrot red hair was pulled back into a chignon, from which several corkscrew curls had sprung loose. She flashed Sarah a smile that displayed more gums than little pearl teeth, but she was still very pretty.

"Why, hello there . . . I'm Hester."

Her breathy voice was pitched so high that Sarah would have thought a five-year-old had entered the room had she not looked.

"Her name is Miss Matthews," the lady's maid replied curtly, motioning toward the gray heap of clothing. "These are to be burned. And those downstairs as well."

Sarah's heart ached all the more. "I've no lice," she said in a small voice. "May I keep my clothes?"

"I am sorry," Marie replied, though her expression did not soften. "You will have other things to wear. Much finer things."

"But what's she going to wear *now*?" the younger maid asked, her brow knitting under the canopy of corkscrew curls. "You ain't going to keep her in that tub all day, are you?"

"Mrs. Bacon will send someone to SWAN AND EDGAR'S when Stanley returns. There is not much to her, so we will have to wrap her with a towel until they send some clothing."

With the discarded clothes in her arms, Hester paused at the door. Marie had spoken to her just as harshly as she did Sarah, but clearly she was not intimidated. "Avis's the thinnest of us," she said in the high-pitched voice. "I'll see if she's willin' to lend her a wrapper. Better than a towel."

The gesture of kindness gave Sarah the courage to ask, "Please, Miss . . ."

"Yes?"

"I've some things wrapped in my bundle downstairs."

She smiled. "I'll see about them, Miss Matthews."

The door closed behind her, shutting off the inflow of cooler air and goodwill, and Sarah was left alone with Marie again.

"Wet your hair," the woman said.

"Yes, Ma—" Sarah began automatically, then cringed at her scowl. "I'm trying hard to remember."

The woman did not reply but sloshed her hands in the water before taking the soap from her. Sarah leaned back on her elbows until her face was an island in the water.

When she raised herself again, she stared ahead and allowed her hair to be lathered. Fingers dug roughly into her scalp, but it was not an unpleasant feeling. After a couple of minutes Sarah's short hair was a bonnet of lather. The maid was pulling a chain attached to a stopper. Water lowered with gulping sounds as if the pipes underneath were thirsty. *But my hair* . . . Sarah protested silently.

Marie turned on the cold-water tap again and said as if by way of grudging apology, "It would take too long to heat more water."

"I'm used to rinsing with bath water," Sarah offered while about half still remained in the tub.

"Bath water? You might as well not bother to wash. Come now, move back a bit."

The water scooped in palmfuls over her hair was chill enough to set her teeth rattling. "Cold, yes?" the maid asked after turning off the tap, when Sarah shivered at the water trickling down her bare back.

Sarah forgot again. "Yes, Madam."

But the maid simply took towels from the cupboard and wrapped one around her hair like a sultan's turban. She motioned for her to stand and wound another towel around

Sarah's torso, tucking in the last corner under her arm. With her assistance Sarah stepped out of the tub and onto the carpet. Marie dried her face, arms, and legs with still another towel. *Three!* Sarah thought. At the home, it was more likely that three girls would share one threadbare towel, and it was almost sodden when it was the unfortunate last girl's turn.

When the maid was finished, having even dried between Sarah's toes as she held on to the side of the tub for balance, she dropped the towel on the carpet. Her frown deepened. "You are even thinner wet. Your arms are like chicken bones."

"I'm sorry." Sarah moved her left hand behind her so that it wouldn't be a target for criticism as well.

"Well, Naomi will fatten you up. Her cooking is typical bland English fare, but as you have never tasted French food, you will be able to stomach it."

"Yes, M—" Giving a sigh, Sarah said in an apologetic tone, "Why mustn't I address you as 'Madam' . . . if you please?"

"Because I am a servant," the woman replied.

"But so am I."

"No. You are Mrs. Blake's ward. You must learn to address people correctly, or you will be thought of as an ignorant little girl with no refinement. Mrs. Blake is the only person you address as Madam, unless one of her prattling friends comes to call."

Sarah nodded and said with even more meekness, "Thank you. I shall try to remember that. But how am I to address you . . . if you please?"

The woman rolled her eyes. "You address me as 'Marie,' for that is my name. The others are to be addressed by their given names as well, except, of course, for Mrs. Blake and Mrs. Bacon and Mr. Duffy."

Mrs. Bacon was the housekeeper, Sarah remembered. So it stood to reason that Mr. Duffy was the butler. But when she asked Marie, the woman made a snort of disapproval. "I would not work here if there were one. English butlers are pompous popinjays. Mr. Duffy is addressed as 'Mister' simply because he has been employed by Mrs. Blake for so long. He is the gardener, but presently he is on his way to fetch Naomi, Madame's cook, from the station, which means meals will once again be merely tolerable instead of barely palatable."

❧ Nine ❧

"You'll be careful with that trunk, now," Naomi cautioned as Mr. Duffy pocketed the harmonica he had played all the way from King's Cross Station, and William unfastened the straps to the hackney's boot. They were in the mews, the road running behind the gardens of Berkeley Street where the stables belonging to Mrs. Blake and the other residents of the square were situated. When the trunk lay on the ground, Mr. Duffy dropped some coins into the cabby's outstretched hand.

"Thank you, guv'nor," the man said with a tug on the bill of his cap. He sat up straight in his box again and reined the horse around in a crunch of gravel. "And that was mighty fine music!"

"Thank you, good sir!" After saluting the departing cabby, Mr. Duffy glanced at the stable, where William and Stanley, the groomsmen, lived upstairs. "Would you

want to be getting your things out now,
William?"

"Almost everything in it needs to go out
with the wash," Naomi answered for him.
"So we might as well bring it to the cellar
now."

"*We*, she says," Mr. Duffy quipped with a
grunt as he and William hefted the trunk to
their shoulders.

They started down the garden path with
Mr. Duffy leading. Naomi, well to the side to
allow them room, looked ahead and spotted parlormaid Claire Duffy advancing
gracefully upon them. She was a Ruben-
esque woman of thirty-five who moved
with the grace of a ballerina even upon the
path stones. Her eyes were a warm hazel,
her cheeks apple rosy, and her acorn-
colored hair dipped into a handsome
widow's peak.

"Yoo-hoo!" Claire called, waving.

Naomi smiled and returned the wave. Mr.
Duffy said, "There's my fair wife. Close your
eyes, boy, I expect she'll be wantin' to kiss
me."

But it was Naomi whom Claire kissed
and then turned to plant one upon William's
startled face. "So good to have you back!"

she declared, a smile dimpling her plump cheeks.

"It's good to be back," Naomi assured her with a wink at Mr. Duffy. "But we've been away only four days."

"Claire wants everyone to stay put," her husband said. "Come, boy. Now that you've finished tryin' to steal my wife, let's move along before my shoulder gives."

The four started for the house again, Naomi and Claire lagging behind. "She's here," Claire said in a low voice.

"Mr. Duffy said she might be." Slowing her steps just to be sure her words didn't reach her nephew's ears, Naomi asked, "What's she like?"

"Only Mrs. Bacon, Hester, and Marie have seen her so far," Claire replied with equally lagging steps. "Mrs. Bacon says Sarah Matthews is her name."

"Matthews?"

"Yes. After the orphanage."

"I see." Naomi smiled. "I've yet to meet a 'Sarah' who wasn't a jewel."

Claire's voice lowered another notch. "Mrs. Bacon sent word around that we're not to look taken aback when we see her hand. It's crippled."

"Oh dear. Can it be mended, do you think?"

"Not by any doctor this side of heaven. It's a birth deformity."

Naomi had given much thought to the girl's plight over the past months, so she felt as aggrieved as if she had found out the news about a dear friend. She would have to warn William as soon as they were alone. Not that he would act anything less than gentlemanly, but surprise sometimes caused one to say the wrong thing. "The poor mite. Bad enough being in an orphanage all those years."

"And then to have the Missus send her up to a bath first thing." The parlormaid grimaced. "Marie's giving it to her now."

"Marie?"

"Hester said she didn't look too keen to be about it."

"What a welcome!" Naomi shook her head. "Let's hope she's not frightening the poor child to death."

"But I have one with my things," Sarah said, pride forbidding her to add that at least a third of the bristles were broken. Still, Marie pressed the toothbrush into her hand. It looked new, with soft even bristles and a rose carved into the wooden handle.

"You will use that one," the lady's maid said, reaching again into the narrow cupboard by the sink to bring out a squat white jar. When it was handed to her, Sarah had to shift the toothbrush between two fingers to hold it. Dr. Ebermann's Tooth-wash was arched on the lid beneath a picture of Napoleon, who stood with one foot on a rock under the caption, "The Best Dentifrice in the World."

Sarah shifted her feet uncomfortably. At Saint Matthew's plain water was used. Did one smear the tooth-wash across one's teeth or dip one's toothbrush into the jar when it was possibly used by others? She gave Marie a helpless look. The maid, apparently assuming her discomfort came from not being able to manage this task one-handed, took the jar, twisted open the top, and held it out. The white paste inside did not appear to have been disturbed.

"Well?"

"I'm not quite sure what to do," Sarah confessed.

Marie gave a long-suffering sigh. "You must dip the toothbrush into the paste."

"Thank you."

"And do not swallow it."

The taste was mildly unpleasant, but Sarah grew used to it the longer she brushed. She rinsed using the glass Marie withdrew from the cupboard and, under the maid's prompting, spat into the basin under running tap water. Marie took the brush from her and rinsed it, propped it in the glass, and returned it to the cupboard.

"I have loosened the lid on the paste so it will be easier to open from now on," she said gruffly.

"Thank you."

The maid shrugged before turning to start across the room. Sarah could do nothing but follow. But at the door Marie turned and frowned toward the table with all the bottles. Sarah hurried over to push the stool back underneath. She almost bumped into Marie when she turned. The maid reached past to pick up an octago-nal-shaped purple bottle with Rummel's Double Distilled Lavender Water on the label beneath a spray of lavender. She took out the stopper and a sweet mild aroma filled the room.

"A young lady should smell nice, yes?"

Marie's face was still set into hard lines, but there was no anger in her tone.

"Yes," Sarah agreed. She was still so intimidated by her that she would have agreed to the opposite just as quickly.

Marie turned the bottle against her finger and then dabbed behind Sarah's ears. "It is not half so fine as anything from Paris, but you are too young for perfume, anyway, so it will do."

"Thank you." The wetness behind Sarah's ears caused her a little shiver. Once the stopper was replaced, the scent didn't seem as strong. And when they were out in the corridor, she could detect only a lingering trace of it on herself. But it was proof that Marie perhaps did not despise her after all, and some of her fear ebbed.

They stopped at the first door on the left, white and paneled, with a crystal knob. "This is where you will stay. It is the guest chamber."

She did not open the door, however, but nodded toward the one directly across the corridor. "I am the only servant to sleep on this floor," she said proudly. "That is so I can be near Madame if she needs me." She looked toward three more doors ahead, one on the right and two on the left. "Madame's chamber," she said with a motion to the right, and to the left, "The far one was Monsieur Blake's. Next to his was their son's."

Sarah had so longed to leave this house that it had not even occurred to her to wonder where she would sleep the night. As she was ushered through the doorway, she halfway expected to see rows of narrow beds. Instead, one bed sat against the opposite wall, with thick wooden posts and curtains of royal blue brocade hanging from a tester. The mattress was as high as her chest and wide enough to sleep a half-dozen girls from Saint Matthew's. That thought was enough to make Sarah's eyes sting, so she pushed it aside and listened to Marie say that the wardrobe dominating the wall to her right was for hanging her clothes—when she had some.

On the right side of the fireplace, against the left wall, was a long window draped with laces and the same rich cloth as the bed-curtains. "You can see the garden and mews," Marie said. There was also a dressing table and bench, a bedside lamp table, and a chair and ottoman upholstered with a satiny blue-and-gold striped fabric. The room seemed more worthy of Queen Victoria than an orphan from Drury Lane. Could she ever grow accustomed to being in a place with furnishings so rich that she feared her very touch would mar their beauty?

Her eyes met a welcome sight. Her belongings, like old friends, were arranged neatly atop a chest of drawers. She had a grateful thought toward Hester, who at that minute breezed through the open doorway, one arm draped with a cloth of sea green satin with tiny pink flower buds.

"Avis says she may borrow this," she said, holding the garment up by its shoulders. "I had to beg it out of her—it was a Christmas present from her mother, and she wants to keep it nice."

"Then I shouldn't wish to wear it, please," Sarah said in her smallest voice, though it was the most beautiful dress she had ever seen. What if she ripped or soiled it?

"Nonsense," Marie snorted. "It is only a dressing gown." To Hester she said, "But it is still too *ample*."

"But we can roll the sleeves and tuck the

waist up into the sash so's she don't trip herself." The maid dipped into an apron pocket. "Oh, and I've a measuring ribbon."

"Good. We will do that first."

Sarah found herself between the two women. One held a ribbon with numbers on it around her towel-swathed waist, from the top of her shoulder to her ankle, and then the length of her arm. Marie went over to the desk and lifted a latch to raise the top. She brought out a pencil and sheet of paper and scribbled while Hester helped Sarah into the wrapper. Soon the lady's maid joined them again, rolling the sleeves and pulling the cloth up through the sash at her waist so that it billowed out like a pillow.

The two maids stepped back appraisingly. Hester covered a smile with her hand, and Marie frowned and said, "She looks like a harlequin. And we have spent enough time on this foolishness. I will bring the measurements to Mrs. Bacon, and you have work to do."

What about me? Sarah thought, fearful of being shut up alone in the cavernous room. She met Hester's eyes in a pleading look.

The younger maid nodded and asked, "But what will we do with Miss Matthews?"

Halfway through the doorway, Marie waved a hand without looking back. "I do not know. Show her around if you must. Just keep her out of everyone's way."

Again Sarah felt the sting of tears. She was to live in this magnificent house, but it was no more a home to her than was Saint Paul's Cathedral.

"Don't worry about her," Hester said with a pat on her back. "Let's comb your hair before it dries, shall we?"

"Yes, Madam," Sarah said before remembering that she wasn't to say that. But the red-haired maid simply laughed and pulled out the bench to a dressing table that resembled the one in the bathroom, only there were no bottles on its surface. It was the first Sarah had seen of herself since her bath, and she did look comical with her turban, sagging shoulders, and billowing waist. Not enough to make her laugh, for her heart was still so heavy, but she wondered if she might remember this day years from now and do so. She hoped so.

"Why doesn't she live in France?" Sarah

asked, seated on the bench. Damp curls were beginning to free themselves as the comb was pulled through them.

"She won't talk about it to us *common* folk, but Avis overheard her tellin' Mrs. Bacon about a beau who were killed in a duel."

Sarah found herself both horrified and fascinated. "He was killed?"

"That's what Avis says." The maid pulled the comb through again, releasing more curls.

In the mirror Sarah could see her freckled nose wrinkle.

"Stanley—he brought you over in the coach—said if they was dueling, they was fighting over who *had* to take her, but I scolded him rightly for that. It ain't proper to make sport of the dead. But Stanley didn't mean nothing by it. He just likes to have a good time."

With no idea how to respond to this, Sarah simply nodded as the maid set the comb on the table.

"There you are, Miss Matthews—not much to that little task. Are you ready for a look about the place?"

"Yes, thank you." Because she was so

amiable, Sarah said after a second's hesitation, "But you don't have to address me as 'Miss Matthews.' No one ever did at the Home."

In the mirror, Hester's reflection wore an understanding smile. "And you ain't used to it, are you?"

"I'm just a child. It doesn't seem right."

"But Mrs. Blake wishes it so."

"But why? Is a ward so important?"

A guarded expression crossed the maid's comely face. Just as quickly the smile returned. "Yes, very important. And now let's have that look about, shall we?"

She still did not understand but rose to her feet and pushed the bench beneath the table. It was at the doorway that she balked. Hester's good-natured attentions had changed the tone of the room a bit, to where it seemed less intimidating than what was on the other side. Marie no longer terrified her, but there was someone who did. She looked up at the maid. Dare she confess her fear?

"What's wrong, love?" Hester asked. "You ain't still afeared of Marie, are you?"

Sarah glanced out into the corridor and decided to take the chance. "Mrs. Blake," she whispered. "What should I say if I see her?"

"Just wait and see if she speaks first. She's had a hard lot, the Missus, with her husband and son dead and rheumatism in her joints. But you've no cause to fear— she's kind enough in her own way."

Sarah felt a tug of sympathy for the elderly woman. Mrs. Forsyth had said she had no family, but she had not had time to consider, even when Marie pointed out the doors to the two unoccupied rooms, that it meant loved ones would have had to *die* for that to be so. She was about to ask how it had happened when Hester said, "Now, we'd best show you around before someone puts me back to work."

After the trunk was delivered to the cellar, it took Naomi and her nephew some minutes to go through it for the few articles of clothing that should not be washed, such as belts, hats, and shoes, along with the small items they had bought—she, a figurine of a shepherdess, and he, a folding pocket knife. Fortunately no one was about, so Naomi was able to have her private chat with William.

"Mrs. Blake has brought a girl here to live. . . ."

"You mean she found her granddaughter," William said, shifting his belongings in his arms. "I didn't leave my toothbrush, did I?"

Naomi blinked at him. "Who told you that?" He couldn't have figured it out for himself, for he did not even live in the household when Mary Tomkin was dismissed. Besides, she had rather hoped he had no knowledge of the depravation of which humans were capable. *He's only sixteen!*

He simply gave her a maddening smile. "Aunt Naomi, I hear talk."

She had taken it for granted that the servants would eventually figure out the identity of the girl. But before she even arrived? "You haven't been spreading talk yourself, have you?"

"Why would I do that? It's none of my affair."

"Well, do keep it that way. And when you see her, try not to look at her hand. Claire says she has a birth deformity."

"What a shame," he said with a grim nod. "But I doubt if I'll even see her. Mr. Duffy says he intends to get as much work as he can out of me before I leave."

Naomi patted his cheek and was stricken to feel faint bristles against her fingers. "When did you start shaving?"

There was amusement in his dark eyes. "Over a year ago, Aunt Naomi. But we left so early this morning I hadn't the time."

Why did you have to grow up so fast? Naomi asked silently, but then asked herself, *Would you have him stay a child forever?*

"Your toothbrush is there in your hand," she said. "And Mr. Duffy will wait till you have some lunch in your belly."

She gathered up her own belongings and went down the corridor into the kitchen, from which wafted the familiar smell of roast beef with garlic cloves—many, many garlic cloves. Trudy turned from stirring a pot on the gas stove. Her face lit.

"Here, take this!" she said to Avis.

The parlormaid took over the stirring with twice as much relief in her expression as there was in Trudy's. In her late twenties, Avis had auburn hair and owlish gray eyes. Her figure was spindly thin in spite of a healthy appetite at the table, and she inter-

jected little laughs into even the most serious of discussions. Naomi believed her
skittishness was due to the eleven years
she spent in the employ of a shrewish
woman in Chelsea before Mrs. Bacon hired
her last year.

Trudy hurried over to throw her arms
around Naomi, belongings and all. "It's so
good to have you back! They've done
naught but complain about the cooking!"

"There, now. I'm sure your meals were
just fine."

"You wouldn't know it by the comments
that was made," Trudy said, with Avis nodding agreement from the stove.

Disengaging herself gently from Trudy's
arms, for the staff of the porcelain shepherdess was digging into her ribs, Naomi
asked, "Were they eaten?"

"Well . . . yes."

"Then they couldn't have been that aw-
ful, could they?"

She went upstairs to change her clothes,
for the kitchen was no place for her serge
traveling outfit, which would have to last for
years to justify the three pounds she spent
for it. Several clean and starched uniforms
hung on her side of the wardrobe. After

slipping into one, she paused at the mirror over her chest of drawers to anchor some extra hairpins into her chignon. *You just can't stay away from the kitchen, can you?* she asked the travel-weary face staring back at her, for neither Mrs. Blake nor Mrs. Bacon would have complained had she waited until supper or even tomorrow to resume her duties.

Downstairs, she took an apron from the cupboard drawer and flapped out the folds.

Trudy shook her head. "You should rest, Naomi."

"And allow you two to have all the fun?"

"Will you be needing me?" Avis asked in a tone that invited refusal.

Naomi smiled understandingly. She had learned long ago that not everyone loved pottering about in a kitchen as much as she did. "I'll help Trudy if you'll lay the cloth."

Avis shot her a grateful look and gave a little laugh. "I'll never complain about dusting again!"

When she was gone, Trudy glanced at the door and said, "You came back not a moment too soon, Naomi. All she did was go on and on about that beau of hers!" Avis corresponded with an Army sergeant on duty in Nigeria—they planned to marry in six years, when his enlistment was concluded. "I know more about him than I know about my own brother."

"She misses him." Naomi opened the oven door with a folded dish towel. A blast of hot air met her face, along with the odor of garlic and singed beef flesh. "We should take this out now," she said, only because saying, "You should have taken this out fifteen minutes ago" would hurt Trudy's feelings and serve no constructive purpose. She was on her way over to the worktable with the hot roasting pan when Hester walked through the doorway with a girl in tow.

"This is Miss Sarah Matthews," Hester said with a hand upon the girl's shoulder.

At least Marie didn't drown her, Naomi thought. She set the pan on the oak table. "Hello, Miss Matthews," she greeted, with Trudy coming over from the stove to echo the same. "We're happy to have you here."

"Thank you."

The girl dipped into a curtsey, then looked a little embarrassed for having done so. Swallowed by a garment that looked

oddly familiar, she had large green eyes under a short mop of pale cherubic curls.
Naomi could see no resemblance to Mary
Tomkin nor to Jeremy Blake. *Perhaps when
she fills out a bit.* She did not have to worry
about showing any reaction to the crippled
hand, for the girl kept it down at her side.

"Thank you for lending me your gown,"
she said to Trudy. "I'll try to take good care
of it."

"Oh, but it's not mine—it belongs to Avis.
But I'm happy it fits you." Trudy pulled a
face as her eyes moved over the garment.
"Well, *almost* fits you."

Hester and Trudy laughed, and Naomi
smiled. And the girl smiled for the first time
since entering the kitchen. It was a tenuous, fragile little movement, but with
enough power to capture Naomi's heart.
Not that that was such a hard battle to win.

❧ *Ten* ❧

After leaving the warmth of the kitchen and its heavenly aromas, Sarah was led to the sitting room on the ground floor. It resembled the parlor in that there were sofas and chairs and tables, but the colors were more sunny and cheerful. A woman with reddish hair—but not so red as Hester's—was arranging silver cutlery upon a small cloth-covered table. "This is Avis," Hester said. "She's a parlormaid along with Claire, who you ain't met yet."

"Thank you for lending me your gown," Sarah told her. "I'll take good care of it."

Avis gave a fluttering little laugh. The wrists protruding from her sleeves were almost as thin as Sarah's as she set a plate upon the table. "You're welcome, Miss Matthews. My mother made it—she's a seamstress in Chelsea. I visit her on my half days off. She says green is most flattering to auburn hair. But the color suits you well enough, though you're dreadfully white. You've not been ill, have you?"

"Not recently," Sarah assured her after a glance at Hester, who winked.

"That's good. My fiancé came near to dying from malaria when he was eighteen, and he says his coloring has never been the same. Edwin Price is his name. He used to be ruddy faced, like his father and brothers, though I suspect it's gin that keeps the glow in his brother Ralph's cheeks. Why, his nose shines like a new penny."

"The Missus has her meals in here most days," Hester said when the parlormaid took a breath. "The dining room table's too big for one person—or two. You'll be joining her."

Sarah's pulse jumped. "Me?"

"You'll do just fine, love." To Avis she said, "Ain't the soup spoons supposed to be on the other side?"

Avis touched her own forehead and made the little laugh again. "Silly me."

"Look about if you like, Miss Matthews. I should see to my work now."

You can't ask her to stay, Sarah ordered herself. She couldn't expect Hester to neglect her duties from now on just to nursemaid her. She glanced around the room. A peek through the doorway was all she had seen during the hurried tour. It would take hours, she imagined, to inspect every figurine, vase, statue, and painting. One glass-fronted cupboard was devoted to serene-faced Oriental dolls, exquisite down to their fingernails and the embroidery on their silk garments.

"Lovely, aren't they?" Avis said.

"I've never seen anything like them," Sarah replied.

"They're from Japan," came a voice from the doorway.

Again her pulse jumped. She turned to find Mrs. Blake entering the room, oddly smaller than she had seemed in the parlor, while Marie hovered at her side. Sarah curtseyed.

"You curtsey very nicely, Sarah, but I shall grow weary of you bobbing like that every time you set eyes upon me."

"Yes, Madam."

"Very well. Come to the table."

There were only two place settings, which surprised Sarah because if *she* was allowed to dine at the table, surely Marie would. But it seemed the lady's maid's only reason for being there was to pull out her mistress's chair. Sarah waited behind hers, just as she had been taught to do at Saint Matthew's— never mind that there were long benches instead of chairs. The courtesy seemed to please both women, for once Mrs. Blake was seated she nodded up at her, and the lady's maid gave her a faint smile before her face reassumed its stern expression.

Sarah had read of people using linen napkins at meals, and after watching Mrs. Blake unfold hers and place it in her lap, she did likewise. But the arrangement of so much cutlery was mystifying. And the plate, almost transparent in its fineness and rimmed in gold, was too beautiful to sully with her food. She became so intimidated by it all that her appetite left her in spite of the rumblings in her stomach. The two maids left the room when another came through the doorway, pushing a trolley clattering with dishes.

"How did she get that up the stairs?" Sarah wondered aloud. "We have a dumbwaiter," Mrs. Blake replied.

Though she had no idea what that meant, Sarah nodded. "I see. Thank you."

Her expression must have mirrored her

confusion, for Mrs. Blake added as the maid, whom she addressed as "Claire," ladled reddish brown soup into bowls, "A dumbwaiter is a contraption that carries things from the kitchen. Do sit up straight, Sarah. A lady's back should not touch the back of her chair at mealtimes."

"Oh, I beg your pardon." Sarah straightened but thought, *Then how does a lady relax?* They might as well have been seated on Saint Matthew's benches. Would that she were.

Claire moved to stand watchfully next to a fireplace of white marble. She was older than Hester and Avis, pleasantly rounded, with light brown hair and a serene smile. Mrs. Blake picked up a spoon from the outside of her place setting, and Sarah followed her lead. Her appetite returned with the first spoonful. She had never known soup could be so thick, with chunks of cabbage, potatoes, celery, and carrots. She had to pace herself so as not to get ahead of Mrs. Blake, who ate so slowly that Sarah thought she would never survive in an orphanage.

After Claire whisked the soup bowls smoothly away, there were pickled beets, sprouts in a white sauce, something Mrs. Blake explained as macaroni pudding with bits of ham, and a thick slice of roast beef. Sarah could recall having had roast beef only on a couple of special occasions, and then only the tiniest sliver. But as the elderly woman picked up her knife and fork, Sarah could only stare at hers. She would rather starve than open herself up to criticism by spearing it with her fork to nibble at the sides, much less pick it up with her fingers.

"Shall I cut that up for you, Miss Matthews?" Claire asked.

Sarah could have wept for relief. "Yes, please."

Mrs. Blake busied herself with cutting up her own beef. Accustomed to silence at mealtimes, and intimidated by her lunch companion, Sarah was grateful that the elderly woman did not attempt conversation or look at her. Sarah kept her eyes upon her own food unless glancing up to see that she was using the proper utensil or eating too fast. She would have been a total wreck were it not for Claire, who smiled at her every time she whisked away one dish to replace it with another.

The sweet was a rhubarb tart covered with cream, heavenly to taste. Sarah was so unaccustomed to having so much to eat at once that she felt relieved when Mrs. Blake put her spoon down beside her half-finished dish.

"But you don't have to stop just because I am," Mrs. Blake said after Sarah put hers down as well.

"It was delicious," Sarah said apologetically. "But I should pop if I ate another bite."

"Dear me. We can't have that." The smile was as ill-fitting to her face as Avis's wrapper to Sarah's frame, but the sight of it emboldened Sarah enough to speak.

"I'm sorry about your husband and son."

Mrs. Blake stared as if she had not quite heard, eventually saying, "Thank you." She turned toward a large portrait on the wall of a man wearing a scarlet coat with a dog lounging at his feet. There were smaller portraits of this same man on other walls and staring back at her from tabletops. Sarah wasn't sure if he was Mrs. Blake's husband or son. The woman did not make it any clearer when she murmured with pale eyes brimming, "My heart died with him that day."

"I'm sorry," was all Sarah could think to say.

Mrs. Blake turned to Claire. "You may go now."

"Yes, mum," Claire said and obeyed with the squeak of trolley wheels upon carpeting. As the door closed, Mrs. Blake looked at Sarah again. "Help me to my feet, child."

Sarah was on her feet at once and pulled out the woman's chair. They walked together to the portrait. Mrs. Blake stared up at it with so much longing and sadness in her expression that pity welled up in Sarah's heart.

"We wake up thinking we will spend our day in the usual way," Mrs. Blake murmured. "Occupied with so many little unimportant things, blindly unaware that by nightfall our lives will never be the same."

That was something Sarah would not have understood only a day ago. Her throat thickened.

"I would give the rest of my life to have him here with me again for just one hour. He was a joy to me from the minute he was born."

The son, Sarah realized. With a respectful tone she asked, "How did he die?"

"He was murdered. Savagely." Mrs. Blake turned watery blue eyes toward her. "I'm going to nap now, Sarah. You may help me up the stairs."

In silence they walked up two flights of stairs, the elderly woman holding the banister with one hand and linking her other arm through Sarah's. At the landing Mrs. Blake said, "I can manage from here."

Unsure of what she was supposed to do with herself, Sarah looked down the corridor. Without Hester, her room seemed no more of a refuge than any other in the house. Besides, she was certain her thoughts would not settle down enough to allow her to nap.

"What is the matter?" Mrs. Blake asked.

"Oh, nothing, Madam." With effort she stretched her lips into a smile. "Thank you for taking me in."

"Are you fond of reading?"

"Oh, very much."

"Then feel free to acquaint yourself with the library until your clothing arrives. It's next to the room where we lunched."

Immediately her spirits lifted. She dared to ask, "May I read one of the books?"

There seemed to be a flicker of amusement in the elderly eyes. "Read as many as you like. You would find my late husband's shipbuilding journals tedious, but there are some novels that will be to your liking."

Sarah gushed her thanks and, when the door was closed, hurried downstairs. The library was more masculine than the parlor and sitting room, with heavy dark furniture and paneled walls. She imagined that the late Mr. Blake and his son spent much time there reading together or perhaps playing chess at the magnificent chess table with tall ivory pieces carved into Roman and Hessian soldiers. A huge map of twelfth-century Britain was framed upon one wall, alongside a portrait of Admiral Nelson. Upon another table sat a toy clipper ship large enough to sail a litter of puppies.

But best of all was the entire wall filled with shelves of books. Most were bound in leather, with titles etched in gilt—not shoddy and worn like Saint Matthew's small donated collection. Sarah felt as if she were in a confectioner's shop, something one of the girls at the Home had described to her, and with penny enough to only choose one sweet. Which book first?

After some time she chose *Barnaby Rudge* by Dickens, and after ten minutes of sitting stiffly upright in one of the leather chairs, yielded to the temptation to sink back into it. Surely a young lady wasn't constrained to perch herself uncomfortably when no one was present to witness her doing so.

"You should have *seen* how kindly Marie was," Hester said at the table in the servants' hall. All were present except for the subject of her observation, who was at her usual solitary tray in her room.

Claire Duffy shook her head while passing the saltcellar to her husband, Roger. "Forgive me for saying so, but I just can't imagine it."

"Neither can I," Stanley Russell drawled. The groomsman was short but muscular, built as compactly as a bulldog. His dark brown hair was wavy, his mustache trim and neat, and his sapphire blue eyes fringed with thick lashes. One front tooth overlapped the other but did not detract from his handsome looks, of which he was well aware. Yet he wore his vanity so good-naturedly that it was impossible to dislike him. "Do you mean kindly as *most* folk mean it, or kindly for Marie?"

"Stanley . . ." Mrs. Bacon gave him a warning look from the head of the table. Yet even she was vulnerable to his boyish charms, for she did so with an indulgent little smile.

He grinned back at her. "I meant no disrespect, Mrs. Bacon. I'm just saying that kindness ain't the same for all folk."

"Now, how can you say that, Stanley?" Naomi asked as her knife sawed at her roast beef. It was a bit tough, but with her having arrived so recently, no one would say anything, for they wouldn't be quite sure whose fault it was. No one complained about Naomi's cooking to her face, for she indulged everyone their little likes and dislikes, such as Mr. Duffy his fried eggs with crispy edges, and Avis the end slices of plum pudding, and even Marie with her antisocial trays. "Kindness is kindness."

"Beggin' your pardon, our fair Naomi, but it depends on who's payin' the kindness." Stanley's words worked their way around a mouthful of roast beef.

Naomi couldn't help noticing the adoring look that did not fade from Hester's face, for the chambermaid loved him to distraction. Which was a pity, Naomi thought, because so did half the female servants in Mayfair.

"That's right, on who's paying it," Mr. Duffy agreed.

"Would either of you care to explain?" Claire asked.

But Stanley had deposited more beef into his mouth and sent Mr. Duffy a helpless look. The gardener cocked his head, his macaroni-laden fork poised above his plate. "Well, a highwayman might think he's payin' you an act of kindness by merely robbing you instead of slitting your throat."

"Mr. Duffy . . ." Naomi and Mrs. Bacon said in unison.

He was no more cowed than Stanley, but he winked at both women and moved his fork on up to its target.

"I think the highwaymen days are over, anyway," Avis said. "Here, at least. But they're still a problem in Nigeria where Edwin is serving duty."

"They're still here too," Stanley argued after an audible swallow. "I know of a fellow from Tottenham who met up with a pack of highwaymen on the Cambridge Road. They took everything he had—his horse, coat, hat, even the meat pie he'd packed for his lunch." He cut his eyes toward Hester. "They took the whole *kit and caboodle*, they did."

"I haven't heard that since I was a girl," Mrs. Bacon said. "My, Stanley, you do come out with some words, don't you?"

He shrugged modestly, while down the table William wore a pleased little smile as if the compliment had been directed toward himself.

You'll have to talk with him, Naomi told herself, though it was tempting to let it pass, since he would be leaving again so soon.

The lighthearted atmosphere caused Trudy to become reckless with her words. "Well, I know why Marie was kind to the girl," she said while swathing butter upon a roll. "It's because she knows who she is."

The silence dropped like a curtain. Naomi held her breath as all eyes went to the scullery maid. Trudy, on the other hand, continued to butter her bread before looking up and realizing she was the center of attention. Spaniel-like eyes blinking, she said in a feeble voice, "Well, why else?"

Mrs. Bacon dabbed her lips with her napkin and set it beside her plate. She was opening her mouth to speak when Trudy squeaked, "I'm sorry, Mrs. Bacon!"

The housekeeper shook her head. "No, I'm glad this subject came about." Pushing her eyeglasses up the bridge of her nose, she moved her eyes from Trudy and glanced at every face. "I understand there has been some speculation going around about a subject which I need not name. We're entitled to our private thoughts, but if I hear of anyone voicing one, you will be sacked on the spot."

It was like being scolded by a loving parent, for everyone knew it would distress Mrs. Bacon to have to dismiss anyone. Yet there was no mistaking the gravity of her words, especially when she added while picking up her fork again, "Do not try me on this."

Later, when everyone resumed their duties and a still pink-faced Trudy was clearing the table, Mrs. Bacon drew Naomi aside. "Do you think that did any good?"

"You made yourself very clear," Naomi assured her.

"What about Marie? Should I give her the same speech?"

"I doubt that is necessary." She believed Trudy to be wrong about Marie guessing Sarah's identity, simply because Marie did not indulge in chit-chat with anyone in the house. And it wasn't likely that Mrs. Blake had told her, because the last time they discussed the subject, her mistress was still adamant that the secrecy be maintained.

Mrs. Bacon gave a fretful sigh. "I'm only surprised that someone hinted at it so soon. But I suppose we couldn't expect to keep a lid on this forever."

"No, sometimes you have to open the lid and stir the pot so it won't boil over." Naomi smiled and patted the housekeeper's arm. "It's going to work out, Mrs. Bacon. God brought the girl here. I'm as sure of that as the day I was born."

Mrs. Bacon's pleasant face creased with a smile. "It *will* be good to have a child about, won't it? And she seems a sweet-natured girl."

"She'll be good for Mrs. Blake."

Unfortunately, Mrs. Blake was not of the same opinion and sent for Naomi later that afternoon. "It was a mistake to bring her here," the elderly woman said as soon as the sitting room door clicked closed. Marie was not about, causing Naomi to wonder if she was upstairs assisting Mrs. Bacon with showing Sarah her new clothing. It would be nice for the girl's sake if indeed Hester had not exaggerated about Marie's uncharacteristic kindness.

She took a chair without being invited to do so. As long as she was called upon to shoulder her mistress's burdens, it was easier to do so seated. With respectful frankness Naomi looked into the pale-blue eyes. "Mrs. Blake, you can't possibly be thinking of sending her back." *I'll resign if you do*. She could think of no greater cruelty than to snatch away the hope for a better life that had been offered the girl.

Mrs. Blake's face wore the indignation of someone misjudged. "You think me capable of such an act, Naomi?"

You sent her mother away, crossed Naomi's mind and then she was ashamed, for she could tell by the sadness in the aged eyes that Mrs. Blake could read her thoughts. *That was fourteen years ago*, she reminded herself. *People change*.

"Why do you say you've made a mistake?" Naomi asked gently.

For some long silent seconds Mrs. Blake pressed her temple with the fingertips of one long blue-veined hand. "I so hoped she would remind me of Jeremy," she said in a frail voice. "It would be almost as if he had returned to me."

"But she looks nothing like him," Naomi conceded.

"I kept watching, hoping to catch a tiny glimpse of one of his mannerisms. Nothing."

"She never had the chance to spend time with him, Madam."

"I realize that." Again a space of silence, and then a mixture of hope and guilt came to Mrs. Blake's face. "You do recall suggesting I send her away to school if her company doesn't please me?"

"I do not, Madam." Naomi would not sit there and have her own words twisted. "What I suggested was that you do so if she turns out to be a brat. Which isn't the case now, is it?"

"Well . . . no."

"And she's apt to be made sport of. Children can be cruel, you know."

The hand went up to Mrs. Blake's temple again. "You pushed me into this, Naomi. What do you suggest?"

Naomi thought for a second. "This house is big enough to keep half of Parliament out of your way. Why not let her stay awhile, at least until you're sure of what should be done? She could even take meals in the servants' hall."

"Impossible." The woman looked as shocked as if Naomi had suggested the girl muck out the stables with a shovel. "She is still my grandchild."

"Then you're willing to continue having meals with her?"

"Well, no . . ."

"Please, Madam. She's used to having people about."

"Oh, very well," Mrs. Blake said at length. She looked somewhat relieved, as if she had hoped to be talked into doing that very thing. "Though she's not apt to learn table etiquette that way."

We don't exactly lick our plates, Madam, Naomi thought but then winced inwardly at the remembrance of Mr. Duffy eating peas with a butter knife and Stanley talking around mouthfuls of food. "We'll try our best to teach her."

The older woman, staring at her son's portrait, nodded absently. When several long moments had passed, Naomi decided her company was no longer required and rose to her feet. "If you'll excuse me . . ."

Mrs. Blake turned her face to look up at her again. "I suppose I should hire a tutor."

"Why, that would be nice."

"I shouldn't wish her to be backward academically, especially if I do send her away to school later. She couldn't have been taught much in that orphanage."

Naomi smiled. "I don't know about that. But they've certainly managed to teach her something just as important as the academics."

A gray eyebrow raised. "Yes?"

"Gratitude, Madam. She's thanked everyone who crossed her path today for the least little kindness. Perhaps you've noticed?"

❧ *Eleven* ❧

As soon as Naomi left the room, Dorothea Blake pushed herself to her feet. Her melancholy deepened with every aching step she took across the carpet. She stopped in front of Jeremy's portrait. While his features were arranged into a serious expression, the artist had captured so capably the waggish glint in his dark eyes.

Gratitude.

Was it true that it was something that could be taught, as Naomi had mentioned? Why else would a child who had had so little be so quick to express her thanks? *She didn't inherit that from her father*.

It stung her that she could have such a disloyal, unmaternal thought. But she could not stop herself from pressing further, as one probes an aching tooth with the tongue. To the beloved figure on canvas she said under her breath, "I thought the more I gave you, the more you would love me." But how many times had he ever thanked her? Few that she could recall, and those were followed immediately by requests for more.

Even in her early years living near the East End docks, she had not wanted the same near poverty for the children she would someday bear. Fortunately Arthur Blake, a ship's carpenter who worked alongside her father, set his cap for her when she was sixteen. He was five years older, brash, and unafraid of taking risks, with an ambition that infected everyone around him.

The world he had promised her did not come all at once. She even had to take in sewing for a while so that Arthur could save most of his salary for a small percentage in a shipment of cotton from the southern part of the States. The weaving of cotton flourished all over Britain, as did his fortunes later.

They were not so fortunate in building the large family Dorothea desired, for she miscarried four times. And then a healthy baby boy arrived! Jeremy was a miracle, not just because Dorothea had long given up on bearing even one child, but because by this time Arthur was so seldom at home. The pain of taking second place to her husband's financial dealings lessened as her son's laughter and antics filled the house. She delighted in Jeremy's high-spiritedness, even though it meant paying dearly for a nursery maid to stay any decent length of time.

You had so much more than I ever dreamed of having. Shelves and cupboards of toys from ports all over the world. Had he merely considered them his birthright? Should she have explained to him that they were the fruits of his father's long hours of labor and those earlier years she spent sewing into the wee hours by candlelight?

Dorothea touched lightly the carved gilt frame before wiping her eyes with the back of her hand. Then she turned away. It was too painful to stand there wrapped in misgivings. And had he been the most grateful young man in Britain, his body would still be lying in Saint George's churchyard.

———

"Miss Matthews?"

On London Bridge a woman was speaking, her blazing eyes turned toward the

coach. Sarah backed away from the win-
dow. She opened her mouth to ask Mr.
Swann to raise the glass, but the words
would not rise above her throat.

"Miss Matthews . . ."

Sarah jumped at the touch upon her
sleeve and opened her eyes. She gaped at
the figure standing over her until she recognized Claire Duffy, the parlormaid.

"Mrs. Bacon says you mightn't sleep
tonight," the maid said. "You've been in
here a good three hours since Marie first
spotted you."

"I'm sorry . . ." Straightening in the chair,
Sarah felt the book sliding and lurched for
it.

"Did I give you a fright?"

"Oh no," Sarah told her, then added, "I
had a nightmare," as if by saying it aloud
the unsettling memory of the woman's face
in her dream would leave her.

"Yes? Then I don't feel so bad about
waking you."

It was then that Sarah noticed the tray
and glass in her hands. Claire smiled, dimpling pleasantly.

"Naomi thought you should have some
lemonade."

Lemonade! And it wasn't even Christmas! Setting the book on the chair arm and standing, Sarah thanked her and took the glass from the proffered tray. The crystal was cool to the touch, just how she imagined diamonds would feel, with bits of pulp tantalizingly clinging to the inside rim. "Would you care for some?" she asked.

"I've already had some. Drink up, and then Mrs. Bacon wants you to try on your new dresses. You can find your way back to your room, can't you?"

"I can, thank you." The lemonade was sweetened liberally so that her eyes did not even water. She resisted the temptation to hold the empty glass aloft and allow the bit of sugar collected at the bottom to trail down into her mouth. After handing Claire the glass she picked up *Barnaby Rudge*, intent upon replacing it on its shelf.

"Why don't you take it with you?" the maid asked.

"Will Mrs. Blake mind?"

"Not if you take care of it. I expect you know how to do that."

With the book tucked under her arm, she left the library and went up the staircase. Stopping at the open doorway to her room, she gaped at the assortment of garments spread over the bed and draped over her chair. A long oval mirror had been moved to the center of the room. Marie was brushing the folds from a gown of pearl gray. Mrs. Bacon held up one of muted green with a white ruffled collar and beckoned her over.

"Come in, dear." Two gowns later, Sarah stood in front of the long mirror in a lace-trimmed silk of narrow purple and white stripes, while at her shoulder Mrs. Bacon said to Marie, "This will need taking in at the waist as well. 'Tis a pity SWAN AND EDGAR'S had only five gowns that were close enough to fitting her."

Marie clucked her tongue. "Only the English would think of such a thing—buying clothes off the peg. They cannot possibly be of good quality."

Sarah brushed her right hand against the folds of her skirt and wondered if the royal princesses had such finery. "But they're beautiful," she offered timidly. "And five is much more than enough." After all, she had never owned more than two at the Home. And had never thought herself deprived for it, for a body could only wear one gown at a time.

"But here you'll change for dinner," Mrs. Bacon told her with an understanding smile. "And so you have here only three days' worth of clothing—four or five if you do your best to keep them clean. Laundry goes out only on Mondays, you see."

Raising her arms to be helped out of the striped silk and into a blue crepe de chine, Sarah was told by the housekeeper that Mrs. Blake's seamstress would be commissioned to make up for what her incredible wardrobe was lacking. Besides dresses there were two nightdresses of embroidered lawn, a rose-colored linen wrapper to wear over her nightgown should she have to visit the bathroom at night, seven pairs each of silk knee-length drawers and wool stockings, seven chemises of white cambric, six embroidered handkerchiefs, two pairs of white gloves, a straw bonnet lined with white satin, a silk nightcap, and a soft knitted shawl of robin's egg blue. The three pairs of white gloves mystified her, until Marie informed her that she should at least wear one on the right hand whenever she went anywhere. There was a pair of soft leather slippers, and she was told by Mrs. Bacon that she would be measured at a cobbler's soon for a pair of shoes and ankle boots.

The last was a cream-colored organdy trimmed with brown satin ribbons, which also needed some taking up in the seams, but Sarah was told to wear it for the rest of the day, as there would be no sense in changing for supper so late.

"I'll send Hester to put your things away," Mrs. Bacon said and patted her head. Marie merely gave her a nod before following the housekeeper out of the room.

Sarah looked around her. She would have started putting things away herself but wasn't quite certain what went where. Even with fine clothes scattered about, the room did not seem any more hers than when she first walked through the doorway. She thought about what Mrs. Forsyth had said about the little maid in Naaman's household and tried to push aside all thought of Saint Matthew's. Reading had helped earlier, and so she sat on the edge of the gown-draped chair and opened *Barnaby Rudge*. She had only turned another two pages when a high-pitched voice exclaimed, "Well, ain't you a sight prettier than before!"

"Thank you." Sarah smiled up at Hester.

"Fond of readin', are you? I never had the notion to learn letters and such, which were good, because we didn't have the money to spare for schoolin'. Anyhows, Stanley says that fellows don't like women to be brighter than they are, and with him barely able to read his name, it would be silly for me to try to learn now."

Unsure if all that information required her to express condolence or congratulations, Sarah put the book aside and rose. "May I help?"

"If you like," Hester replied with a doubt-ful glance at her left side. But minutes later the maid was marveling that Sarah could fold her new underclothing and stockings so quickly and neatly.

"Folding laundry was one of my duties at Saint Matthew's," Sarah explained. "But I wasn't allowed kitchen work, in case I might drop something."

Hester winced. "Does it pain you?"

Knowing she was referring to her hand, and not the something she might drop, Sarah pressed it into a fold of her gown out of habit. "Not unless I injure it . . . just like the other one."

"I'm glad to hear that." The maid talked on, telling Sarah she was nineteen and had been employed at the household for three years. "My folk live up to Letchworth, and there ain't much work to be found there, so Trudy and I came down to London at the same time. We're cousins."

"Do you like working here?" Sarah asked.

"I've heard of worse places. With only Mrs. Blake, there ain't as much to do as if there was little ones runnin' about and makin'—" She stopped herself, her eyes wide. "Not that I'm callin' *you* a little one, mind you. Why, you ain't much younger than me."

Six years seemed a huge gap to Sarah, but she smiled her appreciation.

"William will be glad you're here," the maid went on as she shook the wrinkles from the striped dress. "He's been the pup for years."

"William?"

"He helps Stanley and Mr. Duffy when he ain't away at University. You'll not see much of him though, for he's off again soon."

"Too soon to suit me," said a voice from

the doorway, where Naomi Doyle stood smiling at both of them. She had a lovely face, with unblemished cheeks, a pert little nose, and eyes as blue as Mrs. Kettner's cobalt trinket box. "William is my nephew."

"I didn't think to mention that." Hester held up the dove gray gown. "Why don't you come have a look at Sarah's new clothes, Naomi?"

She came on into the room. After expressing her admiration for all five dresses and the nightgowns, she turned to Sarah. "I've come to invite you for supper in the servants' hall at half past seven. It's just off the kitchen. You'll be taking all your meals there for a while."

Sarah was not fooled by the casualness in Naomi's tone nor her reassuring smile. She had made a poor impression on Mrs. Blake. In spite of the relief that she would not have to repeat the awkwardness of lunch, she felt a stab of sadness. How disappointed Mrs. Forsyth would be if she found out, which could be very soon, if Mrs. Blake were displeased enough to send her back. That would have delighted Sarah, if only the reason could be anything but her own failure. Her spirits lifted a bit when Naomi suggested she play in the garden until supper. She had noticed greenery through the library window.

"Be sure to take an apple with you," the cook added. "You'll see them the hall table by the French doors."

She thanked her and made her way to the ground floor, hesitating at the blue china bowl filled with golden apples until she convinced herself that Naomi would not have offered if she wasn't welcome to one. Few were the times she had had a whole apple to herself and never one so large. She waited to bite into it until she stepped through the doors beside the staircase.

The aromas of damp earth and greenery mingled with the aroma of the apple on the bricked terrace, where white lace cast-iron benches and chairs, round little tables, and plants in carved stone pots were set about. In the wall-enclosed garden a huge man clad in a white smock and dark blue trousers was bent over a patch of flowers. He turned his face toward her as she tentatively set foot onto the stone path. His fierce look suggested he resented this intrusion into his outdoors. Just as Sarah was considering retreating, he smiled and the spell was broken.

"You're Miss Matthews, ain't you?"

She wondered if she would ever get used to being addressed so formally. "Yes, sir. Are you Mr. Duffy?"

"Aye, that I am," he replied, both hands moving toward his back as he straightened.

"Are you hurt, sir?" Sarah asked because she was certain her ears had caught a low groan.

"Old age, 'tis all. Would you care to have a look about?"

"Yes, please." She was self-conscious about eating in front of him, just as she was about drinking the lemonade with Claire. She wasn't certain if she had the authority, but felt compelled to ask, "May I get you an apple?"

He chuckled. "You need them more than I do, little Miss, but thank you." He walked with her, telling her the names of cupped orange crocus blooms, purple anemones, sunny-centered daisies, hyacinth blooms that looked like bunches of blue grapes, and primroses in all shades of glorious color. In the center of the garden loomed a crab apple tree overtaken with fragrant white blossoms. A gardening shed and the high stone walls surrounding the garden were covered with green vines. "Clematis," he told her. "It'll bloom in another month or so. It's a mite early for flowers yet."

"I can't imagine more," Sarah breathed, her eyes drinking in the abundance of color all about her. The space in Saint Matthew's garden not devoted to privy and clothesline had been long trampled to bare earth by small feet. There was even a vegetable patch here with small green leaves emerging atop tidy rows of hills. Just past a brass sundial they came upon a young man painting an ornate wire arch a dark green color. She wondered if he was the nephew of whom Naomi spoke, for though he seemed ages older than she, he was still the youngest person she had seen so far.

"William," the gardener said. "Naomi's nephew."

The boy held his brush still and smiled at her. "Good afternoon, Miss Matthews."

"Good afternoon," she said, but by then he had returned to his painting. The action reminded her that while she had the liberty to amble in the garden, others had duties.

Bashfully she said to Mr. Duffy, "May I show myself the rest?"

"Any time, little Miss," he replied with a smile, then pointed off to the far left. Against the stone wall a post rose some fifteen feet into the air, supporting a barrel circled with three ledges and topped with a peaked round roof. "You might sit and watch the dovecote. There's a bench nearby—but not *too* near by if you understand my meanin'. Just toss your apple core at the base and they'll finish it off."

Sarah thanked him and walked over to a bench woven from boughs, set about ten feet from the post. Three birds with ash-colored plumage walked about on the barrel's ledge, occasionally disappearing through one of the openings, then popping out another and singing a persistent *coo-coo-cuh.* A fourth flew from the direction of the back of the garden with a long piece of straw in its beak.

If only they could see this, she thought, resting her head on the bench's high back and chewing another bite of apple. Her friends at the Home would be at work now, some helping to prepare supper, others tending to younger children. And, of

course, taking in wash, for with such limited clothesline space, Sundays were the
only days on which laundry wasn't done.

"Nanny! Make Rueben throw the ball!"

The childish voice came from her left.
Finishing her apple, Sarah tossed the core
as instructed, rose, and walked over to the
wall a bit away from the dovecote, looking
through the vines for any gaps. She found
none but discovered a spot with a decent-
sized jutting stone several inches from the
ground. Her deformed hand was no obstacle—she had climbed Saint Matthew's wall
hundreds of times to take a peek into a
window of the pen grinding factory behind
the garden. Mindful not to crush any vines,
she stretched to get a grasp at the top with
her right hand, then placed the toe of her
left slipper on the stone and hefted herself
up. To keep her balance she hooked both
arms over the top, automatically covering
her left hand with the sleeve of her right.

"Nanny!"

Sarah smiled at the activity taking place
before her. A servant dressed in the same
black and white as Mrs. Blake's maids rose
from a bench and walked over to a brown-
haired boy of about six as he clasped a

red ball to his chest and shook his head adamantly to three boys who were railing at him.

"Master Rueben, we must share," the nanny admonished.

But he stood his ground. "It's my ball! And David won't stop throwing it at my head."

"Master David . . ."

"You're not even trying to catch it!" said a boy who looked just like Rueben.

"Twins," Sarah murmured with wonder. She had read of identical twins, but the only two to reside at Saint Matthew's had been before her time. The boys were dressed alike in brown knickers with black stockings and loosely fitted coats with patch pockets. But then, so were the other two, who looked older, though not the same age.

The nanny turned again to Rueben, but it was the tallest boy who convinced him to give up the ball. Speaking with authority he said, "If he hits your head again, I'll send him inside."

There was a protest this time from David, but presently the game of "toss and catch" resumed. Sarah's arms were beginning to ache, so she lowered herself to the ground, still listening. Three minutes later she was at her perch again, and that was when one of the twins spotted her. She wasn't sure whether it was Rueben or David.

"Who is there?" the boy said, pointing.

All faces turned toward her. Even the nanny lifted her eyes from her knitting. Sarah gaped back at them and thought about dropping to the ground. But the oldest boy took a step in her direction.

"Do you live there?" he asked in a friendly voice.

"I think so," Sarah replied.

All four boys, who were moving toward the wall, traded smirks. "How can you not know for certain?" the oldest asked.

"I do live here . . . I mean. I just arrived today."

"You've been away? We just returned from Spain last week. Our grandmother rents a villa every winter. Father only stays a fortnight because the bank can't manage without him."

"No, I lived at Saint Matthew's."

"Oh," he said, his knowing tone suggesting he was unwilling to admit that he had no idea where that was. "We've never been there, but I'll wager it's not as warm as Spain. How old are you?"

Fourteen, Sarah began to reply, but remembered what Mrs. Forsyth had told her. Reluctantly she admitted, "Thirteen. And you?"

"Nine," he replied, then added straight away, "But I'll be ten in December."

Only seven months from now, Sarah thought with a little smile. Younger children were so amusing. And being used to having so many of them about, she felt more at ease than she had since her arrival.

The other non-twin boy took a step closer and squinted up at her. "I'm eight. My name is Ben Rothschild." He pointed at the twins, then his older brother. "That's David and Rueben and Mordie."

"Short for Mordecai," said the oldest. "After my father. But no one calls me that. We have an infant sister too. What's your name?"

Four sets of eyes widened at her reply.

"You're a *girl*?" asked the twin holding the ball.

Sarah frowned. "Can't you tell?"

"I thought you were dressed odd," Ben said.

"*Oddly*," his older brother corrected. To Sarah he said, "Why is your hair like that?"

"It's comfortable," she replied evasively. She certainly wasn't going to tell them about the lice.

"You may come play with us if you like," Ben told her.

Her heart jumped. She was good at "pitch and catch," in spite of her hand. And the thought of the boys seeing her deformity wasn't painful now that she had met them and found that they were friendly. It was from adults she felt compelled to shield it.

"I'll have to ask."

"Well, ask," Mordie said.

"Very well." But a glance to her left showed streaks of orange in the darkening sky above the roof, a reminder that supper was not too far away. "I'm supposed to keep my dress neat," she told the boys. "Perhaps tomorrow?"

"Just don't bring any dolls," one of the twins said, causing snickers from his brothers.

"Only if I may borrow one of yours," she replied, then dropped to the ground, smiling at the hoots of laughter from the other side. She walked toward the house through the cool of early evening and wondered if she lived there long enough if the strangeness of the place would fade away just as the daylight was fading now. And if the ache in her chest would eventually lessen, she might actually be glad to have been sent here. What did she expect? To take up much-needed space at Saint Matthew's for the rest of her life? *I'm trying to be grateful, Mrs. Forsyth*, she thought.

William only glanced up from his brush and paint long enough to send her a preoccupied smile when she passed by, and Mr. Duffy asked, "Like the birds, Miss?"

"They're lovely, thank you."

She was nearing the terrace when movement in the second-storey window caught her attention. Mrs. Blake was looking down at her from her late husband's study, the black widow's weeds standing out against the gold draperies. After a quick mental battle over whether it would be best to wave or look away and pretend she had not noticed her, Sarah lifted her hand. Mrs. Blake nodded back and then stepped away from the glass. She did not see the woman when she went to wash her hands.

Twelve

Back in her room Sarah sat in the armchair and read, keeping a look at the chimney-piece clock. Its works were set into a brass-mounted painted plate, upon which an elegantly dressed man and woman strolled beside a fountain. At a quarter past seven she went down to the servants' hall, which was empty, though the cloth was neatly laid. The only decorations were two water-color landscapes on the wall framed simply in wood, but the room seemed far more welcoming than the dining room upstairs.

Faint sounds came from the kitchen. She went to the doorway. Naomi was at the stove, ladling steaming soup into a tureen and singing softly,

Fairer still the woodlands,
robed in the blooming garb of spring;
Jesus is fairer, Jesus is purer,
Who makes the woeful heart to—

The cook stopped and turned her face toward the door. "Why, Miss Matthews. I didn't realize you were there."

"You sing very nice."

The cook took up the tureen by both handles and turned to walk toward her. "You wouldn't be teasing me now, would you?"

"Why, no." Sarah moved out of the doorway, then watched helplessly as she made her way over to the sideboard. "Can you carry that?"

"Oh, quite." Her burden relieved, Naomi turned and smiled. "Don't allow my size to fool you, dear girl. I've carried heavy pots for so long that I'm strong as an ant."

The *dear girl* warmed Sarah's heart. "May I help?"

"That would be nice. I insisted Trudy take a well-deserved rest. But supper is always light, so it'll take us no time."

"Thank you."

"I can't recall anyone ever thanking me for putting them to work. If you'll set out the rest of the food, I'll finish the tea. Can you manage that?"

"Oh yes." The kitchen was a pleasant place, warm and fragrant with fresh bread and cinnamon. Sarah was directed toward the worktable, where there sat a basket of dark rolls, plates of yellow cheese slices, and a crock of butter. She was making her third trip when Trudy appeared and started at the sight of her.

"You don't have to be doin' that, Miss Matthews."

"But I asked to," Sarah assured her.

The scullery maid smiled doubtfully but went on into the kitchen, and Sarah heard her say, "I'll get Marie's."

Is Marie ill? Sarah wondered.

Trudy hurried out again with a tray and began serving it at the sideboard. "Marie likes to eat alone," she said with a quick glance in her direction. "We send her meals up the dumbwaiter."

Others began drifting into the hall, Claire the last after having served Mrs. Blake. "Come, Miss Matthews, you can be first," Stanley the groomsman said, motioning her over to the sideboard while others expressed agreement. Sarah shot Naomi a helpless look. While she could carry things fairly well, she could not hold and serve a plate at the same time.

The cook pulled out a chair. "We'll give her a rest, Stanley. She's been helping me."

"You put her to work?" Mr. Duffy said. "You'll have the little miss afeared of coming down here again, Naomi."

"Oh, but I offered," Sarah told him and smiled at his wink. Avis, first at the sideboard, brought over two filled dishes and put one in front of her before pulling out the chair to her left. While the plate was not as translucent and fine as the one Sarah had been served at lunch with Mrs. Blake, it was still lovely, all white with blue vines and flower buds.

"The Missus' old Blue Willow," Avis whispered, pointing to a tiny chip in the side of her own plate. Hester pulled out the chair on Sarah's other side, the rest of the places filled quickly, and Mr. Duffy said grace. Having learned about life outside the orphanage mostly from novels, Sarah had always assumed there was no enjoyment to be found in a life of servitude. She was glad to find the atmosphere quite jovial, for she was already beginning to develop an affection for the people surrounding her. They were kind and solicitous, and beyond some polite questions regarding the comfort of her room and if she had enjoyed the garden, they did not pressure her into conversation. The combination of their camaraderie and warm lentil soup helped to soothe away the ache in her chest a little more.

After supper she bade them all a shy good-night and read for a little while before changing into her nightgown and wrapper. She did not see Mrs. Blake on her way to or from the bathroom. *Perhaps a "ward" is someone from whom you hide*, Sarah thought as she opened her door again. Guilt struck her, for she had been given a home and so many nice dresses. Surely if Mrs. Blake was planning to send her back, she would not allow her to spend the night. Back in her room, she found Hester tossing the bolster pillow into the armchair.

"I'm supposed to help you dress, but I'm too late, ain't I?"

Sarah went to the other side. Together they pulled down the covers. "I don't need help preparing for bed," she told the maid, hastening to add, "but thank you."

"Oh, but Mrs. Bacon wouldn't have that. Besides, it's just a stop on my way upstairs. If you're ready to hop in, I'll catch the lamp."

"Thank you." She felt like a small girl again, being tucked in. Hester patted her shoulder.

"Good night, love. Shall I leave open the drapes?"

"Yes, please. Good night."

When the door closed, Sarah slipped out of bed and knelt on the carpet.

"Father, please forgive me for still wanting to go home."

Just whispering the beloved word caused her vision to blur. For several seconds she blinked her eyes and willed the tears away.

I will try to love it here and make you and Mrs. Forsyth proud of me. She prayed for her loved ones at Saint Matthew's, for Mrs. Blake and her servants, and even for Mr. Swann.

"If I forgot to thank him for showing me the bridge, please let him know somehow that I am grateful for his kindness."

"Are you very tired?" Aunt Naomi asked William. The two sat out in the garden in the woven bench, as was their custom two or three times weekly when he was home. It was a pleasant opportunity for catching each other up on the events of their days or for relating something either had read in the newspaper or even in a novel. Other times they pointed out constellations and listened to the crickets in the grass. Tonight a milky haze obscured only the brightest of stars and a three-quarter moon. But the crickets were in concert, sounding like so many rusty hinges.

"My eyes were drooping after lunch," he told her while covering a yawn. "But Mr. Duffy put me to painting, and my second wind came along. And you?"

"I wasn't until just now," she said, then covered a yawn herself.

Which caused William to yawn again.

"Stop," she ordered.

"Stop what?"

"You're doing that on purpose."

William shook his head. "I wasn't, Aunt Naomi."

"Then I beg your pardon," she said, though slanting a suspicious look at him.

"You have it." And as mindful as he was that being an underclassman at Oxford made him too dignified for such silliness, he could not resist feigning a yawn this time, and loudly. "Sorry," he said with a teasing little smile.

She only smiled back. "You should go on in to bed. But first we need to talk about Stanley."

William looked out toward the back, where a window could be seen lit above the garden wall. The former groomsman, Jack Umberly, had shared those rooms over the stables with his wife, Nora, a parlormaid, until eighteen months ago. Stanley was hired when the couple returned to Midhurst to tend Jack's ailing parents, and William moved from his tiny attic room to the stables as well. His aunt protested at first but reconciled herself to it when Mr. Duffy advised her that the boy needed the company of men. It helped when she realized he would continue dropping in at the kitchen to raid the biscuit tin or apple barrel and that they could still sit outside on an occasional evening.

He enjoyed being out there in the mews, listening to other groomsmen along the gravel road swap stories and jokes. He even didn't mind the constant horse and hay smells breezing through the open windows. And Stanley's aversion to being cooped up indoors allowed him plenty of solitude for studying. "What about Stanley?" he asked, though he suspected he knew. "Do you fear he'll corrupt me after all this time?"

She shook her head. "No. I fear you might look up to him, to be truthful."

"But I do admire how he handles the horses. And *you've* laughed at his jokes."

"True. But do you think it's right . . . using women that way?"

He had assumed it the other way around, judging from the way women seemed to flock to Stanley. And yet there was something that vaguely disturbed him about it, for it had taken him but days to discard the hope when Stanley first arrived that he would be the one to marry Aunt Naomi.

William was certain it was his own fault that men did not court her. Over the years he had noticed many an admiring look sent her way on the half-Mondays they spent together and at Saint George's. Invariably the looks took in himself at her side, and the interest faded. He had hoped his being away would change that, but she was a bit of a loner, and without his company she seldom ventured any farther than the sub-scription library, her charity meetings, and church.

When you finish your schooling . . . be-gan the promise he had made to himself long ago. *You'll earn decent wages, and she'll have her own cook.* And with all her new leisure time, he would urge her to get out and meet people by joining book ap-preciation societies and perhaps even tak-ing riding or painting lessons. *Somewhere in London there is a man who will appreci-ate . . .*

He realized she had started speaking again and put his thoughts away.

"You saw how he used that *kit and ca-boodle* nonsense on Hester," she said.

William had to admit he had and still found it amusing. "But he likes Hester. What was wrong with that?"

Aunt Naomi raised a hand as if it would help her to articulate but then lowered it to her lap again. Moonlight reflected from her blue eyes. "Why do you think he strives so hard to win her affection? Does he love her? Is he planning to ask her to marry?"

William scratched his head. Hester was pretty, but then he had seen Stanley with other women just as pretty. "I'm not sure," he replied, then repeated for lack of anything else, "But he's fond of her."

"Enough to give up courting other women?"

"He doesn't confide in me about things like that."

"Thank God for that."

"But I doubt he would give it up," William had to admit. "He does seem to crave the attention."

"And that's why I say he's using women. When you purposely cultivate someone's affection with no intention of loving that person back, it's wrong. Is breaking every female heart in London the only way Stanley can maintain a lofty opinion of himself?"

"I don't—" Frowning, William switched his train of thought. "Why are we discussing this now, Aunt Naomi? Surely you've known how he is before this."

He felt the light pressure of her hand upon his arm. "Because I didn't realize you had a part in it," she said in an earnest tone.

"Just by supplying him with an occasional word or phrase?"

"Thereby handing him ammunition. Will

you be here, William, to help comfort Hester when he breaks her heart? I'm aware that most fellows admire and even envy men like Stanley. I just hope you'll never be tempted to be that way."

As she spoke those words William listened with a defensive ear, reminding himself that he was more educated and knew a little more of the world than did she. But such thoughts lasted only long enough for him to realize it was concern for his well-being and not criticism that had prompted this discussion. Besides, what she was saying struck a chord with him. He patted the slender hand resting upon his sleeve. "I wouldn't want to be like that, Aunt Naomi. It just amused me to see how Stanley carries on. But I'll not lend him any more help."

She gave him a relieved smile. "You're a dear boy, Will."

Even after almost eight years, he still loved the endearments she lavished upon him, something he had not experienced during his first nine. He assumed his parents had loved him, in spite of his father's explosive temper and his mother's withdrawn silences. If only he had some tender moments from those days to press into his mind's memory book. As Aunt Naomi had explained some years later, his parents had not been able to escape the way they themselves were reared. When he asked her how *she* had managed to do so, she had replied in her calm manner, "A person can do anything if it's important enough."

He meant to return her smile but found himself caught up in a genuine yawn. She laughed and moved her hand from his sleeve to tousle his hair.

"Off to bed with you, William Doyle."

———

"I forgot to give you this," Trudy said up in their room as she reached for a book from atop her chest of drawers.

Naomi would have surely thought it odd had she noticed it there first, for the scullery maid cared for reading nothing but recipes. "What is—" Naomi began automatically, but then had it in her hand and stared down at *Phineas Finn* stamped into the leather binding. Dumbstruck, she looked up at Trudy's grinning face.

"The notice came in the post yesterday mornin', so Mrs. Bacon said I could nip over for it. Are you pleased?"

"Pleased?" Naomi turned the book over in her hands. For four months her name had crept up the roster at the Clarendon Subscription Library for this second of Trollope's *Palliser* series. She had read all seventy-eight novels in Mrs. Blake's personal library at least once. But there were none recently published, as her mistress had lost all interest in reading when her son died. "Very pleased! How thoughtful of you, and with having to take charge of the cooking and all."

"It weren't nothin'. I was glad for the fresh air."

Trudy's delighted tone belied the casual words, and Naomi switched the book to one hand and embraced the scullery maid. "But the fee . . ."

"The gentleman at the desk said that you could pay next time you stop by, since you're a regular patron." She added quickly, "But I had brought along tuppence, just in case."

"You're a dear," Naomi assured her and hastened to ready herself for bed so that she could have a little reading time.

Within five minutes she had slipped beneath her covers and stacked two pillows behind her shoulders. She had just reached the part where Geoffery Haredale was being introduced when Trudy, at the dressing table wrapping her coarse blond hair with strips of rags, said, "Promise not to be angry if I ask you something?"

Naomi looked up from the novel and said pleasantly, "I don't make promises, Trudy." To do so seemed contradictory with Jesus' admonishment to allow one's yea to be yea and nay to be nay.

The maid wrinkled her nose. "I forgot. Then just tell me you won't be—"

"Of course I won't be angry. What is it you would like to ask?"

"Why else would the Missus bring an orphan here, if she weren't . . . well . . ."

Quietly Naomi sighed. "Why *not* bring one here? Don't the Scriptures instruct us to be kind to widows and orphans?"

"That's been in the Scriptures all the Missus' life, even longer, I expect. Why did she wait so long?"

"There's a first time for everything, Trudy."

The scullery maid shrugged and combed out another section of hair, which caused Naomi to assume it safe to return to the novel. But when Trudy rose from the bench, she came over to sit on the foot of her bed. Naomi moved her feet to make room.

"Avis says she wouldn't choose an orphan with such a flaw . . . not when she could have picked another one. You know how fussy she is."

Naomi closed the book and wrapped both arms around her covered knees. "Trudy, do you wish to keep your position here?" she asked bluntly.

Trudy's spaniel eyes widened. "I'm just telling you my thoughts, Naomi. I know you ain't going to go spreading them."

"But you've already spoken with Avis about the subject and no doubt Hester as well."

She opened her mouth as if to protest but closed it again.

"I don't care to have to go training someone else, Trudy." The flush on the young woman's cheeks caused Naomi to soften her tone. "And I rather like having your company in the kitchen. So it will behoove both of us if you'll forget any gossip you've heard and put your mind to work on things that won't get you sacked."

Trudy gave her a sheepish smile as she rose from the bed. "I'll try, Naomi."

"Try very hard. And put out the light, will you?"

The feather mattress lapped around Sarah's limbs like the water around a boat. Yet she had napped too long in the library, and too many pictures of the events of the day played themselves across her mind. And each of the three pillows was too plump. So she lay awake in the darkness and wondered who was sleeping in her bed. Was she someone newly rescued from the London streets or one of the younger girls from downstairs? Did she also feel alone and strange, and was she staring at the same three-quarter moon through the window?

From somewhere she could hear soft music. Sarah eased her head up from the pillow and held her breath. There was a piano in the parlor. Mrs. Blake would surely be the one playing, for what servant would risk waking the household? The melancholy tune seemed to have been written just for her in her homesickness, but that could not be so.

A picture of Mrs. Blake standing before the portrait came to her mind. Their situations were completely different, but she began to feel a tenuous bond with the woman who had brought her here. In the dark of night while the whole of London slept, they were both kept awake by longings for something forever lost to them.

❦ Thirteen ❦

The next morning Sarah awoke to a light knocking sound. She sat up in bed and looked around the room until recognition pierced her groggy mind.

"Good morning, Miss Matthews." The door opened and Mrs. Bacon entered, clothed in a gown of blue and green plaid. The ring of keys upon her apron string jingled faintly as she came over to the bed. "Did you sleep well?"

Sarah was torn between lying and offending her. Honesty won out. She rubbed her aching neck. "The bed is very comfortable, thank you. But the pillow . . ."

"Hmm." Mrs. Bacon pushed her eyeglasses up the bridge of her nose and studied the pillow Sarah had pushed aside sometime in the night. "Too plump?"

"Yes, Madam," she replied without thinking, but Mrs. Bacon did not seem to notice the slip. It was still so unnatural, to speak to adults as if they were her own age. And being addressed by them as Miss Matthews was completely unnerving. She envied the servants, who knew their places in the household. What purpose did a ward serve?

"I'll see to it. It's time to dress for breakfast. And Mrs. Blake's doctor will be here later to examine you."

"But I'm not ill."

"But of course you're not," she said with a smile. "Mrs. Blake would just like to be certain you're as healthy as you should be. And her dressmaker is to call at two, so please don't fall asleep somewhere where we can't find you."

"I won't." Sarah moved her knees to the side and dropped to the carpet. As was her habit, she turned right away to made the bed, but the housekeeper touched her shoulder.

"That's not for you to do, dear."

It seemed futile to protest. Hester came shortly afterward and helped her into the muted green gown. They made the bed together. As they walked down the corridor, Sarah realized she had forgotten to ask Mrs. Bacon about the boys next door. Out

of habit her appetite was prepared for porridge, but the aromas that greeted her on
the staircase suggested something even
better.

The servants had already formed a
queue at the sideboard. Timidly Sarah returned their greetings, relieved they had not
waited. Naomi directed her to the same
place where she had sat last night and put
before her a plate of fried eggs, smoked
fish, and toast. And bacon, which Sarah
had tasted only twice in her recollection.
After Mr. Duffy prayed, she picked up a
strip and bit into its savory crispness. It
was only as she chewed the second bite
that she became aware that her eyes were
closed in rapture. She opened them to discover smiles directed her way.

Stanley winked. "That pig did not die in
vain, did he, Miss Matthews?"

Gladly Sarah would have slid under the
table. She looked at Naomi, whose smile
was affectionate and not mocking. A
glance around the table told her it was the
same with the others. Struck with what a
picture she must have made, she was able
to smile back.

"It's very good bacon," she said in a

small voice that caused Mr. Duffy to chuckle. His laughter was contagious. Even William, who hardly even looked at her, joined in. And as Sarah laughed, the fist in her chest loosened its grip upon her heart a little.

After breakfast Mrs. Bacon escorted her upstairs. Sarah's knees grew weaker with every climbing step. "Doctor Raine is a kind man," the housekeeper assured her at the parlor door as if reading her thoughts.

"Thank you." Gathering her nerve, Sarah asked, "Will you stay with me?"

"But of course." They went into the room. The housekeeper pulled the piano stool to the center and twisted the round seat to its highest setting, boosting Sarah up onto it. They filled the waiting gap with Mrs. Bacon telling about a hot-air balloon that had lifted from Hyde Park on Easter Sunday. "We'll take you to see it if they do it again next year."

A year, Sarah thought with a wooden smile. A bell sounded from downstairs. Soon afterward Claire ushered a portly man carrying a black bag into the room and then left. Doctor Raine had thick horn spectacles, hair and mustache a stark shade of black, and extraordinarily white teeth.

"Why, you did not inform me she was such a fetching young lady, Mrs. Bacon," he admonished while making a little bow.

The examination was nothing equal to Sarah's fears. He looked into her mouth and ears while keeping a running monologue about the antics of his beagle, Ishmael, who could paw doors open and enjoyed having his teeth cleaned. "I use salt on his brush, just as I do mine. He has the whitest teeth of any dog in England."

"Salt, Doctor Raine?" Mrs. Bacon asked.

"Since my youth. Only, you must first grind it down with a mortar and pestle, or it will wear away the enamel. Now let's listen to your heart, shall we?"

Under his direction, Mrs. Bacon unfastened just enough of Sarah's buttons to loosen her collar so that the doctor could use a tubing device he referred to as a stethoscope against her chest and upper back. He examined her left hand last, holding it gently and manipulating her wrists. "Does it ever pain you, Miss Matthews?"

She shook her head. "No, sir."

"That is very good." Offering his arm, he

said, "Now, will you stand for me? We must see if you have rickets." Having the bones of both stockinged calves probed was embarrassing but completed within less than a minute. Marie came into the room as he was replacing his stethoscope into his bag.

"Madame would like to speak with you in the sitting room, monsieur."

Doctor Raine bade Sarah and Mrs. Bacon good-day, made another little bow, and left with Marie. "Mrs. Blake will send for you as soon as he leaves," Mrs. Bacon said when the door closed behind the two. "Naomi and I have a meeting to attend. Will you be all right in here alone, or shall I ring for someone?"

Sarah glanced around the gilt and crimson finery. Being in the company of Doctor Raine and Mrs. Bacon had distracted her from the discomfort she felt in this room when she had first stood under Mrs. Blake's and Marie's scrutiny. As if she were a rusted tin cup on a silver tray. Still, she nodded. "I will."

"That's a good Miss."

Alone, Sarah lowered the stool again and carried it over to the piano. Its cabinet glowed with rich wood, and though she dared not raise the lid, she was certain there were no missing ivories, as in the piano at Saint Matthew's. She moved to the stuffed peacock. Its glass eyes gave the bird a look of deep introspection. Carefully she touched the soft feathers of its breast. She jerked back her hand at the sound of the door being opened.

"Madame will see you now," Marie said.

She accompanied the maid downstairs and into the sitting room. Mrs. Blake set her teacup and saucer on a table and invited her to join her at the divan, while Marie slipped into a chair.

"Did you sleep well last night, Sarah?" the elderly woman asked.

"Yes, Madam." A prick of conscience reminded Sarah that was not the case. But she was too in awe of Mrs. Blake to correct herself.

"And your breakfast?"

This time she could be honest. "It was delicious. Especially the bacon."

"Very good." Mrs. Blake folded her long hands. "Doctor Raine insists you put on some weight, but with Naomi's cooking that should be easily accomplished. Another concern is your paleness. Fair coloring is to be desired for a lady, but not so much that one resembles a ghost. So you are to spend a couple of hours every afternoon in the garden."

So far, the news had been good. "Yes, Madam," Sarah told her. "Thank you."

"The reason I stress 'afternoons' is that Doctor Raine has recommended a tutor of sterling reputation, and as soon as my solicitor verifies his qualifications, you will be spending mornings at lessons."

The last statement was delivered in the tone of one who will quarter no argument. But to Sarah, it had the same effect as demanding she have chocolate cake every day. Lessons! She had assumed her education had ended. Suddenly the thought of staying here wasn't quite so distressing. "Oh, thank you!" she gushed.

Mrs. Blake leaned her head thoughtfully to the side. "I was of the opinion that young ladies these days do not care for schooling."

"I've always liked to learn things," Sarah confessed. But so had many of her friends at the home. She thought that perhaps Mrs. Blake did not know too many girls.

"I'm glad to see that you're appreciative

of this opportunity. Had Jeremy a tutor who inspired him to live up to his potential, he surely would have been a brilliant scholar and excelled at University. But it was as if a curse hung over us, for one after another failed him."

The tragedy of this touched Sarah. What a difficult life her son must have had! Which made her realize that wealth could not solve every problem. "I'm sorry." The woman closed her eyes, her lined face filling with grief. In a panic Sarah turned toward Marie, who shook her head.

Presently Mrs. Blake looked at her again. "You had schooling at Saint Matthew's?"

"Yes, Madam. Mrs. Kettner was a good teacher, but we had few texts and they were very old."

"Well, we shall see that this gentleman has the most current texts. If you wish to learn, you should have the proper tools."

"Thank you, Mrs. Blake!" Sarah exclaimed, heart racing for joy. The thought struck her that she was being selfish. "But you've already spent so much money on me."

"That is the one thing I have in abundance. You may go now, Sarah."

"Yes, Madam." Sarah got to her feet, though she would have liked to have lingered to soak up more of the unexpected warmth the woman was showing her. Suddenly she remembered the boys and asked respectfully if she might play with them later this afternoon.

Mrs. Blake shook her head. "You may not."

The immediacy of the reply caught Sarah off guard. *It's because they're boys*, she thought. She hoped she wasn't being too forward by explaining, "We were just going to play catch. I would keep my dress tidy."

"You may not play with them ever, Sarah. They are Jews."

"Jews?" Of course she knew about Jews. They were Abraham's descendants and left Egypt with Moses. She even was aware that dozens, perhaps even hundreds, resided in London. But forbidding them as playmates seemed as irrational a reason as if they had freckles. "But they were very well-mannered," she said meekly.

"Manners has nothing to do with it." Mrs. Blake wore a weary frown, as if explaining was sapping her strength. "How many Jews were in your orphanage, Sarah?"

"Well . . . it was a Methodist home."

"Exactly. Because Jews have their own orphanages. Even *they're* aware that we're not to keep society with each other. Do you understand?"

"No, Madam," truth compelled her to say, albeit just above a whisper.

"Then you may not play with them because I order it so."

That, Sarah had no choice but to understand.

———

Mayfair boasted several ladies' charity societies, most centered around Saint George's Church and the smaller chapels. The Dorcas society, which met on every first and third Wednesday morning in the vestry of Berkeley Chapel, was one whose memberships were comprised exclusively of servants.

Naomi had been a member for three years, Mrs. Bacon even longer. Donated funds—a good bit from servants but most from employers simply because they had more available to give—purchased lengths of sturdy wool that were stored in the chapel cellar. Either the workhouse population was sadly expanding, or London's winters were growing colder, for the blankets the society hemmed were always in demand.

"I just hope the bee has left Mrs. McBride's bonnet," Naomi murmured after a glance over her shoulder as she and Mrs. Bacon turned from Hill onto shadowy John Street. It was their turn to provide refreshments, and she held a large tin of crisp arrowroot biscuits and the housekeeper a basket containing tea leaves, sugar, and milk. The chapel's rounded dome peeked through the branches of a budding oak ahead.

Mrs. Bacon pushed her eyeglasses up the bridge of her nose. "You're just going to have to be blunt, Naomi."

"I've not wanted to embarrass her."

"Alice McBride? Why, her skin is as thick as yesterday's cream."

"That makes it worse." From painful family experience, Naomi understood that most insensitive people were unable to withstand the slings they so freely shot at others. She sighed, almost wishing she had it in her to be dishonest. It would be so much simpler to state that she already had a beau. *A soldier, just like Avis's.* She wouldn't be expected to produce this fictitious fiancé if he were on a tour of duty.

Seventeen women were assembled by the time tea and biscuits were served. Mrs. Landon, a housekeeper from Upper Brook Street, was tenacious about allowing only twenty minutes for refreshments so that the focus would be on their benevolent labor. Still, there was ample opportunity for socializing as the women sat in a large circle with cloths draped over their laps. Naomi enjoyed the chatter, too, though mentally she managed to draw away from it to send up a prayer for the poor soul who would be warmed by each blanket she completed.

Unfortunately the bee still occupied Mrs. McBride's bonnet, just as it had since the day eight months ago that she seized Naomi's hand and declared, "You *must* meet my brother!"

"Dear Miss Doyle!" the woman began after dropping into the nearest unoccupied chair, which happened to be the fourth from Naomi's right. Her voice was so like her brother's, loud and allowing no contradiction. "Healy was crushed not to see you at church Sunday."

The scattered conversations around the circle faded within a matter of seconds. As uncomfortable as they made her, Naomi could not fault the others for being amused at these attempts to match her with Healy Robbins. And the attention only encouraged Mrs. McBride. Her sharp-featured face heightened in color as her voice increased in volume.

"He brought hothouse roses for you, he did. Had to hold them the whole time."

"William and I went to Leicester," Naomi mumbled into her sewing. Her ears caught the sound of a smothered giggle.

"Yes, that's what your gardener said. If you would ha' only told me the week before, I wouldha' warned Healy not to buy them. Cost him a whole florin."

"Do you think that church is an appropriate place for presenting flowers?" It was Mrs. Bacon who made this attempt to come to Naomi's rescue.

"It is when a *certain* woman is too uppity to grant him permission to call!"

Naomi jerked the needle through the wool and tangled the thread. She could feel all faces turned toward her as she began picking at the knot with her fingernails.

"Of course a florin's a small matter to Healy, what with him bein' bailiff at the Doulton factory. I trust I've mentioned his fine cottage on Sloan Street? Now, there's a good living . . . if *only* that certain woman was bright enough to realize that she ain't getting any younger."

In all her brazenness, Mrs. McBride had never pushed so far. All motion suspended in the hush that dropped over the circle. Naomi's pulse pounded in her temples as if her blood had turned to treacle.

"What's the old saying?" the woman went on, heedless to the tension in the air. *"Defer not till tomorrow to be wise, tomorrow's sun to thee may never rise."*

Dragging her eyes from the tenacious knot, Naomi said with restrained quiet, "It is very kind of you to be concerned for my welfare, Mrs. McBride. But if you mention your brother's name to me again, I will box your ears."

After a stunned silence Mrs. McBride gasped as if having difficulty catching her breath. "I say there!"

"And please tell him that if he approaches me at church again, I will do the same to him."

Mrs. Landon cleared her throat loudly. "Perhaps we should—"

"Well!" Mrs. McBride snorted. "You could ha' told me you weren't interested a long time ago instead of leadin' my brother on!"

"I've told you a dozen—" Naomi began but stopped herself, for humiliation was already thick upon the woman's face. She sent up a quick apologetic prayer for grace. And it was granted, for she was able to say with no effort, "I beg your forgiveness for the threat I just made, Mrs. McBride. I certainly would do no such thing. And now may we return to sewing? You stitch so beautifully that I'm inspired to do my best just from watching you."

"And I as well," Mrs. Bacon agreed hastily.

"You should see some of her other needlework," said Miss Jones, a young brown-haired parlormaid from King Street. "I seen some at the May Fair last year. They should be in a museum, they were so fine."

Mrs. McBride raised her chin and said with injury still in her voice, "It's all in the length of the thread."

"The thread, Mrs. McBride?" said Mrs. Landon.

She nodded, her expression and voice softening a little. "Too many of you cut it too long so's you'll not have to thread the needle so often. But it's easier to manage a shorter thread and worth the trouble."

"That turned out rather well," Mrs. Bacon said as the two walked back together with tin and basket much lighter. They returned the wave of a Hill Street gardener who was perched upon a ladder and weeding a flower box in a second-storey window.

"I had to pray my way through it," Naomi told her. "I assumed the Doyle temper had left me long ago, but I can see it's only been hiding."

"There are some of us who would have paid to watch you box her ears."

In spite of her repentance, Naomi couldn't help but smile. "Do you think she's finally given up?"

"I believe so. She left arm in arm with Miss Jones."

"Oh dear."

They shared a chuckle, and Mrs. Bacon gave her a sideways look. "Any regrets?"

"About Mr. Robbins?"

"He has that fine cottage on Sloan Street."

"But unfortunately he's part of the parcel." Linking her arm through the housekeeper's, Naomi said, "I don't expect at thirty-two to find the love you and Mr. Bacon enjoyed. That is reserved for the young, I think." Mrs. Bacon's husband had passed away when he was twenty-four from blood poisoning brought upon by a ruptured boil. "But I would want a husband I at least liked."

"I understand that. But don't despair of love quite yet, Naomi. Perhaps it will find *you*."

Naomi smiled wistfully. "If that be so, it's going to have to look in the kitchen."

And it was in the kitchen that afternoon that she flipped through the pages of *Mrs. Beeton's Book of Household Management*. "As I recall," she said to Trudy, "the recipe calls for three quarts of white stock. If that's so, we won't have to make more."

Trudy, seated in a chair near a tin tub, reached down into the water for another oyster and pried its shell with a shucking knife. "I would rather have them fried than in soup, myself."

"Of course," Naomi agreed. "There is no comparison."

"But you would have to have lots more than this."

"Quite so. But that was all that was delivered. The season's almost over." She ran her finger down a page. "Three quarts it is."

"Naomi?" said a small voice.

Naomi straightened and looked over at the slight figure in the doorway. "Do come in, Miss Matthews."

"Will I be underfoot?"

"But of course not."

The assurance was echoed by Trudy, who just before plunging her hand into the water again, said, "If you'll come and stand close, we might spot a pearl."

"A pearl?" The girl's eyes grew even wider as she walked toward the scullery maid. "You have oysters there?"

"Aye. For soup. You've tasted them?"

"I've only read about them."

Naomi folded her arms, leaned against the worktable, and smiled as the girl stepped close to Trudy to stare at the opened shell in her hand. "You eat *those*?"

"And beg for more. You'll see why once you've had a taste."

She looked politely doubtful. "Have you found a pearl?"

"Once last year," Trudy replied. "Which is why I don't complain about shucking them. I sold it to a jeweler and bought a right fine winter cloak. Red, it is, just like Riding Hood's."

Good soul that she was, Trudy had offered to share the profit, but as the scullery maid's wages were less than half of hers, Naomi had insisted she keep it herself. She busied herself in gathering eggs, vinegar, oil, and cream while the girl watched Trudy. But there was no pearl. Miss Matthews thanked Trudy for allowing her to watch and then came over to the table. "Would you like to mix the mayonnaise?" Naomi asked.

"May I?"

She handed over the spoon. "Don't stir too swiftly now."

"Like this?" the girl asked as she made smooth circles around the inside of the bowl.

"Very good." Naomi was aware that she could be called upon the carpet one day for assigning work to Mrs. Blake's granddaughter. But it made sense that one remedy for homesickness was being allowed to take part in the routine of a household. And the girl was clearly homesick. Something else seemed to be troubling her as well, for she glanced up a couple of times as if weighing whether or not to speak.

It was only after Mr. Duffy had come and helped Trudy carry the tub outside to clean it and dispose of the shells that Miss Matthews looked up from the mayonnaise and said, "Do you like Jews?"

"Jews?" Naomi echoed, not certain if she had heard correctly.

The girl nodded.

"Why, it depends on which Jew . . . just like anyone else."

"Do you know why Mrs. Blake doesn't like Jews?"

"Why do you ask that?"

The girl told her. The irony of it was that Mrs. Blake was only too willing to trust the Rothschild children's banker father with her money. "There are many people of the same opinion, I'm afraid," Naomi said.

"But why? What have they done?"

Naomi set down the measuring tin she was using for the white sauce. How could she explain to a child what she didn't understand herself? "It makes no sense to me, Miss Matthews. They're accused of killing Christ, yet our Lord himself was a Jew. And it's held against them that they prosper in business, but why shouldn't someone prosper who is diligent at his work?"

Disappointment pinched the girl's pale face. "Will she never change her mind?"

"I'm afraid people get set into their ways as they grow older. They're less likely to question their own beliefs or how they even came to have them."

"I see."

"But you mustn't allow this to blind you to her good qualities. She did allow Trudy to keep the pearl, when by all rights it was hers."

Miss Matthews nodded after a second. "I'm grateful that she gave me a home and so many nice things."

The words did not quite match the glistening in the green eyes. Naomi decided it was time to change to a more cheerful subject. "I hear you're to have a tutor."

It worked, for the pinched expression eased a bit. "With the latest texts."

"Yes? Before long you'll be walking

about the place speaking in Latin, and we won't know what to make of you."

"I wouldn't do that," the girl said, smiling. She tipped the bowl. "Is this thick enough?"

Naomi returned her smile. "Perfect."

✵ *Fourteen* ✵

Madame Gauthier was an attractive older woman who wore her dark brown hair piled high into ringlets. Trying not to steal too many glances at the two symmetrical spots of rouge on her cheeks, Sarah submitted to another measuring, even though Marie informed the seamstress that she and Mrs. Bacon had already performed that task. Madame Gauthier had replied something in French and continued, pausing to scribble into a little notebook, but Marie clearly did not take offense, for the words between them flew back and forth in an affable manner.

When the measuring was finished, the seamstress took from her satchel a book of sketches of young women wearing various articles of clothing and a pouch containing several small squares of fabric. "You would like to choose?" she asked Sarah while

Marie refastened the buttons to the pearl gray gown behind her back.

Choose? She had worn plain linsey-woolsey for almost all of her fourteen years. *Thirteen*, she reminded herself. What did she know about such things? The only suggestion that came to mind was, "Could you put the buttons in front of all of them?"

"If you wish. And the styles?"

Thankfully, Marie took the sketchbook. "Doctor Raine has ordered Miss Matthews to spend every afternoon in the garden. I will help you choose."

This seemed more than acceptable to Madame Gauthier, for by the time Sarah had slipped on her shoes and collected the copy of *Barnaby Rudge* from the top of her chest of drawers, the two were chattering happily in French again. Outside she traded greetings with Mr. Duffy in the vegetable patch. He was tying a row of fragile-looking plants to tall wooden stakes with strips of cloth. "For the beans to climb," he explained. "Else they'll get top-heavy and droop to the ground. Makes for easier picking too."

She set the novel on clean grass and

bent to touch a tiny leaf. "How long before they're ready?"

"The beans? Oh, six weeks or so." To her inquiry about the hill absent of any plant growth, he replied, "I'll be planting cauliflower there in a bit."

"But I thought this was a vegetable patch."

"Why, they *are* vegetables." He handed her a packet from a pocket of his smock. *Webb's Early London Whites* was printed in fancy lettering above the picture of something looking like handfuls of snow set into a green garland.

"What do they taste like?" she asked.

"Taste? Hmm." He scratched his forehead. "You ever have broccoli?"

She shook her head.

"Cabbage?"

"Yes, sir. Many times."

"Sort o' like cabbage, then."

As she handed back the packet, a whinnying sound came from the direction of the stable. She turned her head to look at the back gate. She had paid little attention to the horses that brought her here yesterday.

"Why don't you pay them a call?" Mr. Duffy asked.

"May I?"

"William's curryin' them now—he'll be proud to show them to you."

Though she was tempted, Sarah decided to head for the bench instead of the gate. *I'll wait till he goes back to University.* Even in the orphanage she had been quick to blame any aloofness from another person on her deformed hand. It was only during the past few months she began to suspect she was not giving people credit for kindness, as some could be afflicted with the same shyness that came over her at times. But whatever reason the boy had for practically ignoring her, she would not force her company upon him.

She was relieved to hear no sounds from over the wall. *Perhaps they're inside.* They were so much younger than she was and may have even lost interest in her. She could accept that better than having to tell them she couldn't play.

A greenfinch perched upon the back of the bench with a piece of straw in its mouth and angled its head curiously at her. Sarah stopped and took shallow breaths. Another finch joined the first, and then both flew off into a high branch of the crab apple tree.

Sarah wondered if some silent communication had passed between the two. Had the second warned the first that the unfamiliar girl watching them could be up to mischief?

Or maybe they think I'm a boy, she thought. She was just opening the novel when she heard over her left shoulder, "When are you coming to play?"

Oh no. Turning, she spotted the oldest Rothschild boy peering a couple of feet down from the spot where she had looked at them. She rose and walked toward the wall. "Good afternoon," she said, forcing a smile. She could hear the voices of the other three at play on the ground.

"Nanny has mixed us up some bubbles," Mordie told her.

"For washing?"

He rolled his eyes. "No, for hoops. Have you never blown bubbles?"

"I've never even heard of such a thing."

Mordie turned his head and looked below. "Rueben—send up some."

A second later at least a dozen bubbles as big as eggs floated past his right shoulder, sparkling in the sunlight. One even drifted over the wall toward Sarah. It had a faint bluish sheen and popped before reaching her. Awestruck, Sarah said, "Do send some more, please."

"More, Rueben!"

"If you'll come over, you can make all you want," the boy said while another batch of bubbles floated upward.

Sarah shook her head. "I'm sorry. I can't."

"But why?"

"Master Mor-die?" His nurse's voice came from several feet behind him. "You shouldn't be climbing that."

"She thinks I'm still five years old," the boy grumbled before turning to call, "I'm not climbing—I'm chatting with the girl next door!"

In that space of time Sarah discovered a tactful way to refuse the invitation. She could only hope that God would forgive her for not being completely forthright. Moving her left hand from the folds of her gown, she held it up for him to see. "I'm not as good at games as other children."

The boy gaped at her. "What happened to you?"

"I was born this way."

"Does it hurt?"

Why must people always ask that? She shook her head. "It's not injured. It's just made differently."

"May Ben have a look?"

Sarah sighed. She had had virtually no contact with children of the male gender, but she was a little surprised at their morbid curiosity. "Very well."

Mordie's head disappeared and presently Ben's took its place. His face filled with delighted horror. "Did you do that last night?"

"It would be bandaged, wouldn't you think?"

"I want to see it!" came a younger voice over the wall

But Sarah had displayed herself for long enough. "I'll be returning to my book now," she said. "Have a pleasant afternoon."

"Now you're good and tidy, old girl," William Doyle said to Gypsy, the yellow cob horse, as he hung the currycomb back upon a post of the stall. He slipped a head-collar on her and led her out of the stall, pausing at the open door of the coach-room. Stanley, clad in his Wednesday-afternoon-off coat and trousers, was uncapping a pot of black varnish and squinting at the underside of the footboard in search of scratches.

"Wouldn't you like me to do that?" William asked.

The coachman looked at him. "I'm just markin' time till Hester gets back from the shops. Only one fellow showed up for cards, so we didn't fancy stealin' from each other."

Stanley and Hester often spent their shared half-Wednesdays together, strolling in Hyde Park, boating on the Serpentine, or taking an omnibus to other parts of London. It had not dawned upon William until last night how Stanley seemed to find time to spend with Hester only when other plans had fallen through. He rather wished Hester would take her time shopping—but he had a feeling she usually rushed through her errands in the hopes that Stanley would be waiting. He cleared his throat uncomfortably. "Then I'll see what Mr. Duffy has for me to do."

"Tell the old codger not to work you too hard."

"I'll do that," William replied, his stock reply to Stanley's oft-made bit of advice. He led Gypsy out to join Dudley, a bay cob, in the stable yard. On his way through the garden gate, he brushed horsehair from his fustian work shirt. Miss Matthews was seated on the bench near the dovecote. It occurred to him that they shared something in common. Only he was not reared by strangers, but by an aunt who had made him feel cherished from the first day he was put into her care. What would it be like to live in an orphanage? Did she miss the other children, or had they been cruel and was she happy to get away?

She doesn't look very happy right now. But it was none of his business. And little girls had an annoying tendency to mistake common courtesy for affection when it came from a male even remotely their age. He closed the gate and hooked the latch.

As his boots clumped the brick path, he glanced at her again and wondered if she had ever been near a horse. *It's none of your affair*, he thought. And so it was with annoyance at his own softness that he veered his steps toward the bench. She lowered the book to look at him.

"I don't suppose you would care to look at the horses, would you?" *Say no*, he coached silently. That way, his being considerate enough to ask would be enough of a good deed.

He felt a little guilty at the hope in her expression. "I shouldn't wish to be a bother."

"You'll not be. As long as you don't do anything foolish. They're not accustomed to children."

She set her book upon the bench. "I'll be careful."

He wasn't sure if she was following until he unlatched the gate and turned to find her stepping back out of the way, her face flush with excitement. "Have you ever petted a horse?" he asked.

"I touched one once."

William had to smile. "How so?"

"I was fetching the mail for Mrs. Forsyth when the landlord of the building next door left his rig outside. I had never seen a horse that was completely white, so when the coachman ducked into the public house, I went closer."

They stopped at the stable yard, where William rested his folded arms upon the top railing and turned to her. "Where did you touch him?"

"On Drury Lane."

"No, I mean on his body."

"Oh. The side of his neck."

Dudley and Gypsy, having ignored them just long enough to maintain their dignity, began moving closer. The girl took just a small step backward, which was wise, William thought. Give them time to get used to each other. "And what did the horse do?"

Eyes wide upon Dudley and Gypsy, she replied, "He shook his head and made that blowing sound with his mouth."

William willed himself not to smile again. She would stop if she thought he was mocking her. He didn't know why he was interested, but the thought of this timid-looking slip of a girl daring to seek out a new experience was strangely touching.

"You mean like this?" He blew out a fluttering stream of air between his lips.

She covered a smile with her hand. "Yes."

"Horses do that all the time." William turned to nuzzle Dudley's velvety nose. Gypsy pressed close for attention, as if he hadn't just spent a half hour brushing her. "Now, Gypsy, don't be selfish."

"What is the other one's name?"

"Dudley."

"Gypsy and Dudley. Will they have a colt one day?"

"Never. Dudley's a gel—" William began but then stopped himself, remembering her age and gender. "They're Welsh cobs."

She seemed to accept that as a logical reason and stepped up next to him, holding out a hand in a tentative manner as if she might snatch it back. Gypsy moved over to take a sniff. "Just hold still," William told her, catching the noseband to Dudley's head-collar so that he would not attempt to join the other horse.

Gypsy moved closer and the girl backward, until the long neck hung over the rail and could advance no farther. Eventually Miss Matthews moved her hand up to rub the side of the animal's head. After a little while, as her strokes grew bolder, she said, "I believe she likes this."

William nodded. "Imagine not being able to rub your own face."

They spent another quarter of an hour like that, hardly speaking except to the horses, then he told her he would need to help Mr. Duffy. "You shouldn't be out here without one of us until they're used to you," he warned. "Dudley tries to nip fingers when he's in a mean mood."

Thankfully she did not whine or beg him to allow her to stay longer. As he held open the gate again, she said, "It was very kind of you to show them to me."

"You're welcome," William told her, and found himself adding, "Perhaps if I've time tomorrow you can visit them again."

"Thank you," she said with a shy smile.

"But of course if Stanley is out there, you may visit then as well," he felt compelled to add to make it clear that their acquaintance was no more special than anyone else's.

"Are you quite certain he won't mind?" the girl asked.

"I'm certain," William replied, relieved that there was no crushing disappointment in her expression as there had been upon the faces of the little girls who tearfully bade him farewell in Leicester.

❧ *Fifteen* ❧

Sarah woke much more refreshed on Thursday morning, due in part to a growing familiarity with her room, but mostly because Hester had presented her with a more comfortable pillow. She helped Trudy clear breakfast dishes from the table, and Naomi suggested she take a turn about the square.

"By myself?" Sarah asked.

"You can hardly get lost," the cook said. "You should let Mrs. Bacon know your whereabouts, though."

Mrs. Bacon, writing in her account book in her tiny cellar office, raised her head to affirm that it was a good idea. "Just be sure to wear your bonnet."

That was something Sarah didn't have to be told. She had not realized before how odd a sight her short hair was. Traffic was light on Berkeley Street, composed chiefly of fine carriages and coaches. The square was cool and earthy with flowers growing in scattered patches of sunlight. Nursemaids pushing prams or holding the hands of small tots visited in one corner. An elderly gentleman with a book sat upon a bench. Farther south, two elegant-looking ladies and a young gentlemen chatted at one of the lacy black cast-iron tables across the street from GUNTER'S CONFECTIONERY, which Mr. Swann had mentioned.

At the sight of the Rothschild boys and their nursemaid, Sarah crossed the street again for fear they would spot her. She had just reached number 14 when below to her right the tradesmen's door opened. Mrs. Bacon had exchanged her apron for a straw bonnet trimmed with cherries and maroon ribbons that matched her calico gown.

"I was going to look for you," the housekeeper said, climbing the steps. "You may as well come along with me to market, and we can make a stop at the cobbler's."

Sarah took the housekeeper's offered arm and hid her left hand in a fold of her gown. Mrs. Bacon seemed in no hurry, and they ambled north with the square to their left. Pedestrians from the opposite direction traded greetings with the two, except for those who were attired very finely—they simply nodded or ignored them completely. They turned to the east upon Bruton Street, which was graced with more mansions, then Old Bond, narrow and lined with shops.

Their first stop was a greengrocer's, not in the open air like Mr. Brody's, but enclosed with a large bow window displaying short crates of carrots, turnips, parsnips, onions, and cabbages. "Why do you buy vegetables when Mr. Duffy grows them?" Sarah asked.

"Because he can't possibly grow enough to feed all of us," the housekeeper explained. "And between the two of us, it's more of a hobby that Mrs. Blake allows. Mr. Duffy was reared in the country and can't bear not having some sort of vegetable crop in the ground."

The owner's son followed Mrs. Bacon with a large basket while she inspected and chose heads of broccoli, celery stalks, lettuces, spring onions, apples, and rhubarb, in addition to ordering four dozen eggs. "Brown, if you please," she reminded the boy, who looked to be Mordie's age. He nodded absently as if he had heard this many times before and sent Sarah a shy smile.

They passed the chemist's, draper's, and glover's shops. "I never stop here anymore," Mrs. Bacon said with a scathing glance at the fishmonger's establishment. "Twice they sold us bad fish." They went another half block, and were just about to enter L. UNDERHILL, COBBLER, when a woman came out of the door and almost collided with Mrs. Bacon.

"Dear me, Annie!" the woman exclaimed with a giggle. She wore a gown of lavender print with vibrant pink flowers, her hair bound up in a hat from which sprouted pink ostrich plumes. "Shame on me . . . woolgathering and not minding my steps!"

"Theodora," Mrs. Bacon said, and the two embraced. "Are you over your head cold?"

"Quite, thank you."

Mrs. Bacon made introductions, informing Sarah that Mrs. Mallet was the housekeeper at number 17, three houses from Mrs. Blake's. "Mrs. Blake's ward?" the woman said, small hazel eyes studying Sarah's face. "I heard she was takin' one in. How good of her. And how old would you be, dearie?"

"Four . . ." Sarah began, then amended. "Thirteen."

"Thirteen, eh?"

"And now we must go," Mrs. Bacon said, threading her arm through Sarah's again. "So much to do today." The cobbler's shop smelled of leather and polish. Two young apprentices sat upon tall stools at a table, one tapping tacks into the sole of an up-turned boot with a small hammer, the other sewing the back of a slipper. Elderly Mr. Underhill measured both of Sarah's stockinged feet with a cloth tape, then gave her a peppermint drop from a glass jar. Sarah fought an inner battle over whether to save it for savoring later or pop it into her jaw. The popping won.

A hog's head grinned at them from under a garland of linked sausages behind the glass at L. WARNER'S FINE MEATS, WHOLESALE AND RETAIL. The bell tinkled a welcome when Mrs. Bacon opened the door. A woman in servants' dress nodded at them, then returned her attention to the man behind the counter who wore a blood-stained apron. The odor of raw meat was overwhelming. Sarah began taking shallow breaths, grateful for the peppermint to mask some of the smells.

But by the time the bell tinkled the previous customer's exit and Mrs. Bacon had stepped up to the counter, Sarah could stand it no longer. She asked, "May I wait outside?"

"Of course. But wait . . ." Mrs. Bacon opened the drawstring to her reticule and drew out a navy blue button the size of a farthing. Pushing her spectacles up the bridge of her nose, she said, "WATNEY AND SONS is just across the street. Look through the button rack and see if you can match this one, and I'll join you when I've finished. But do be careful crossing, mind you."

The responsibility was an awesome one. Sarah held the button tightly in her hand as she dashed across after a dray wagon rattled past carrying crates of tinned goods. WATNEY AND SONS was a popular establishment, for at least a dozen women and men looked over tables and racks and shelves of everything from handkerchiefs to walking canes, toothbrushes to stockings, and hair ribbons to furniture wax. Sarah located the button rack against one wall, long hooks upon which hung cards of buttons in all sizes and colors. While she looked, she could not help but overhear two women in conversation nearby.

". . . I was just hired on as chambermaid—that's how I recollect that it was '56—and Mrs. Young—she was housekeeper then, God rest her soul—saying that pitiful creature had come to the back door begging for work."

After a clucking sound of disapproval came another voice. "You would ha' thought she would ha' known better than to look in these whereabouts . . . and in a family way yet!"

"That's what Mrs. Young told her, and I expect she took heed and went off somewhere. But not before blubbering that he had promised to marry her, but now he wouldn't even speak with her, and his mother accused her of tryin' to ruin him. All that money from them ships—you would ha' thought they would set her up somewhere out of the city."

After more clucks, the second voice lowered. "It ain't right to speak ill of the dead, but once he spattered my best Sunday dress, racing by in that little runabout after a rain. I could ha' sworn it weren't no accident. He didn't even stop."

"Beastly rude, he was. And as I've always said, sooner or later the chickens come home to roost."

"And you're positive this girl's his—"

Curious at the abrupt silence, Sarah glanced over her left shoulder. Two women were hurrying down an aisle in the opposite direction. The one in lavender looked back and met Sarah's eyes. Pink feathers quivered as she turned away quickly.

On her way back down Bruton Street, Sarah thought about the discomfort on the fleeing woman's face. But why? No names had been mentioned, save the housekeeper Mrs. Young, who was no longer living and had not seemed to have done anything wrong. She looked up at the housekeeper beside her. "Mrs. Bacon?"

"Mmm?" Mrs. Bacon's weak eyes were kind behind the spectacles.

"That lady you almost bumped into . . ."

"Mrs. Mallet?"

"Is she your friend?"

"Why, yes. We play cribbage every Friday evening."

That information stifled Sarah's inclination to go further. And thankfully, Mrs. Bacon did not ask why she wanted to know.

Back at the house Sarah could hear Mrs. Blake's and Marie's voices as she passed the sitting room. Upstairs, Jeremy Blake's door stood open. Sarah passed her own room and peered cautiously inside. She saw Hester standing at a writing desk and making swift little motions with a feather duster against a lamp, causing the crystal teardrops clinging to the glass shade to clink together softly.

The maid looked up and asked in her childlike voice, "Did you enjoy the square?"

"Yes, thank you. May I come in?"

The chambermaid hesitated. "I suppose it's all right, seeing as how you live here now. Just mind you don't touch anything."

With that kind of dubious welcome, Sarah took only three steps into the room. She looked about her. It was as if someone still lived there, for a folded nightshirt lay upon the foot of the bed, and a dressing gown was looped over the tall back of an armchair. On a bureau in a silver tray a pipe was propped against a rectangular tin of Pioneer Tobacco. There were also an ebony-handled brush and comb set, a shallow wooden trinket box, and a pair of leather gloves.

"What was he like?" she asked.

It seemed Hester was about to ask of whom she was speaking, but then she gave a little nod while continuing to dust. "I only came two years ago, so I never met him."

"Oh." Sarah looked about some more, staying in the same spot. A jar of peppermint sticks sat on the edge of a writing table, their strips wavy because of the design cut into the glass. As much as she had enjoyed the peppermint the cobbler gave her, these did not tempt her in the least. It would have been too irreverent and even macabre to accept a treat that had probably been purchased by Mr. Jeremy himself. When Hester moved to dust a wardrobe, Sarah said, "I went to market with Mrs. Bacon too."

"What fun! Did you buy anything?"

"I was measured for boots and shoes." Casually she added, "And I found some buttons for Mrs. Bacon while she was at the butcher's."

The maid smiled and continued dusting.

"I overheard some women talking about someone."

"Talkin' about who?"

"I don't know." Sarah had no choice but to admit the part that somehow made this relevant. Taking another two steps forward, she said, "But one looked at me in an odd way as if I wasn't supposed to be listening, then they hurried away."

Hester stopped dusting. "What they was sayin'?"

Sarah lowered her voice to tell her. She left out the part about the woman who looked back being Mrs. Bacon's friend because she feared it might somehow reach the kindly housekeeper. She had no sooner finished when Hester unpursed her lips and began dusting again. "That's odd all right."

"Do you know what it means?"

The duster began moving almost furiously. "Maybe they was talking about somebody royal and there wasn't supposed to be anybody hearing. It's against the law, you know, talking bad about the royals."

"You mean the queen?"

"Well, perhaps not her, but there's royals living all over Mayfair. Why, Stanley and I seen Prince Edward ride by in a carriage once, probably visitin' one of his kin."

"You did?"

"He looked right handsome, with a white gardenia on his coat. He tipped his hat to me, and it made Stanley jealous because he said, 'Maybe you'd rather be with him than me,' and I said, 'No, that ain't true, the prince is married,' and Stanley frowns and says, 'Oh, then if he wasn't married you would want to be with him?' and I said, 'That ain't what I meant. Of course I'd rather be with you.' "

She said all of this without seeming to draw breath, and when the flood of words stopped, Sarah nodded. "That must be it. Someone royal."

"There, you see? So it's best not to concern yourself with what a couple of old busybodies said."

"Yes, I see," Sarah said, though she was actually more confused than before.

Lunch was fried sole with anchovy sauce, spinach, and stewed rhubarb. Already Sarah imagined she could feel the flesh growing around her protruding ribs. She had to smile at the way Stanley drew back his lips to flash his teeth at Hester when she teased him about having spinach between them. *They must be in love*, Sarah thought, for his name came up in Hester's

conversations almost as much as Avis's fiancé did in hers.

She helped clear away dishes and considered asking Naomi about what she had
overheard in the shop. But she couldn't do
so without Trudy overhearing. As fond as
she was growing of the scullery maid,
Sarah had a feeling it would not be prudent
to confide in too many people, judging on
how nervous the question had made Hester.

When she went upstairs to fetch *Barnaby
Rudge* to take out into the garden, she met
Marie in the corridor in Sunday dress.
"Have a pleasant afternoon," the maid said
with a rare smile.

"Where are you going?" Sarah asked automatically, followed with, "Forgive me, I
wasn't thinking."

A tan glove waved away her apology.
"There is no shame in being curious. I have
three sisters who also work in Mayfair, and
we share the same half-day off. Today we
take an omnibus to the National Gallery to
look at paintings."

Outside, Mr. Duffy was bent over a row in
the vegetable patch while William dug a
hole farther down the path. "Little Miss!"

Mr. Duffy called, straightening, a smile across his roughhewn face.

"Yes, sir?" Sarah thought it reasonable that anyone addressed as Mister was due that extra expression of respect. She was much more comfortable doing so, and he had yet to correct her.

He was stepping out of the patch. "Might I have a minute?" When they met, he withdrew some lengths of string from a pocket of his smock. "And might I have your hand?"

It was obvious which one he meant. Sarah extended her left hand, surprised at herself in that she felt no awkwardness about doing so. With soil-stained fingers he turned it palm up and stared at it for a minute, his brow furrowed in concentration. He circled the first string from the arc between her nub of thumb and where her fingers should have begun and then down to the wrist.

Sarah's curiosity finally got the better of her. "Why are you doing that, Mr. Duffy?"

He winked. "I'll tell you soon enough, Little Miss." The second string he looped from the same arc to where her wrist began on her right. This one went into his right pocket. With one hand holding her wrist steady, he circled still another string about three inches up her arm from the heel of her hand and tied it. After easing this one down past her hand, he simply looped it over his thumb, said, "Very good!" and turned for the gardening shed.

"What was going on there?" William asked when Sarah reached him. An evergreen shrub with roots encased in sacking lay across from the deepening hole.

"He asked to measure my hand."

"Why?"

"He wouldn't say. I think it's to be a surprise."

"Ah." William pushed the shovel down into the hole with his boot on the top of the blade, then hefted the unearthed soil onto the mound at his right. "Then I'll ask him."

"You will?" Even though he had shown her the horses yesterday, Sarah still felt shy in William's presence. But the common goal they now shared emboldened her enough to step a little closer and lower her voice. "Just be sure he doesn't see you telling me, please."

"Hmm." He covered the tip of the shovel handle with his leather-gloved hands and rested his chin upon them. "I don't recall offering to share that information."

Sarah blinked. "I just assumed . . ."

"That I would betray the man who taught me how to work a garden and could conceivably order me to dig a dozen holes before nightfall?"

"No, of course—" Embarrassment dulled her wits to where she had no idea what should follow. But she did manage an apology before turning for the refuge of the house.

"Wait, please."

Reluctantly she turned.

"Do forgive me." He gave her little smile. "Digging is dull work, and I couldn't resist having a little fun at your expense. I forget what it's like to be the new person."

Posture easing, she asked, "Like your first time at Oxford?"

"And as a servitor yet," he replied with a grimace. "You've only an inkling of the mischief of which males are capable."

"Do they treat you terribly?"

"Nothing unbearable, and it only strengthens my resolve to get an education, so there is good in everything. But

truly, I wouldn't want to spoil your surprise."

Sarah couldn't help but smile back. "I
shouldn't have asked anyway."

"There's no law against curiosity." Posi-
tioning his gloved hands upon the handle
of the shovel again, he said in an affable
tone, "And now you'd best run along so I
can finish this. Stanley should still be at the
stable. Why don't you visit Dudley and
Gypsy?"

"Yes, thank you." Her book tucked under
her right arm, she walked to the back. She
heard a giggle just as the gate swung
halfway open. Stanley stood at the stable
yard with one arm loped around the shoulder of a young woman in servant's dress
and lace cap. Sarah was just about to turn
for the garden again when he spotted her
and waved with his other hand.

"Good afternoon, young Miss! Gypsy
and Dudley was just asking about you."

That brought a fresh spate of giggles
from his companion. Her mouth was too
wide and her eyes too close together to be
pretty, but she was comely enough for
Sarah to dislike her on Hester's account.

"He's been around horses too long!" the

woman said to Sarah, though her eyes never left Stanley's grinning face. "Thinks they talk to him!"

"I'll come back later, thank you," Sarah murmured.

More female giggles trailed her on her way back through the gate. "We've gone and embarrassed her. It weren't like we was *kissing*!"

Sarah felt almost sick to her stomach as she walked the path. William stopped digging to give her a pained look.

"I'm sorry, I didn't realize he had company."

"Some other time," Sarah said with forced casualness. But she wished she had spent the day in her room. It was only afternoon, and already she had heard something she wasn't supposed to hear and seen something she wasn't supposed to see. She could barely look at Stanley at supper, yet he seemed to feel no discomfort, even teased Hester as before. That made her more aggrieved with him than with the woman who had been with him, for *she* might not have been aware of Hester's feelings, as Stanley surely *had* to be.

❧ *Sixteen* ❧

That evening Sarah had just finished her bedtime prayers when three quick raps sounded at her door. She lifted her head from the pillow, and Marie entered in a circle of candlelight. Through the open doorway drifted faint strains of the same haunting piano music. "You are not asleep yet?" the lady's maid asked in a gruff voice.

"I-I'm sorry."

"No, that is good. You must go downstairs and comfort Madame."

Stupid with shock, Sarah gaped at her.

"Well, will you come now?" the lady's maid asked in a tone that did not invite argument.

Sarah found her voice. "How can I do that? She doesn't even want me near her."

"I do not know. But Mrs. Bacon is asleep, and I cannot find Naomi. Perhaps having a child about will make her act like an adult. Come now."

She could see that it was useless to argue. And so reluctantly she slid from the bed and allowed the lady's maid to help her into her wrapper and slippers. With knees of jelly she was steered down the flight of stairs. *The worst she can do is send me back*, she thought at the parlor door, which gave her enough courage to touch the knob.

She turned to Marie, who nodded her on. "Aren't you coming?"

The maid shook her head. "I am going to my room. Just ring for me when she is ready to go to bed."

Remember Naaman's servant girl, Sarah told herself and drew in a deep breath.

Dorothea Blake was forty when she hired her first piano tutor in pursuit of a dream she had kept inside since she was a small girl in East London. Mr. Gordon, her father's and, later, husband's employer, opened his magnificent Victoria Park house every Christmas to the shipbuilders and their families. While the women pretended they were used to such fine furnishings and hovered over their children for fear of cake crumbs or spilt punch, and the men in ill-fitting suits gorged themselves and pretended the camaraderie they shared with Mr. Gordon was an every-day occurrence, Dorothea would stand at the piano, enraptured, while Mr. Gordon's daughter played carols.

As they both grew older, the girl allowed her to turn the pages of the songbook whenever she nodded, a responsibility Dorothea did not take lightly. The slender fingers rippled over the keys like water over stones, the girl's expression one of serene detachment, as if she were unaware that dozens of people were watching and listen-ing. Back in the Leman Street cottage, Dorothea would sit at the foot of the bed she shared with two older sisters and pre-tend the footboard was a piano. She even nodded at appropriate intervals to the imaginary little girl at her side, who has-tened to turn pages and watched her with the same awe that filled the faces of the imaginary people all about her.

Music became her companion and com-fort later during the nights that her husband poured over ledgers in his study and Jeremy was who-knows-where with his friends. But she could no longer summon up such solace after Jeremy died, and so the piano sat idle. Even the most beautiful music could not take the place of a beloved son. Lately she had taken up playing again to drown out the accusatory thoughts that had begun to plague her, thoughts of how she might have failed Jeremy by overlooking his faults.

The tear that clung to her chin until it grew cold finally dripped to the bodice of her gown as her fingers explored the overlapping melody of Bach's "Little Fugue in G Minor." Though meant for the organ, the notes adapted well enough to the piano and to her memories. To her left the tall torchère lamp shed just enough light to illuminate the keys and sheet music. The ache in her chest had spread itself to her joints and even constricted her throat until swallowing was painful. How could Marie understand, strong woman that she was? It was a relief when the maid gave up trying to bully her into going to bed and left the room in a huff.

The fingers of her left hand moved down an octave to introduce a more somber layer of the melody when she heard the door open. *Just go away!* she wanted to plead, asking herself for the hundredth time why she allowed such an overbearing servant to stay in her employ. But Marie's sharp voice did not come. And a moment later a much smaller presence stood at her right, just as she had stood at the side of the girl in the mansion so many Christmases ago. Dorothea glanced at her through weary eyes. She looked like a pixie with her short flaxen curls, delicate features, and huge waifish eyes filled with fear. Turning back to her music, Dorothea said, "Turn the page whenever I nod."

She played on, the girl obediently turning pages. When Dorothea eventually paused to wipe her nose with the sodden handkerchief in her lap, Sarah asked, "Shall I get you a fresh one?"

"Yes. On the arm of my chair." She was not finished with the composition, but the desire to continue was gone, and she closed the lid. "Marie sent you down here, didn't she?" Dorothea asked when the girl returned.

"Yes, Madam."

What had she expected? Some affection and concern? From the girl whom she could hardly bear to look at for the guilt she felt and the disappointment that she was not more like her son? *And if she only knew the rest . . .*

Yet there was pity in the voice that said, "Shouldn't you go to sleep now?"

Arms that had resigned themselves ages ago never to hold a grandchild fairly ached to embrace the girl. But the moment passed, and the impulse died with it. She would have to reveal their relationship if she were to do that. And the thought still terrified her. So instead she motioned toward the small teakwood chest of drawers by the door. "Take a candlestick from the top drawer and walk me upstairs."

Later, after Marie had helped her into her nightgown and tucked the covers around her, Dorothea lay with darkness pressing against her eyes and thought about the pale little face beside her at the piano. Even though she wasn't ready to claim the girl as family, she was glad that Naomi had talked her out of sending her away.

The lamp, Sarah thought, just as her limbs were beginning to melt into their nest of clean sheets, soft mattress, and pillow. The longer she put off getting up, the more difficult it would be, so she swung her legs over the side of the bed and pushed her feet into her slippers. Enough light seeped in through the window for striking a match to light the candle on her bedside table. She pulled her wrapper over her night-dress, took up the candleholder, and padded across the room and down the quiet corridor in a trail of beeswax scent.

Downstairs, she opened the parlor door to darkness. *Marie*, she thought. Just as she reached the staircase again, she heard soft footsteps on the steps below. The hairs upon the back of her neck rose. She would have taken flight had her legs not rooted them-selves to the floor, so she held her breath and watched the faint amber circle rise upon the wall of the half landing. And then Naomi ap-peared, bathed in candlelight.

"Naomi," Sarah breathed as her heart still pounded.

The cook took three more steps before looking up and smiling at her. At the top of the landing, she said softly, "Miss Matthews? Are you having trouble sleeping?"

Sarah explained about the lamp. Noticing the lace of a nightdress above the collar of the wrapper Naomi wore and the reddish-blond hair hanging thickly to her waist, she asked if there was anything wrong.

"I didn't want to disturb Trudy, so I sat in

the kitchen." Naomi lifted her other hand to show her a book. "*Phineas Finn.*"

"You like to read?"

"Almost as much as cooking. You should be getting some sleep or you'll be a zombie tomorrow."

"A zombie?"

"Why, the living dead."

They walked up the flight of stairs, the cook continuing with Sarah to her room. "I shouldn't have said that about the zombies," she said as if to explain why she was there. She eased the door closed behind her. "There is no such thing, you know."

"Don't worry, I never have nightmares," Sarah assured her, then corrected herself. "But I did have one in the library my first day here."

"I should imagine. That was a difficult day for you, wasn't it?"

"Some parts were nice," Sarah had to admit. And partly out of curiosity, but mostly because she was loathe to part with the cook's company just yet, she asked, "Do you ever have nightmares?"

"Mine have more to do with falling soufflés," Naomi said, taking her candle and then motioning her toward the bed.

Sarah untied the sash to her wrapper and hung it over the chair. "Mrs. Blake was crying at the piano. That's why I was down there earlier. Marie said I should comfort her."

"Yes? Why, that's very good."

"I don't see how. We barely spoke."

"Trust me. You were just the person she needed to see."

After climbing into bed, Sarah settled herself upon her pillow. Naomi set both candles upon the night table and tucked the covers over her shoulders. "Have you said your prayers?"

"Yes. Earlier."

"Very good. Well—"

"Could you stay just a little longer?" Sarah said impulsively.

"But of course," Naomi replied. "It takes some time to get used to a new place, doesn't it?"

"I'm used to the room. But some things happened today that I can't stop thinking about."

"Then move over a bit and let's talk about them."

Sarah pushed her pillow toward the middle of the bed so that Naomi could sit upon the side. Because Stanley and the young woman were the foremost thing on her mind Sarah mentioned it first. "He wasn't even embarrassed that I saw him."

There was no surprise on Naomi's face. "Hester and Stanley aren't betrothed, so he feels he has the freedom to see whomever he pleases."

"But he acts as if he loves her. And I believe she's in love with him."

"So do I. But Hester wouldn't want you to worry yourself over this. She knows how he is."

"She doesn't mind?"

"She minds." Naomi shrugged helplessly. "Hester is young, Sarah, with stars in her eyes. We've tried to reason with her—Mrs. Bacon, Trudy, me—about Stanley so many times that I don't even think she hears us anymore."

"Stars in her eyes?"

"It's just a saying that means she's not quite seeing clearly. She tells herself that she can make Stanley love her enough so that he'll change one day."

"Do you think he will?" Sarah asked.

"I doubt he feels the need to," the cook replied frankly. "Not if she's going to love him anyway."

"Would it be interfering to pray that God removes the stars from her eyes?"

Cool fingers lightly brushed back Sarah's curls. "We'll both do that. I confess I've given up on Hester, but we're supposed to continue in faith, aren't we? And what else is troubling you, dear girl?"

Sarah wished they could stay like that forever. *It must be like this to have a mother.* But it was inconsiderate to keep Naomi away from her own bed for much longer, so she quickly told her about the conversation in the shop. This time she did not leave out the parts about meeting the other housekeeper earlier and that she was Mrs. Bacon's friend, for she knew instinctively it would go no further. "She gave me such an odd look. And I don't believe she was talking about royals."

"Royals?"

"Hester said it was against the law to say bad things about them."

It seemed for a second that Naomi would smile, but then her expression sobered. "I wish people wouldn't gossip like that."

"Do you know what she meant?"

After a pause, she nodded. "But it's something I haven't the liberty to discuss."

Sarah could not help but sigh. "You haven't?"

"Will you do something for me?" Naomi asked abruptly.

"Yes. Anything."

The fingers smoothed Sarah's curls again. "Trust me enough to accept that it's a memory you should put out of your mind?"

Though she had to stifle another sigh, Sarah nodded. "I'll try."

"There's a good girl."

"Thank you." Sarah returned her smile. "I shouldn't have kept you awake so long."

"Not at all, I enjoyed our chat. You'll be all right?"

"I'll be all right." She watched Naomi collect her book and candle, snuff the candle on the table, and pause at the door to send back another smile. The last thoughts Sarah had before drifting into nothingness were of how pleasant the cool fingers had felt against her forehead.

———

"Good morning, Miss Matthews!" came the voice after the knock.

Sarah raised her head from the pillow

and blinked at Mrs. Bacon's smiling but blurred face. "Morning?" But she was in the parlor just a moment ago, drinking lemonade with Naomi while Mrs. Blake played the piano.

"I heard you had a busy night," the housekeeper said with a sympathetic look in her eye. "May I help you wash?"

Sarah propped her raised shoulders up with her elbows and smiled. "No, thank you. I'm awake now."

"Very good! Hester will be here shortly."

"Thank you."

When the door clicked shut, Sarah's head dropped again to the pillow. She would wait just until the cobwebs left her head. But her next awareness was of someone gently shaking her shoulder. She opened her eyes to gape at Hester.

"I see you ain't picked out a frock yet," the maid said.

"Oh dear!" Sarah tossed aside the covers and bolted out of bed. "I'll be back!" She sprinted to the bathroom without taking time for wrapper and slippers. Thankfully, she did not run into Marie or Mrs. Blake on her way back to her room, where the chambermaid pulled the nightgown

over her arms and replaced it with the pur-
ple-striped dress with two fluid motions.
Four passes through her hair with the
comb, and then they took the stairs side by
side, Hester laughing at Sarah's frettings.

"Naomi won't throw out our share," the
maid assured her. "And we'd have to do
more than be late for breakfast to raise
Mrs. Bacon's ire." The usual hum of conversation was going on in the servants' hall.
Instead of reproving looks, Sarah and Hester were met with greetings when they hurried through the doorway. Mr. Duffy got to
his feet, and a hush fell over the room.

"I've somethin' for you, little Miss."

"Yes, sir?" On her way to the head of the
table, Sarah could not help but glance at
William, who simply raised an eyebrow and
smiled. Mr. Duffy held a small square
wooden tray with raised one-inch sides,
sanded smooth. He turned it over to show
her the leather straps upon the back.

Before he could even ask, Sarah offered
her hand. He winked at her and, turning
down her palm, directed her to ease her
hand through the first strap until her arm
below her wrist felt snug. The next two
straps formed an inverted V—she was able

to fit the heel of her bit of thumb into the smaller, while the other slanted across her hand to the other side.

"Now turn it over," he directed. When she obeyed, he set a plate into the tray. It fit securely into the square, the corners of the tray open for lifting it out again.

Sarah stared at the contraption upon her hand, rocking it a bit. The plate did not move, nor did the tray tip. She looked up at the gardener and said with wonder in her voice, "I can serve myself now."

"We'll have to change the straps as you grow, but 'tis no great chore." At his side, Claire was wiping her eyes with her napkin. Sarah glanced down the row of faces and spotted Naomi doing the same.

"Try it out, Miss Matthews!" Stanley said.

"Yes, do," said Trudy. "We've been on such pins and needles!"

Scraping sounds accompanied her to the sideboard as servants on the back side of the table turned their chairs. Hester hung back from serving herself, and Sarah realized it was to not impede their view. So she stood a bit to the side, lifting a spoon from the rim of a dish of creamy buttered eggs. With a glance back at her audience, she dished a serving onto her plate. There was applause, and more when she forked a piece of cold ham. All the while the tray remained steady above her upturned hand.

There was not one unsmiling face in the room as she approached the table. Avis started rising as if to help, but Sarah shook her head respectfully. It was a simple matter to take hold of the plate from an open corner, set it down, then pull the tray from her arm. Simple but profound, in that it represented a lessening of her dependence upon others.

"Thank you, Mr. Duffy!" Noticing tears in the creases of his rugged face, Sarah moved to the head of the table, hesitated a moment, then embraced him. His great arms wrapped around her, his hand pounding her back enough to rattle her breath.

"I were afeared it might not work," he said thickly. "Them straps . . ."

Eventually she was back in her place and Hester in hers. Mr. Duffy prayed between sniffs, and Stanley then lifted his teacup and proposed a toast. "To our Miss Matthews!" While cups were raised she forgot to be angry at him and was in danger of weeping herself. More toasts followed in the jovial atmosphere. One was made to Mr. Duffy for his inventive mind, and then two to William, who would be leaving to- morrow and turn seventeen the following day.

William came over to Sarah's side after finishing his meal. "I'll be leading Gypsy and Dudley out to graze in a bit. You may come along if you like."

She replied that she would enjoy that. "Should I wait in the garden?"

He shook his head. "I've packing to fin- ish, so I'm not sure how long it'll take."

"Then I'll stay down here and help Naomi."

When the last chair had been pushed out, Avis began dusting them with a cloth, while Trudy and Sarah cleared the table. "What kind of cake is Naomi making?" Avis asked.

Trudy did not look up from scraping scraps from a plate into a pail. "Chocolate iced."

"What a good omen—that's Edwin's fa- vorite. It must mean I'm to get a letter to- day."

"Omen!" Trudy snorted. "So you would

expect no letter if William's favorite was plum cake?"

Avis looked crestfallen but then brightened again. "Not at all, Trudy. Edwin is almost as fond of plum cake!"

Smiling at their banter, Sarah balanced a butter crock upon her tray and brought it into the kitchen. Naomi looked up from mixing batter in a large bowl. "I see you've found another use for it."

"It doesn't even slide as long as I keep my palm flat," Sarah told her, holding it out to demonstrate. "I wish I had something to give to Mr. Duffy. I don't expect he would care for a fossil."

"Oh, but you've given him more than you can imagine."

She recalled the emotion upon his face and realized not all gifts were able to be held in the hand. Such as the one Stanley had given by declaring her *Our* Miss Matthews.

When the table was cleared, Sarah asked permission to look through the half-dozen cookery books on another cupboard shelf. Most fascinating was a new-looking brown, cloth-bound book titled *The Household Cyclopedia of Practical Receipts and*

Daily Wants. Not only were there recipes but also advice on how to seat according to rank at dinner parties, how to raise domestic pets, apply for a patent, crochet, play parlor games, lease a home, and dress minor wounds. There was even advice on the etiquette of courtship and how to choose a husband or wife. The latter intrigued her more than anything, for she had been in the company of so few married people in her lifetime.

"What does it mean, please, to be a thorn in someone's pillow?" she asked Naomi, who was rubbing the skin of a plucked goose with lard.

"I beg your pardon?"

Sarah read aloud: " 'No extent of accomplishments will compensate for the lack of amiability. A lady who answers her mother petulantly will prove a thorn in her husband's pillow.' "

After trading glances with Trudy, who was kneading dough at the worktable, Naomi replied, "I assume it means he'll never rest well because of all the grief she will give him."

Trudy nodded. "You can be sure that if she answers her *mother* petulantly—whatever that means—she'll do the same to him."

"It means 'ill-temperedly,' " came a voice from the doorway, and William walked into the kitchen. "What are you allowing that child to read?"

"It's a book of recipes and the like," Sarah replied but closed and replaced it lest he come over to look. She was sure there was nothing shameful in reading advice concerning courtship, but the amusement on his face suggested he would make sport of her for doing so.

"It's nothing that will harm her," Naomi said. "Have you finished packing?"

"Just now." He walked over to the oven and drew in an appreciative whiff. "Chocolate?"

"If you don't go slamming the door and making it fall," Trudy warned.

"Then I had best get away from the temptation." To Sarah, he said, "Do you still wish to come along?"

"Yes, please," she said, relieved that he had not forgotten the invitation.

❧ *Seventeen* ❧

Hyde Park was dotted with nursemaids airing children as fresh as the daisies nodding in the flower beds. William smiled when Miss Matthews looked about her and confessed, "I didn't realize it would be so vast. How nice to look about and not see buildings everywhere!"

They stood between one of the paths and the waters of the Serpentine, and he drew up the courage to ask her about Saint Matthew's. He had hesitated because he wasn't certain what he would do if she were to break into sobs. "Was it like *Oliver Twist*?"

"It wasn't at all like that," she replied, holding Gypsy's lead rope as if she expected her to bolt any second, while the docile creature pulled at grass with little snorting sounds.

"But it's obvious that you didn't get enough food," he pressed carefully.

She pulled her wrap closer about her,

and he wondered if it was because of the cool of the April morning or in an effort to hide her thinness. Bits of conversation floated their way from strolling nursemaids with their charges, family groups, and sometimes courting couples. "But there was no Mr. Bumble begrudging us every morsel. Mrs. Forsyth—she was the headmistress—would have gladly fed us more. And she did so when it was available."

"You were never mistreated?"

"Never. But I was fortunate enough to have been there since infancy."

The lead rope tugged as Dudley strained his neck toward a patch of clover. William took a couple of steps in that direction and looked back. "You consider that fortunate?"

Her green eyes widened with sincerity. "Some of the girls have lived in alleys and had to dig potato peelings and rotten vegetables from garbage piles. We've had little ones brought there with bruises and broken bones from having been beaten. Even a baby like that once, but she died."

So bleak a picture from real life and not from the pages of a novel saddened William. And yet he could not help but admire that she was so grateful to have been spared that. What she did not understand was that the alleys and orphanage were not the only two paths set before her when she was an infant. There was another, one of tutors and clean clothes, a fine home, and plenty of food. But she had not been allowed in that direction. Until now. Even so, it was as if she had been slipped through the back door, not quite belonging. Why wasn't she allowed to know that Mrs. Blake was her grandmother?

And he was certain that it was so, even though it was the one thing his aunt Naomi would not discuss, except to caution him not to listen to rumors. In order not to do that, he would have had to walk about with his fingers in his ears. Even Stanley had told him that a parlormaid from a house on the west side of the square had speculated that the arrival of an orphan girl could have something to do with the notorious Jeremy Blake.

"Do you miss your friends?" he asked.

"Everyone is so good to me here," she said quickly.

"That's not what I asked."

After a hesitation, she nodded.

"Why don't you ask if you may visit them?" There were many days that Stanley took the coach out just to give the horses exercise, so a trip to Saint Matthew's would be no inconvenience to anyone. Mrs. Blake wasn't a completely unsympathetic person—she had proved that by allowing him to come to live with Aunt Naomi when his parents died.

Her face clouded a little. "Mrs. Forsyth said I shouldn't write. I don't think she would want me to visit either."

"I'm sorry." Impulsively he opened his mouth to invite her to write to him, only to dismiss the thought just as quickly. She had Aunt Naomi, Hester, Trudy, and the others for company. And there were more than enough demands upon his time at University without corresponding with a little girl, no matter how much he pitied her.

"What about you?" she asked when calm once again overtook her features. "Have you any memory of your parents and brother?"

"I can vaguely remember little Stephen," he replied. "And I don't know if I should remember my parents so well if not for their portrait." He could see their somber faces every morning as they stood in wedding clothes with shoulders not even touching. It was Aunt Naomi who kept the silver frame on his chest of drawers polished.

"Do you miss them?" she asked with surely the same cautious expression he had worn while asking about the orphanage.

"I did when Naomi first brought me here. She was virtually a stranger, however kind she was. I have an uncle in Leicester, you see, but his wife didn't want another child to tend. I can remember weeping here every night for a little while. But I think it's easier to bounce back when you're young. I was only nine."

"I'm glad you have her and even your uncle and aunt. It would be terrible not to have any family, like Mrs. Blake." Her comment held no hint of irony, as if she had forgotten this was her own situation, or at least what she assumed it to be.

"Yes," he agreed. A welcome thought came to him. "I'm glad you spend time in the kitchen. Perhaps Naomi won't miss me quite as much this time."

"I should never replace you in her affection. But I do like to chat with her and Trudy. You don't think I'm in their way?"

"Quite the contrary. I know for a fact they enjoy your visits."

She smiled and William smiled back. Remembering the horses still chomping happily, William said they would need to return. "They're not used to fresh grass—it's just a treat we allow every now and again."

In companionable silence they walked back up Charles Street, the horses following. They had just reached the square when she asked why he had chosen to study chemistry. "I like understanding the order there is to the universe," he explained, though he was certain a thirteen-year-old girl would not understand. And sure enough, she gave him a blank look.

"You do know what elements are, don't you?" he asked.

This time she nodded. "They're what everything is made of."

The next part was what had fascinated him for the past two years, ever since reading his schoolmaster's copies of *Chemical News*. "But they haven't all been discovered yet."

"Which ones?"

"We don't know yet. But they're out there, waiting to be found."

She cocked her head and raised her eyebrows.

"Well, what is it?"

"If they've not yet been discovered, how can you possibly know they exist? Isn't that like saying there are animals out there we've not yet discovered?"

"Well, that's entirely possible, isn't it?"

"Yes. But we can't declare that for *certain* until they're actually found."

William nodded, impressed that someone of thirteen could think of such an analogy. They were entering the mews, and he returned the wave of the groomsman harnessing a team to a carriage behind GUNTER'S. Patiently he said, "We know for certain because of the gaps in the atomic table."

"Gaps in a table?"

That led to an explanation of atomic weights. She listened attentively, with no silly questions, and he found himself saying, as he opened the gate to the stable yard behind Mrs. Blake's garden, "You may write to me if you wish."

"I may?" she asked in a hopeful tone, as if she feared he would change his mind.

"Just not too often. I shall be very busy, you know."

So she's returned. From the window of her late husband's office, Dorothea watched Sarah walk through the stable gate and up the garden path. The girl had accompanied William to Hyde Park, according to Mrs. Bacon. Dorothea doubted Sarah realized just how closely she kept informed of her whereabouts. *It would probably frighten her to know*, she thought.

She realized it was up to her to bridge the gulf between them. But how could she bring herself to do so when every sight of her brought such guilt? Telling the girl of their kinship would increase the distance, for how could she explain driving her mother away, and that it was loneliness, not compassion, which prompted her to search for her? And that had Jeremy married and produced legitimate heirs, she would not have bothered to look at all?

The girl stopped to chat with Mr. Duffy. Dorothea touched the glass and murmured, "If I had only known you were in an orphanage . . . and so pitiful with your crippled little hand. I would have sent for you sooner."

She had to believe that about herself.

The mood for the farewell party was festive in the hall that evening, with chocolate cake after supper and little gifts for William from the servants. Marie even came downstairs long enough to present him with an aluminum pencil case from herself and a shiny gold guinea from Mrs. Blake. Naomi, who gave him a new coat for the occasion, kept her tears in check during the celebration and again the next morning on Paddington Station's platform as she waved until she could no longer see the train. Then the acrid smoke that still lingered from the London-Northwestern locomotive's stack gave them excuse to flow freely.

She sat with folded hands in the coach while Stanley maneuvered the horses through the traffic of Bayswater Road. In spite of her tears on the platform, she discovered that her heart was not quite so heavy this time. He always came back, and late June was only two months away.

How blessed she was to have someone to love! How terrible it would have been to go through the rest of life keeping that love bottled up inside until it grew stale and perhaps even bitter from disuse. *Is that how you feel about us, Father?* she asked as she stared at the stream of humanity passing on the pavement. *Did you have so*

much love inside that you felt it would over-
whelm you if you didn't create a people to
lavish it upon?

———

"Marie is very good at braids," Hester
told Sarah the next morning as she fastened the buttons to the blue crepe de
chine for her. "Trudy and I coax her into
doin' our hair when she's in a good mood.
When your hair grows, it'll be fun to make a
fine lady out of you."

Sarah looked at herself in the cheval mirror. However they primped her, she could
never look so pretty as Hester, whose hair
seemed even redder against the yellow of
her ruffled gown. The back had a marvelous
bustle, which Hester said made one's sil-
houette so feminine that it was worth the
discomfort of not being able to sit comfortably. Sarah was glad that the servants were
not required to wear their uniforms to
church and looked forward to seeing how
the rest were attired at breakfast. "I'll be allowed to sit with you, won't I?"

"With us? Why, Mrs. Blake wouldn't hear
of that."

Her heart made a little lurch. She had

seen very little of Mrs. Blake since that night in the parlor, and at those times only received a nod and mild greeting. "But I'm allowed to have meals with you."

"That's different. Other folks don't know that."

Sarah had no idea what that meant and was pondering whether she should ask when the maid said, "You'll have time to collect your bonnet and wrap after breakfast. Are you excited?"

"Yes." *And frightened*, Sarah did not add. While she was certain that the Church of England worshiped the same God she did, she wasn't quite sure what would be expected of her. Would she be pressured to give up the Methodist faith she had been taught since an infant? *I won't do that, Father*, she promised.

Breakfast was no sooner over than Saint George's bells started ringing as if they had planned it so out of consideration for their parishioners' nourishment. "Why don't you wait in the sitting room?" Mrs. Bacon said to Sarah while most of the servants left to collect their things.

Naomi stepped up to the housekeeper's side. The sapphire blue gown and narrow-brimmed straw bonnet with blue scarf wrapped around the crown brought out the blue of her eyes, gave a flush to her clear cheeks, and made her appear younger. "You'll like Vicar Sharp," she said, smiling. "Don't allow the name to fool you—he's a gentle soul. And if you'll look over to your left, you'll be able to see us in the gallery."

That made Sarah feel more at ease. She bade them farewell and hastened to the ground floor, halting just inside the open sitting room doorway. Mrs. Blake was seated on the divan, dressed in her usual black and reading a newspaper. Marie, wearing a gown of camel brown and a hat trimmed with olive green feathers and mauve ribbons, stared out the window from her chair.

"Forgive me . . . I've made you wait?" Sarah asked.

Both faces turned toward her. Mrs. Blake folded the newspaper and set it upon the lamp table. "Newsprint will stain upholstery," she explained as if Sarah had asked. "And you are not late."

"Yes, Madam," Sarah replied.

"You may sit down, Sarah," she said with a motion to the unoccupied part of the divan. "We have another eight minutes."

Sarah obeyed, and in the silence that followed, she stared at her gloved right hand clasped over her bare left one and wondered if she was expected to say something. Mrs. Blake seemed of the same mind, because when their glances met once, she looked away.

"Did you rest well?" Marie inquired before the silence could completely unnerve Sarah.

"Yes, thank you. And you?"

"I sleep like a stone every night."

Mrs. Blake finally spoke again. "I trust you do know how to behave in church, Sarah?"

"Oh yes, Madam."

"A young lady does not fidget, nor does she draw attention to herself by singing more loudly than the rest of the congregation," she went on as if Sarah had not just assured her. "And it will behoove you to pay attention to the sermon."

"It is time to leave, Madame," Marie said, rising to her feet.

Sarah followed the two down the corridor. Stanley waited at the front door, handsome in top hat, black coat with brass buttons, white breeches, and shiny black boots that reached to his knees. Touching the hat's brim, he said, "Good morning, ladies . . . lovely day out there."

He seemed nonplused when Mrs. Blake and Marie only nodded in reply and even had the good nature to wink at Sarah as he held open the door to the coach. She smiled back before remembering she was supposed to be angry at him.

On the pavement, groups of people walked up Berkeley Street carrying hymnals and prayer books, reticules, and folded umbrellas. Servants, she supposed, even though they wore Sunday dress, for the owners of the mansions surely took coaches, as did Mrs. Blake. Some familiar figures came into her sight. Waving furiously as if she had not breakfasted with them less than an hour ago, she cried from the window, "Naomi! Hester! Mrs.—"

They were sending smiles and waves back to her, and she would have named them all had she not heard Mrs. Blake's voice. "Sarah!"

She had forgotten she was not alone. She sat back in her seat. Mrs. Blake had a look of one whose patience was being sorely tried. "I allow you to take meals with the servants so you'll not be lonesome. But a lady does not act so familiar with them in public if she wishes to gain the respect of her peers. Goodness knows you'll have a difficult enough time of that."

Sarah nodded, pushing her left hand into the small of her back as tears stung her eyes. Last night's feeling of belonging evaporated. She turned her face again toward the window and willed herself not to cry.

Dorothea's words hung in the air like hateful things. Even Marie sent her accusing looks. She wished she could snatch her words back, explain that she wasn't referring to the misshapen hand. But the explanation would be far worse. The girl was too young to understand that it was her circumstances of birth that posed a far greater hindrance to her being accepted by polite society. Even if her parentage could successfully be kept a secret, the fact that she had lived in an orphanage since infancy was proof enough for most that she was born out of wedlock.

She cleared her throat. The girl beside her did not turn from the window.

"We will share my prayer book and hymnal," were the only words Dorothea could think of to fill the thick silence. When Sarah glanced at her, she said, "I will have Mrs. Bacon purchase a set of your own for you this week."

"But I don't mind sharing," Sarah murmured.

But of course you wouldn't, Dorothea thought. If only the girl had been a brat, loud, and ill-kempt as her mother had been. Then with a clear conscience she could have sent her away to a fine school, there to reside until some fortune hunter discovered the connection between her and the Blake shipping fortune. And Dorothea would have gladly contributed a fine dowry, a final penance on Jeremy's behalf.

But she was far from a brat. *And she's the only family you have*, Dorothea reminded herself. If only she could summon up again the fragile bond they had shared in the parlor that night. Again she cleared her throat as the coach began slowing to a halt in Hanover Square in front of Saint George's. "We will get you a matching set."

"Madam?" the girl asked.

"Prayer book and hymnal. I have even seen young ladies carrying lovely white ones, with gilded pages."

Concern filled the young face instead of the pleasure she had expected. "They must be frightfully expensive. You've spent so much money on me already."

"I have more money than sense, child. And very few years left to use both."

The girl's eyes widened in shock, which strangely amused Dorothea. But she restrained herself from smiling and, as Stanley opened the door, said, "Remember . . . a well-bred young lady does not fidget."

———

The vicar's voice rang out strong and dramatic, as if he were Nehemiah encouraging the people of Jerusalem to rebuild the city's walls.

"Beloved brethren, the Scripture moveth us, in sundry places, to acknowledge and confess our manifold sins and wickedness; and that we should not dissemble nor cloak them before the face of Almighty God, our heavenly Father; but confess them with a humble, lowly, penitent, and obedient heart; to the end that we may obtain forgiveness of the same, by His infinite goodness and mercy. . . ."

Because she so desperately wanted to

prove that she could be a young lady, Sarah did not allow herself to gawk at the Corinthian columns leading up to a gilded ceiling, the stained-glass windows, massive organ, or candelabra. But she did venture a glance above her left shoulder during the space when she and the rest of the congregation were getting to their knees. Those in the gallery not looking at their prayer books had their eyes closed, but she was comforted just by the sight of Naomi and Mrs. Bacon and the rest, except for Marie, who was seated somewhere else with her sisters. Mrs. Blake did not kneel on account of her age but bowed her head and held her *Book of Common Prayer* open so that Sarah could read along with the others.

"'Almighty and most merciful Father; we have erred, and strayed from Thy ways like lost sheep. We have followed too much the devices and desires of our own hearts. . . .' "

As the service progressed, she was overjoyed to realize that she would not be asked to abandon her faith after all. She even had to send up a quick prayer of repentance for the disloyal thought that she was grateful Vicar Sharp did not glare and roar as did Reverend Howe on his Sundays at Saint Matthew's, invariably causing some of the youngest girls to weep and have to be hurried from the room.

After the closing hymn was sung, worshipers filed out of the pews and strolled down the aisles in small groups, filling the church with the hum of quiet conversation while the organist played "Oh My Soul, Bless God the Father." "I know that one," she whispered.

"Very good," Mrs. Blake returned with a little smile, then leaned closer. "I will introduce you to the vicar. But you must linger only long enough for politeness' sake, as others will be waiting."

Sarah had not reckoned on that. In the pew she had been one face among many. What if he asked her about herself? How did he feel about Methodists?

"Vicar Sharp, this is my ward, Sarah Matthews," Mrs. Blake said at the door. The vicar seemed older at the door than he had in the pulpit, with a few lonely strands of steel-colored hair resting atop a head otherwise as bald as a stone. His sidewhiskers were magnificent, sprouting from his wrinkled cheeks like weeds.

"Indeed?" He scooped up her gloved hand and smiled warmly. "Welcome, Miss Matthews."

"Thank you." She dipped into a bob with her hand still in his, almost weak with relief that the word *Methodist* had not passed between them. On the pavement Marie caught up with them but then lagged behind a bit when Mrs. Blake steered Sarah by the elbow toward two women in huddled conversation. The pair stepped apart and smiled.

"Mrs. Gill and Mrs. Stafford, may I present my ward, Sarah Matthews?" she said after greetings were exchanged and with her hand upon Sarah's shoulder.

Like Mrs. Blake, Mmes. Gill and Stafford had softly lined faces and gray hair peeking from bonnets. But only Mrs. Gill, short and buxom, was dressed in black. Mrs. Stafford's taller, though no less buxom, frame was swathed in a gown the color of marigolds.

"Welcome to Berkeley Square, Miss Matthews." Mrs. Gill had a curious habit of blinking her eyes often, as if not even aware that she was doing so.

Focusing her own eyes upon the lower

part of the woman's face so as not to be rude, Sarah thanked her and curtseyed. She kept her left hand in a fold of her dress.

"Have you been ill, dear?" Mrs. Stafford said.

Her voice was so nasal that Sarah wondered if she were ill herself.

"Not since the ague last winter," she answered before it dawned upon her that the woman was referring to her thinness and pale skin. The sympathy in the woman's expression compelled Sarah to assure her, "I've had much more to eat since I came here, so I'm growing stouter every day, and there is so much more sunlight in the garden than there was in—"

There was a spasmodic tightening of Mrs. Blake's fingers on her shoulder. "You may wait in the coach with Marie now, Sarah."

Even though Sarah's eyes did not stray from the hands in her lap, she could feel Marie's seething stare as they sat in the facing seats. Only five days ago she was inspected for lice, her clothes even burned. Was it a shameful thing living in an orphanage? She couldn't imagine why. It wasn't as if children had any say-so about whether or not they should have parents.

"Do not despair yourself," Marie said eventually.

Sarah looked up.

The lady's maid threw a contemptuous look out of the window. "They are sharp old hens. And you have not even met Mrs. Fowler, who is the worst of the lot." She did not appear concerned about possibly being overheard when seconds later Mrs. Blake was assisted through the open door by Stanley.

"I'm sorry," Sarah told her, still not sure why she should be.

Mrs. Blake nodded, a tight smile at her lips. "From now on you will simply reply to questions with as little embellishment as possible. Do you understand?"

"Yes, Madam."

They rode in silence, Sarah with a sick feeling in the pit of her stomach. She had done it again! She supposed Mrs. Blake regretted having her here more now than ever. Just when she was beginning to feel more at home at Berkeley Square, she had put herself at risk of being sent back to Saint Matthew's. And she realized she didn't want to go.

Please don't let that happen, Father, she prayed.

———

By noon the next day she breathed a little easier, for there had been enough time for Mrs. Blake to pack her off if she had thought Sarah's behavior at church unforgivable. The matter of her origin still troubled her, however, so she broached the subject to Naomi after a lunch of chicken cutlets with gravy and vegetables. The cook stood at the worktable carving bits of ham for supper's yellow split-pea soup while Trudy washed dishes at the sink. Sarah sat on the ledge of one of the cupboards, polishing jars of spices and dried herbs and then replacing them on the freshly dusted shelf.

"Shameful to come from an orphanage?" Naomi sent her a curious look. "Why would you ask that?"

"I'm just wondering." Sarah did not want to relive yesterday's embarrassment by giving details.

She was prepared to have the whole notion dismissed, perhaps be told that she was too young to worry about such things.

Instead Naomi said, after a brief silence, "Miss Matthews, there is nothing shameful about a person who lives a decent life. God is no respecter of persons, as the Scripture says. But you will occasionally happen upon people who take issue with anyone born into circumstances different than their own."

"But no one can determine how he's to be born."

"It's just the way society ranks people. A duke is seated higher than an earl at dinner parties, no matter if the earl is a doctor who has saved thousands of lives. And the gentility look down upon those in trade, no matter how educated or cultured those in trade might happen to be."

"But wasn't Mr. Blake in trade?" Sarah asked hesitantly.

The cook gave her a wry smile. "My tongue set a trap for me, Miss Matthews. But no matter what your social standing, there are others perched upon the same rung of the ladder. Mr. and Mrs. Blake were never wanting for friends."

"And I had friends at Saint Matthew's," Sarah reminded her.

"There, you see?"

Sarah nodded. Orphans surely clung to the bottom rung of the ladder or perhaps to the rung just above beggars and thieves. She had no idea what rung she occupied now, being not quite a servant yet not the same as well-bred people. But she didn't think she would like to be in society. The five minutes in front of the church had been more than enough. She held up the jar she had just dusted that was filled with interesting-looking rolled brown sticks. "May I ask what this is?"

"Cinnamon bark. We'll put a bit in your tea today if you like." Turning the ham to the other side, Naomi began chiseling off more bits. "Unfortunately, it's not just the upper crust, Miss Matthews. Even among servants, there is pride over rank."

"And a scullery maid is the lowest of them all!" Trudy snapped as she shoved another dripping dish into the rack above her.

Sarah marveled at the sharpness in her tone, but Naomi smiled and said in her soothing tone, "Trudy will be a cook in a fine house like this one day, you may mark my words."

❧ *Eighteen* ❧

Three more pages, William told himself on the evening of May 21, four weeks after moving back into the garret room of Staircase Sixteen. He lifted his eyes from Dmitry Mendeleyev's *Principles of Chemistry* to steal a glance at the pasteboard box upon his chest of drawers. It had sat there since the afternoon post and had become his motivation not to waste a minute of the day.

Unfortunately, young Lord Holt had chosen that particular day to go punting in an inebriated state and took a topple into the River Cherwell. To prevent the underclassman's fine Wellington boots from hardening, William had had to remove them from the fireplace fender every hour and give them another rubbing with saddle soap. That, along with his other duties, such as collecting Mr. Kendrick's laundry from a washerwoman on Brasenose Lane and delivering a supper tray to Lord Holt, whose clothes would dry out before he did.

And then there were his studies—he had vowed to himself never to fall behind. Mr. Mendeleyev's words on periodic law sometimes fused into blobs of gibberish, but when he finally slammed shut the text, it was with a sense of accomplishment. Yawning and stretching out his aching shoulders, he rose from his writing table. He cut the twine with his pocket knife and lifted the box's lid, to be greeted by the buttery aroma of Scotch shortbread. Pressed into the top of each square were toasted almonds, just the way he liked them.

Aunt Naomi, you're worth your weight in gold. There were also a half-dozen Dutch pippin apples and a parcel of cracked walnuts. After taking out a square of shortbread, he gave his attention to the envelope tucked into the side. He had received two letters from his aunt since returning to Oxford. This time two pages were folded together. A glance at the signature of the second told him that Sarah Matthews had finally written. He read his aunt's letter first, settling sideways into his chair with an arm loped over the back. She told of her days in the kitchen since she last wrote, her delight to have borrowed a copy of *Lorna Doone* from the lending library, and the activities of the other servants.

This morning Mr. Duffy brought in several of the Crecy carrots you helped him sow. Trudy and I were amazed at their sweetness, and she talked me into another carrot pudding.

As usual she apologized for having nothing exciting to tell, but it was the routine domesticity of her letters that was soothing upon his print-weary eyes. He could almost smell bread baking and hear his aunt's singing softly as she did only when she thought no one was listening.

In her last paragraph she wrote,

Miss Matthews cut the shortbread for me. It was I who suggested she write. She feared you were only being kind when you offered. It would be like you, dear person that you are, but as there was so much hope in her face, I insisted you would be happy to hear from her.

William thought again how perfect the timing was, the girl moving into the house. It was as if God had orchestrated it so on his aunt's behalf. He brushed away crumbs from a fold in the letter before moving it behind the next one.

Dear William,

Please put this aside if you are too busy to read it. I hope that your lectures are interesting and that the weather there in Oxford is pleasant and not so foggy as London. Mrs. Blake sat with me in the garden for a little while last Thursday and said that she has found a tutor of excellent repute, a Mr. Colby, but that he will not be available until June tenth. I am to keep my mind occupied until then by reading two books he has assigned, Aids to Reflection *by Samuel Taylor Coleridge and* History of Civilization in England *by Henry Buckle. I hope that Mr. Colby has some knowledge of chemistry, however, I do not think I should wish to be a chemist. Please do not take offense; I know that you will be a great chemist one day and discover at least one of the missing elements.*

William marveled at the painstaking neatness of the lines of script, with only two small blots to mar the conformity of it. He could imagine the gravity in her pale face as she labored over the page. And he realized this was probably the first letter she had ever written.

Naomi allowed me to cut the dough for your shortbread and press in the almonds. We made macaroons on May Day. Everyone except for Mrs. Blake and Marie walked to Hyde Park. Hester pinned so many flowers to my hat that you could not see the brim. The May Pole was lovely, with garlands and children frolicking about singing sweet little songs.

I confess to you that I disliked the Punch and Judy show and only pretended to laugh because everyone expected me to do so. When Naomi excused herself to leave, I asked to accompany her. The others assumed I was fatigued on account of my age.

Naomi said she had heard enough quarreling when she was a girl and that she did not care to be reminded of those days.

On Saturday evening past, I read the final chapter of Frankenstein *in Naomi's room while she polished her Sunday boots and Trudy sewed a button onto her pink dress. It is hard to imagine Mrs. Blake ever reading it. Naomi said she had also enjoyed the story as a girl and that it serves as a reminder that even a person of mild nature can be corrupted by ill-treatment. And that if everyone strove to follow Jesus' commandment "to do unto others as we would have them do unto us—"*

"—all of society would be the better for it," William murmured, smiling. "Aunt Naomi and I had that same discussion, Miss Matthews."

The closing lines were terse.

Thank you for not minding the time I spend with Naomi. Please do not go to the bother of replying to this letter. It is kind enough that you invited me to write.

Very sincerely yours,
Sarah Matthews

Guilt pricked his conscience as he folded the letters and put them in the drawer. He had written to his aunt only once since his arrival this term, and though she assured him that she understood about his time limitations, he knew how much she loved to hear from him. Tomorrow after chapel he would make time to compose another. And he supposed as long as he would have to ink his pen anyway, he could scribble a note to the girl.

As tempting as it was to fall across the bed without even removing his shoes, William crept down the silent corridor to clean his teeth, bathe with a flannel, and change into his nightshirt. He felt as if his brain had been scooped out and replaced with pudding, rendering him incapable of anything but the most rudimentary thought. When he finally pulled the covers up over his shoulders, he mumbled a prayer into his pillow and apologized for the brevity of it. He sank into a sleep so deep that when his eyes opened to a still-dark morning, he could vaguely recall a bit of only one dream, his aunt walking up the street with a pale girl wearing a hat decorated with flowers.

———

By the Sunday morning of May 29, four of Madame Gauthier's dresses hung in Sarah's wardrobe alongside the ready-made ones, which were beginning to feel tight around her waist and bodice. Fortunately the seamstress had allowed for growth in the new dresses. Though Sarah was still thin, even after six weeks of Naomi's cooking, she was delighted that her ribs no longer protruded like the black keys of Mrs. Blake's piano. And she even seemed a wee bit taller, for she could now stand on tiptoe and brush her fingertips against the top of her doorframe.

"What will we do with the dresses I outgrow?" Sarah asked while Hester fastened the buttons to her newest gown, a yellow silk with a white eyelet lace pinafore.

"I suppose the Missus will give them to one of them charities she sends money to," Hester replied.

Sarah thought that it was a shame they

couldn't be sent to Saint Matthew's. But then, Mrs. Forsyth would never allow finery to only a handful of girls. As much as she enjoyed the new clothes, she felt guilty that one person should have so much.

"Have you picked out a hat?"

In addition to the new dresses, there were three bonnets as well. But Sarah's mind was not on choosing, for it was then that she realized Hester's voice had not its usual lilt. She turned from the mirror. Hester, in turn, averted her eyes toward the window.

"Hester, what's wrong?" Sarah was not nearly so meek anymore, at least not in the company of the servants, in spite of an occasional slipped "yes, Madam" or "sir." They seemed now like caring aunts and uncles—even Marie and Stanley, though she still disapproved of the way he treated Hester.

Hester's lips trembled as if she was straining to keep her emotions inside. "I'm just out of sorts this morning. Nature and all that. You'll learn when you're older."

Having spent most of her life surrounded by girls—some streetwise beyond their years, Sarah reckoned she had been well-versed in "all that." Sympathetically she said, "Perhaps you should sit down?"

But then a sob tore out of Hester's lips, and she buried her face in her hands. "If only I didn't love him so!"

Sending a helpless glance to the door for help that did not materialize, Sarah patted the maid's heaving shoulder. She had not the courage to voice what she was thinking, that Hester could *choose* not to love Stanley. That the solution was so simple to her surely meant it was more complicated.

"If only he would marry me!" Hester whimpered.

Sarah could bear it no longer. "But why would you want to if he makes you so unhappy?"

"The heart can't choose whom it loves, Miss Matthews."

"I see," was all Sarah could reply, though she didn't see at all.

The chambermaid did not accompany her downstairs, saying she wasn't hungry after all. "Stanley gave Vera Mifflin a ride in the wagon yesterday," Trudy muttered to Avis in Sarah's hearing. "And it weren't the first time." Both sent sharp looks at the groomsman, who went on heaping marmalade onto his toast. Even Naomi seemed put out at him, for she merely made a tepid smile at his declaration that the rain was so heavy last night that he had to dog-paddle out to the stable. But Mrs. Bacon and Claire and Mr. Duffy chuckled with enough enthusiasm that Stanley didn't seem to notice the four who didn't.

———

Sarah was becoming a little more at ease in Mrs. Blake's presence. Eventually it had dawned upon her that the elderly woman felt just as awkward in her company, though there were moments when there seemed to be a tenuous bond between them. Such as during the ride to church that morning. Sarah sat with gloved right hand resting upon the kidskin-bound *Book of Common Prayer* and *Hymns for the Church*, listening to Mrs. Blake and Marie speculate over the theme of today's sermon. Suddenly Mrs. Blake pointed out her window to the left.

"See the little lad behind the lamppost?" Sarah leaned forward, as did Marie from the other side. Indeed, a small boy stood as still as the post itself and waited for the small group walking in his direction.

"He ran ahead, and his family is pretending not to notice so he can pop out and frighten them. But I do hope he'll mind that puddle behind him."

"Does Madame wish me to call out warning?" Marie asked in a droll tone.

"Why, of course not. That would spoil the surprise." Mrs. Blake turned again to them. "Jeremy used to crouch behind a lamp table when he was small. He thought if he kept perfectly still, no one could see him."

The smile faded and her pale eyes glistened. Marie gave her mistress a weary look. Impulsively Sarah said, "There is a girl at Saint Matthew's who would hide whenever it was her turn to bathe."

Now under the scrutiny of both sets of eyes, Sarah wondered if she had blundered. But then Mrs. Blake blinked. "Indeed?"

"Hannah. She's one of the younger girls—about six years, so she must have been four in those days."

"Naughty child!" Marie said, but with a little smile.

"Not necessarily, Marie." Mrs. Blake's face was serious. "She could have been afraid of water. Was that the reason, Sarah?"

"It was the soap," Sarah replied. "She said it made her skin itch. Mrs. Forsyth bought a cake of Star soap just for Hannah after the time it took us two hours to find her."

"A prudent move. But where was she hiding?"

"In Mrs. Forsyth's wardrobe."

To Sarah's relief, Mrs. Blake smiled. "The cheek of the girl, hiding in the headmistress's room! We had a hideous pink sofa when I was a girl, mended in several places. I was hiding behind it when my sister Edith's beau asked for her hand. Thought I was quite clever, I did, until my parents came into the room, and I had to sit perfectly still for what seemed like hours. To make matters worse, all I could think about after a while was how desperately I needed to use the privy."

Marie chuckled, but Sarah was too stunned to do anything but gape at this same woman who had lectured her about the proper conduct and conversation of a lady!

"What is it, Sarah?" Mrs. Blake said. "You look as if you've seen a ghost."

"Madame has shocked the child," Marie admonished.

"No . . . I merely . . ." Heat rushed into Sarah's cheeks; however, nothing rushed into her mind to rescue her. But when the two women laughed, she joined in.

Mrs. Blake's lighthearted mood lasted all through the worship service, and afterward it was probably the impetus for inviting to Thursday tea Mmes. Gill and Stafford, and a Mrs. Fowler, to whom Sarah had been introduced three weeks ago. Mrs. Fowler was the eldest of the circle of friends, for the hair visible beneath her black bonnet was snow-white, and her face as wrinkled as a walnut shell. Graciously the three accepted. Mrs. Gill, blinking, clasped gloved hands together and chirped, "It's been too long since we've had a good chat!"

"And what do you think we're doing now?" Mrs. Fowler asked. Sarah could not tell if the irritation in the throaty voice was genuine or in jest, as Mr. Duffy and Stanley were wont to do.

"It's not the same when the vicar is just a few feet away," Mrs. Stafford said, dropping her voice to a nasal stage whisper. "I certainly don't wish to hear a sermon about *gossip* next Sunday."

In the midst of the schoolgirlish giggles

that followed, Mrs. Blake seemed pleased, even a little relieved. She said to Mrs. Stafford. "And, Augusta, do bring little Becky so the girls may play."

"I'll certainly try," the woman agreed after a lightning-quick glance in Sarah's direction. "Though it's quite probable that she'll have a riding or dancing lesson or something of that sort. I scolded Francis just yesterday for not allowing the children opportunities to amuse themselves, but you know how these University women are—all caught up in modern notions about child-rearing. And there is only so much you can say to a daughter-in-law without being accused of interfering."

Others began taking issue with their daughters-in-law except for Mrs. Blake, who excused herself and Sarah at the first lull in the discussion. She was pleasant enough while bidding her friends good-day, but wore a tight-lipped expression on the way to the coach and stared out of her window all the way home.

"Has Madame taken ill?" Marie finally asked as they waited for Stanley to hop from his perch and open the door.

"I'm quite well, thank you," Mrs. Blake

replied in a tone that suggested otherwise. Sarah wondered if the change in mood was because she too was aware that, lesson or no, Mrs. Stafford's granddaughter would not be at tea Thursday. She wished she had the mettle to assure her that it didn't matter, that she had gotten quite used to playing alone.

Hester appeared for lunch with shadows under her eyes. She picked at her meal and spoke only when addressed. If Stanley noticed the strained atmosphere, he did not let on but was his usual bantering self.

After the lunch dishes were cleared and Trudy was in the garden collecting basil, Sarah wondered if she should mention the apparent snub at church to Naomi. She had burdened her with so many of her misgivings. What if Naomi grew weary of having her come down to the kitchen for chats? She didn't think she could bear such a thing.

"Penny for your thoughts?" The cook's voice broke into her reverie. They were both seated at the worktable, Sarah mixing cocoa powder, sugar, and a bit of salt to store in a crock for making hot chocolate. Naomi chopped vegetables for the soup

that would be the main part of supper—
Potage Printanier, Naomi had explained,
also known as Spring Soup.

Putting aside her gloomy thoughts for
the moment, Sarah asked, "Why do we
have soup every night?" Quickly she
added, "I'm not complaining . . . I like it
very much." Especially with the recipes so
varied, for it seemed that Naomi had
dozens, from pheasant to parsnip, calf's-
head to cabbage.

Naomi's knife made little thumping
sounds against the board as it minced
through a long carrot. She did not look up,
which was a relief to Sarah because she
would not wish the dear woman to lose a
finger.

"Mrs. Blake believes a light supper is
better for sleeping afterward. It makes
sense to me, not having our stomachs
overtasked with digesting. And it's pleasant
getting out of the kitchen for a little time to
ourselves in the evenings instead of having
to clean up after a big meal."

"I'm glad," Sarah told her.

"I do enjoy cooking, mind you. But anything can become tedious if you're not allowed a break."

"How did you come to be a cook?" Sarah wondered why she had never thought to ask before. Obviously Naomi wasn't born and reared in Mrs. Blake's kitchen.

"I was a kitchen maid first and learned as I went along. But I already had some experience with plain cookery, for my family had no servants." She explained that as the daughter of a tenant farmer, there had been few opportunities for employment in Leicester.

"Was it very difficult for you? Coming to London by yourself?"

"Very," Naomi replied with a nod. "I was eighteen, and it was my first time away from home. But I wanted desperately to make a better life for myself. And I was able to send part of my wages to my parents while they were living."

Sarah wondered why Naomi had never married. She was certainly pretty, even more so than Hester, though that had not dawned upon Sarah until several days after her arrival. She was beginning to understand that there was more to beauty than just the arrangement of eyes, nose, and mouth, that one's character had a way of drawing attention to the attractive or not-so-attractive features, depending on the quality of the character. Mr. Duffy, whose visage had frightened her at their first meeting, she now found endearing because of his kindness and humor. And Naomi's serenity was just as comely a feature as her cobalt blue eyes and smooth cheeks.

"What happened at church, dear girl?" Naomi asked.

Sarah stopped stirring cocoa powder, which by now was as completely mixed as the bread dough rising upon the cupboard ledge. "How did you know?"

"You were very quiet at lunch."

She had to smile. "I'm always quiet during meals."

Naomi smiled back at her. "There is happy quiet and sad quiet."

In the warmth of the kitchen and of Naomi's companionship, Sarah could almost convince herself that the snub didn't matter. But the memory still gave her a little stab, so she found herself relating Mrs. Stafford's overeager assurances that her granddaughter wouldn't be available.

Incredibly Naomi's lips tightened as if in

anger, but her expression smoothed into its usual serenity a second later. The carrots pushed aside into a mound of coins, she switched to potatoes. "Tell me, Miss Matthews, the few times you were in Mrs. Stafford's vicinity, did you do or say anything to offend her . . . even accidentally?"

Sarah didn't even have to think about that one. "No, nothing."

"Hmm. Then tell me this. In the days when you were ignorant of Mrs. Stafford's very existence, were you terribly unhappy about it?"

"But when I didn't know Mrs.—" Sarah stopped herself and smiled. "I shouldn't concern myself over this, should I?"

"I expect your cocoa will taste just as sweet whether she thinks well or ill of you." Sobriety overtook Naomi's expression again. "During your lifetime not everyone will be fond of you, Miss Matthews. I wish I could say otherwise, but there are few good people in this world who have no detractors. But why dwell upon the few who may not care for you, when you can spend that time thinking about the many who do?"

"Who do what?" asked Trudy, coming

through the doorway with a handful of greenery.

"Adore Miss Matthews," Naomi replied.

"Oh, but we do, don't we?" The scullery maid patted the top of Sarah's head as she dropped the leaves into a heap upon the table. "And I believe your hair has grown an inch since you got here. You'll look like a proper girl yet, won't you?"

Later, while Sarah looked through the pages of *The Household Cyclopedia,* she ran her fingers through her hair. Perhaps it would grow another inch by the time William returned for summer break. Not that it mattered, she told herself.

Her eyes lit upon something on the page that reminded her of Hester and her despondency. Respectfully she waited for a pause in Naomi's and Trudy's discussion over tomorrow's lunch menu to ask, "May I borrow this for a little while?" She hoped neither would ask why. As friendly as Trudy was, she was still Hester's cousin and could possibly take offense.

Naomi simply smiled. "But of course."

✵ *Nineteen* ✵

Sarah spotted Hester in Marie's room from the corridor, red curls bound up with a cloth as she polished the fireplace grate. From the doorway she asked, "May I visit with you?"

"Come on in, Miss Matthews." The face turned in Sarah's direction wore the expression of a person just hoping someone would happen along to relieve the solitude. When Sarah hesitated, Hester grinned and said, "Marie won't bite."

She stepped into the room, decorated in uncharacteristically subdued colors of mauve, cream, and pale green.

"Just don't get too close or you'll muss your frock. And pull up that bench so's I don't have to crane my neck."

Mindful of scraping the hardwood floor near the hearth, Sarah shoved the book under her elbow and picked up the bench from the dressing table. She settled three feet away from the fireplace and tucked her gown behind her knees.

Hester smiled at her. "What have you there?"

"It's Naomi's," Sarah replied, holding up the book. She was aware that Hester would not be able to read the title but hoped the still-shiny gilt lettering would be impressive enough to lend authority to the words.

The maid gave it a benign glance and went back to polishing with a black-smeared cloth. "You ain't going to read recipes to me, are you?"

"It's a book of advice." Sarah drew a deep breath. "I thought you might care to hear what it says about courting."

The maid's polishing slowed a pace. "I didn't know there was things in books about courtin'. Well, what's it say?"

Opening the book, Sarah found her place and read: " 'Choice of a husband . . . As few ladies are privileged to initiate proposals in reference to spouses, directions may only be given with respect to the acceptance of offers.' "

"Now tell me again in Queen's English," Hester grumbled good-naturedly.

Sarah thought for a second. "It means

that most women have to wait to be asked, but we have the choice as to which proposal we accept."

"Thinkin' about marriage already, are you, Miss Matthews?"

"Oh, not me . . ." She intercepted Hester's wink and realized she was being teased. Smiling, she looked to the page again. " 'Do not encourage the advances of a gentleman who is believed to have jilted a lady; you owe this to your sex and to society.' "

When Sarah looked up, Hester was sitting back upon her heels, cloth idle in her hand. "Explain that part again about owing to my sex and all that."

"I believe it means that if *all* women wouldn't have anything to do with men who treat them less than decently, the men who aren't decent would have to become so."

She was about to apologize for her muddled tangle of words and make another attempt, but Hester nodded thoughtfully. "I don't suppose they would go to all that trouble of putting it in that book if it weren't true. Is there more?"

"A little." Sarah read on. " 'Never believe any one whose protestations of love are intense at first sight; you may better judge the sentiments of the man who loves you by his manner than by his words.' "

"And what's *intense* mean?" Hester asked.

"With his whole heart. As if he would die for you if you asked him." She grasped for an example. "Like William Dobbin's love for Amelia Sedley."

"Who?"

"Forgive me—they're from *Vanity Fair.*" And when the maid still wore a blank look, Sarah added, "It's a storybook." Literary characters were discussed so often on Saint Matthew's third storey that Sarah sometimes forgot they were not real people.

"You might know he wouldn't be a real fellow." Hester frowned. "Stanley says that very thing . . . that he would die for me and all that. But his actions don't say that at all. And when I say the courtship is over, he promises—*intensely*—that he'll change his ways."

"But he doesn't?" Sarah asked in spite of knowing the answer.

"For maybe a day or so. You know . . ." she said with green eyes narrowing, "it's just like having a dog lick your hand whilst it piddles on your foot."

Sarah bit her lip and forced herself not to smile.

"But does it say in there how a girl is to make herself *stop* loving a man like that?" Hester asked with eyes wide.

"No . . . I haven't read all of it, but I don't think so."

"Well, ain't that just jolly keen! They row you to the middle of the pond and then take away your oars."

"Perhaps if you prayed about it?" Sarah suggested timidly. "I asked God to take away my homesickness for Saint Matthew's and He did."

"You was that sad?"

Her eyes clouded a bit at the memory. "I even thought about running away."

"Poor lamb," Hester said. "And He took it away, like that?"

"Well, not all at once. But it's gone now."

"Hmm." She rubbed the tip of her nose, leaving a smear. "I'm a Christian girl, mind you, but I never seen as how God had time to concern himself with the goings-on of a chambermaid, what with the wars and such in the world."

"Mrs. Kettner would remind you that God even knows when a sparrow falls."

"Who?"

"My teacher at Saint Matthew's."

"Oh." Hester picked up her cloth again. "It were good of you to tell me all this, Miss Matthews. You'd best run along now and leave me to do some thinking."

"Have I made you angry?"

"Angry?" She smiled and held her blackened thumb and forefinger slightly apart. "Not even this much. But Mrs. Bacon will be if I don't tidy up this grate."

Sarah took *Aids of Reflection* out into the garden for the rest of the afternoon, ignoring the sounds of play from over the wall. The text was written for someone above her years, but she studied each paragraph meticulously until she could absorb the gist of it. She was mulling over Coleridge's distinction between Reason and Understanding when Mordie's head appeared at the wall.

"Is your hand better?"

"I'm afraid not," she replied with an apologetic smile.

"You could play croquet one-handed. We would do the same to make it fair."

Sarah could no longer meet his eyes directly. "That's very kind of you. But I have to study."

Hester came to the supper table in a fresh uniform, the soot scrubbed from her nose. As at lunch, she abstained from the usual banter and answered any question put to her with an economy of words. But Sarah detected a subtle difference. Whereas before she had seemed despondent, now there was a preoccupied air about her. Even Stanley seemed to notice, for Sarah caught him sending more than one curious look in her direction. And his attempt at humor—telling of a stableman down the mews who tended a horse that would whinny if he hit a high note while whistling—elicited from her no more than an absent smile.

"That's why you borrowed the book, isn't it?" Naomi said in a low voice when Sarah brought the butter crock into the kitchen.

"I was going to tell you later. The part about courting seemed so perfect."

"And she obviously listened. It just bears out the Scripture . . . *and a little child shall lead them.*"

As much as she loved being complimented by Naomi, Sarah could not help but wince. "Thirteen isn't so much a little child, is it?"

The cook smiled. "Thirteen is a young lady. And a very wise young lady at that."

———

It was on Mondays that Naomi missed William the most. She could not bring herself to go to any of the old places without him. But on impulse after breakfast the following day, she knocked at the sitting room door.

"You may enter," came Marie's voice.

Naomi walked inside. Mrs. Blake, seated on the divan, and Marie, in a nearby chair, worked needlepoint from hooped canvases. Marie gave Naomi a bored look and resumed sewing, while Mrs. Blake rested the hand holding the threaded needle in her lap. "Yes, Naomi?"

The voice was flat, her expression tight. Naomi wondered if yesterday's conversation outside the church was still lingering in her thoughts. That was another reason she was here. If the girl wasn't allowed to play with the Rothschild boys and was to be shunned ever so cordially by polite society, she should be given opportunity for experiences not confined to the bounds of 14 Berkeley Square.

"I'll be taking my half-day after lunch, Madam."

"Very well, Naomi," Mrs. Blake said with a slight lift of brows, for it wasn't Naomi's usual custom to remind her. Even Marie looked up again.

"May I ask your permission to invite Miss Matthews to accompany me to the theatre this evening?"

"The theatre?" She spoke the word as if having never heard it.

"*The Enchanted Wood* is at the Adelphi. I've read the reviews, and it seems perfect for a young—"

"That is very kind of you, Naomi. Please do not take offense, but it would not be appropriate for Sarah to be out socially with a servant."

"I see." Naomi raised her chin a bit. She had worked hard all of her life and had never allowed herself to feel ashamed of her station. "Then if you'll excuse me . . ."

"You may leave us," Mrs. Blake interrupted again, only the order was directed toward the chair. Marie stabbed her canvas

with her needle, set it aside on the armchair, and pushed herself to her feet with
exaggerated motion.

"I shall be upstairs."

In spite of the recent injury to her own
dignity, Naomi felt sympathy for the lady's
maid. Surely even Marie had figured out
Sarah Matthews' identity, so how long did
Mrs. Blake intend to keep pretending? As it
was, the secret had almost become an en-
tity among the servants, a presence that
lurked in corners and shadow, and growing
larger every day that they pretended not to
see it.

"Do have a seat, Naomi."

"With all due respect, Madam," Naomi
said, lowering herself into a chair adjacent
to the divan, "Marie doesn't engage in gossip. Surely it's wearisome to have to watch
what you say every minute you're together.
May I ask why you've not told her?"

Mrs. Blake looked even more weary.
"Too many already know."

An understatement if there ever was one,
Naomi thought.

"And she would try to prod me into
telling Sarah. She's grown very fond of the
girl."

"Then why *not* tell Sarah? She's very bright, and it's just a matter of time before she figures—"

"No!" A frown tugged at the creased lips. "She'll despise me."

"I don't believe that, Mrs. Blake. She'll be confused at first, of course, but she'll grow to love you. You're her *grandmother*."

Such longing came into the woman's face that Naomi thought she was on the verge of agreeing. But her expression hardened. "The proper time is for me to decide. And she may not accompany you to the theatre, Naomi. Even though her father did not give her his name, she is still a *Blake*."

The inflection upon the *Blake* seemed a little pretentious to Naomi, who was aware of their less-than-aristocratic roots. "I attend theatre in Sunday dress. No one would know that she's in the company of a servant."

"And if one of my acquaintances happened to be there?" She shook her head. "I admit I have allowed the girl to overstep the bounds of propriety by digging in the dirt with Mr. Duffy and loitering in the kitchen, simply because she lacks playmates. But it will be difficult enough for her to be accepted without flouting social convention."

"Very well, Madam." As there was nothing else to discuss, Naomi rose from the chair. "If I may take my leave now . . ."

"Wait, Naomi." Her mistress's expression softened. "This is no reflection upon you personally, you must understand. I have always admired your straightforwardness and the character you've instilled in William. Had I been so mindful of Jeremy's . . . well, perhaps things would have been different."

It was impossible to bear a grudge against such transparency. "Thank you, Madam," Naomi said. "And if I may be so bold . . . there is a point when we choose our own way. You can't blame yourself forever."

"Very kind of you to say so, Naomi. Do ring for Marie on your way out."

Naomi did as instructed. And decided she would spend her half-day in legendary Exmoor in the company of *Lorna Doone*.

When the door closed, Dorothea rested her head against the pillows between the divan and the wall behind it and stared up at the beloved portrait. *But I will, Naomi.* And why not blame herself?

How many sermons had she heard on The Prodigal Son? It was a picture of forgiveness, a lesson on how God longs to restore fellowship with His straying children. But another key lesson had escaped her.

The son did not mend his ways until he was sick of the pigpen.

Oh, she was familiar with pigpens— enough to make her friends recoil in horror if they only knew. For almost every year of her upbringing her father had penned a sow in their tiny garden to be sent to the butcher's in the fall. When one sister died and the other married, the task of carrying out the pail of slops became Dorothea's. There was little space for the poor creature to do anything but wallow in its own filth, so she would hurry with mouth closed tight while taking shallow breaths. Not a place that a person would choose to stay.

You never allowed Jeremy to reach that place, she told herself. Instead, she softened the sharp edges of life for him, paying off gaming debts and having Mr. Duffy wait up to put him to bed when he stumbled in reeking of debauchery, if he came home at all. She even unfairly dismissed a girl who had been ill-used by him—as much as it pained her to admit it to herself.

There was no comfort in reminding herself that his father's nurturing was directed chiefly toward the business. That she loved the boy more gave her the greater responsibility to see that he turned out right. She was David weeping over Absalom, wishing in vain that she could have died instead.

———

"Mrs. Blake wishes to see you after breakfast," Sarah was told by Mrs. Bacon three days later just as she was removing the plate of broiled whiting, poached egg, and buttered bread from her tray in the servants' hall.

"Very well," Sarah replied. "I'll hurry."

"Bad for the digestion, Miss Matthews," the housekeeper said. "She said you were to have a proper meal."

Avis whispered to Trudy in Sarah's hearing, "It wouldn't do to have a stomach rumblin' when those hoity-toity ladies are to tea."

It's Thursday, Sarah thought with spirits sinking.

"In other words, Miss Matthews," Stanley said, his thickly lashed eyes sending a glance Hester's way, "you shouldn't leave until you've eaten the whole *kit and caboodle*."

Mr. Duffy guffawed and slapped his knee, but Sarah reckoned the dear soul would do so if Stanley recited the alphabet. Others made polite laughter. Sarah smiled at the groomsman because she had been the one addressed. Stanley was capable of greater wit than that, but his efforts at humor had a desperate quality to them lately.

And the red-headed reason for this simply spooned quince jelly onto her bread and said in her childlike voice, "You know, I saw a cloud yesterday that looked just like a fox."

After breakfast, Mrs. Blake's instructions to Sarah concerned the afternoon tea. "You will have to study your texts this morning." She looked anxious, as if one loud handclap would give her a fright. "But don't linger for too long in the garden. Your cheeks are pink enough—we can't have you looking like a plow girl."

"Madame should remind Miss Matthews to eat a proper lunch," Marie said, not lifting her eyes from her needlepoint, which would eventually become a likeness of Jesus Christ praying in the Garden of Gethsemane.

"Goodness, yes!" Mrs. Blake agreed. "A young lady does not come to the table with an empty stomach and gorge herself in the presence of guests."

"Yes, Madam," Sarah replied, though quite certain her stomach would be so twisted in knots at tea that she would have to force herself to eat for the sake of courtesy.

"Mrs. Bacon will see that you have a bath after lunch and change into your nicest gown."

"She has not worn the green silk yet," Marie offered.

Mrs. Blake gave the maid an approving nod. "Very good. And, Sarah . . ."

"Yes?"

She pressed her lips together, as if weighing her words carefully. "You're not too young to understand how important it is to cultivate the favor of people of quality. It is not an overstatement to say that your future happiness depends upon it."

It seemed very much an overstatement

to Sarah, even as she nodded. Wasn't her future happiness more secure in God's hands than in Mrs. Stafford's lace-gloved ones?

"You must be vigilant at all times of the impression you are making," Mrs. Blake continued and went on to a half-dozen other admonitions concerning how to socialize with one's elders. Sarah's apprehension had developed into full-blown terror by the time she was dismissed to study in the garden.

After lunch Avis attended to her bath. "My fiancé, Edwin, bathes in the River Niger," the maid said as her fingers briskly soaped Sarah's scalp. "He says he would give a month's wages to soak in a proper English bath. Only the officers are allowed them, you know. It ain't fair, if you ask me."

"I think it would be fun to bathe in a river," Sarah offered.

"Mayhap in some nice little English river. But not when you have to hire native boys to beat pots with sticks to frighten off the crocodiles."

"Oh." The afternoon tea suddenly seemed a little less fearful by comparison. But only a little. After she was dried, turbaned, and helped into her wrapper, Sarah walked with Avis down the corridor to her room. Hester, laying out Sarah's gown on the bed, looked up and frowned.

"But you've washed her hair," she said to Avis.

The parlormaid touched her forehead. "Oh dear! And the Missus already snappin' at everybody like a badger!" She took in a gulp of air and looked at Sarah with owlish eyes. "Do forgive me, Miss Matthews. It's just that—"

"Well, it can't be helped now," Hester cut in with a stern tone. "Just lay a fire. And leave the door open so's it don't get too stuffy." As Avis hastened to the fireplace, Hester motioned Sarah to the dressing table and began unwinding the towel from her head. "It's a good thing your hair dries so quickly."

"Yes." But Sarah's mind was still on the anxiety in Avis's face. When the parlormaid was gone and Hester had used the towel so briskly that her hair stood in all directions like a madwoman's, she asked, "Why did she apologize?"

"Avis? Why, it ain't good form to speak against the Missus."

"But why did she apologize only to me?"

"Hmm." In the mirror, Hester's brow furrowed in concentration. "Well, Avis's head is filled with thoughts about that fiancé, so she don't think too clear about anything else. Look how she forgot she weren't supposed to wash your hair."

"She *did* talk about him," Sarah conceded.

"There, you see?" Hester's gums and small teeth appeared with her smile. "Now, up with you and I'll scoot that bench over to the hearth."

Sarah's fine hair was prone to tangles now that the very tips were long enough to curl up around her earlobes. As the comb worked at a nest of snarls, Hester said, "I turned down Stanley's invitation to the Park yesterday. We both have Wednesday afternoons off, you know. Do tell me if I hurt you."

"You did?" Sarah asked, making an unsuccessful attempt to turn her head.

"Hurt you?"

"No . . . turn him down?"

"I told him I was going to shop for paper and a sweet little frame so Avis could paint a picture for my mum's birthday."

All thought of the afternoon tea emptied itself from Sarah's head. This was better than any intrigue in any novel. "What did Stanley say?"

"That he would come along with me. Stood there with his hands in his pockets, grinnin' like a brewer's horse because he knew I wouldn't turn him down. But I did."

"Did you give him a reason?"

"Well, I figgered if I acted cross, he would know it was on account of his courtin' other women and think I was just trying to get him to pay more attention to me. So's I just smiled and said maybe some other time, that I fancied a little solitude." The comb paused. "That is a proper word, ain't it?"

"Solitude? Why, yes." Sarah smiled to herself. "The perfect word for this situation."

"Anyhows, when I got back, I spent the rest of the day mending clothes. I had some buttons threatenin' to come off and just couldn't take the time to do it, what with saving Wednesdays for Stanley."

"Were you lonesome?"

As the tangles unsnarled, Hester raked her fingers through Sarah's hair, fluffing it so the heat from the building fire would reach her scalp. "You know . . . I never thought about it until just this minute, but I enjoyed my solitude a lot more than I expected to. It ain't so much fun being with a man who can't keep his eyes off other women. I was always a nervous wreck, and we would end up having words about it."

Sarah's heartbeat quickened. She wished she could jump from the bench and race down to the kitchen to tell Naomi. "So you don't love him anymore?"

"Why, of course I love him." A note of uncertainty crept into the childlike voice. "I'm just saying that I used to *live* for my afternoon off, but I didn't miss him as much as I thought I would."

"That is no wonder," Marie said from the open doorway. She walked into the room, arms folded and amber gold eyes knowing. "There is more to life than being at the beck and call of a man who will not be faithful. I assumed only Frenchmen were that way, only to find it the same in England."

"Not *all* men, Marie," Hester said, taking no umbrage. She came around to fluff up the fringe over Sarah's forehead, curling sections with her fingers. With a wink at Sarah she said, "Look at Mr. Duffy."

"The rare exception. And why should it

not be so when there are so many silly women willing to accept that behavior?" Marie frowned. "Why did you wash her hair? Madame will be sending for her soon."

"It's almost dry. And why ain't you off with your sisters?"

"I told them I would be a little late. It is important to Madame that the child is dressed appropriately."

"Well, you *could* pick out a bonnet and glove if you want to save time."

The lady's maid blew out an aggrieved sigh, but she walked over to the wardrobe and brought out a hat of white straw trimmed with teal green velvet ribbon, white lace, and crystal beads. "This will be appropriate," she said, setting it on the foot of the bed next to the gown. But she stood at the open glove drawer long enough for Hester to send her a curious look.

"Marie?"

Marie looked back as if in a trance, then walked out of the room with a pair of white gloves in hand.

"Perhaps there was a spot?" Sarah speculated.

"Perhaps," Hester replied. "But what an odd duck she can be."

Twenty

Sarah got up to close the door when her hair was dry. The teal green silk floated down over her arms like falling leaves and rustled the lace of her cambric petticoat. Hester was tying the parchment-colored lace sash in back when there was a knock at the door.

"Marie must have snapped out of her trance," Hester muttered. "Come in!"

But it was Naomi who opened the door, paused in the doorway, and smiled. "Why, you've become such a beauty!"

"Ain't she, just?" Hester said.

"Thank you," Sarah replied self-consciously, aware that both would say the same thing if she wore oat sacking. She brushed at a fold in the skirt. "This would make anyone look nice."

"I can't picture it doing quite the same for Mr. Duffy." Naomi reached into her apron pocket. "I mustn't stay or Trudy will panic.

We're making dainties downstairs. But I wanted to give you William's letter."

Sarah reached for the folded page. Staring down at the *Miss Matthews* written on a blank side, she still asked, "To me?"

"That's your name, isn't it?" Naomi asked, smiling again. "It was in the envelope with mine."

Marie bustled through the open doorway, advanced upon Sarah, and held out her open palm, upon which lay a pair of white gloves. Only, the fingers and thumb of one were stuffed like little sausages.

"Cotton," was Marie's only explanation. "Give me your hand."

Sarah tucked the letter into the sash around her waist and complied, too timid to argue that she would prefer keeping her hand down at her side. Hester leaned close to watch, but Naomi's face was expressionless as she excused herself and left the room. The glove slipped easily over Sarah's hand. Marie fastened the pearl wrist button, then took a step back and folded her arms under her generous bosom.

"What a clever idea!" Hester said.

Sarah held up her hand in wonder. The hand did indeed look whole, except the fingers were too fat for her thin wrist. And they stood out from the palm like the spikes of a garden rake, even when she lowered it to her side.

"Hmm." Marie's forehead dented. "Too much."

"Too much," Hester agreed.

"Well, no matter." Taking the glove from Sarah's hand, Marie began pulling cotton from the fingers. "We will try again."

But this time the fingers were too limp, dangling with Sarah's every movement.

"I know what's wrong." Hester held up a hand. "We curve our fingers in when we ain't using them—like so."

"That is so." With an absorbed frown Marie removed the glove. She bent a stuffed finger. "That could be done with a running stitch at the tips, I believe."

Though grateful for this effort to make her less conspicuous, Sarah felt compelled to offer feeble protest. "Actually, I could just keep my hand in my skirt like—"

"It will take me but a moment," Marie cut in before bustling out of the door again.

Hester shrugged and picked up the towel from the bench. "You might as well read your letter. I'll tidy up."

"Thank you." Sarah went over to the bed and propped herself against the mattress for fear of wrinkling her gown by sitting. Slowly she unfolded the paper, wishing to savor the moment. She may have been raised in an orphanage, but the nation of England deemed her important enough to commission a postman to carry a letter to her all the way from Oxford! It struck her with no less awe to remember that hers was included with Naomi's—had hers been the only one, she would still be holding it. William's words were printed in hurried block letters.

Dear Miss Matthews,

Thank you for your interesting letter and for helping Aunt Naomi make the shortbread. Like a greedy Achan I have hidden the tin under my bed so that I am not compelled to share. Were it anything but shortbread with almonds, perhaps I might be more generous . . . perhaps!

In case you are curious, I print because of poor penmanship at scripting. It is not as tedious as you may think, for I have grown accustomed to it over the years.

Sarah smiled at the thought of what Mrs. Forsyth would say to giving up like that. No one left Saint Matthew's with anything less than perfect penmanship. But she reckoned that the headmistress, knowing how limited the opportunities were, wanted to give her girls at least one advantage.

I shall be very interested in meeting your Mister Colby. It speaks well of his ability that he should assign work so that your mind will not grow idle. Do not be intimidated at the thought of studying Latin. Because you are fond of reading, you will be intrigued to discover how many of our good English words have roots in the language. Take, for example, the Latin word for hand, manus, from which is derived manual, manipulate, manage, manacle, manuscript, manufacture, and at least a dozen more.

The weather here is cool in the mornings and most pleasant. From my window I often hear the laughter of people poling boats (it is called punting) on the River Cherwell. Lectures are vastly interesting, though I confess my mind often wanders during "Anglo-Saxon Folklore." I remind myself that an Oxford man should be well-rounded in all subjects. What a sad state I should be in if I were to be able to analyze the properties of table salt and yet be unable to recognize a fairy should I happen to stumble upon one. Do not think me cynical, Miss Matthews. I am deeply grateful for this opportunity for a fine education, just as you are looking forward to yours.

The last short paragraph expressed his gladness that she seemed to feel at home in Berkeley Square, and he closed with *Very truly yours, William Doyle.*

"Well, how's our William?" Hester asked, folding Sarah's wrapper over the chair.

"Very well." And because that was such a vague reply, Sarah added, "He said he hides the shortbread under his bed."

Hester smiled and fortunately did not ask her to read it aloud. It was not that the printed lines were intensely personal, but

Sarah felt something of it would be lost if she were to share it. *There is a bit of Achan in me too, William*, she thought, tucking the folded sheet under her pillow so she could read it again later.

Naomi stopped at the girl's open doorway and spotted Hester pinning on Miss Matthews' hat. There was no sign of Marie, which was an answer to the silent prayer she had sent up from the staircase. She turned and crossed the corridor.

"You may enter," came Marie's voice to her soft knock. Naomi opened the door. The lady's maid sat at her dressing table, stabbing the tips of the white glove furiously with a threaded needle. "Yes, what is it?" she asked with only a glance up at Naomi.

Before replying, Naomi stepped inside and closed the door behind her. "A moment of your time, please. I must take issue with what you're doing."

"And did you take issue with Mr. Duffy's tray?"

"The tray is functional. You're going to make her feel she should be ashamed of her hand."

Marie lifted her eyes only long enough to scowl. "Have you not noticed that already she is ashamed of it?"

"Then we should be teaching her that she shouldn't be."

"And will you run ahead of her everywhere she goes and ask people not to stare or make comment? Or ask Madame's snooty friends not to give her pitying little smiles so that they can tell themselves how compassionate they are?"

Opening her mouth to snap a reply, Naomi realized she had none available. She had learned only too painfully from her own family how cruel people could be. With a sigh she said, "I don't know, Marie. It seems she should be learning to stand up against that kind of treatment."

"I agree." This time when Marie looked up, her expression had softened a little. "But not yet, Naomi. Mr. Duffy protects his young plants in little pots until they are strong enough to bear the weather and weeds and the insects of the garden. What is so wrong about doing the same for a child?"

There was nothing wrong with that, Naomi realized after one by one the argu-

ments that rose in her mind proved themselves weak. At least not when there was
something that could be done about the
situation. "You're right."

"Of course." Frowning, Marie pulled the
needle through another glove tip. "I am in a
hurry, and you have distracted me long
enough. Close the door after yourself."

Naomi's smile lasted all the way down
the staircase. *At least she makes life more
interesting around here.*

Sarah turned the glove to study every
angle after Marie fastened the button at her
wrist. The stitches were barely visible at the
tips of the cupped fingers. Surely no one
who wasn't aware of her deformity would
look twice at her.

"It's a miracle. . . ." Hester breathed.

"Look at yourself," Marie commanded.

The two accompanied her to the long
mirror and peered over her shoulders. Allowing both hands to fall slightly to her
sides, Sarah was amazed at how normal
she looked. She had felt like an oddity for
as long as she could remember. Light slanting in from the window gilded her curls, and

the green gown brought out the roses in her cheeks.

Why, I'm . . . pretty?

Guilt came on the heels of that thought, for Mrs. Forsyth had always stressed inner instead of outer beauty. *A fair woman without discretion is like a jewel in the snout of a pig* was a verse copied countless times in the girls' penmanship tablets. But she wondered, while basking in the compliments of the two maids, if the words were not a condemnation of outer beauty, but a reminder of which was the most important.

Father, thank you for making me look nice, she prayed while tears stung her eyes. *I'll try very hard never to become vain.*

In the glass, Marie was wiping her eyes. Sarah turned to embrace her. "Thank you!"

"You are welcome." Marie endured the embrace stiffly and then stepped back. "You must not weep or your face will splotch." To Hester, who was blowing her nose into a handkerchief, she ordered, "Give one to Miss Matthews."

"Yes, Marie," Hester said and went to the chest of drawers. "That were a kind thing you—"

"*Was*, Hester," Marie corrected on her way to the door. "Not *were*. It is a pity that the English cannot speak their own language." She turned in the doorway to admonish, "Miss Matthews, you must conduct yourself with *sang-froid* this afternoon. They are no better than you are."

She was gone before Sarah could thank her, or even ask the meaning of *sang-froid*. Grinning, Hester handed over a handkerchief. "Didn't I tell you she were a odd duck?"

But a split second later she corrected herself. "*Was* a odd duck."

———

There is nothing so attractive as silver against a white cloth, Dorothea thought, looking over the parlor table. On silver trays and gold-rimmed dishes perched an assortment of delicacies: petite crustless sandwiches of cucumber slices with butter, cream cheese with walnuts, smoked chicken with raspberry mayonnaise, as well as the almost mandatory Victoria sandwiches—actually finger-sized cake slices layered with gooseberry jam. Lemon curd,

gingerbread, and a bowl of plump strawberries completed the menu.

The tea, which she would serve herself,
would be its usual crowning touch. The orange pekoe leaves, delicately scented with
jasmine flowers, were imported from a
small Yangtze Valley plantation and only
available to Emperor Manchu and provin-
cial Chinese leaders. *And* to Arthur Blake
and later, his widow, in exchange for occasional shipments of Wedgwood Jasper-
ware to Governor Tseng Kuo-fan for his
number-one wife. One of the many advan-
tages of owning a shipping line. Oh, Hazel
Fowler would make prim little faces as if
sipping vinegar, but that would not stop her
from holding out her cup for refills a half-
dozen times.

*Why do you even invite them over if you
don't enjoy their company?* Dorothea
asked herself, already knowing the answer.
Friends—or at least friendly acquaintances—were a necessary part of life.
When she and Arthur moved up in the
world, she had desired for Jeremy the ad-
vantages that only well-situated people
could provide. What good was money if
you weren't invited to the best parties of

the season or to fox hunts in Rutland? Where was he to find a suitable wife—had he lived so long—if not through the introductions of those whose places in society were well-established?

And just when she had decided that she no longer required their connections and that their company was too fatiguing, there was Sarah to consider. If her friends would attend social occasions where Sarah was present now and then, observe how courteous and humble she was, and see her so attentive at church, surely they would be understanding and accepting when the time came to reveal that she was Jeremy's child out of wedlock.

"Good afternoon, Madam."

Dorothea's eyes moved from the lavish table to where Sarah stood in the doorway, a mixture of waif and young woman in her silk dress. *Your granddaughter*, Dorothea told herself while Marie nudged the girl forward.

"Does Madame notice anything different?" Marie asked when the two stood side by side in the room.

"Different?"

Sarah gave an uncertain look to Marie,

who nodded. When the girl held out her hands, Dorothea's breath caught. "What did you do?"

Marie smiled. "Cotton. Does it not look real?"

Tears dimmed Dorothea's eyes over what could have been and her part in the reality of what was. Who knew what kind of living Mary Tomkin had made for herself in the slums? Could a lack of proper meals have adversely affected the child she was carrying? *If only* . . .

"It looks real," she said finally. And a little ray of hope entered. It was possible that her friends were not aware of Sarah's deformity. After all, the girl kept her hand hidden in public. It would certainly be easier if one less obstacle barred the path to social acceptance. "Quite real."

"Very good," Marie said and glanced at the long-case clock. "Now I must fly to meet my sisters."

As the maid's shoes clicked upon the oak flooring, Dorothea knew she should say something about the rest of Sarah's appearance. There was such hopefulness in the girl's expression. Why? What did the approval of an embittered old woman matter, when she had won the hearts of the whole household?

"You look very nice, Sarah," Dorothea murmured, and pained by the gratitude that flooded the young face, she added brusquely, "Do remember to ask Mrs. Stafford about her lilies."

"They will not flower until late in August, you understand," Mrs. Stafford replied nasally, seeming pleased that Sarah had asked. The woman wore a pink print gown with ruffles that seemed intended for someone far younger. "The Auratum, or Golden-rayed Lily, if you will, requires a warmer climate. That is because it is indigenous to Japan."

The party of five sat in three upholstered chairs and the sofa, casually arranged about the tea table and its polished silver tea service. Avis stood unobtrusively at the larger table behind the sofa when she was not passing around a tray. Dishes laden with dainties were perched upon linen-draped knees, teacups and saucers held in gloved hands. As proud as Sarah was of her glove, to her dismay it turned out to be a nuisance, for the stuffed fingers got in the way of using the hand to help balance her portion. She constantly had to make sure that she was not bending it back unnaturally. All this while keeping her back an inch from the back of her chair. Mrs. Blake seemed to sense her discomfort, for with a meaningful look she poured only a manageable one-third of the usual amount of tea into Sarah's cup.

"I have never cared for gardening." Mrs. Fowler held out her cup for yet another refill. It was not the wrinkles that made her appearance so forbidding, for Mrs. Kettner had just as many in a pleasant, comforting face. "What is the sense in paying a gardener if one intends to soil one's own hands?"

"Lots of people take up gardening as a hobby, Hazel," Mrs. Blake said in Mrs. Stafford's defense.

Mrs. Gill, her short, buxom frame swathed in widow's garb, delicately pushed the remains of a sandwich past her teeth and batted her eyes at Mrs. Fowler. "It's no different from working needlepoint when one has a seamstress, is it?"

"I suppose not," Mrs. Fowler conceded

and then raised her white brows impishly. "Then you may consider my hobby doing all I can to keep my money out of the hands of relatives who despair that I've managed to live so long."

Amid the giggles Sarah set her empty cup upon the saucer in her lap, grateful that the conversation had taken off on its own and no longer required her participation. Much less chance of embarrassing Mrs. Blake this way. But it was not to last, for during a lull in discussion over how ludicrous it was of the rector's wife to wear a brown wig over her gray hair, Mrs. Gill turned to Sarah and asked, "How do you find Berkeley Square, Miss Matthews?"

"It's very nice, thank you." It occurred to Sarah that such a benign question could lead to one about the orphanage. To steer the subject away tactfully, she added, "I like to look in the shops on Bond Street too."

"Ah, shopping," Mrs. Gill said with a nod. "And what female doesn't?"

That brought smiles from the aged faces, even after Mrs. Fowler snapped, " *I* don't!"

"Admiral Nelson lived on New Bond for a time," Mrs. Stafford said to Sarah. "You've studied him, I presume?"

"Yes, Madam."

"But of course, bright girl that you are." Her approving smile made Sarah forget all about the snub at church. Perhaps young Becky *had* made other plans for today. "My grandfather served under him at Toulon. He was such a fearless commander . . . even after losing an arm."

"And an eye as well?" Mrs. Gill offered in a hesitant manner.

Mrs. Stafford nodded. "It goes to show us that physical infirmities can be overcome where there is courage."

"When I was a girl in Camden," Mrs. Fowler said, "the postman made his rounds faithfully in spite of a lame foot."

"And Beethoven still composed after he went deaf," Mrs. Gill said, blinking.

Sarah's padded hand slid down between her side and the chair arm, while the smile froze upon her face. Was she imagining that the casualness of the discussion seemed forced? *How do they know?* But then, any discussion of Admiral Nelson must surely include his injuries, which would remind the women of other examples.

When Mrs. Fowler said, frowning, "It's a

pity Lord Nelson couldn't overcome certain *character* infirmities," Sarah could not help but glance from the corner of her eye toward Mrs. Blake. She wore a tight little smile and held her cup poised above the saucer.

"What do you mean, Hazel?" Mrs. Gill asked.

"Why, taking Lady Hamilton as mistress. And while already married."

Mrs. Stafford arched a knowing eyebrow. "Well, *she* certainly came to no good end, even with sizable annuities from the old lord *and* Admiral Nelson. I have it on good authority that she threw money about shamefully between shopping and gambling."

"Money doesn't always equal common sense," Mrs. Blake said in a tone that suggested she was still not at ease with the conversation, yet did not quite know how to steer it in another direction.

"Any grammar school child can tell you that water seeks its own level." Mrs. Fowler's lips puckered like a drawstring purse. "She started out as a servant—why would she be expected to end up any better?"

Mrs. Gill sighed. "I suppose it's true . . . you can't make a silk purse from a sow's ear."

"I wonder what ever happened to their daughter," Mrs. Stafford said.

"You mean their *out-of-wedlock* daughter?" Mrs. Fowler took another quick sip of tea. "If she's accepted into gentle company at all, it's only because of her father's fame. A statue in the center of London does tend to impress people. But I shouldn't wish to be her, always wondering what people are saying behind their fans."

Instead of feeling relief that the conversation had drifted from physical infirmities, Sarah oddly found herself so ill at ease that the nerves between her shoulders prickled. She fairly jumped at the sharp *click* from beside her. All eyes went to Mrs. Blake, who had set her cup and saucer down on the tea table and was rubbing her brow.

Mrs. Gill blinked at her. "Dorothea?"

Avis stepped closer while Sarah wondered if she should excuse herself to look for Mrs. Bacon.

"Just a sudden headache," Mrs. Blake murmured.

"You poor dear," Mrs. Fowler said with a

sympathetic pursing of lips. "Perhaps we should take our leave."

"No, I'm fine now." But there was something disquiet about her expression when she turned to Sarah to say, "Why don't you go on out to the garden, Sarah?" She turned to the others. "Doctor Raine has ordered a daily dose of fresh air, and we mustn't give him cause to scold."

"Ah . . . Doctor Raine," Mrs. Stafford said while the other two nodded.

Almost limp with relief, Sarah handed her cup, saucer, and dish to Avis, who had hastened over for them. "Good afternoon," Sarah said, smiled politely at their reciprocal farewells, and left the room. She took her time moving down the hall, just in case the sounds of her shoes against the oak flooring should drift past the door. It would embarrass Mrs. Blake to hear evidence of her eagerness to leave. But on the staircase her speed increased with every step. She pulled off both gloves and set them on a terrace table, then started down the path toward the stables in the hopes that Stanley would allow her to help with feeding or grooming. After the past hour, the company of two horses seemed vastly refreshing.

❧ *Twenty-One* ❧

It was a struggle for Dorothea to maintain a pleasant expression while her guests chatted. *They know*, she thought, staring at Turner's *Crossing the Brook* hanging on the wall just beyond Hazel Fowler's shoulder. How could she have been so naive as to think they wouldn't? Oh, they were subtle about it, too genteel to humiliate a child except to condescend to her about her infirmity. The message was intended for her.

By sheer will she kept tears in check. How many servants no longer in her employ had carried gossip to their new situations? Were the people of Mayfair whispering behind gloved hands at this proof of her son's infidelity? *But you were going to admit she's your granddaughter at the appropriate time*, she reminded herself. It was little comfort.

The subject of conversation drifted from complaints about aches and pains to complaints about the ineptitude of most servants. *How shallow we are, for all our years!* she thought amid painful remembrances of her own part in such discussions. When empty plates were surrendered to Avis, and Dorothea had refilled cups, she dismissed the maid. This was not her usual custom, so her friends turned questioning looks to her.

"Is your head better, Dorothea?" Augusta Stafford asked.

"Yes, thank you." And because she could think of no roundabout way to approach the subject, Dorothea took a deep breath and said to the three, "Please tell me . . . how did you find out?"

Florence Gill's lash batting ceased. "Find out what, Dorothea?"

Dorothea had to remind herself that if she had misjudged them, then she would be simply making an announcement earlier than she had desired. She cleared her throat. "About Sarah."

Their expressions told all, even though Augusta said after a quick glance at Hazel Fowler, "Why, whatever do you mean?"

"I believe you know."

Augusta began worrying the pink ruffle

on her collar while Florence ran her bottom teeth against her top lip and resumed blinking. The pendulum in the long-case clock clicked the seconds. It was Hazel's throaty voice that broke the silence.

"Everyone knew about the scullery maid, Dorothea. We figured it was just a matter of time before a child appeared on your doorstep."

"These things happen, Dorothea," Augusta Stafford said. "And in the best of families. My sainted mother never got over the scandal surrounding her cousin-twice-removed."

Dorothea nodded, pressing lips together.

"Does Miss Matthews know?" Florence's voice rose barely above a whisper, as if Sarah might be right outside the door.

In actuality, Dorothea figured the girl was as far from this room as possible. *All that rot about Nelson's arm.* "She does not," Dorothea admitted. "I needed some time."

She was comforted by the three nods and murmurs of understanding.

But then Augusta leaned forward intently. "We admire that you're attempting to make up for the past, Dorothea . . . though I must confess I would have done the same as you did in those days. One slatternly servant can destroy the moral composition of even the most decent home."

"What we *cannot* fathom," Hazel said when Augusta had settled herself upright again, "is why you brought the child here when there are outstanding boarding schools all over England."

Florence Gill nodded. "With her gracious little ways, she would certainly be accepted by the other children in spite of her hand. And you could keep her background secret."

"I'll even ask Carl to recommend one," Augusta offered. Her son had served four years on the Taunton Commission, which studied the English secondary school situation.

With such counsel from three whose opinions had influenced everything from her choice of wardrobe to choice of house furnishings for over twenty years, Dorothea found her thoughts drifting along those lines. But only until the memory surfaced of how intensely miserable she was before Sarah came. And far more compelling was the thought of how devastated the girl would be to be sent away. Even though they had not yet formed a bond of kinship, she could tell that Sarah was thriving here.

"I won't do that," she said, and when Hazel Fowler opened her mouth to argue, she repeated herself. "I won't."

Her guests exchanged glances again. It was Florence who spoke next. "Think of the girl, Dorothea. Would you have her go through the rest of her life being shunned by decent company?"

The *decent company* stung the most, for Dorothea judged Sarah as decent as any of them. For the girl's sake, however, she allowed that to pass. "But it doesn't have to be that way, don't you see? I intend to make her my legal heir one day."

"The queen herself could adopt her, and it wouldn't undo what has already been done," Hazel Fowler said with the same disapproving expression she wore while tasting the tea. "Out-of-wedlock is out-of-wedlock."

"Sarah had no say in that, Hazel." Dorothea had to think, had to make them see that she wasn't on some crusade to undermine the respectable morals of Mayfair's residents. "I'm only asking for some compassion. You're all respected by everyone in the community. If your families will accept her, others eventually will."

"We have the utmost compassion, Dorothea." The pitch of Augusta's nasal voice rose, while she held a hand to her chest as if accused. "I'm sure God loves her just as much as any child. And you certainly have the right to invite her to take tea with us in your own home. But what we cannot do is keep society with her beyond that."

Those latter words sounded achingly familiar, though Dorothea was too crushed to recall when she had said them herself or why.

"Nor will we ask our grandchildren to do so," Florence said, at least having the decency to wear a regretful expression.

Hazel sealed their collective sentiment with the statement, "Unfortunately, one is judged by the company one keeps."

Dorothea felt as if she had been slapped. Not only did her heart ache for Sarah, who was being politely elbowed out of society, but for herself and even Jeremy. Would they not even bend for old time's sake or the sake of the son who had charmed them with his witticisms when he was living?

"Dorothea?"

At the sound of Florence's voice, Dorothea opened her eyes, not even aware of when she had closed them. There was nothing more to say, so she put a hand to her temple. "I should rest now."

Augusta clucked sympathy. "Your headache is back?"

"Yes," she lied.

Relief washed across all three faces. They gathered wraps and reticules, their gaiety forced after having risen from such a somber discussion. Florence advised her to lie down with her feet elevated, and Augusta insisted they would show themselves out. Hazel stopped to pat her knee and say, "Think about what we said, Dorothea. She would be better off away at school."

Their footsteps still carried faintly from the staircase when Mrs. Bacon bustled through the doorway with an anxious face. Mrs. Blake shook her head at her offer to bring some Beecham's Pills.

"I'm just fatigued. Help me to my room."

In her bed, she stared up at the embroidered underside of her canopy and wondered how she would go about breaking the news to Sarah. The longer she waited,

the more likely the chance of the girl overhearing one of the servants discuss it—for
if Mmes. Stafford, Fowler, and Gill knew,
they surely did.

But she felt so drained from the confrontation with her friends. And from the
pain of realizing that had this situation occurred in someone else's family, she would
have been just as quick to cast stones.
God forgive me, she murmured, closing her
eyes. How long since she had really
prayed? *And don't let this girl hate me
when I tell her.*

Leftover dainties from tea accompanied
the turnip soup in the servants' hall that
evening. Sarah's appetite returned twofold
in that companionable atmosphere. Stanley
praised her horse-currying skills, and Avis
made an imitation of Mrs. Fowler's
pinched-face way of sipping tea that
caused Mr. Duffy to chuckle, Claire to
choke in her napkin, and Mrs. Bacon to
give warning.

"I didn't care for the glove," Sarah confessed in the kitchen while Trudy washed
dishes and Naomi put away the few left-

overs. "I couldn't use my hand at all, and besides, I'm sure they already knew about it."

Naomi paused from ladling the soup tureen into a smaller bowl. "Were they unkind?"

"Oh, not at all." At least Sarah didn't think they were. But the suspicion still lurked in her mind that the discussion of others with infirmities was not coincidental with her being present. As self-conscious as she was about her hand, she would have felt less ill at ease if the women would have mentioned it directly rather than hinted about it.

The three faces in her mind faded, to be replaced by one with dark ringlets. "Will Marie be angry if I don't wear it again?" she asked Naomi.

"I'll lay odds on that!" Trudy muttered from the sink.

Naomi glanced her way and then smiled at Sarah. "Just be honest with her, Miss Matthews. I have a feeling she'll understand."

Hester came into the kitchen to say that Mrs. Blake wished to see Sarah.

The woman was seated alone on the divan in the sitting room when Sarah entered. Both long hands clutched the frame of a small picture. "Sit here with me, Sarah," she said.

As she obeyed, Sarah asked, "Does your head hurt again?"

"No, thank you."

Sarah glanced curiously at the picture. With a wan smile, Mrs. Blake held the frame sideways for her inspection. Captured in oils were the blue bowl and apples from the hall table. "Did Avis do that?"

Mrs. Blake shook her head. "Jeremy. He was twelve years old. It's the only thing he ever painted. I keep it on a table in my bedchamber."

"It's very nice." She thought what a pity it was that he didn't go on to paint other things. Perhaps he would have been a great artist, and Mrs. Blake would have walls filled with his work to comfort her.

"His tutor at the time . . ." The woman's brow furrowed. "I can't recall his name, but he was artistically talented. Anyway, he desired to teach Jeremy to paint and play the violin. Jeremy showed promise in both, but he complained to me that the lessons were boring. His father had no use for art, and I didn't want my son unhappy, so I instructed the tutor not to pressure Jeremy until he was ready. Which never happened."

It was the first time Mrs. Blake had suggested that her son had been anything but perfect and failed by other people. Sarah nodded, not sure what she was expected to say.

Mrs. Blake laid the picture down in her lap. "Even a person who commits some wrong acts can possess some good traits and talents, Sarah. And because he chooses to ignore those good traits doesn't mean they can't be passed down to his children."

"Yes, Madam." She hoped Mrs. Blake wasn't about to cry, especially without Marie there. They sat for three minutes without speaking, Sarah clasping her hands and watching the pendulum of the chimneypiece clock. The corner of her eye caught two glances sent her way from Mrs. Blake. Tendrils of fear began wrapping themselves around her heart, like Mr. Duffy's rambler roses upon their arch. Surely she hadn't been summoned just to be told about the painting. Had Mrs. Blake been so humiliated at tea that she could no longer bear having her here? Was that what brought on the headache?

"I was proud of how you conducted yourself today," Mrs. Blake said at length.

Sarah eased out a cautious breath. "Thank you."

"And I apologize for the discomfort my guests caused you."

"But they were just trying to encourage me," Sarah hastened to assure her.

"Hmph! I'll allow that might have been their intent. But one would have thought they were just hoping someone would lop off one of their limbs so they could be so blessed. The fact that you hide your hand should have made it clear to them it was something you wouldn't care to discuss."

The fear of being sent away began to ebb, being replaced by the fear of being at the center of discord between long-standing friends. And the fear mingled with confusion, for who was she but a ward from an orphanage? "Please don't be angry at them," Sarah nerved herself to say. "I wasn't offended."

"Ah, but you wouldn't, would you?" Mrs. Blake's pale eyes studied her face sadly.

"You've a good heart, Sarah. You didn't deserve the lot that was handed to you."

Again Sarah felt confusion, for she thought the lot handed to her was very nice, especially recently. She did not receive an explanation, for the door opened and Marie burst into the room, complaining that London omnibus drivers were all lunatics and that the meat pie she had purchased from a vendor was cold. Her praises were reserved for Madame Tussaud's likeness of Napoleon Bonaparte, which looked "so lifelike I would not have jumped if he had sneezed."

Mrs. Blake, who seemed oddly relieved at the interruption, asked Marie to sit and tell them about other exhibits at the wax museum. Presently she turned to Sarah. "I've kept you long enough, Sarah. You should prepare for bed now."

Later, Sarah had just finished her prayers when soft footsteps sounded from the corridor. She held her breath. When she heard the soft click of Marie's door, she slid out of bed. The opposite door opened to her light knocking, and the lady's maid stood in an aureole of lamp light.

"Why are you still awake? And in your bare feet!"

"May we speak?" Sarah whispered after a helpless glance toward Mrs. Blake's door.

"Come in, then," Marie said, lowering her voice as well.

Sarah remembered her manners after the door closed behind her. "I'm glad you had a good time with your sisters."

"Yes. You got out of bed to tell me that?"

"No . . . I . . . ." She took a quick breath and started over. "It was so good of you to make the glove for me. But I would rather not wear it anymore. It wasn't comfortable, and I shouldn't wish to be considered vain, like the vicar's wife is for wearing her brown wig."

"Then do not wear the glove."

There seemed no injury in Marie's voice, but just to be certain Sarah said, "But it was good of you to make it for me."

"You are welcome," Marie replied. "And the longer you stand there in your bare feet, the greater your chance of catching a chill." She went to her dressing table and pulled two pins from her hat, sticking them into a red velvet pincushion. "At least stand upon the carpet."

"I think they already knew about my hand," Sarah told her after moving closer.

"Ah . . . servant talk. I should have known."

"Servant talk?" She had not even considered that distressing notion. Would Mrs. Blake's servants, the closest to a real family she had ever known, gossip about her?

Marie had removed her hat and was pulling a brush through her dark hair, crouching just a bit so she could see the mirror. "You must not feel betrayed. Some of Madame's servants may be silly, but we are not malicious. And we have great affection for you."

"But if someone told . . ."

"We have great affection for you *now*, Miss Matthews. But when you arrived, you were a stranger to us. Is it too difficult to believe that one or two might have said to a friend that Madame has taken in an orphan with a crippled hand? Not in a critical way, but as a statement of fact."

With it put that way, Sarah could understand.

Marie put down the brush and turned. Her amber gold eyes were apologetic, even sad. "I told my sisters at that time. I do beg your pardon."

"You have it," Sarah replied, moved almost to tears that her forgiveness would matter so much to the woman who could still intimidate her.

"Thank you." The maid smiled and nodded toward the door. "Now go to bed, Miss Matthews, and allow me to do the same."

❧ Twenty-Two ❧

Under a darkening sky, Mrs. Blake only exchanged tepid greetings with her friends after church Sunday. Sarah kept her gloveless hand buried in a fold of her skirt amidst mingled feelings of relief over passing them by and angst over having caused this disharmony. After Stanley had helped Mrs. Blake into the coach, Marie looked back toward the huddled trio and muttered something—the only discernible sounds reaching Sarah's ears were *day lwah*.

"Day lu-wah?" Stanley asked, extending an arm to assist Marie. "What's that mean?"

Marie gave Sarah a little smile. "I was thinking of the geese on my father's farm."

Hester did not appear at lunch. "She's taking reading lessons at the Baptist chapel," Mrs. Bacon explained when Stanley commented on the empty place at the table.

"Oh dear," Claire said, wincing at the rumble that rattled the casement windows. "She had her umbrella with her, didn't she?"

"She did," Trudy replied.

Sarah could not help but send a covert glance toward Stanley, who could not have appeared more stunned had he just heard that Hester had run off to join the army. He wore a forced smile as the meal progressed and even while telling Mr. Duffy of his plans to go out on the Thames on a cousin's fishing boat on Wednesday.

As Sarah helped clear the table afterward, Trudy had more to say about Hester's action. "It was what you call one o' them spur-o'-the-moment notions. After church we overheard a chambermaid from Brook Street goin' on about the lessons. They're free, the lessons are, and they even serve sandwiches, since most servants can fairly well get Sunday noon off. Mrs. Bacon told her to go ahead and give it a try."

"Weren't you interested?" Sarah asked.

The scullery maid placed another dish on her tray. "I've already had a bit o'schoolin'. There weren't so many of us crawlin' about in our cottage as in Hester's folks'. I can read recipes and write home for the both of us, so why would I need to learn any more?"

Naomi, smiling with arms folded, said from the kitchen doorway, "Wouldn't you enjoy a novel now and again, Trudy?"

"Made-up stories?" Trudy snorted. "When you find one about a scullery maid who becomes Queen of England, I'll give it a try. Or mayhap I'll just wait and let Hester read it to me." She sent a wink at Naomi. "I would have given my last shilling for one o' them cameras when Stanley heard what she was up to."

Sarah had to agree with Trudy, though with some guilt on account of having just come from church. And she recalled Hester's declaring that she had no interest in reading. Was this just to make Stanley jealous? That would mean the chambermaid still cared desperately about him. She couldn't help but hope that wasn't the case, at least not until he mended his ways.

She was delighted to learn that night as Hester helped her prepare for retiring that the maid had enjoyed her first lesson.

"Never were an hour and half so short, Miss Matthews!" her girlish voice declared as she plumped up pillows while Sarah laboriously buttoned up her nightgown. "There was seven of us there—five girls and two fellows. I've a card of alphabet to copy on paper for practice. After the third lesson, I'm to be lent a storybook!"

"I could help you study during the week," Sarah offered.

"That's so very nice of you. I would ask Trudy, but she grumbles as it is about writin' home so much for me." She paused, pillow in hand, and said with wonder, "Why, I'll be writing my own letters home one day."

Sarah could stifle the question no longer. "What made you change your mind?"

"About readin'?" The maid rolled her eyes sheepishly. "I only went there to show Stanley that he's no right to be tellin' me what I should or shouldn't do if he ain't willin' to marry me. But when Mr. Smith said he never seen anybody learn vowels so quick, I was so proud I wanted to learn more right away."

"Mr. Smith?"

"He's the vicar, only they don't call 'em vicars. Got himself soaked to the gills even with a umbrella going out to flag a couple o' hackneys. Said he didn't like the sound of that thunder and that we should be inside as soon as able. Wouldn't think of us repaying him either. It were so nice to be in the company of a gentleman!"

————

"Did Madame not rest well?" Marie asked in the sitting room the next morning.

"As well as ever," Dorothea muttered, her mind wandering again from the blue stitches on her needlepoint canvas, which were to form the blooms of delphiniums in the garden of a thatched-roof cob cottage. *Why can't you just call her in here and say the words? She has a forgiving nature.*

"Perhaps in the mornings you should try some coffee instead of tea."

Dorothea made a face. "I tried coffee once. It was hours before the taste left my mouth." *Forgive that you sent away a girl not much older than herself, on the word of a son you knew was lying? That you lived in comfort while she suffered lice and near starvation in the slums? That she will spend the rest of her life the subject of gossip because you cannot bear to move from this house?*

And then her mouth worked independently of her thoughts, for she looked at Marie and said, "How long have you known about Sarah?"

More forthright than Mmes. Gill, Fowler, and Stafford, Marie replied calmly while continuing to stitch, "Almost from the beginning, Madame."

"It's true, then. Everyone knows."

"Everyone but *her*."

Dorothea pushed her needle into an unworked section of canvas and set her hoop on the chair arm. "I'm considering asking Naomi to tell her. They've grown very close."

Marie looked up at her. "Madame would do such a thing?"

After a minute of being stared down by the Frenchwoman, Dorothea glanced away. "No. Of course not."

"The words will come to Madame when it is the proper time," Marie said with softened tone.

"But if she overhears before then?"

"She would have heard by now if the servants did not take pains to be careful. And as she has no relationships outside . . ."

"Relationships outside," Dorothea echoed bitterly. "No, my *friends* have seen to that."

Marie set her canvas in her lap. "May I offer a suggestion, Madame?"

———

"Breakfast was excellent, Naomi," Mrs. Blake said.

"Thank you, Madam." Standing in the sitting room, Naomi could not think of anything she and Trudy had done differently to alter the usual Monday morning fare.

"And you'll be taking your afternoon off today?"

"Yes, Madam. But I'm willing to take another day if—"

"Oh no, today is quite fine."

Another dance, Naomi realized, taking in Mrs. Blake's self-conscious expression and Marie's impatient one. And so she waited, as if it were the most natural thing in the world to be standing there upon the carpet with hands clasped.

At the time Marie looked ready to burst, Mrs. Blake cleared her throat. "We were just discussing what you mentioned last week."

"Last week, Madam?"

"About Sarah seeing some of London. It's quite a shame to be surrounded by so much history and culture and never experience any of it."

"There is nothing like firsthand experience, to be sure."

"I would accompany her on excursions myself had I a stronger constitution. I'm not inclined to hire a governess who'll be sitting idle most of the time when Sarah begins her lessons on Thursday. And it would not be appropriate for Mr. Colby to escort her about town, even as his pupil."

"I reminded Madame that you are well-acquainted with the city," Marie said with a self-important tone and critical squint at her canvas.

Bless you, Marie, Naomi thought. *You're full of surprises lately, aren't you?*

". . . *and* as for Miss Matthews being out socially in the company of a servant," Marie went on, "there is little difference between a cook and a governess anyway. Yes?"

"Yes." *Unless you would care to have a meal at some point*. The dance was taking so much longer than necessary. She was delighted Mrs. Blake had changed her mind, but there was much to do in the kitchen to prepare lunch *and* supper's soup so that Trudy would not be overwhelmed this afternoon.

Mrs. Blake inclined her head musingly. "I wonder if your offer still stands to have Sarah along?"

In keeping with the tempo of the dance, Naomi did not answer right away.

"You would have the use of the coach, of course," Mrs. Blake jumped into the silence to add, as if fearful that refusal was imminent.

"We would enjoy ourselves more if we didn't have to concern ourselves over Stanley having to wait, Madam," Naomi said forthrightly. Better to have all matters understood at the beginning than misgivings later.

"Then he could deliver you to places, and I would pay return cab-fare. As well as admissions . . . the best theatre seats, naturally." Warming up to the subject, she added, "And that would include William between terms. I wouldn't want to hinder your times together."

Naomi smiled. "That's very generous of you, Mrs. Blake."

"Compensation for your sharing your

Monday afternoons. Then your offer still stands, may I presume?"

"Of course, Madam." She glanced at the clock. "But . . . if we're to have time to go anywhere today, I must ask to be excused now."

"Very well." With a relieved smile, Mrs. Blake added, "And thank you, Naomi."

But Marie's voice stopped her at the door. "I suggest Madame inquire about her shoes."

"Her shoes?"

With a quiet sigh, Naomi turned to face the two again.

"When you are escorting Miss Matthews," Marie said primly, "you will not wear those men's shoes . . . yes?"

Boy's, actually, Naomi thought, wiggling her toes. "Yes. I mean . . . no, of course not."

Mrs. Blake's eyebrows lifted. "Men's shoes?"

———

"We're actually here. . . ." Sarah breathed as she walked with Naomi through the western door. Westminster Abbey revealed itself in all its solemnity, from its lofty roof and pointed arches to its range of noble supporting pillars and connecting chapels. She had read of the Abbey in Oliver Goldsmith's *Citizen of the World*, one of the worn books in Saint Matthew's collection. "I never thought I would ever see it myself!"

"And we've barely scratched the surface, as you'll see," Naomi said, fishing in her reticule. She looked more schoolgirl than cook, her strawberry blond curls clamped with a comb behind her straw hat and trailing down the back of her plaid gown of mauve, blue, and beige. Sarah panicked when she withdrew some coins and handed her sixpence.

"But I didn't know we were supposed to—"

The cook patted her arm, her blue eyes lively. "Courtesy of Mrs. Blake, who insists that we enjoy ourselves."

They were shepherded into a group of five adults—three women and two men—by a wiry, stoop-shouldered elderly man who collected sixpence from each of them. He wore the expression of a doting mother when explaining how, for the sake of preservation, one must restrain oneself from touching the sculptures and tombs of royal personages.

But at the base of Shakespeare's monument in the Poets' Corner, Sarah was so awestruck that she did not realize she had reached out a hand until she felt cool marble beneath her fingers. The copy of *Julius Caesar* at Saint Matthew's was so yellowed and spotted that Sarah had initially believed one of the older girls who told her Shakespeare had printed it himself. Guiltily she withdrew her hand and glanced at the tour guide, who gave her an understanding smile.

"He is not buried here, you know. Stratford has that honor."

Later, when she gave him a questioning look at Queen Elizabeth's tomb, he nodded. "She's here, all right." The guided tour lasted over an hour, and Sarah and Naomi spent another three ambling about the nine chapels on their own.

"Have you any idea where you'd like to go next week?" Naomi asked as the hired hansom moved northward under a violet-and-orange streaked sky.

Sarah could hardly believe her ears. "Next week?"

"And the next, and so on," the cook replied. "Mrs. Blake wishes you to have more exposure to London."

"How kind of her. I'll be sure to thank her."

"She would like that. And be thinking during the week of where we should go."

"I already know," Sarah said after a hesitation.

"Yes?"

"Marie spoke about a wax museum. . . ."

"Madame Tussaud's." Naomi smiled. "Now, that would be fun. I've not been there in years."

Sarah hoped the week would fly. "Then you don't mind chaperoning me?"

"Perish the thought! I was missing my outings with William. And he'll be along when he's home."

William. Sarah had his letter practically memorized. What fun they would have, the three of them! She breathed in air that smelled of gaslights, coal fires, and evening meals, and thought of the warm bowl of soup awaiting her. "You know, I was convinced the morning I left Saint Matthew's was the worst day of my life."

Naomi gave her arm a squeeze. "And it turned out to be the best day, didn't it?"

"Not the best."

"No?"

Smiling at her questioning look, Sarah replied, "*This* is the best day."

Stanley's befuddlement over the new Hester lasted into the week, for he sulked like a small boy during lunch Wednesday, with her not even seeming to notice. While clearing the table afterward, Trudy said Hester had turned down Stanley's offer of an afternoon boat ride on the Serpentine. "He's miffed 'cause he couldn't get her to change her mind. She wants to practice her reading."

"But he was already planning to go fishing on the Thames anyway," Sarah said, picking up the butter crock. "Don't you remember his talking about it just a few days ago?"

The scullery maid smirked. "I think Stanley's been askin' around . . . found out that Baptist vicar ain't old and ain't married."

Sarah went upstairs to the attic when the kitchen was clean and Naomi and Trudy were preparing supper's soup. "Help me study?" Hester said after answering the knock. "What a love you are!" They sat on her bed, and Hester held up a pasteboard card just a trifle worn at the edges and sounded out words such as *cat* and *bat* in her high-pitched voice. She had come to *hat* when a rattling sound startled both of them.

"Hailstones?" Hester said, turning toward the window overlooking the garden.

"It sounded like them."

The chambermaid got up and crossed the floor. The yellow dimity curtains were drawn aside, so she raised the window and leaned out.

"Have you gone daft, throwing rocks like that?" she called.

From behind Sarah could see nothing but the dovecote and top of the crab apple tree. But it was unmistakably Stanley's voice rising from the ground.

"Come now, Hester! Please don't be treatin' me this way!"

"You can find a dozen silly old girls to go boatin' with!"

"Ah, but they wouldn't be as lovely as

you, now, would they? And I wouldn't be asking them to marry me!"

"I've heard that talk before!"

"This time it comes from my heart, Hester! We'll call on the vicar today!"

"Just what's going on here, Stanley?" Mrs. Bacon's voice was not as loud, but filled with enough ire to lift it three storeys and an attic. Hester drew herself in so quickly that she bumped her crown. Her hand flew up to her head, but her green eyes were shining with triumph.

"Did you hear that? I knew it would work!"

Sarah could only gape as Hester snatched a brush from the top of her chest of drawers and pulled it through her red curls. *All he has to do is make another promise?* If that was the usual way of courtship, she was glad for her crippled hand and that she had no dowry. Better to be a spinster like Naomi and Marie.

The chambermaid turned at the door. "He just needed to be taught a lesson, Miss Matthews. Thank you for showin' me that."

"What about your reading lessons?"

"Why, there's naught will change about that." But there was a trace of doubt in her voice. She gave a little wave, and her footsteps sounded on the corridor, landing, and top steps. But they stopped. Sarah went out to the corridor just in time to see red curls appear in the staircase, and then Hester. The chambermaid gave Sarah a sheepish smile. "You know that book you was readin' to me when I was cleanin' Marie's grate that day?"

"It's just downstairs."

"Would you mind readin' it to me again?"

Sarah's heart leaped. "I'll get it right away. But what are you going to tell Stanley?" Try as she might, she could not help but feel some compassion for the man who praised her horse-grooming abilities and told jokes at mealtimes.

"He'll find another to dry his tears soon enough," Hester shrugged, regret passing across her face. "It's just his pride that's hurt. Will you fetch the book now, love, before I get weak and change my mind again?"

As Sarah flew toward the landing, she heard behind her, "Mayhap I could even pick out some of the words myself. Just the little ones."

❧ Twenty-Three ❧

Thursday afternoon was so fair and cool and the garden so awash with scents that Sarah took *History of Civilization in England* and a ripe pear out to the bench near the dovecote. Mr. Colby would be arriving tomorrow, and she didn't know how he would feel about studying out-of-doors, so she wished to take advantage of as much of the day as possible. Because privacy was almost nonexistent at Saint Matthew's, she had learned to keep her mind focused upon what she was reading in spite of what was going on about her. She was easily able to ignore the coos of doves and the tinking of a hammer in the gardening shed. Only when the faint strains of dreary music stopped was she aware that they had been drifting down from the third floor.

"I'm fine." Dorothea turned from the open score of Berlioz's *Symphonie Fantas-*

tique, fifth movement, to send a dismissing wave toward the parlor door.

But Marie, bedecked in chartreuse silk, hat, and gloves, heaved a sigh. "I will have Stanley send word to my sisters. We were only going window-shopping. Madame cannot sit in here all day feeling sorry for herself playing sad melodies."

"I'm not—" But another urge to sniff could not be ignored. Dorothea scooped the crumpled handkerchief from the piano ledge and turned her face so that Marie would not see her use it.

"Aha!" came from behind and footsteps approached.

"You forget your place, Marie, and that I could sack you this moment."

"Yes? Madame forgets how much in demand are French servants. My sisters and I will warn all French people we know that Missus is too bad tempered to work for."

"If they're all as overbearing as you, I want them nowhere near me." She blew her nose again, swiveled on the bench to face the maid, and arranged a pleasant expression on her face. "I'm much better now."

"Yes?"

"Yes. My hands were starting to ache anyway. Now go!" Dorothea watched her hurry to the door like a bird being released from its cage and felt a twinge of envy over Marie being so close with her sisters. Stretching and closing her hands, she rose from the piano and went to the window to look out over the square. By cruel coincidence Florence Gill happened to be walking toward GUNTER'S, accompanied by a brood of grandchildren.

"Mrs. Bacon says I'm to take your place, Naomi," Avis said in the kitchen with all the enthusiasm of a soldier approaching the hottest part of the battle. "The Missus wants you in the parlor."

"Very well." Ignoring Trudy's martyred expression, Naomi replaced her apron with a fresh one from the cupboard drawer. By the time she left the kitchen, Avis was telling Trudy about the time her fiancé, Edwin, broke out into hives from eating cinnamon biscuits.

Mrs. Blake sat at one end of the sofa with arms folded as if to comfort herself. The pale blue eyes looked beseechingly up at her, and her first words were, "I'm so tired."

"Then you should take a nap, Madam. Why don't I help you up—"

"I'm tired of being afraid, Naomi."

Naomi sat down next to her. "What are you afraid of?" she asked softly, though certain she already knew. Sometime during her three decades she had learned that voicing one's fears often helped sort the rational from the irrational ones.

"Everything. Of being poor . . . my husband preferring his business to home . . . of people discovering I was reared in a hovel with a privy and pigsty . . . of my son not loving me if I didn't give enough." She made an audible swallow. "Of dying with no one to grieve me. Of God punishing me for what I did to Jeremy and Sarah . . . and Mary Tomkin."

Naomi allowed a space before replying, to make sure that her mistress had emptied herself. "We would grieve for you, Mrs. Blake. The girl as well."

Tears trembled on the lower lashes. "I don't see why."

You've promised wisdom to those who ask for it, Father, Naomi prayed. *Could you send perhaps a double portion right now?* It was only when the assurance came that she was not stepping out in front of divine guidance that she said, "Have you asked forgiveness for those things you mention, Madam?"

"Of course," she replied peevishly. "Many times."

"Well, with the Scriptures saying God is *faithful and just* to forgive the sins we confess . . . it seems a little rude to me not accepting what He's offering you."

"You sound just like the vicar, Naomi," Mrs. Blake said, rubbing her forehead.

"Yes? I wonder if he can cook."

Her attempt at mild humor brought only a wary look from her mistress, but Naomi was undeterred. "What about victories in your life, Mrs. Blake? Good things? Such as being able to provide a livelihood for *nine* servants, not to mention what you give to charity." She thought it best not to mention Miss Matthews just at the moment for fear of bringing on another wave of remorse.

"Those have been . . . nice," the woman finally conceded. She glanced about her. "I have loved this house. My piano. Seeing the trees from the window." After a silence she added, "Were it not for my husband's success, I would have probably had to work at a factory all my life, Naomi. That would have been far worse than being a servant."

Naomi smiled to herself, taking no offense.

"Then why am I so constantly haunted by fears?"

"It's a simple matter of faith, Madam. Don't you believe that the God who caused the good things in your life is capable of carrying on to the end?"

"I obviously don't. Why should He?"

"Then why should He have done so in the past? You're His child." The almost overlooked verse to a cherished hymn came to Naomi's mind. She took the liberty of touching Mrs. Blake's arm and quoted,

"Through many dangers, toils and
  snares,
I have already come;
'Tis grace hath brought me safe thus far,
And grace will lead me home."

Tears again came to the aged eyes. But her expression was more thoughtful than anxious. *"Brought me safe thus far,"* Mrs. Blake echoed softly.

"It kept you from the factory, Madam. It'll lead you home, as the song says. Don't you think it's time to cast fear to the wind and live a little more recklessly?"

"Recklessly? I'm an old woman, Naomi."

"Moses and Abraham were old men, Madam."

"Yes." Mrs. Blake sighed again. "Thank you, Naomi. You may go now."

"Yes, Madam." She rose from the sofa. *Why did you have to add that "reckless" part?* she asked herself as she moved toward the door. Surely God hadn't led her in that direction.

"Naomi?"

"Yes, Madam?"

"Do you know where Sarah is now?"

"Why, in the garden." Naomi's heartbeat quickened just a bit. "She stopped by the kitchen on her way out."

Mrs. Blake nodded. "Help me down the stairs, will you? It's time I had a talk with her."

For how long the unfamiliar sound had been going on, Sarah wasn't certain. But she replaced her marker, set the book aside, and got to her feet.

Weeping?

It came from the Rothschild garden. Were the boys teasing her? If so, she certainly intended to scold them for the chills running down her back. She went to her former perch at the wall and pulled herself up.

All four were gathered around their nanny at the bench. One twin rested his head against her arm while she wiped his face with a handkerchief. The other covered his eyes with the crook of his arm and leaned against Ben's shoulder, while Ben wiped his own face with the back of his hand. Mordie stood next to him with glistening cheeks.

"What is wrong?" came a whisper from Sarah's side. She turned her face toward Mr. Duffy.

"I don't know," she whispered back. "They're all crying."

He eyed the wall and turned for the shed. Meanwhile Mordie looked up at her and spoke to the nanny, who glanced up at Sarah and then nodded. By the time he trudged over to the wall, Mr. Duffy had returned with a step stool and raised himself beside her.

"Ruthie . . ." the boy said between sniffs. His eyes were puffy, his face splotched crimson. "She had the croup."

"But will she be all right?" Sarah asked.

The boy shook his head and covered his face.

Mr. Duffy gave her a somber look, then told him, "We're sorry to hear it, lad."

"We're so sorry, Mordie," Sarah echoed, eyes filling.

Mordie turned toward his nanny again, and Mr. Duffy motioned to Sarah that they should get down. In silence they walked toward the house. It was when they reached the terrace that she became aware of Mr. Duffy's big hand wrapped around her right one. A face appeared through the glass of one of the French doors. Mr. Duffy turned the knob, and Mrs. Blake stepped outside.

"There you are, Sarah. I thought we might—" She stopped. "What is wrong?"

"The baby's dead," Mr. Duffy said with a nod toward the wall.

"No!" she gasped.

Little images came to Sarah's mind, infants who had died at Saint Matthew's, since she was old enough to remember. She could almost hear Miss Woodward weeping, and see Mrs. Forsyth's grim expression. Yes, babies were ushered straightway into the arms of Jesus, as Mrs. Kettner always said. But it was still such a sad thing that a person so small and trusting and helpless should suffer, even for a little while.

With a stricken expression and a hand up to her throat, Mrs. Blake stared at the wall. Anger quickened Sarah's pulse. This pity for people who were not worthy even to be playmates? "You should be happy," she heard herself say through trembling lips. "There's one less Jew next door."

———

"Sarah?"

Sarah turned her cheek against her sodden coverlet. She had expected someone to come eventually, most likely Mrs. Bacon, to tell her the coach was ready. But she had not expected *that* voice at her bedroom door. She could still see Mrs. Blake's face, which had frozen in horror when Sarah spat those hateful words before pushing past her and fleeing upstairs.

The knob turned, the door opened, and she heard soft footsteps approaching.

Pushing herself up from the mattress, Sarah sat up on the edge and stared into a pair of pale watery eyes.

"I'm sorry," Sarah told her. Not out of desperation to stay, though she wanted to badly. Sometime during the half hour that she had lain there, reason—or perhaps God's quiet voice—had convinced her that Mrs. Blake would not have wished harm upon the neighbors. "I'll understand if you send me back."

Incredibly, Mrs. Blake scooped Sarah's left hand from her lap and pressed it against her ashen white cheek. Her eyes closed, and when they opened, fresh tears clung to the lashes.

"Out there . . . you looked as if you hated me."

"How could I hate you?" Sarah shook her head for emphasis, her own eyes clouding. "You've been so good to me, taking me in and giving me—"

"Because I deserve your hatred," she said just above a whisper. "You have no idea."

"But I know you wish the baby were still—"

"I'm your grandmother, Sarah."

Sarah blinked at her. "That's not possible."

"It's true. You're Jeremy's daughter."

"But I was left at a church. Mrs. Forsyth doesn't even know who my parents were."

"She knows. I had Mr. Swann request that you not be told."

Sometime over the course of the next half hour Mrs. Blake moved to the striped chair, while Sarah sat on the ottoman at her knees. And once the initial shock lessened, some things Sarah had puzzled over during the recent past came into focus. Such as the fragment of conversation she overheard in the shop on Old Bond. Why Avis would apologize to her and not Hester for the remark about Mrs. Blake. And especially, why *she*, flawed as she was, would be the orphan chosen to come here.

"But why didn't Mr. Jeremy marry my mother?" she asked. She could not bring herself to refer to him as "Father," nor Mrs. Blake as "Grandmother." This was all too new.

Dorothea's fatigue grew, until every movement was labor. Strong was the temptation to reply that Jeremy had se-

cretly married Mary Tomkin. No one but the girl would believe it, and only until someone like Augusta Stafford took it upon herself to inform her of the whole truth. There had been enough lies. "Because he swore the child was not his," she replied, glancing away from the green eyes. "And I chose to believe him."

"Why? Because she was a servant?"

"Yes, Sarah. But then, I would have believed him over anyone."

The look that had so disturbed Dorothea downstairs passed across the young face again, though the child was quick to iron it out. "He never even wondered what happened to me?"

"I'm sorry." Dorothea shook her head. "He didn't like to think about things that caused him any discomfort."

"Then he was an evil man."

Yes, Dorothea thought.

"What happened to my mother?"

"She went back to live with her family. It was her father who put you out."

"Is she still living?"

"Yes."

"Then she'll want to see me." Sarah's eyes were wide. "Won't she?"

Tell her about the fifty pounds, Dorothea thought. That would make closing that door simple. But she could not bring herself to be so cruel. "I don't know, child."

"Couldn't we visit her and ask?"

That, she could not allow, even if her mother lived next door instead of in another town. Not without risking greater hurt to Sarah. "You may write to her and ask," Dorothea said, and when the girl appeared about to protest, she added, "She does not reside in London."

Sarah nodded, suddenly seeming older than her years. Within the space of less than an hour, the girl had gained and yet lost both parents, perhaps irrevocably, unless Mary Tomkin Hogarth regretted selling her maternal rights. In spite of her intense desire to keep Sarah to herself for as long as possible, Dorothea forced out the words, "But to save time, I'll hire Mr. Swann to deliver your letter and bring a reply, if he's available."

"Thank you!" the child said as if she had been offered gold.

Even though she could understand the hope in the drawn face, Dorothea's anguish deepened. How could she have been so naive to think that *she* would be enough for the girl? *God forgive me*, she prayed, remembering suddenly that nearby others were suffering something more terrible than her own wounded feelings.

"Let's wash our faces, Sarah," she said quietly. "We have a call to make."

✳ *Twenty-Four* ✳

Naomi and Trudy had left for the greengrocer's after Claire came into the kitchen with Mrs. Bacon's request that they prepare something to send next door. Naomi's acquaintance with the neighbors and their servants was limited to nods and smiles when passing on the pavement or in the square. Still, she was relieved to have something useful to do for them. The Rothschilds were Orthodox and therefore unable to accept anything she would have cooked or baked, but Naomi was almost certain the huge basket of apples, cherries, apricots, and walnuts compromised no Jewish dietary law.

"You're back," Mrs. Bacon said, coming through the doorway just as Naomi placed the last washed apricot on top of the heap. "Just in time."

"Didn't you see Trudy? I sent her up to tell you."

"We must have just missed each other." Stepping up to the worktable, the housekeeper glanced back at the door. "I don't know if Claire told you, but it was Miss Matthews who first heard about the baby."

"Oh dear." In her haste to leave for the greengrocer's, Naomi had not even wondered if the girl knew. "How is she?"

"She snapped at Mrs. Blake right in front of Mr. Duffy and ran up to her room. I believe that's what led the Missus to tell her who she really is. So sad, that it took such a tragedy to bring it about."

"I see." It seemed to serve no purpose to mention that that was the reason Mrs. Blake went out into the garden in the first place. "How is Miss Matthews now?"

"She's fine. Apparently the talk went well. They'll be going next door together."

When Trudy reappeared, Mrs. Bacon thanked them both and left with the basket. Naomi wished she could see if Sarah was truly all right. But if the girl was with her grandmother, she had no place intruding. So she sent up a prayer placing the situation in far more capable hands, then busied hers with supper preparations.

Black crepe already marked the windows of the Rothschild home where callers were received by Mrs. Rothschild's sister, who assumed duties for the distraught parents. When Sarah and Mrs. Blake returned home from paying their respects, the elderly woman pleaded exhaustion and asked Mrs. Bacon to help her prepare for bed early.

"We'll start having meals together tomorrow," she told Sarah, then gave her a worried look. "Unless you would prefer to continue in the servants' hall."

That was exactly what Sarah would have preferred, but she replied otherwise. She was already beginning to feel a certain responsibility for Mrs. Blake that went beyond gratitude. They were family, something she never imagined she would have. And if they were to become close, they would need to spend more time together.

No mention was made of the Rothschild infant during supper in the hall, but the atmosphere was subdued. On her way from the sideboard, while most others were still filling plates, Naomi leaned down to ask if she was all right. Sarah nodded, not sure if the cook was referring to the death or what she had found out about herself this afternoon. Both, she suspected.

What little conversation there was gave over to perplexed silence when a lone church bell started tolling in the distance, soon joined by another, until it seemed every bell in London was ringing. Sarah thought it was a touching, sad tribute to the Rothschild baby. But Hester whispered, "Someone royal must have died."

The service entry door opened, footsteps came through the kitchen, and Marie entered the hall in her Sunday clothes. "I have already dined, thank you," she said when a stunned Trudy offered to dish up a tray. After a self-conscious pause, she said, "The bells ring because Charles Dickens has died. I know you English loved him. I am sorry."

She left then, and an even grayer pall was cast over the meal. Though Sarah had met neither Mr. Dickens nor the Rothschild baby, she grieved the man because of the characters he had penned and the child because of tears she had witnessed on her brothers' faces.

But a spark of hope within her burned

that night as did the candle on her writing table. She feared turning on the lamp in case Marie or Mrs. Bacon should notice light beneath the door and insist she go to bed. She would not be able to sleep until she poured out in ink all the love she had stored up inside for a mother, without even being aware that she had one.

Mrs. Blake says I may visit if you are agreeable. I shall be most anxiously awaiting your reply, dearest Mother. . . .

———

Two days later Jules Swann was seated again in the Hogarth parlor, which now boasted furniture with purple velvet upholstery, landscapes in gilt frames, and a colorful Oriental rug on the floor. A pianoforte sat against one wall. "For our Lucy," the former Mary Tomkin offered when she saw him glance in that direction. "She has a ear for music, her piano tutor says."

"Very good." Jules smiled at the girl, who ducked her head timidly. To his relief she did not offer to demonstrate her ability. And to his greater relief, little Georgie was in good humor, content to sit on his bare haunches and chortle while his brother teased a calico kitten with a flue brush. In two hours the last London train would be leaving Crewe, and Jules hoped to spend the night in his own bed instead of the railway inn. To Mrs. Hogarth he asked, as he had in April, "May we speak privately?"

She obliged without hesitation this time, ordering Lucy to take the middle brother and even Georgie and the kitten out to the tiny garden. Jules watched them leave the room and wondered at the lack of any family resemblance between them and Sarah Matthews. But then, they were half-siblings.

"You found my little girl?" Mrs. Hogarth asked when the door closed.

"In a Methodist orphanage and well cared for. She was given the name 'Sarah.' "

"Sarah," she echoed, her mouth pulling into a frown that seemed more from habit than negative thought.

"She lives in the Blake mansion now," he said carefully.

"What does she look like?"

"Wide green eyes. Her hair is blond and

curly. She was on the thin side when I delivered her to Berkeley Square, but I'm told she's filling out."

Mary Hogarth smiled dreamily. "She was such a perfect little thing, just like a China doll."

"Yes?" Jules fought the temptation to ask about the hand. What would it prove? If she were to insist that there was no deformity, he would have to bear in mind that she had just given birth and had barely had opportunity to hold the infant. Far more plausible than the brief notion that flitted across his mind, that Mrs. Forsyth would have misled him or was mistaken. *Impossible*. Reaching into his coat pocket, he said, "I've a letter from your daughter."

The frown reappeared. "Why? I thought we wasn't supposed to know each other."

"The situation has changed, Mrs. Hogarth. Mrs. Blake has given her permission to contact you." He took the folded page from his coat pocket and started to get up from his chair, but she held a palm out in front of herself. *But of course*, he thought, embarrassed at his lack of sensitivity. He had had to read to her the document she signed in April before she could affix a barely legible scrawl. He cleared his throat. "Shall I read it for you?"

"No."

Looking past the page he had already started to unfold, Jules said, "I beg your pardon?"

Sadness washed across the square face. Still, she shook her head adamantly. "Beggin' your pardon for saying this, Mr. Swann, but don't come back here again."

"But I assumed—"

"I'm glad to hear that the girl's being cared for, even if it's by that witch Mrs. Blake. But like I said before . . . my pa kept me hidden away till she was born. I don't want my Bob finding out. He's got high morals and might hold it against me."

"I could take the letter back with me after I've read it to you, Mrs. Hogarth."

Again she shook her head. "I don't want you readin' something that's going to make me long for her. We ain't fancy like the Blakes, Mr. Swann, but we've a good little life here, and I want to keep it just the way it is."

Jules did not argue. He was certain Mrs. Blake would be relieved not to have Mary Hogarth included in Sarah's life. But having not been able to resist peeking at Sarah's poignant words on the train, he felt compelled to ask if there was any message she would care to send the girl.

"Just tell her I'm glad she weren't ate by a dog or froze to death in that pail," Mrs. Hogarth replied after a long moment's thought. "But that we can't have nothing to do with each other. See that she understands that, will you, so she won't be knockin' at this door when she's grown?"

"Very well." Jules got to his feet. But at the door, as she took down his hat from a gleaming brass rack, he swept another glance through the refurbished room. "May I ask how you explained all of this to your husband?"

She gave him a sheepish smile. "I told 'im a uncle passed on and left me some money. Bob's morals are high, but he ain't real bright."

With his duty concluded in far less time than he had allowed, Jules ended up waiting on a bench in Crewe Station for over an hour. Evening had descended upon London by the time he stepped out onto King's Cross Platform. He flagged down a hackney with the intention of going on home to his family and waiting to conclude his business tomorrow after church. But he told the driver, "14 Berkeley Square." He had not seen Sarah Matthews yesterday when summoned by Mrs. Blake, but he knew instinctively that she was anxious for a reply. It was just a pity that he could not deliver a good one.

The red-headed maid who took his card left him standing inside the hall and knocked softly on the sitting room door before going inside. Presently Mrs. Blake came out alone and approached him. With voice lowered she said, simply, "Well?"

Jules shook his head. "She didn't even want to see the letter."

"I see." The elderly woman sighed. "I don't know whether to be disappointed or overjoyed."

"I understand." He meant it. The terror in the girl's face upon their first parting had haunted him for weeks. He was pleased to discover yesterday that she was regarded with affection by the whole household, for not only had she *not* been sent off to school, but she had been informed of her kinship with Mrs. Blake.

Mrs. Blake glanced back at the sitting

room door. "You must be the one to tell her, Mr. Swann. I wouldn't want her to think . . ."

She didn't have to explain. As much as Jules would have wished to avoid this part of his duty, he nodded and accompanied her up the corridor. Sarah Matthews smiled at him from a small checkered game table upon which were arranged about a dozen round draughts pieces. The red-headed maid and the dark-haired French one, who did not scowl at him this time, left the room while the girl pushed out her chair.

"Good evening, Miss Matthews," Jules said, returning her smile. He was glad now that he had come inside. His wife would be happy to hear of the color in her cheeks and the flesh softening the angles of her face. "Draughts?" he said in an inane attempt to postpone the inevitable.

"Mrs. Blake is teaching me."

"I was surprised I could still recall the rules," the older woman confessed with a wan smile toward the girl. Worry still lurked in the pale blue eyes. Worse yet was the anticipation shining from Sarah's green ones.

Get on with it, Jules thought, and as gently as possible, he said, "I'm afraid it's not good."

Dorothea was surprised at how well Sarah took the news, that she even had the presence of mind to inquire about Mr. Swann's daughters before he left. It had never occurred to Dorothea to wonder if the solicitor even *had* children. Whether because being raised in an orphanage taught one not to raise one's expectations too high, or if Sarah did not wish to cause her discomfort by showing her unhappiness, the girl had simply blinked away a few tears and assured her that she wanted to finish the draughts match.

Later upstairs, when outside sounds of carriage wheels and hoof beats had ceased, Dorothea took up her candle and padded down the dark corridor to the bathroom. She paused at Sarah's door on the way back, leaned her cheek faintly against the smooth wood, and held her breath. The silence was not reassuring, for if the girl were weeping, she would do so quietly.

Should I knock, Father? Would the girl resent her grief being intruded upon by the person who had sent her mother away?

She had spent so many years blaming God that she had no right to ask for direction, but in her circle of candlelight she felt a presence, an answer. *Not now.*

She went to Jeremy's room, instead, and held up the candle to peer at his bed, not slept in since her son's last night in it, the gloves on his chest of drawers, and his silk dressing gown across the chair. *Was the pleasure worth it, Jeremy? Did you ever consider who would have to clean up the rubbish you left behind?*

Not that Sarah was rubbish. Far from it. She was a reason to get up in the mornings again. What a joy to discover that the heart in her aged chest was capable of producing something besides pain!

"I shouldn't have wakened you," Sarah said again to Naomi. For the past half hour they had sat on the top step of the garret landing, the candle behind them throwing grotesque shadows against the slanted ceiling.

"I'm glad you did." The cook's voice was as soothing as the hand resting upon Sarah's shoulder. "It's a terrible disappointment."

Sarah wiped her eyes with the sash of her wrapper and wondered if it were possible to run out of tears. "But if it would make her husband angry to know about me . . . well, she shouldn't risk her marriage to tell him."

"That may be so, but it doesn't make it any easier to hear."

"But I really do understand." She wiped her eyes again. "She has to think about the other children too." *A sister and brothers I'll never see?*

Naomi smiled sadly. "I admire your capacity for understanding, Miss Matthews. But soothing away your grief with understanding is the same as . . . well, tying a bandage over a splinter. The problem won't go away until it's given proper attention."

"Proper attention?"

"By allowing yourself to cry it out whenever you feel the need. I never shamed William for his tears those years ago, and once he was able to put his grief behind him, he was able to thrive in his new life."

It was such a relief *not* to be reminded that she had never really expected to know her mother anyway. That she was still far better off than when she lived at Saint

Matthew's. That she should be grateful for a grandmother and a household of people who were good to her. She wiped her eyes again and mustered up a smile for the woman beside her. "I feel better, Naomi. Thank you. And I'll go on to bed now."

Concern was still evident in the shadows of Naomi's face as she reached back for the candle. "Shall I come downstairs and sit with you for a while?"

"Oh no. Please get some sleep yourself."

Sarah hurried down the staircase a little calmer than when she had climbed it. Now that she had permission to weep, she no longer felt such an overwhelming need to do so. She had just stepped into the dim corridor and noticed faint light coming through Jeremy's open doorway.

Didn't you ever wonder about me . . . Father? she thought, approaching the room. *How I looked, or even if I were a boy or girl? If I had food or shelter?* She reached the doorway expecting to see Marie. Instead, there stood a much smaller figure in white. Mrs. Blake turned, squinting at Sarah's candle. Her wrinkled cheeks glistened.

"In spite of all he did, I can't make myself stop loving him," she said apologetically.

"I understand," Sarah said for the second time that night. She meant it, even though her understanding was tinged with envy that *her* mother could not afford to have such fierce love for her.

"But if I could start all over again, I would do everything in my power to keep him from heading down that road." She studied Sarah's face. "You're still the same good person you were before, you know. You shouldn't feel shame for anything he did."

"Thank you," Sarah said, only to ease the worry in Mrs. Blake's expression. It was one thing to suspect her parents had never married, but another to know the whole sordid story.

"Are you terribly upset about your mother?"

"Not so much anymore. I just had a talk with Naomi."

"Oh, well, that's good." A sad smile came and passed. "She's a comfort."

Sarah nodded but wondered at the sadness. Could it be because she chose to pour out her disappointment to someone else and not her? It struck her, incredibly, that though Mrs. Blake may have brought her here out of some charitable obligation or even guilt, she had somehow grown to love her. She could see it in the aged eyes, even in the dimness of candlelight. For the first time since arriving at Berkeley Square, Sarah felt a great sense of belonging to someone.

She blinked a tear away and set the candle on the chest of drawers so she could hold out her arms. Smiling, she said, "Grandmother."

Part Two

January 28, 1875

London

❧ *Twenty-Five* ❧

"And just what are we doing, pray tell?"

Sarah jumped and turned. "I wasn't going to peek, Mrs. Bacon!" Raising her arm so that the housekeeper could see the lap quilt folded over it, she said, "But Grandmother asked me to fetch this from the sitting room, and . . ."

Her excuse was met with a knowing nod. "And someone foolishly left the door open?"

"Yes . . . open." She could not help but turn her face again toward the gap in the doorway. It was just wide enough to reveal the white cake on the center of the dining room table, decorated with iced pink honeysuckles.

But Mrs. Bacon reached past her and pulled the knob until the soft *click* sounded. Her expression was firm, in spite of the affection in the hazel eyes behind the wire spectacles. In the almost five years since

Sarah's arrival at Berkeley Square, Mrs. Bacon's brown topknot had grown a little more gray, the spectacle lenses—as well as the aproned waist—a little thicker. "You'll disappoint everyone if you don't slip away at once, dear."

"Yes, of course." Smiling, Sarah stood on tiptoe to kiss her cheek. She hastened upstairs and eased open the parlor door so as not to interrupt what Vicar Sharp was saying.

". . . and so with Mr. Mumford moving on to take a parish in Yorkshire, I'll be taking on another curate as soon . . ."

But he stopped and smiled up at her as if she had not been sitting in the same room just minutes ago. His appearance had changed little since she had first made his acquaintance at the door of Saint George's. Only a few less steel-colored strands stretched atop his balding head, and just a bit more gray frosted the thick side-whiskers. "Oh, to be eighteen again, Miss Matthews!"

"Now, now, Vicar." Sarah's grandmother raised her cup and saucer so that the quilt could be tucked around her frail figure. She exchanged smiles with Sarah and asked, "Are your golden years so wretched?"

"Why, on the contrary, Mrs. Blake. My life has been such a grand adventure that I would wish to relive it."

"Heaven forbid! Once is enough. See to the good reverend's tea, Sarah."

"Yes, Grandmother."

The vicar shook his head and handed Sarah his cup and saucer. "I've other calls this afternoon."

"You'll not forget dinner, will you?" Grandmother asked.

"Mrs. Sharp and I will be here at seven . . . sharp." He left chuckling at his own joke. After Sarah poured her grandmother some more tea, she was directed toward the nearest empty chair.

"Sit down, Sarah."

"Are you tired, Grandmother? Perhaps you should nap for a little while?"

Sarah worried so lately about the woman's health. Doctor Raine came by weekly to listen to her heart with his stethoscope, as if he feared it would stop any day now. Why would he do so if rheumatism were the only affliction? But whenever she caught him aside to ask, he would simply smile and say, "The body requires more care as it ages, just like an old house."

"I feel well, child." Deeper were the lines of her face, and her hair had whitened to the color of snow. But a smile curved her lips. "And I wish to give you your gift."

"Now?" Her grandmother was lavish with gifts but also delighted in presenting them in the midst of fanfare and celebration. And Sarah could see no wrapped parcel, however small, in the vicinity. "Wouldn't you rather wait until this evening?"

"No, I would not care to do that. Not this time."

Sarah smiled with affection and even anticipation. It had taken a couple of years to get to the point where she could accept a gift without guilt over causing her grandmother another expense. She was fond of giving them, too, oftentimes spending her allowance on others in the household. A crown weekly was modest for a shipping heiress, but her grandmother feared encouraging any improvident traits that may have been passed down from her father. It was more than enough in Sarah's view, considering that any material need was provided simply by asking Mrs. Bacon to add it to her shopping list. "Then what is it, Grandmother?"

The old woman hugged herself with her frail limbs. "I'm purchasing a fine old mansion in Hampstead. It will require a new roof and a bit of restoration, but I'm told the garden is two acres and lovely."

A house? How many times had her beloved matriarch declared she could never move from Berkeley Square? "I'm afraid I don't understand."

"It's for us, dear girl." Grandmother pressed fingers to her smiling lips. "Where there will surely be bright young people to befriend you."

So generous a gesture robbed Sarah of speech so completely that finally disappointment took her grandmother's smile. "Have you nothing to say?"

Sarah hastened out of her chair to kneel beside her grandmother's. Carefully she scooped up a spotted hand. "That is the kindest thing anyone has ever done for me."

"I only regret not plucking up the courage to do this years ago." Tears lustered the pale eyes. "I know how you enjoy the city, but we'll only be a bit more to the north. Yet away from Mayfair."

"Please don't regret anything. You've been so good to me. But please . . . may we stay here?"

"Here? In this wretched place?"

Her critical tone did nothing to assure Sarah that moving would be wise. At her grandmother's age, the cords of memory were not so easily broken—which was why Jeremy's room still was kept up as if he would return any day. And there was the familiarity of one's longtime home. Surely the strain of a new place would be too much upon her declining health.

"I've been happy here for over four and a half years, Grandmother. So how can it be wretched?"

"But friends . . ."

"This house is brimming with them." And there were the Rothschild brothers—in Spain for the winter—who taught her how to play lawn tennis. The tidy parsonage Hester now shared with her husband and infant son was only six blocks away. And William was back in London to stay, having been awarded his Master of Studies in Chemistry in early December. His position kept him busy, but he still found time to join her outings with Naomi almost every Saturday afternoon and to come for Sunday lunch in the hall.

But she had to admit it did pain her, catching the occasional knowing glance sent her way. Hearing a hush come over the group of chattering young women at an outside table at GUNTER'S as she passed. If she were to discover cures for every known disease, people in Mayfair would likely remember her as "the illegitimate daughter of the late Jeremy Blake."

"Sarah?" Grandmother said, uncertainty filling her expression.

Sarah pressed the hand she held against her own cheek. "Forgive me for spoiling your surprise. But is it possible to resell the house?"

"I've not actually signed the final papers yet. But you're not asking this because you think I'm not strong enough for the move, are you?"

Father, forgive me. "Not at all."

After a space of silence, Grandmother straightened in her chair. "The surprise is not spoiled. In honor of your birthday, we will give the house to Saint Matthew's."

Sarah's breath caught. "You would do that?"

"The fresh air and room to romp would be good for the children."

"I can't imagine a gift that would please me more, Grandmother!"

"Very good." Her lined face grew thoughtful. "But I doubt if there are many orphans running about Hampstead. How would they replace the ones who grow up and leave?"

The disappointment that struck Sarah was fortunately short-lived. "Most girls were brought in by ministers and policemen who found them in the streets. Surely they wouldn't mind delivering them up there, knowing they'll have a better place."

"I'll send word to Mr. Mitchell to conclude the transaction right away and to hire someone to begin repairs." Even though Mr. Mitchell ran Blake Shipping, he continued to handle Grandmother's personal legal affairs. "Perhaps you would like to be the one to tell them at Saint Matthew's?"

If Sarah was happy a minute ago, she was now euphoric. She had seen the home's facade only once since moving to Berkeley Square, and only after coaxing Stanley to drive her past during the course of another errand. But she had caught not even a glimpse of Mrs. Forsyth or any of the staff or girls. What a joy it would be to visit and with such good news! "May I go there now? There's time if I—"

"Not today, I'm afraid. The servants are too busy with party preparations."

"Stanley isn't. Couldn't he drive me?"

"*Unescorted?* Down Drury Lane?"

"Well . . ."

"A coachman is not the same as an escort, Sarah," Grandmother replied with a firm shake of the head. "Some miscreant could break down the door and make away with you before Stanley could climb down from the box. You will wait until Saturday afternoon and have William and Naomi accompany you."

"Yes, Grandmother." Sarah leaned forward to kiss her soft cheek. "You're still a dear."

The old woman looked pleased. "And *you* haven't played draughts with me in weeks. Come now, Marie is helping Naomi, so it's up to you to amuse your old grandmother."

"Killed in a duel?" At the worktable, Marie's amber eyes lifted from the chain she was making from strips of colored paper and wallpaper paste. "From whom did you hear that?"

Naomi winced, though her fingers continued to dredge oysters through the seasoned flour to put aside for frying, one of Miss Matthews' favorite dishes. They would not have been speaking so candidly if Trudy—who never seemed to get in on any good conversations—were not upstairs helping Claire and Avis lay the dining room cloth. "I can't recall, Marie. Someone must have misinterpreted something you said and . . . well, you know how stories like that tend to spread."

Even though their relationship had evolved into something between a truce and friendship over the past four years, Naomi was surprised when Marie showed no sign of anger.

"It was my sister Patrice's fiancé," Marie replied calmly.

"The eldest?"

"Yes. As you can imagine, her heart was broken. The man who killed her fiancé was from a wealthy family who owned most of the land in Bernay, even our father's farm. She would have had a life of privilege had she given in and married the other man, but she sold the wedding dress our grandmother made for passage to England. We adored her—Leona, Nicolette, and me—and so as Patrice saved for our passages and found positions in Mayfair, we joined her one by one and then helped her save for the others."

"Your parents gave consent?"

She pasted another loop onto the chain. "We were mouths to feed, could not work as hard on the farm as our five brothers, and were too homely to find husbands—except for Patrice. Our papa complained we would be a burden to him for the rest of his life. And our mamma was too cowed to take our side."

"I'm sorry," Naomi told her. Not only for Marie's painful past, but for her own critical thoughts over the pains the maid took at her appearance.

"Sorry? But it was a good thing coming here. We make our own way, my sisters and I. And every week we spend time together."

"But you dislike England." *Or we English*.

Marie shifted in her chair and looked a little embarrassed. "I admit I had . . . what is the word . . . *prejudice*?"

Before Naomi could confirm that it was, Marie nodded. "Yes, prejudice, as did my sisters."

"I see." Naomi felt no insult—all her life she had heard ridicule of the French, so it stood to reason that they would return that scorn. The last oyster dredged, she went to the sink to wash and dry her hands, then peeked at the pair of chestnut-stuffed pullets in the oven. They were a mild crispy gold, almost ready. She lifted the lid from a back-burner kettle and pushed a spoon against the stewed Rump of Beef a la Jardinière, satisfied that it was almost tender enough. Next she stirred the julienne soup. After a glance at the rolls rising on a cupboard ledge, she pulled out the chair next to Marie's and reached for some colored strips.

"If you'll paste the ends, I'll loop them," she offered. "I'm free for the next ten minutes or so."

Marie nodded, and the chain lengthened much faster. Presently the lady's maid said, as if she had mulled it over in her mind the whole time, "It was our oldest brother,

Aubrey, who taught us to dislike the English. He served in the army during the Crimean War."

"But we fought together on that one."

"Yes, but the troops had very little contact. Aubrey delivered messages from General St. Arnaud to the British commander—and the English soldiers he passed talked through their noses to mock him. Aubrey despised them more than he did the Russians. They called him a 'frog'!"

"Oh, Marie . . . I'm sorry," Naomi said for the second time. And she hoped her cheeks weren't flushed. Had she a farthing for every time she had heard that label while growing up, she supposed she would have quite a nest egg.

Marie shrugged. "Now that I am older and have read some, I can see they were bitter because they bore the brunt of the fighting at the River Alma and lost so many men. One doesn't think about that when she is young. I was certain that the servants here did not care to have a 'frog' in their midst, so I was determined to show that I did not care."

And so by her standoffishness she had fulfilled her own prophecy, Naomi thought.

Still, she wished she had put forth more of an effort to understand Marie in those early days. She held out one more strip to be pasted, and when it was another loop on the chain, she rose to her feet. "I should see to those hens now." But she stood there for a few seconds and said, impulsively, "I'm glad you brought that down here. We so seldom get to chat."

Marie shrugged again. "There is too much going on in the dining room, and I thought it a waste to heat the library for only one person."

"Of course." *God forbid you should admit to wanting anyone's company.*

But minutes later, when the pullets had been transferred to a covered platter and Naomi had put a kettle of water on to boil for the potatoes, the accented voice said from the table, "But it has been pleasant visiting with you like this."

Twenty-Six

Under festoons of colored paper chains, the long table practically groaned with Sarah's favorite dishes—julienne soup, fried oysters, crispy pullets, stewed rump of beef, parsleyed new potatoes, grilled mushrooms, artichoke bottoms, macaroni with parmesan cheese, stewed turnips, fresh rolls, and in the center of it all, GUNTER'S butter cream cake. Her birthday, Christmas, and Easter were the only occasions the servants celebrated in the dining room with other guests. By the time Avis and Claire whisked away the entrée dishes, spread a fresh cloth, and returned to their seats, Stanley was groaning, "I'm full as a tick!"

At the head of the table Sarah glanced to her right and saw her grandmother's and Marie's tightening lips. Farther down the row, Claire Duffy planted an elbow into the groomsman's ribs. Though Stanley had become quieter, more thoughtful since Hester's marriage, he still seemed unable to break the habit of causing at least one woman to scold him during the course of a meal. And why should he, with so appreciative an audience as Mr. Duffy, whose cheeks reddened from the effort of containing the chuckles he would have released in the servants' hall?

"But you'll take just a sliver, won't you, Stanley?" Mrs. Bacon coaxed as the server in her hand sliced through a cluster of iced honeysuckle.

"Only out of fondness for our Miss Matthews."

"For Miss Matthews?" Trudy asked from his other side. "Or for your sweet tooth?"

He raised a hand to his chest. "It wounds me that you would have to ask, Trudy."

Down the table, Hester exchanged smiles with her husband, Mr. Addison Smith. He was not nearly as handsome as Stanley, with his tall gangly body, protruding Adam's apple, and beak nose. But he treated his wife with quiet respect and affection, and often when he looked at her, he wore the expression of someone who cannot quite believe his good fortune.

Mrs. Sharp, seated across from Grandmother, said in a half-teasing tone, "Well, because I am fond of our Miss Matthews *and* of GUNTER'S, I will have more than a sliver, if you please, Mrs. Bacon." She was some ten years younger than the vicar and still wore the ill-fitting brown wig that was probably still the subject of discussion in Mayfair's parlors. Occupying the other chairs on that side were the vicar, Avis, Mrs. Bacon, Hester and her husband, and Sarah's tutor, Mr. Colby, who was leaving in a fortnight to join an expedition making preliminary plans to scale the Matterhorn.

On Sarah's right sat Grandmother, Marie, Mr. Duffy and Claire, Stanley, Trudy, Susan, the brown-haired cockney who took Hester's place, Naomi, and William. The latter was staring at her a little oddly, as if she had icing on her face. Sarah ran a hand over her mouth and, coming up with nothing, raised an eyebrow at him in silent query. But he simply winked at her and once more became the same dear William she had quietly loved since the day he introduced her to Gypsy and Dudley.

A quarter of an hour later, William eyed the tissue-wrapped box in the collection assembled at the head of the table and kicked himself mentally for giving her yet another toy. He and his aunt Naomi had accompanied Sarah to see *Killarney* at the Adelphi just Saturday past. On Sunday he sent her a little wave from Saint George's gallery and chatted with her in the garden after lunch. She couldn't have matured so much in just four days—why was he just now noticing?

Though she was still slender, she had developed feminine curves over the years, and her pixyish cap of blond hair had grown into the mass of curls caught up in a comb at the crown of her head. No longer did her cheekbones jut from a pinched little face. William wondered if it was because her green eyes were still large and waifish that he continued to think of her as a little girl. But at the head of the table stood a poised young woman, stylishly adorned in a plum-colored silk trimmed with black embroidering.

"She's grown up on us, hasn't she?" his aunt murmured as Sarah, thanking Trudy warmly, angled a small box for all to see the hair ribbons inside.

William gave Aunt Naomi a wry smile. "I just wish I would have noticed earlier. What did you get her?"

"*Middlemarch*. And yourself?"

He told her about the eight-inch model of the HMS *Victoria* that he had altered with a tobacco tin underneath to hold sodium bicarbonate and vinegar to give it motion. He had even tied twine to the stern so that she could sail from the bank of the Serpentine, but now he wasn't certain. Did eighteen-year-old girls care for that sort of thing?

"She'll adore it," Aunt Naomi said as if reading his mind. "Trust me, there is still some child in her yet."

"Yes." He patted the hand resting upon his arm and watched Sarah slip her finger-less left hand into the handle straps Mr. Duffy had fashioned and attached to a white parasol. She had stopped hiding her hand in public over a year ago, telling him that reading Thoreau's *Journal* convinced her she had consumed herself with worry long enough over how people perceived her. William had complimented her maturity back then but, ironically, never equated it to growing up.

And while some changes happened too

rapidly, others crawled. At twenty-one he was the youngest, most recently hired, and, therefore, most underpaid investigator for the Hassall Commission, formed in 1872 by an act of Parliament to stem the widespread adulteration of food, drinks, and drugs, particularly in poor neighborhoods. He enjoyed his work tremendously, but it pained him that his dream of enabling his aunt Naomi to become a lady of leisure would take much longer than he had anticipated.

He came out of his reverie to notice Sarah lifting the lid from his gift. She scooped the ship from the box and looked over the decks and smokestacks before turning it to the underside. "For fuel?" she asked.

"Sodium bicarbonate. It's in the smaller box. And that's vinegar in the bottle."

"Sodium bi—what?" Mr. Duffy asked.

"Baking soda," Sarah answered, sending William a smile. "It's wonderful, thank you. You'll help me launch it when the weather turns, won't you?"

"Yes, of course." The knots in his shoulders eased. He felt lighthearted enough to accept the second slice of cake Mrs. Bacon pressed upon him.

"Last one!" Trudy exclaimed, pushing a dripping plate into the wall rack to dry overnight. She turned to hold out her apron to Naomi. "Look at me—I'm soaked to the skin!"

Naomi stretched to hang the copper pot she had just polished onto a hook over the worktable. "You'll dream of dishes and soap, won't you?"

The scullery maid feigned a shudder. "Not if I have any say-so about it."

"Why don't you go on upstairs? I'll pass a mop under the sink and be along."

"You don't mind?"

"Not at all," Naomi replied. She worked quickly and hung the mop back on its nail just inside the pantry. When she came out again she sensed a presence and looked toward the doorway leading to the servant's hall.

"Stanley!" She put a hand to her heart. "I thought you were Trudy."

That he would allow that to pass without jesting gave her an indication of his mood. *Hester*, Naomi thought, giving him a sympathetic smile. "You didn't enjoy tonight, did you?"

He shrugged. "My own fault."

Naomi could not argue with that. "Would you care to sit for a little while? I'll make hot chocolate."

"None for me, thank you. But you ain't tired?"

"It's a good tired," she replied as she pulled out a chair from the worktable.

Dropping into the seat across from hers, he propped his chin upon his stacked fists. "I thought I didn't care about her anymore."

"I'm so sorry, Stanley."

"Ah well."

"It's just going to take some time."

Again he shrugged. "I'm glad she's bein' treated good . . . truly. His bein' a religious fellow and all."

In his current mood, Naomi wasn't certain if she shouldn't allow the latter remark to pass. But it wasn't often that he showed so vulnerable a side. Nor was it often that they had the opportunity to chat privately. She had watched his frantic search for happiness for almost seven years now and thought *someone* should encourage him to look up. "It's not his being religious that makes him treat Hester well, Stanley," she said gently.

"What do you mean?"

"Well, Jesus' harshest words were for people who were so religious that they make Mr. Smith seem like a heathen."

He stared at her as if she had announced that she despised cooking. "But if they was religious . . ."

"Religion is what *made* them so harsh. They were proud of themselves for keeping the rules so well, yet they did not take care of their elderly parents, nor show charity to widows and orphans. And they hated Jesus for telling them that it was their hearts which mattered most to God."

"Then, why do you go to church if religion is bad?"

She had to grope for words to explain that one without undoing what she had just said. "True religion is loving God and having compassion for your fellow man, Stanley. That's not bad at all. And part of loving God is gathering with other Christians to worship Him . . . not to show everyone how righteous we are."

"Other Christians." He frowned pensively. "You know . . . I've waited outside

Saint George's every Sunday for years, Naomi. And my ears have caught some spiteful things at times."

"Granted," she said. "Again, we're back to what's in the heart. Attending church doesn't make anyone a Christian, Stanley, any more than walking into the stable makes one a horse. It's repenting and asking Jesus Christ to be Lord of your life."

"Repenting?"

"Turning away from your sins."

He blew out his cheeks. "That's a hard one, Naomi. I couldn't keep that up."

"Nor could Saint Paul, one of the greatest preachers who ever lived. Nor can I. But if you truly repent, Stanley, Jesus will help you. He said it's the sinners who need Him, just like it's the sick who need a doctor."

"Hmm." After another long silence, he narrowed his eyes and smiled. "You're a crafty one, Naomi."

"Crafty?" She was truly surprised. "Why do you say that?"

"We were talking about Hester and ended up talking religion."

"You're the one who first brought up the subject, as I recall," she said, returning his smile. "But seriously, Stanley . . . what could it hurt for you to consider these things?"

A sheen came over his eyes, and he turned his face a bit as if embarrassed. "I'm going to think hard on all this, Naomi," he said with voice softening.

"I'm glad."

"Well . . . good night." He pushed out his chair and rose, but instead of leaving, he stood behind it with hands hooked over the back. "I always thought you weren't too fond of me."

"Not fond of you?" Naomi smiled again. "I've always been fond of you, Stanley. Even the times I've wanted to box your ears."

It didn't matter to William that his Farringdon Street flat was tiny because he spent so little time there. What mattered was that it was cheap, enabling him to put as much of his wages aside as possible. He could have saved a little more had he moved back above Mrs. Blake's stable as she had offered, but with his having no time to do gardening or stable work, and her refusing to accept rent, he could not bring himself to become dependent upon her again.

He had no such qualms about allowing her to pay his expenses for the Saturday outings, for Aunt Naomi had convinced him that Mrs. Blake felt more than compensated for the companionship they brought to Sarah. It was the thought of these outings that kept him lying awake in his bed that evening. He had come to take them for granted—happily so, as one takes for granted the blackberry scone with Sunday tea. It had never crossed his mind that they would end one day.

Even though her socializing was limited, surely there were others in Mayfair who were aware of Sarah's beauty and grace—young men not influenced by the gossip of their mothers and sisters, and, unfortunately, more inclined toward marrying money than earning it. Once suitors began asking permission to call, Mrs. Blake would have to devote her ebbing energies to seeing she made a proper match for Sarah. And Sarah's time would be taken up with all the activities that went along with courtship. The idea pained him so much that he suspected what he felt for her had grown deeper than brotherly affection.

He almost wished that were not so. Mrs. Blake demonstrated great broad-mindedness by allowing Aunt Naomi and him to show Sarah all the sights of London. But it had taken thirteen years for her to reconcile to the fact that the Blake bloodline had been tainted with a servant's. She would not tolerate having it happen again. He knew that she was fond of him, but he also knew that it would not matter that his servant days were behind him nor how many Oxford degrees he earned.

Just please watch out for her, Father, he prayed under his breath as his eyelids grew heavier. *At least give her the decent man she deserves, who'll treat her well and be faithful. Not a money chaser*.

Rarely was he struck with a sense of divine assurance after praying, and he blamed himself for that. His job absorbed so much of his time that often his prayers were routine or hurried so that he could get some sleep. But his foggy thoughts were invaded just then by a profound knowledge that his prayer would be answered in that fashion. That should have comforted him, but actually it made him feel worse and robbed him of another hour of sleep.

❧ Twenty-Seven ❧

Mr. Mitchell came the next morning while Sarah was at her lessons in the library. The broad-shouldered, graying fifty-three-year-old had barely begun his professional career when Dorothea's husband hired him. A novice was all Arthur Blake could afford in those days. Now Mr. Mitchell had charge over two additional solicitors, three engineers, and a host of employees from clerks to shipbuilders and ship's captains. In spite of his vast duties, he had yet to send an underling to conduct business with Dorothea, and she appreciated that. It was he who had amended her will so that Sarah was named legal heir, also setting aside generous amounts for the servants based upon years of service.

"I strongly advise that you wait to sign these *after* you've presented the house to Saint Matthew's," he said from the sitting room chair after draining his fourth cup of tea. His protruding brow and thin lips gave his face a shadowy, roughish look, incongruous with the integrity he had demonstrated all these years. "You don't want it on your hands if they're not willing to use it."

"That's reasonable," Dorothea replied, even though the purchase would barely dent her fortune. There was no sense in throwing money about just because she could. "We'll find that out tomorrow. Sarah is pulling at the harness to tell them, but I won't allow her to go there unescorted."

He reached down for the satchel at his feet and started replacing papers. "Would you like me to escort her today?"

Dorothea considered his offer but then shook her head. "She's grown so close to my cook and her nephew that I'm positive she'll want them along. And the nephew has only half-Saturdays and Sundays off."

"Very well, then. Shall I return with these on Monday?"

"Yes, do."

He was getting to his feet when the matter that had hovered in the back of Dorothea's mind for weeks nudged itself to the forefront. "There is something else."

"Yes, Mrs. Blake?" he said, settling back into his chair. His dark brows lifted. "Nothing terribly bad, I trust?"

"Oh, it's nothing you should worry yourself over," she replied, and then grew amused at herself for jumping so quickly to reassure him. The concern lingering in his face made her decide not to disclose the part known only to Doctor Raine and the vicar. It would only make him uncomfortable, and she would have to listen to his regrets and little homilies about not giving up. Mr. Mitchell was bright enough to know that people her age tended to pass on sooner or later. "It's Sarah. Can you assure me that the will is completely binding?"

His expression eased a bit. "It is absolutely binding."

"Even though she hasn't the Blake name?" It had been a hard pill to swallow four years ago, Sarah's request to keep her name. Now Dorothea was glad she had not pressed the girl into it. Jeremy had not bothered to do so, and changing the name would only provoke more ridicule from the community.

"Even though, Mrs. Blake."

Dorothea nodded, though still not quite

satisfied. The ache in the hands resting upon her lap quilt was worsening, so she straightened and curled her crooked fingers for relief. Doctor Raine's edict last week was that she take her meals unsalted, saying she would eventually notice the difference in her joints. But there was nothing he could do about her heart. She had reconciled herself to dying but couldn't help but wish the process were a little more comfortable physically. "At the moment, I see no possibility of her marrying before I pass on—"

"Is there something you're not telling me, Mrs. Blake?" Worry creased his jutting brow again.

"One should think ahead, Mr. Mitchell. I won't always be here to guide her. Neither will you." That was what robbed her of sleep the most. As bright as her granddaughter was, she was inclined to be too trusting and did not yet have the life experience necessary for taking on an oftentimes cruel world.

"True, Mrs. Blake. Then do go on."

"I pray daily that she will marry wisely. But I have lived long enough to see how infatuation can make even wise hearts foolish. It will be tragic enough if she ends up marrying a fortune hunter, and worse if he squanders away her inheritance at the card table or through sheer incompetence."

The solicitor nodded. "Unfortunately, I have known of that happening."

"Are there any other measures we can take now to protect her?"

"Those have been done, Mrs. Blake. Thanks to the Married Women's Property Act of 1870, Sarah will control all property bequeathed to her, as well as the income generated from the same. A husband will only have access to the money insomuch as she allows it, and she will not be liable for his debts."

"Then I may breathe a little easier." But not quite yet, she realized a fraction of a second later. "What if Sarah *allows* this husband to control her fortune? What if he takes on the notion to run the company?"

"If he is capable and will allow us to teach him what we've learned over the years, that would be a good thing." He blew out a long breath. "I'll not deceive you, dear Mrs. Blake. A wastrel of a husband could still cause Sarah some problems if she were to allow him that control.

That is why you should continue to pray that she marries wisely."

His footsteps had no sooner faded into the hall than Mrs. Bacon appeared to collect the teacups and tray and ask if she needed anything.

"Where is Marie?" Dorothea asked her.

"Down in the kitchen, Madam. Shall I send for her?"

"Yes." Now that simply rising from her chair was so painful, she was becoming more and more dependent upon the maid. "And have her bring up more tea. Mr. Mitchell drank the pot dry—he must have given up smoking again."

Five minutes later the Frenchwoman appeared with a tray in her hands and Naomi at her side. Both wore expectant looks.

"Well, what is it?" Dorothea asked.

The two traded glances. It was Naomi who spoke first as Marie poured tea. "We're concerned about Miss Matthews' education, Madam, what with Mr. Colby leaving next week."

Dorothea had an idea of what was coming next, for Marie had dropped little hints lately about how good it was that young women were being encouraged to go to college these days as well as young men. *" 'The Sandhursts,' where my sister Leona is employed, send their two daughters to Girton,"* she had just so happened to mention last night while helping her prepare for bed.

"I will not send her away," Dorothea told the two.

"But of course not, Madam," the cook said. "Why, we would be the first to protest."

Narrowing her eyes, Dorothea reminded herself to remain stalwart against the soothing voice that had talked her into other radical changes in the past. That the changes had blessed her life made little difference. There would come a time when others would have to make decisions for her. She would surrender to that only when she had no other choice. "Then the matter is settled, is it not?"

It was obviously not, in their minds, for Marie said, "We have heard of a reputable day college for young ladies, Madame. The North London Collegiate School."

"Only six hours of study daily, no boarding," Naomi hastened to add, as if that fact would fall on glad ears. "And half-Saturdays off."

"Six hours." *She might as well be boarding*, Dorothea thought, what with time devoted to travel back and forth, sleep, and homework. For thirteen years, her own selfishness had robbed her of the blessing of having Sarah in her life. Now a different kind of selfishness made her want the girl home as much as possible. Even when they weren't together, such as the time Sarah spent in the library at her lessons, it was a comfort knowing she was under the same roof. "That simply will not do." Dorothea watched as the two traded glances again, leading her to long for the days when they were enemies.

"Madame knows how much Miss Matthews enjoys learning," Marie said. "And she needs the company of young ladies her age."

Dorothea had them there. "I'm also aware that Mr. Colby says she has completed every secondary text he has assigned to her, which is why his employment will terminate soon, Matterhorn or not. And I don't ascribe to this notion of girls going to college. It isn't as if she'll have to get out and earn a living."

And as for having the company of other

young ladies, Sarah had plainly stated that she was not lonely when she turned down the offer of the house. The tea was growing tepid in her cup. Dorothea took a sip. She was weary of the argument, but with needlework and the piano too painful for her hands, arguing with maids seemed the only activity open to her at the moment. "You both may as well sit. I can see that you've more to say. I can only hope Trudy's not burning our lunch."

"Lunch is taken care of, Madam," Naomi said, smiling as the two took seats upon the divan. She smoothed out her apron. "Forgive me, but have you ever asked Miss Matthews how she feels about having her education concluded?"

"I haven't seen the need to." But try as she might, Dorothea was not able to maintain the barricade her will had erected against them. How many times had Sarah enthused over something she had learned, such as the average person being subjected to an atmospheric pressure of 40,000 pounds, or that the literal meaning of the legal term *Habeas Corpus* is "You may have the body"?

"Asking her would serve no purpose anyway." Marie rolled her amber eyes. "She would only tell Madame what she wishes to hear."

"Then we seem to be at an impasse," Dorothea said. "Unless you have any other suggestions."

"I have," Naomi said after a moment. "If you don't wish to send her to college, why not bring the college here?"

Even Marie turned a puzzled look to her. "Here? To this house?"

The cook smiled and shook her head. "Someone qualified to teach on the University level."

Dorothea protested that that was impractical simply because she had never heard of it being done. But wisely, the two gave her opportunity to think instead of taxing her patience with more persuasion. In the end, she shrugged. "I suppose if we don't give her something to do, she'll idle away her time with novels and lawn tennis. Mr. Mitchell is stopping by Monday. I'll ask him to look for someone. That is, if Sarah is willing."

"Oh, she will be willing," replied a smiling Marie. "I can assure Madame of that."

"I'll thank you both not to presume yourselves more knowledgeable about my granddaughter's likes and dislikes than I am," Dorothea chided, even while admitting to herself that the maid was probably correct. But it was a wise mistress who reminded her servants of their places now and again.

However, Marie's and Naomi's celebratory smiles suggested that they were well aware of their places.

———

When Sarah's grandmother had mentioned purchasing a "mansion," the picture that attached itself to Sarah's mind was something identical to their own home, tall and relatively narrow. But the next afternoon she marveled that three Berkeley Square town houses could have fit easily into the great stone mansion on Albion Grove in Hampstead.

"Six chimneys." William's awestruck voice came out in smoky vapor, while a bracing end-of-January wind whipped his hair around the brim of his bowler hat. The four stood just inside a walled garden large enough to bear the frolic of hundreds of small feet without danger of trampling the dormant flower beds and vegetable patch.

"I would love to see the kitchen," Naomi breathed, her pert nose pinked.

"The stables," Stanley said with the same reverence.

Sarah returned the wave of the man, presumably the groundskeeper, who had unlocked the front door. Burrowing again into her wool cloak, she said, "A fireplace would suit me." Actually, she was far more eager to pay the call upon Mrs. Forsyth than to tour the house. Judging from the outside, it would more than suit the needs of the orphanage. But she had to consider her companions' wishes. And so she nudged them toward the door. "We'll stay warmer if we walk quickly."

Some two hours later Sarah was staring out the coach window as it labored down Oxford Street, clogged with vehicles and horses. "Why can't people stay home this time of day?" she muttered, for window lights were beginning to show through the fog.

"The ones behind us may be asking the same thing," William told her.

She turned. "I'm sure they aren't on so great a mission as we are."

"We'll accomplish our noble mission, Sarah. Why don't you relax?" When he had officially left the ranks of servanthood, Sarah had asked him to cease from addressing her as "Miss Matthews." It seemed silly for friends to be so formal. She wished she could ask the same of Naomi, but there were some rules that Grandmother would never bend.

"Perhaps we should save this for tomorrow after church?" Naomi suggested. "Mrs. Blake will fret if it turns dark on us."

"But we've been to theatre much later than this." Sarah realized even as she spoke that she was rationalizing. Grandmother feared the slums, probably because she was raised in them and was aware of their dangers. She touched the cook's gloved hand and said, reluctantly, "If we haven't reached Drury Lane in a half hour, we'll ask Stanley to turn back. What time is it, William?"

He took out his watch. "Exactly five o'clock."

"I think that's wise," Naomi said.

William, clearly attempting to tease his aunt out of her uneasiness, said, "I believe Mr. Turner took a liking to you, Aunt Naomi.

I noticed he took extra pains to show you every cupboard and rack in the kitchen."

Naomi sent him a composed smile. "He used snuff."

Twenty minutes later the coach turned down Drury Lane. There were still no street-lamps in that north section, and loiterers huddled in darkened doorways in spite of the cold. But Sarah could barely sit still for the excitement. When the coach finally halted in front of Saint Matthew's, she reached for the door handle. But William put his hand over hers.

"I should go first. Just in case."

There was nothing to do but allow him to be the gentleman, and by the time Sarah stepped onto the pavement, Stanley was at William's side. The coachman eyed the trio seated on the pavement in front of the public house, slurring out the song, "John Barleycorn."

Then they sent men with scythes so
    sharp,
To cut him off at knee;
And then poor Johnny Barleycorn,
They served him barb'rously. . . .

"I'll stay with the horses," Stanley said to William as he assisted Naomi from the coach.

Sarah thought it was a good idea, although she could have told him it was the ones who *didn't* sing who were far more dangerous. She stared at the orphanage's sooty facade, so familiar and yet no longer home.

"You know, I was near this spot just a fortnight ago," William was saying. "We received a complaint about a greengrocer adding ground chalk to flour. Gave him a hefty fine and threatened him with prison if it happens again. But I had no idea this was Saint Matthew's."

"They always had trouble keeping signboards," Sarah said. *Will they even remember me?*

A hand rested lightly upon her shoulder. "We should hurry, dear," Naomi told her.

Some minutes after William's knock, Lily Jacobs squinted out at them from the open doorway. Other than the yellow cast of her skin from the lamp in her hand, she appeared the same as when Sarah bid her farewell almost five years ago.

"Lily?" Sarah said, smiling.

"Yes, Miss?"

"It's Sarah. I lived here once."

"Yes? Well, do come in."

As they stepped into the room that was no less frigid than the outdoors, the lack of recognition stung until Sarah reminded herself that hundreds of girls had left Saint Matthew's over the years, and that her name was a common one. But even in the lamplight, with the door closed again behind them, Lily only smiled politely, causing Sarah to wonder, *Have I changed that much?*

"We should ask to see Mrs. Forsyth," Naomi suggested from her side.

"Yes . . . Mrs. Forsyth. May we see her?"

Lily nodded, but before she could turn to limp for the inner door, Sarah said, "Wait, please," and withdrew her left hand from her cloak pocket. Even before she completely pulled off the short wool stocking that kept it warm, recognition flooded the worker's face.

"My word! It's *you!*"

Sarah was seized into an embrace and kissed upon both cheeks—which were by now wet with tears. She heard Naomi sniff beside her.

"The girls are just about to go to supper," Lily said, still gripping Sarah's shoulders. "Of course those your age are gone, but most of the younger ones will remember you. Do come!"

Sarah didn't think Mrs. Forsyth would approve of anything so disruptive before a meal, but in her excitement she followed and beckoned Naomi and William to do the same. The youngest, or at least those old enough to walk, were just forming a queue outside the dining room, along with nine older girls who would help with feeding. All nine left their younger charges to gather around Sarah, peppering her with questions such as "Do you really live in a mansion?" and "Is he your husband?" which caused William to blush and Naomi to smile.

"Young ladies—return to your places at once," came a recognizable voice. The girls scurried away, and Sarah turned to face Mrs. Forsyth. Her face showed signs of aging, the hazel eyes were a little more careworn, but she smiled and said, "You can't imagine how many times I've thought of you over the years."

After introductions, Mrs. Forsyth led the

trio to the schoolroom, still fairly warm from lessons, where they sat on aged benches and talked. The headmistress expressed relief that Sarah was treated so well, and sympathy for the ill health which confined her grandmother to home. "What a comfort you must be to her," she said in a tone that was almost questioning, as if she wished to be reassured that this was indeed so.

"Sarah is the light of her eyes," Naomi was quick to say.

Sarah smiled at her, then turned again to Mrs. Forsyth. "My grandmother would like to give you a house."

"I beg your pardon?"

Warming to the subject, she said, "She's buying a fine old mansion in Hampstead. You should see the garden, and it even has water closets."

"And six fireplaces," William said with a glance at the few dying chunks of coal in the grate.

Sarah had never known the head-mistress to be demonstrative, so she did not expect her to leap to her feet and dance with joy. But neither did she expect the anguish that washed across her face.

"That's not too far away, is it?" Sarah asked.

"Far away?" Mrs. Forsyth was staring absently at the faded portrait of John Wesley next to the chalkboard.

"The air is much more healthful," Naomi offered.

"There are six fireplaces," William repeated.

Cognizance returned to Mrs. Forsyth's face. She gave Sarah a sad smile. "Please thank Mrs. Blake for such a generous offer. But I'm afraid we cannot accept it."

"But—"

"I'm sorry, Sarah."

She did not offer a reason why, and her voice was firm. Sarah had known her long enough to realize that she would not be swayed. With a heavy heart she rose from the bench and nodded at William's suggestion that they return to Berkeley Square as soon as feasible.

The dining room was filled with older girls, save the nine who had dined earlier. Those who resided in the home when Sarah left in 1870 still remembered her, despite the age difference. Her spirits lightened as she exchanged swift greetings from table to table. Mrs. Kettner and Mrs. Abbot caught her up in fierce embraces, as did Miss Woodward in the nursery. She left promising to return one day and turned from the coach to wave at Mrs. Forsyth in the glow of the doorway.

Her mood became as dark as the lane that Gypsy and Dudley traveled, more swiftly now that most Londoners were at their supper tables. William and Naomi gave her sympathetic looks, but she was grateful that they did not attempt to cheer her. The surprise she had so looked forward to presenting was spoiled. Girls would not play games in that beautiful garden and take baths in a real porcelain tub, and there was nothing anyone could say to make any of that better.

❧ Twenty-Eight ❧

Morning mist dampened the gray stones of Drury Lane on Sunday morning. "You'll be careful, won't you?" Lily Jacobs asked from the doorway.

"I'll be careful," Olivia Forsyth looked back to reply. In her twenty-five years at Saint Matthew's, Olivia had only missed three chapel services and then only when illness confined her to bed. As she walked toward the omnibus stop, four blocks south in the much safer theatre section of the Lane, the only affliction she suffered was the heaviness of soul that came from almost five years of self-recrimination. And added now to that mixture was guilt over how this would affect Sarah.

She won't be tossed out into the streets, Olivia reminded herself, stepping around the scatterings of a broken bottle and clutching tighter the frayed wool cloak that was part of her trousseau. If Sarah were indeed the "apple of her eye," surely Mrs. Blake would have the decency not to blame the girl and would offer to help establish her in a position somewhere, perhaps as a governess. If not, there would always be a place for her at Saint Matthew's. But both were far cries from her present lifestyle. Why, the salmon-colored cashmere gown she wore yesterday evening was probably of French design, not sewn together by some factory seamstress.

Will she hate you? Olivia asked herself. Unless the trappings of wealth had changed the girl's character dramatically, Sarah would forgive her with time. That would be worse. Olivia needed rage directed at her just as a fakir needed a hair shirt. How could she have ever talked herself into such grave deception? That her purposes were noble was of no comfort in the wee hours of each morning when guilt pricked at her heart.

At the corner of Berkeley and Piccadilly Streets she stepped down from the omnibus to the chiming of "Gloria Patri" by not-too-distant bells. Mentally she added the words to the tune: *Glory be to the Fa-*

ther . . . But the Scriptures said to lift *holy* hands to God. How she longed for the time when she could do so again.

Oh, Father, if this is not from you, please strike me dead before I get there.

She started walking north, her gloveless hand occasionally moving from the warmth of its pocket to draw tighter the hood of her cloak. Surely by the time she reached her destination, Sarah would have left for church. Ten minutes or so later she looked to her left at Berkeley Square, majestic in spite of its bare trees, and felt a pang of regret for the garden in Hampstead that her girls would never see. *And so you must put it out of your mind*, she thought, hastening her steps. It wasn't meant to be.

A thin woman in servant's black-and-white answered her ring at number 14, panting slightly as if she had just run up or down a staircase. Olivia had no social life beyond Saint Matthew's and therefore no card to present, so she simply identified herself.

"Will you wait here?" the maid asked with a motion toward a settle in the hall. Olivia sat without removing the cloak. It would serve no purpose to do so if Mrs. Blake refused to grant her audience. It could be that she was insulted that the offer of the house was turned down. The maid came again down the staircase and up the corridor, giving her a nervous smile. "Mrs. Blake will see you. May I take your cloak?"

"Thank you." She took it off and handed it over, and even in her troubled state of mind, she managed to be amused at the maid's attempts not to stare at her short hair. She was led to a parlor dressed out in rich colors and presented to the white-haired woman seated in a velvet-upholstered chair. "Mrs. Blake," Olivia said with a respectful incline of the head. "Thank you for seeing me."

"I've little else to do, as you see," the woman said. She nodded toward the chair facing her. "Will you have some tea?"

"No, thank you." Truth was, she had left Saint Matthew's in such haste that she had not taken her morning cup, and her mouth fairly watered at the offer. But she had taken enough from Mrs. Blake, and under false pretenses. It made no difference that a cup of tea cost pittance.

"Then what may I do for you? You've reconsidered the house?"

"No, Mrs. Blake. But your kind offer prompted me to come today." Olivia glanced at the maid, who stood a few feet to the side of her mistress's chair. "May we speak privately?"

"Very well." Mrs. Blake turned to the maid. "You may leave us, Avis."

When the door closed, the woman's pale eyes rested questioningly on Olivia. There was no way to soften the blow, so she had no choice but to confess her crime. She could only pray that Mrs. Blake had the stamina to bear it. "I can no longer live with the iniquity I have borne in my heart for almost five years, Mrs. Blake."

In the silence that followed Mrs. Forsyth's terrible story, Dorothea could only sit with hands clinched. The pain in her joints was nothing to the ache in her chest. Sarah, not Jeremy's daughter? And to learn that she had contributed to her infant granddaughter's death by sending Mary Tomkin away was far worse than the guilt that had plagued her over Sarah's thirteen years in the orphanage.

Eleven years, she thought, recalling the confession she had just heard. Brought in at the apparent age of three by a drunken fisherman, which made the girl actually closer to nineteen years instead of the eighteen they had just celebrated. *No wonder she's so mature for her age.*

"Mrs. Blake?"

"Why did you do it?" Dorothea blinked at her through tears. "For the money?"

"That was part of it. I wish I had it to return to you. But mostly I wanted Sarah to have a better future. I didn't have enough faith to trust God to do that."

"Are you aware that I've established legal guardianship? That she's the primary benefactress of my will?"

Mrs. Forsyth's hazel eyes lowered, her voice barely above a whisper. "I'm sorry. But surely that can be remedied."

"It can. My solicitor is stopping by tomorrow, in fact."

"I just ask . . . please . . . that you not hold Sarah accountable for my misdeeds." The headmistress' hand lifted from the faded blue reticule in her lap. "If I could only go back and undo—"

"But you can't, can you?"

"No. I can't."

Dorothea stared at her visitor. The agony

in her face was familiar—she had seen it in the mirror countless times while grieving over her own failures. What had Naomi said years ago? *"Regret is a hard burden to bear."*

She had every right to be furious with the woman for her willful deception, even to bring this matter to the police. Fraud was still a crime in England, and Saint Matthew's had accepted two hundred pounds from her under false pretense.

But she came here today. And she could have accepted the house and no one would have been the wiser.

A remnant of another conversation with Naomi came to her mind, easily, for Dorothea often reminded herself of it whenever pain or fear struck. *Grace will lead me home.*

Mrs. Forsyth had given her Sarah, who demonstrated more love to her than Jeremy ever had. The act was dishonest, but it had saved a bitter old woman's life. And there was nothing anyone could do to bring her real granddaughter back to life, God keep her tiny soul.

Amazing grace. Dorothea imagined it pouring over herself like a sunbeam. She realized that in her gnarled hands lay the power to keep things just the way they were before Mrs. Forsyth rang her doorbell. Why did anything have to change? Because Sarah was no blood relation? That would have mattered once, but being on the waning end of life made her more reflective about most of the notions she once took for granted.

You gave me a second chance, Father, when you sent that girl here. I'll not fail you . . . or her.

"How many people have you told about this, Mrs. Forsyth?" Dorothea asked.

"Only God," she replied in a flat tone.

"Then do you see any reason why it cannot stay that way?"

The headmistress stared, her expression uncomprehending, then incredulous. "Mrs. Blake . . . are you suggesting you wish to keep Sarah here?"

"I've not much longer to live, and—"

"Oh . . . I'm so sorry . . ."

Dorothea shook her head. "I have reconciled myself to that, Mrs. Forsyth. But had you not sent Sarah here, that would not have been possible, for I spent my days constantly looking inward. Loving her, caring about someone else's needs, and being loved in return has been a tonic to my soul. I think you understand how that is."

"I do." Tears brimmed in the hazel eyes.

"Besides, I *feel* grandmotherly toward her."

"Mrs. Blake, if you could only know—" But Mrs. Forsyth covered her face with her hands and wept silently.

Dorothea wiped her own eyes and at length cleared her throat. "Do you need a handkerchief?"

"No . . . thank you." The woman dug a folded bit of linen from the reticule and swabbed at her face. "Forgive me for becoming so emotional, Mrs. Blake. But you will never know what a burden you've lifted from my shoulders."

Dorothea smiled. "Actually, I believe I do. And now will you lift one from mine?"

"Anything," she replied in the tremulous tone of a soldier taking the oath to defend Crown and country.

"Will you accept that house in Hampstead and make my granddaughter happy again?"

Mrs. Forsyth stared at her, seemingly unable to compose a reply. "*And* my solicitor will see that your coal bills go on my ac-

count. With six fireplaces, you'll need it."
Dorothea cocked a wary eyebrow. "You're
not about to burst into another round of
tears, are you?"

For the first time since entering her parlor, Mrs. Forsyth smiled, wiping her face
again. "I'm actually quite stoic most of the
time. And yes, my dear Mrs. Blake, we will
accept that house *and* the coal." She rose
from the chair and, after a slight hesitation,
bent to press a kiss upon Dorothea's forehead. "What a sweet soul you are."

Sweet, Dorothea thought when she was
gone. No one had ever accused her of
sweetness, even in her best days, but she
found she rather liked it. Later she tried to
keep from wincing while Avis rubbed her
hands with an oil mixture of rosemary and
camphor. Saint George's bells began chiming "The Genevan Psalter," meaning Sarah
would be home soon. She could hardly
wait to tell her about Saint Matthew's and
the house. Mentally she followed the notes.
"Praise God from whom all blessings flow!"

———

The following Saturday after lunch, Sarah
read from the *Daily Telegraph* to Grand-

mother and Marie in the sitting room. It had become a routine as her grandmother's hands could no longer manage the pages, and Marie could speak English far better than she could read it. Sarah perched at the end of the divan because of the bustle to her moss green silk gown and held the newspaper aloft to keep the print from smearing.

Serbian peasants in Herzegovina, unable to pay taxes due to crop failures, revolted again against the Ottoman Empire in a series of uprisings. . . .

A faint knock sounded at the door and it eased open. Sarah lowered the newspaper long enough to smile at William, who motioned her to continue. But Grandmother shook her head. "I don't want to hear any more news about fighting."

"I do not like it either," Marie murmured over her needlepoint.

Sarah wondered if she was thinking about France's humiliation by Prussia only four years ago.

Grandmother turned her head to where William still stood just inside the doorway. "Well, don't just stand there eavesdropping, William. Come sit here and cheer us."

He advanced toward Grandmother's chair, and Sarah noticed how nice he looked in his dark gray tweed suit and knotted cravat of midnight blue.

After leaning to take up Grandmother's hand gently and kiss it, he said, "And how can I possibly cheer you, Mrs. Blake? I can't sing or dance."

He was teasing, for he knew exactly what she was after. Marie knew as well, for her face wore a little smile while he settled into the chair next to hers.

"Well?" Grandmother prompted.

William sent a pointed glance toward the door as if about to divulge state secrets, when actually he had confided to Sarah that he was at liberty to share the commission's findings except for those involved in current court cases. "This week we fined a canning company and destroyed their stock of pickles for coloring them with copper salts."

"Pickles." Disappointment colored Grandmother's tone just as the copper colored the pickles, but her chin dipped into a polite nod. "And you threw them out, you say?"

"Copper is a poison. The owner faces prison if we catch them at it again." He withdrew a blue bottle from his coat pocket. *"And . . .* we put the makers of Filby's Pyretic Saline out of business for selling salt water."

"But salt water isn't harmful," Sarah told him.

"No, but at six shillings a bottle, it's highway robbery. Especially with these claims." He turned the bottle and read the label:

"Provides immediate relief for colic, feverish colds, fainting fits, typhus, scarlet fever, jungle fever, lassitude, prickly heat, smallpox, measles, liver complaint, skin eruptions, lumbago, cholera, and various other altered conditions of the blood."

"How absurd!" Grandmother exclaimed, her expression animated again. "And you put them out of business, William?"

"We did indeed. Oh, they'll eventually regroup and find some other means to pick people's pockets."

"But you will go after them again, yes?" Marie asked, the same excitement in her amber eyes.

"Like Hannibal after Scipio," William assured her.

Both women chuckled over that, and then Grandmother said, "You've indulged us long enough, William. Where are you and Naomi taking Sarah today?"

William gave Sarah a hopeful look. "Aunt Naomi is upstairs changing, so I've not asked her opinion . . . but The Polytechnic Institution just added a diving bell and water tank."

"I'd like to see that," Sarah said.

"There, it's settled," Grandmother told him. "For you know your aunt will be nothing but obliging."

"You say a bell for under the water?" Marie said with brow furrowed. "What is so special about that? Who would hear it?"

Sarah excused herself that moment to fetch her coat, hat, and gloves from upstairs, leaving William to explain to Marie. She returned to kiss her grandmother's cheek and promise, as always, to be careful. Naomi, lovely in her sapphire blue gown, met her and William outside the door. As the coach rumbled east toward Cavendish Square, Sarah asked, "What will you tell them if a week passes with no fraud to report?"

"Unfortunately, we're backlogged as it is," William replied. "It's a wonder that we're allowed half-Saturdays."

"But you still enjoy your work, don't you?" Naomi asked from Sarah's left.

"I do, Aunt Naomi." His dark eyes lit. "Why, I almost equate us with Scotland Yard. We try to protect the public from thieves and even poisoners who would feed them copper to save a quid or two. Quite fulfilling, especially when it's the poor who suffer the most from their hands. They'll pay for some miracle tonic when they can't afford a doctor."

He winced. "There, I've gone on and on about it again."

"Oh, but we love to hear it," Naomi assured him.

Sarah nodded agreement. Her heart felt a stirring of pride, not so much for the Commission but for dear William, that he was using the education for which he had labored so hard to serve others. She was about to tell him so, when he changed the subject.

"Aunt Naomi tells me you're to have another tutor."

"I only hope Mr. Mitchell finds someone soon. I can feel my mind beginning to rust."

"Mr. Colby's been gone for how long?" Naomi wore a little smile. "Three days?"

"Let's just hope your new tutor has no interest in scaling mountains," William said.

———

The gunmetal gray diving bell was the size of a small coach, and the threesome watched as it was lowered into and raised from a metal tank by a series of pulleys and a ship's capstan cranked by two burly men. William could hardly be more fascinated if it were the fictitious *Nautilus*. For a steep half-sovereign each, two people at a time could take a five-minute submerge. Or at least two *males*, for the narrow hatch and ladder would not accommodate skirts and bustles.

"Go ahead, William," Naomi urged when he looked longingly at the queue. A dozen men and boys waited, even at that price. "We can amuse ourselves without you."

"Grandmother always says to spare no expense," Sarah reminded him.

William shook his head. Any side activity that did not include Sarah was something he should pay for himself. *A whole half-sovereign?*

He was teetering between practicality and desire, and his aunt was able to nudge him into desire with no effort by simply asking, "How often in a lifetime does a person get to do something like this, William?"

"Very well. If you don't mind looking about without me." The corner of his eye caught sight of a fairly large group of males striding in the direction of the queue. Before hastening away, he gave them a grateful smile and said, "But I'm paying my own way."

The young man at the end watched him all the way over and grinned when William took his place—just seconds before the group fell in behind him. "Well, if it isn't Mr. Doyle! Fancy meeting you here!"

William recognized the drawl, with its studied mixture of boredom and sophistication. "Lord Holt," he said and shook the proffered gloved hand. Lord Holt's face had taken him aback, for gone were the auburn side-whiskers, replaced by a narrow mustache. He was as elegantly attired as from

Oxford days, from his top hat's silk sheen to his black wool suit's fine weave to the fine gloss of his Hessian boots.

"Not as good a shine as yours, old chap," the young lord chuckled when William glanced down at the boots. "Remember how we would advise you to give up books and open a boot-polishing stand?"

William's jaw tightened. He had to stifle the impulse to mention his Commission work. Besides, labor did not impress men such as Lord Holt. They went to Oxford only to learn to be gentlemen or to follow in the footsteps of their fathers.

The man in front of Lord Holt, dressed equally as fine, turned to send William a quick appraising glance. He seemed much younger than Lord Holt, but clearly the two were acquainted, for they exchanged amused smiles before he resumed reading a brochure. The message was as clear as if they had spoken it: This person in the cheap tweed suit wasn't worth introducing.

Mentally William kicked himself for not taking notice of who stood at the end of the queue before joining it. He thought of excusing himself with the pretense of needing to find a drink of water, but with so many now standing behind him, he didn't want to keep Aunt Naomi and Sarah waiting any longer than necessary. Nor could he make himself abandon the idea of going under-water.

Lord Holt was still watching him, so out of courtesy and awkwardness he nodded toward the diving bell and said, "Impressive, isn't it?"

"I suppose," Lord Holt drawled, hands in his pockets. "My cousin Clive dragged me here. He's from Yorkshire and is determined to see everything in London in three days. But speaking of impressive, who was that striking lady with you?"

"There were two striking ladies with me," William replied evasively, though he suspected he knew of whom he referred.

"Indeed. But the younger. Don't tell me you've gotten yourself married."

"No, but I—" William stopped, repulsed by the interest now showing in the same blue eyes that had attached themselves to such things as the interior of every George Street brothel and the French cards he passed around for leers and snickers. *This isn't Oxford*, he reminded himself. *And you're not a servitor anymore.* Just because a member of the leisure class asked a question did not obligate him to answer. And so with polite bluntness he said, "I would rather not discuss either lady, if you please."

At first Lord Holt stared as if he could not believe his ears. Then a sneer curled his mustached lip. "Just making conversation, Doyle." He turned his back to William and leaned forward slightly to murmur to his cousin. William's ears burned. But now he was more determined than ever to stay in queue, it becoming a matter of pride not to slink away from their ridicule.

When only a half dozen stood ahead of him, a remarkable thing happened. Lord Holt, who had ignored him for the past half hour, turned a penitent face to him.

"Beastly rude of me to get your goat like that, old chap. I've been put out at Clive all day and took it out on you."

The apology was so disarming that William smiled and took the hand he offered again. "I shouldn't have been so short with you."

Lord Holt smiled and jabbed a thumb in the direction of the bell, just rising from the tank with water pouring from its metal exterior. "I'm just hoping it doesn't decide to spring a leak when I'm in there."

"There's faint chance of that. But at least you won't be on the ocean floor."

The young lord chuckled appreciatively. Though memories of the man's Oxford misdeeds were too fresh for William to desire ever to see him again, it was a relief to shed the ill feelings he had worn for the past thirty minutes.

They exchanged waves when Lord Holt stood on the platform with his cousin, waiting for the current occupants to exit the bell. William even chuckled as the young man, just before descending through the round hatch, made a big show of holding his nose.

A worker atop the platform sealed the hatch, and it was lowered with a ratcheting of chains and pulleys. William handed his half-sovereign to a man at the foot of the ladder and was ushered up as soon as the two who had preceded Lord Holt and his cousin reached the bottom.

"Remarkable!" Lord Holt said on the platform some six minutes later. Clive even made an enthusiastic nod.

William forgot all about them as he stepped down into an interior as cool as a cavern. A gentleman of about forty followed. They folded themselves side by side on a metal bench to look out the round window, and a shiver ran through William as the hatch was sealed. After a second of disorientating motion, the bell began its descent, water lapped against the window until the glass was covered.

"What a bore," the gentleman said, for all that was visible was the tank's inside wall.

William's mind carried him beyond the wall, down to the deepest explored depths of the sea. *The best half-quid I've ever spent!*

Ten minutes later, he hurried past exhibits of working machinery and spotted Sarah and his aunt near a demonstration of pressure-cooking methods of canning foods. They were not alone. Sarah noticed him first and smiled. Lord Holt, his side to William, turned and brightened as if greeting his fondest friend.

"There you are, good chap! I took the liberty of informing these charming ladies that you were diving and would be by very shortly. Can you believe, my cousin is in queue for another turn?"

"Indeed." Especially grating to William's nerves were Aunt Naomi's and Sarah's unsuspecting smiles. Sarah had youth as an excuse, but his aunt knew that women shouldn't chat with strange men without being properly introduced. "We must be off now, so . . ."

"Lord Holt was just telling us you were friends at Lincoln College," Aunt Naomi said as if not having even noticed she was interrupting.

E tu Bruté? William thought. "Well, we lived in the same staircase."

"I'm not in the habit of approaching unescorted ladies, old chap," Lord Holt explained, nonplused, "but as I had noticed the three of you together earlier . . ."

"It was very thoughtful of you," Sarah told him, green eyes warm.

"You are too kind, Miss Matthews. And if you won't think me terribly presumptive, I'm often in Berkeley Square on errands of mercy. . . ." He made a theatrical pause, just long enough for concern to enter both female faces, then raised his brows impishly. "Mother is terribly partial to GUNTER'S ices, you see."

Sarah smiled as if he had said the cleverest thing, while William wanted to growl, *Can't you tell by looking at him that he's never run an errand in his life? He wouldn't even hang his own towels!*

He could bear it no longer. While the temple in his vein pulsed, he said, "I'm sure your cousin would appreciate your company."

"William?" Aunt Naomi's hand touched his wrist.

As he had in the queue, the man gaped at him. "If I've said something to offend—"

"It's what you've *done* in the past."

Lord Holt turned to Sarah. "I assure you, Miss Matthews, that I've no idea what he means. Gossip was rife at Lincoln, especially against those with titles."

"William doesn't lie," she said, frankness replacing the warmth in her expression. "Please leave us now."

The man's eyes shot daggers at William. But he nodded at the women and pivoted on the heel of his polished Hessians. Aunt Naomi and Sarah watched his retreat for a second or two, then turned again to William.

"This is my fault," Aunt Naomi said. "He seemed so amiable. . . ."

"He's not lacking in charm, Aunt Naomi," William told her. "But trust me, he was the basest sort of scoundrel at Lincoln." And then his anger cooled enough for him to realize how surprised and pleased he was that Sarah would take his word with so little explanation. "You do still believe me, don't you?" he could not help but ask her.

"Of course." She smiled at him, her face filled with trust. "I know you would never lie to me, William."

I would die for you, Sarah, was the first thought that entered his mind.

⚜ *Twenty-Nine* ⚜

Eleven days later on the seventeenth of February, Sarah stood at the sitting room window looking out past streamlets of water running down the glass. The occasional unfortunate pedestrian passed by, always a man with his head swallowed by an angled umbrella. Beyond the gray curtain of rain stretched out an even grayer Berkeley Square, not yet showing evidence of the approaching spring.

She wondered if the rain was also reaching Saint Matthew's. If so, the girls would have already set out pots under the leaking roof. *But not for much longer*, she told herself, smiling at the thought. Grandmother refused to disclose exactly how she had convinced the headmistress to change her mind. Still, Sarah was impressed to be related to the one person in England whose will was stronger than Mrs. Forsyth's.

A team of horses and a coach seemed to

slow down just in front of the house. But the driver did not look her way as it passed on by, just sat with his head drawn into his Macintosh as much as possible, like a tortoise halfway burrowed into its shell. Sarah looked back and read nine-thirty on the chimneypiece clock. Thirty minutes late. Yet how could she fault him when the deluge had prevented Naomi and Mrs. Bacon from attending their charity sewing meeting?

He'll be here sooner or later, she reminded herself. Days from now she would not be standing at that same window, anxious to meet the person who would lead her into the realm of higher education *if* he passed Grandmother's interview. Less than five minutes later her pulse gave a little jump at sight of the hackney cab stopping, another Macintosh man at the reins. An umbrella sprang open just outside the hood and then bobbed as the legs and torso visible beneath it stepped down to the pavement. The man paused to shout something to the driver before advancing upon the steps. Sarah hastened out of the room to the door and opened it before he could ring.

"Whew!" the man, his back to her, was saying from the cover of the porch. He was snapping the umbrella open and shut rapidly to shake off the water. When he turned, their eyes met. His posture seemed to go rigid.

"Forgive me for startling you, sir," Sarah told him, realizing that the rain had muffled the sound of the door.

"Ah—not at all."

He had an oval, clean-shaven face with trim side-whiskers. She had expected someone at least as old as Mr. Duffy, but he was more Stanley's age. And the intensity of his gray-green eyes gave her discomfort. He seemed to notice and shifted his attention to the number on the open door. "This is the residence of Mrs. Arthur Blake?"

"Yes, it is."

"Terribly sorry about the hour, but I almost despaired of ever hailing a cab." His eyes flicked over her navy dress with red and gold trim. "You're not the housekeeper, are you?"

"No, sir." She understood now why he had studied her. And as the cold damp air pouring into the house was bad for Grandmother, she said, "Please, come inside."

He thanked her and stepped across the threshold. Taking his folded umbrella, she pushed it into the brass stand. When she straightened again she remembered she had not yet introduced herself. "I'm Sarah Matthews."

"My name is James Rayborn," he said with a smile and little bow. "And I'm delighted to make your acquaintance, Miss Matthews."

———

William shook the rain from his umbrella on the portico of the Middle Temple. There was nothing he could do about the wool trousers clinging to his calves from dashing through puddles he could not see for the rain. Fortunately, the satchel containing his papers was dry. His ring was answered straightaway by a young white-gloved manservant who took his umbrella and nodded approvingly while William dried his boots as much as possible on the entrance rug.

This was his third visit to the Inn, which contained offices and housing for attorneys and senior lawyers, so William knew to open the door himself to the second-storey apartment. In the outer office Mr. Howitt's secretary turned from the top drawer of a filing cabinet and peered at him through spectacles twice as thick as Mrs. Bacon's. "Mr. Doyle," he greeted. "Mr. Howitt is expecting you. Please do go on in."

William shot a panicked glance toward the wall clock.

"You're not late," the man reassured him, then lowered his voice. "Until I locate the Burnet file, he has nothing to do but twiddle his thumbs."

Still, William opened the inner office door with apologetic carefulness. Behind a massive oak desk, Mr. Howitt looked up from a stack of papers. "Come in and have a seat, Mr. Doyle." And before William could close the door behind himself, the man called out, "And I would have Mr. Allen know that I do not twiddle my thumbs!"

William smiled and took the armchair facing the desk. He opened the worn satchel he had carried off to Oxford—which today had miraculously stayed shut through all the jostling—and thought how grateful he was that his first exposure to the legal side of his profession was with someone so down-to-earth.

"Will the rain ever let up?" the attorney asked, throwing a glance at the bespattered window behind his shoulder.

"I don't know, sir." His calves flinched against soaked wool as he rose to hand the file containing his laboratory findings across the desk. "I believe I found every puddle from our office to the Inn."

Mr. Howitt chuckled affably. He was young for someone in his position, probably not yet forty, with thick facial features and blue eyes quick to fill with gaiety at his own witticisms or with indignation at the cases William brought before him. Cases such as today's evidence against Webber's Pills, guaranteed to cure gout and rheumatism "in thirty days," which were discovered to be nothing more than a mixture of morphine and opium.

"And so the unfortunate user is addicted before the thirty days are over," Mr. Howitt muttered. "And obviously the fine did no good."

"They're making too much money. They simply waited six months, moved from Holborn Viaduct to Lambeth Road, and changed the name from 'Webb's.'"

"Webb's to Webber's? At least they could have used a little more imagination. Well, I'll be meeting with Mr. Bailey this afternoon."

Mr. Bailey was the sergeant who presented the cases in court, but as the Commission could not engage the services of a barrister or sergeant directly, Mr. Howitt took care of that, as well as the required paperwork. William watched him pen notes and thought about how nice it would be if Aunt Naomi would meet someone like him. He was probably not married, as he lodged here at the Inn. He showed no sign of being fond of snuff. That he was not particularly handsome would be the last thing to concern Aunt Naomi.

And he doesn't seem the type who would look down his nose at a servant. Especially if he were to meet one such as Aunt Naomi. But how did a person go about introducing people from two totally different walks of life? Especially when one was his aunt, certain to balk at any attempt of his to matchmake.

He realized he was rudely staring and that Mr. Howitt was staring back with an odd look. Before William could explain himself, the attorney said, "Before I forget to ask, Mr. Doyle, was that you I spotted in a box at the *Prince of Wales* on Saturday past?"

Thank you, God, William prayed under his breath. A discussion about the production of *Prayer in the Storm* would surely lead to Mr. Howitt inquiring about the two lovely women in the same box. "Did you enjoy the play?" William asked.

"Very much. But then, I've loved theatre since I was a small boy."

"Really?" *Aunt Naomi, you're going to meet this man if it's the last thing I do!*

"Oh yes. I would have gone into acting had my father allowed it."

"I'm sorry."

"Oh, but don't be. The law's a good living." He gave William a chummy wink. "But you don't get to rub elbows with beautiful actresses. I would give my last guinea for a tumble with the likes of Genevieve Ward."

William was unable to hide the shock on his face, and Mr. Howitt's smile vanished. "I've embarrassed you."

"No, it's just, well . . ." William stammered for wont of anything else to say.

"Forgive me—I forgot how young you are."

"I'm fine, really." He smiled just to prove it, then nodded toward the file on the desk. "May we return to the case now, sir? I shouldn't take up too much of your time."

His vexation when he left the Inn thirty

minutes later was not at Mr. Howitt but himself. What mattered most to Aunt Naomi was not wit, nor theatre, nor a sociable personality, but Christian morality. And that had not even entered his mind.

Having decided that the presence of a certain physical basis or peculiar form of matter is essential to the manifestation of vital phenomena, we may next pass on to consider whether organization, or the presence of a certain definite structure, is one of the essential conditions of vitality.

After stabbing the full-stop key to the Remington typewriter, Daniel Rayborn cracked the knuckles of both hands, then stretched back in his chair to work away the catch between his shoulder blades. *You need some tea, old man*, he told himself. In his stockinged feet he carried his empty cup from the parlor to his kitchen, picked up the teapot from the stove, and gave it a gentle swish. Lukewarm tea filled his cup—he decided it was less troublesome to drink it that way than to make a fresh pot, most of which would grow stale anyway. He returned to his parlor desk and looked out the wide sash window. Sunlight glistened off Surrey Street's wet cobblestones. Hooves and wheels splashed through puddles while pedestrians skirted them on the pavement.

There was a former nursery atop the narrow three-storey terrace house that would have made a roomier study, but the windows were too high to peer out of from a deskchair. Just because his chosen occupation required solitude did not mean he had to cloister himself away like a monk in a bell tower. At least he could feel a small part of the stream of humanity by simply lifting his eyes from his work.

An hour later he was reading a stack of mail that included some requested notes from Mr. Lewins, a don at the University of Edinburgh, on the alternation of generations in Hydroid Zoophytes. A knock sounded at his door. It was a rare but welcome sound. This time Daniel fished his shoes from beneath his desk and pulled them on.

"Good afternoon, Daniel!" greeted the man on the porch.

"James!" Daniel stepped out to embrace his younger brother. "Wonderful to see you!"

"And you as well."

"But where is Virginia? And the girls?"

"Oh, still in Malta, packing up the house. I've been here only three days—"

Daniel folded his arms. "*Three* days?"

His brother looked sheepish. "I wanted to wait for the time for a good long visit. Between interviews and house hunting, it's been hectic. I despise the frantic pace of this town, but Virginia wants the children to know their grandparents."

Daniel raised an eyebrow. "And their uncle?"

"*Especially* their uncle," James said, smiling again.

"Well, where are you staying? Because you're more than welcome . . ."

"Thank you, but Virginia's parents insisted I stay with them." He glanced over his shoulder at a waiting coach. "Fetch your hat and coat and take a ride with me, will you?"

"A ride? Where?"

"Oh, I'd rather not say just yet. But trust me, you'll not be disappointed."

Only the shine in the gray-green eyes prevented Daniel from protesting that after four years apart he would rather have a quiet talk than inspect some potential homes for his brother's family. With a stifled sigh he lifted his bowler hat from a stack of books and undraped his overcoat from the back of a chair.

"You still writing that zoology text?" James asked as they sat side by side in the coach, moving along with the light traffic of Surrey Street.

"Finished last year. I'm slogging along on another biology—this time college level."

"Slogging?"

Daniel pulled a gloveless hand from his pocket to show him the calluses on his fingertips. "My publisher wants everything typed now. Horrid instrument with ribbons that tangle incessantly, but he says it makes editing easier. And you? How went your position in Malta?"

"Young Mr. Laurier passed his locals with flying colors and is at Oxford, where he is likely spending his days in riotous living, if he hasn't already been invited to leave by the administration."

"How sad."

The regret that washed across James's face belied his shrug. "You can lead a horse to water and so forth. I did my best,

but the die was cast long before I happened along."

Daniel shook his head. He had spent
nine years lecturing at nearby King's College, University of London, and it saddened
him to hear of any young person throwing
away his life. "Well, then you mustn't fault
yourself. And I've been pleasantly surprised more than once to witness maturity
creep up on such hopeless cases."

James paused, narrowing his eyes in
mock suspicion. "You're including me in
that category, aren't you?"

"You were never hopeless, James."

"Oh, but Mother and Father would have
argued that one, God rest their souls."

"And so you pleasantly surprised them."
The street noises faded into the background as the two indulged in memories of
their shared childhoods and of the years
that James occupied Daniel's guestroom
and studied at King's College. They had
spent many evenings at the table pouring
over subjects that his brother was unable
to grasp in a lecture setting. How gratifying
to now see him devote his life to bringing
education to other seemingly hopeless
cases.

As the conversation continued, there was one topic they avoided discussing so studiously that it seemed to occupy a place between them in the coach. And even after seventeen years, it was a bruise upon Daniel's heart.

It was only when they came to their final stop that Daniel looked out the windows and took notice of his surroundings. To his left stretched a square that must surely be magnificent when the tall trees were in full leaf. To his right, a fine stone mansion joined with others on either side.

"Berkeley Street," his brother said.

"Very impressive," Daniel replied with sinking spirits. James had never been one to pinch pennies, but this was surely more house than he could afford even with the assistance of wealthy in-laws. He angled his head in a vain effort to see all the way up to the roof. "But expensive, wouldn't you think?"

"Expensive? Oh, frightfully so, one would imagine."

Then why are we here? The coachman had not come around to the door yet, so Daniel automatically started to reach for it. He felt a touch upon his shoulder and turned again to his brother, who grinned as if he would burst from having to hold a secret for so long.

"I instructed him to give us time to talk."

Daniel sighed audibly this time. "James, what is this about?"

Still grinning, James glanced past him toward the house. "Something incredible happened today, Daniel. It still gives me the shivers."

"Yes?"

"Two days ago a note from a Mr. Mitchell, a solicitor, was delivered to my in-laws' house, asking that I call at his Cannon Street office as soon as possible. The old fellow and I got along famously—turns out he's Virginia's father's cousin, three or four times removed. He asked me to call on a Mrs. Arthur Blake, who is seeking a tutor for her granddaughter. Is the name familiar to you?"

"Sorry." One of the ironic results of spending most of one's time in academia was an ignorance of practical matters of the world. Daniel had not even heard of the typewriter until his publisher, William Blackwood and Sons, had one delivered to his home. And then there were the five years he spent besotted by drink—it was only God's grace and the small stipend from King's College that saved him from losing his house. "Were you offered the position?"

James nodded. "I asked for time to consider it."

"Why?"

"Because of what I discovered. Your daughter lives here, Daniel." Daniel could only stare at his brother.

"It's her, Daniel! Sarah!" James exclaimed. "Alive and well just beyond that door!"

"But how?" Daniel asked, scarcely able to draw breath.

"I don't quite know that."

"And it's been almost seventeen years. How would you even recognize her?"

"The evidence is overwhelming," James replied. "First, she's almost the mirror image of her mother. I almost fell backward when I first saw her. She has your green eyes, though."

"But you said she was Mrs. Blake's granddaughter."

"Adopted, Daniel. And Mr. Mitchell had already informed me that she spent most of her life in an orphanage."

"An orphanage . . ."

James's voice softened. "She has a crippled hand. Her left hand, Daniel."

"Her left hand?"

"The same, Daniel."

"Then she didn't drown?"

"She didn't drown."

Fear replaced the doubt in Daniel's mind. He had prayed for years for such a miracle. But the hollow spot in his heart was for the two-year-old who sat on his knee and tugged at his beard and addressed him as "Father." How weak was his faith! Had he believed God could save Sarah from the waters that claimed his tormented wife, his mind would have allowed her to age accordingly.

"What should I do?" he asked after a long look through his window at the door.

James rested a hand upon his shoulder. "First, you take some deep breaths. Your hands are shaking."

"They are?" Daniel held them up as if seeing them for the first time. Indeed they trembled, as well as his knees. He drew in some equally shaky breaths that had no effect upon his hands and knees. "Now what?"

"Why, we get out now." James looked wounded that he should even ask. "You have every right to claim your daughter. And the proof she's yours, should Mrs. Blake prove obstinate."

That was so. In a cigar box in Daniel's bureau were three yellowed *London Times* articles. The first, dated August 12, 1858, gave eyewitness accounts from two prostitutes and a bridge sweeper of the unidentified woman who leaped from Waterloo Bridge the night before with a small child in her arms. The article of two days later gave Daniel's name, told of the discovery of Deborah Rayborn's body washed ashore in Woolwich, and mentioned the police speculation that the child's body was presumed to be washed out to sea. The third article told of Deborah's burial in the section of Brompton Cemetery reserved for Dissenters—suicides were not allowed in consecrated grounds—and quoted his father-in-law, who accused Daniel of being a Blackheart who refused to allow his wife to bring their crippled little daughter to see her grandfather.

Mercifully that was all, unless there had been other printed accounts of which

Daniel was unaware. Parliament's transfer of the Indian government from the East India Company to the Crown took up most newspaper space during that time.

Why didn't I look for help? He would not have dreamed of having Deborah confined to Bedlam, but surely in all of England there were places devoted to healing tormented minds. He had lied to himself, hanging on to the false confidence that it was the strain of childbearing that had altered her behavior so radically.

"You did not kill your mother," he must have told Deborah a thousand times, hoping each time reason would take root. "An infant has no control over any complications of birth. It was unspeakably cruel of your father to lay that charge at your feet. And God isn't going to punish you by taking our baby."

It wasn't enough to his wife that she lived through the delivery of her own infant. She could barely look at their daughter, forcing Daniel to hire a nursemaid. The malformed hand, which stirred such pity and tenderness in his heart, was proof to Deborah that her father's curse still hovered over her.

"Daniel?"

Daniel blinked, refocusing his attention on his brother.

"This is too much to absorb, Daniel," James said with an understanding nod. "But Sarah will want to see you."

"She won't even remember me." He glanced again at the magnificent house. What had he for her but a narrow town house, cluttered with stacks of books and papers? Only the twice-weekly efforts of the charwoman kept it from total disaster. Did he have the right to barge into her life and take her from a good situation simply because he would give his right arm to see her and hear her call him "Father" again?

"She's yours, Daniel," James pressed.

"And that obligates me to put her needs ahead of my own. There has been enough harm done to my family because of a father's selfishness."

"And so you'll go on as before?"

"Of course not. But I'll not act rashly." He rubbed his eyes, grateful that James allowed him some space for thought. At length he looked again at his brother. "You said she came from an orphanage. Would you know the location?"

❧ *Thirty* ❧

In Saint Matthew's schoolroom two hours later, Olivia pressed steepled fingertips against her chin and thought about how much better her life had been over the past several days. Mrs. Blake had forgiven her, guilt no longer cast a pall over her prayers, the girls would soon be in a new spacious home, and she slept like an infant again.

And with her now, two brothers waited for explanation, their proof in a cigar box on a child's desk. Newspaper clippings, and even more compelling, the familiar face staring back from a tintype of the Rayborns on their wedding day. The young bride could have been Sarah's twin.

Mrs. Blake had asked her not to tell anyone that Sarah wasn't her granddaughter. *But they already know that.* In fact, they knew enough to fill in the gaps in Sarah's history.

"As you saw by the clippings, it was in

the newspaper," the younger Mr. Rayborn said with faint accusation in his tone.

Olivia gave him a pained smile. "I've not read a newspaper since Coronation, Mr. Rayborn. The fisherman said she lived with them for almost a year, until they could no longer afford to keep her. I did not believe his remark about 'fishing her out of the Thames' because he reeked of gin. Instead, I assumed some relative had pressed the child upon them earlier. Even if I had overheard something about a child in the river, I probably wouldn't have connected two events so many months apart."

"You could have gone to the police—questioned his story."

"Yes, of course." She sighed and wished, truly, that she had. "But most of my girls have obscure backgrounds. They're brought in from doorways and alleys and abandoned warehouses . . . and frankly, until today, no one has ever come around looking for one."

"What's done is done, James," the older Mr. Rayborn said. "And I should have pressured the police not to give up searching. I'm just grateful the fisherman happened to be there. Surely there aren't usually boats out at midnight."

"Eel fishermen," his brother told him. "That's when they go."

"I see." Daniel Rayborn's expression filled with both dread and the need to know the truth as he asked, "Does Sarah remember any of that night?"

"She doesn't." Olivia watched the relief cross his face and thought how, in spite of the stir this was sure to cause, it was good to know that Sarah had once had a home and at least a father who loved her. So many of her girls' pasts were blank pages. And he did resemble Sarah, faintly, or at least he had the same straight nose and green eyes. He seemed just a bit older than forty, his close-cropped light brown hair sprinkled with some gray that had not yet crept down into the trim beard.

"She was fair, like her mother," he said, as if reading her mind.

She gave him a sad smile. "What will you do?"

"James says this Mrs. Blake is very protective of her. I don't want to disrupt her life. Yet I can't *not* see her. And I can't help but think she might wonder about from where she came."

"She doesn't," Olivia said in a dry voice. It was time to confess all. The two men listened, Sarah's father's tall frame leaning forward on the short bench. Their faces betrayed misgivings concerning her character, and she longed to blurt out, *But aside from this, I've actually striven to live my life with integrity!*

When she was finished, the older Mr. Rayborn rubbed his eyes. His brother said with more question than statement in his voice, "Yet Mrs. Blake doesn't want Sarah to know they're not related."

"She's dying. And she draws great comfort from having Sarah think of her as a grandmother. In a way, I think she's also trying to make amends for the actual granddaughter's death." She turned again to Sarah's father. "You have suffered terribly, and I've no right to ask you this. But please . . . if you would wait just a little while longer—you'll have the rest of your life to be Sarah's father again. Mrs. Blake may not last the year."

"You can't be serious," the brother said.

Sarah's father blew out his cheeks. "I

don't know if I can do that. And even if I
could, it would be grossly unethical, standing aside until my daughter inherits a
fortune . . . then popping up into the
landscape."

Olivia explained that Mrs. Blake already
intended to leave the bulk of her money to
Sarah, in spite of their lack of family ties.
She could not tell from his expression if
that made any difference. An idea came to
her. "Her solicitor is a Mr. Mitchell. He's
called here twice concerning a house Mrs.
Blake is donating to the children and obviously has her best interests at heart."

"I've actually met him," said the younger
Mr. Rayborn. To his brother, he said, "He
struck me as a conscientious fellow."

"He could settle your legal and ethical
questions," Olivia told him. "Please at least
speak with him before you do anything
else."

She was relieved when Sarah's father
agreed to do so. Olivia walked with them
through the entrance parlor, useless in winter for lack of heat, and watched them button overcoats. The elder Mr. Rayborn
pulled gloves from his pocket but held

them in one hand and turned to her. She offered her hand and said, "Will you ever be able to forgive me, Mr. Rayborn?"

"Yes, of course." He took her hand and smiled. "My brother and I had God-fearing parents, and I've tried to live the same way. Yet I spent five years besotted with alcohol and self-pity, even cursing God. We all do things we regret."

Barely able to look at the understanding in his green eyes, Olivia whispered, "Thank you."

"It is I who must thank you, Mrs. Forsyth. For your compassion for my daughter, something even her own mother couldn't give her."

After the two bade her farewell and left, Olivia moved her hand from the knob and turned at the sound of the inner door opening.

"Beggin' your pardon, Mrs. Forsyth, but the sink pipes are frozen again, and—" Lily Jacobs stopped and cocked her head. "Is something wrong?"

"No, not at all." Olivia brushed fingertips across her eyes and started across the tiny frigid room. Smiling at the bemused face before her, she said, "Is there anything sweeter than forgiveness, Lily?"

"It's about time yer got here!" was how the driver greeted Daniel and James at the hansom. "It's cold as a carp, and I've had to fend off beggars the whole time!"

"We'll throw in a crown for your trouble," James assured him.

As the suddenly more agreeable driver snapped the reins, Daniel watched Saint Matthew's dreary facade until it was no longer in his line of vision. "Hard to believe she lived here for so long," he said, then turned to James on his right. "But, you know, perhaps it was better than with an insane mother. I wore such blinders back then, always so sure she would eventually warm up to her child."

"You loved her."

"Yes." Daniel smiled. "And there were some happy times."

"I remember."

They rode in silence up the Strand, Daniel wrapped in memories. In the kitchen, where they sat over a fresh pot of tea and tin of Huntley & Palmer's Lemon

Biscuits, James asked, "Will you really speak with Mr. Mitchell?"

Daniel had to finish chewing the bite of biscuit he had popped into his mouth. He couldn't believe how ravenous he was. *Nerves*, he thought. "As soon as possible."

He owed this Mrs. Blake something for wanting to be family to his daughter, even while knowing the truth. How could he outright ignore her dying wish?

"I'll go with you," his brother said.

"You will?"

"I'll even send a wire to his office on my way home and fetch you in the morning." James smiled and shrugged. "You might as well do this properly."

That night Daniel labored at his desk until past two in the morning. It would have been pointless to retire until exhaustion muffled all anxious, regretful, and even hopeful thought. He was only cognizant enough, as he lay on his pillow, to thank God again for not turning His back upon him during those days when he shook his fists at heaven, and for allowing James to find his daughter. Then he asked that God would bless those guardian angels who had been put into her life, such as Mrs.

Forsyth and Mrs. Blake, and a gin-soaked eel fisherman.

———

The hammering was coming from somewhere in back of the house. Daniel followed it through the parlor and kitchen and out to his small garden. His father sat on his heels under the pear tree, attaching a leg to a squat three-legged stool. "For little Sarah," he said, smiling up at him.

The hammering sounded again, the image vanished, and Daniel eased his head from his pillow. Another series of knocks came from downstairs. He got up and shrugged into his dressing gown, resentful of the intrusion into his dream, for faintly he could still feel his father's presence.

"What a sight you are!" exclaimed his brother.

Daniel ran fingers through his close-cropped hair. "I worked late."

"Well, some bacon and scotch eggs will wake you," James said, holding a parcel away from his coat, for there were dark circles in the brown paper. "I'll put the kettle on while you dress. Mr. Mitchell is expecting me at ten."

"You?"

His brother grinned. "When you pay by the word, you don't explain. He'll simply assume it concerns the tutoring position."

By quarter of ten they were seated on a leather sofa in a walnut-paneled outer office, while a male secretary's fingers snapped out a steady rhythm of the keys of a Remington typewriter just like Daniel's. Five minutes later a door opened and a graying head stuck out. "Oh, Mr. Rayborn. I thought you might be early. Do come in."

Daniel could see the question in the man's face as he got up to follow. His brother introduced them at the door, and after shaking hands, they were settled onto yet another leather sofa in another walnut-paneled office, while Mr. Mitchell rolled his chair to the front of his desk. He held Daniel's newsclippings and tintype and listened thoughtfully to James's explanation of why they were there.

"Incredible!" he exclaimed when James fell silent. "I need a smoke, if you'll bear with me."

The solicitor handed back Daniel's cigar box and rolled his chair to a small Oriental chest with brass pulls. He took a briar pipe from the holder on top and fished for matches and a tin of Pioneer Tobacco from the top drawer. After lighting it and taking three quick puffs, he sank back in his chair and let from his thin lips a stream of musty-sweet smoke. Then he did a curious thing, taking the stem from his mouth and setting the smoldering pipe back in its holder. "I promised Mrs. Mitchell I would quit. She says its a vulgar habit. But my nerves need a little soothing at the moment."

Returning to the matter at hand, he said, "I can confirm that Mrs. Blake is dying. I sought out her doctor recently when I became concerned about the obvious deterioration of her health. Ordinarily I would not be sharing this information with anyone else, but . . ." He made a helpless gesture.

Daniel nodded. "Have you an opinion on what Mrs. Forsyth asked of me?"

"I join her in urging you to wait," the solicitor said without hesitation. "Though I can appreciate your longing to be with your daughter, Mrs. Blake dotes upon the girl. I've never seen her more content, even through the physical pain."

"This would be an easier decision if she weren't so wealthy."

"I understand. But if it will reassure you . . . after Mrs. Blake told me of Mrs. Forsyth's confession, she drilled me again over the validity of her will. She has always feared that Sarah's illegitimacy—"

Daniel winced. "She's not—"

"Forgive me . . . *presumed* illegitimacy . . . would put a hitch in the inheritance. I assured her that under British law a person with no direct heirs may leave his money to the local street sweeper if so desirous. *And*, once Mrs. Blake is sadly taken from us, you'll have Mrs. Forsyth and the two of us to assure Sarah that you aren't stepping into the picture just because of the inheritance."

"She wouldn't think that of him anyway," James said a little testily.

"I'll be a stranger to her," Daniel reminded him.

Mr. Mitchell smiled, tapping fingertips together. "But you *would* have opportunity to make her acquaintance now and again if young Mr. Rayborn here were to become her tutor. He could keep you informed as to how she's faring. And when the time came to tell her the truth, you wouldn't be strangers."

The suggestion took some of the agony out of having to wait. "That would help," Daniel said.

But James, wearing an enigmatic smile, shook his head. "I've a better idea."

Daniel and the solicitor looked at him. "*You* should be Sarah's tutor."

"Me?"

"Him?" Mr. Mitchell said.

Now it was Daniel who shook his head. "Impossible, James. Staying in the background is one thing. Concealing my identity is quite another."

"Why would you have to conceal it?"

"Well, the newspaper—"

"How many local stories do you recall from seventeen years ago, Daniel? Anyone who happened to read the accounts won't recall the names of the parties . . . in the unlikely event that they remember anything about it at all."

"That sounds reasonable," Mr. Mitchell said, reaching again for his pipe.

Daniel's heart lightened just long enough for practicality to set in. To his brother he said, "I'm not a tutor. And you're the one looking for a position."

"I've other offers to consider, remember?

And wealthy in-laws." James's smile did not diminish, nor did the eagerness in his gray-green eyes. "It's straight out of the pages of Exodus, Daniel! Was it wrong for Moses' mother to hire herself out as a nursemaid for her own child?"

"No, of course not."

"You've lectured whole classrooms at King's, so don't say that you're not a tutor."

"King's College?" Mr. Mitchell said between puffs.

James nodded. "And as to the textbook, you would have evenings and weekends free. And you did mention that typing consumes most of your time. Simply hire someone to do that part."

"Hmm." Mr. Mitchell cocked his head at a reflective angle. "I can't say that you haven't the right to apply to teach your own daughter. Not considering the sacrifice you're making."

Faintly Daniel could still hear the tattoo of typewriter keys. Someone with similar skill could accomplish in one hour what took him four. But at what price? "I'm not sure I could afford—"

Mr. Mitchell took a final puff and replaced

his pipe. "You're forgetting the extra income."

"It wouldn't be a matter of money," Daniel insisted. "You can't very well offer to work for supposed strangers for nothing," James persisted. "That would certainly raise eyebrows. And Mr. Garrett out there . . . with six children and another on the way, he may even be eager to take on the typing."

The idea was beginning to feel more comfortable, even like a gift from God. But to be certain, Daniel asked for time to pray about it.

"But of course." Mr. Mitchell glanced at the pipe but kept his place. "I'll need a couple of days to investigate your background. No offense intended, Mr. Rayborn, but it's standard procedure for everyone who works in that house."

"I understand," Daniel said, raising a hand to ward off his brother's protest. Just because he was Sarah's father and James's brother didn't mean he hadn't just gotten out of prison.

"*And*, Mrs. Blake will want to interview you." Hesitantly, he said, "She has some rather strong opinions. If she turns you down, you won't reconsider your generous gesture . . . will you?"

"No," Daniel responded after needing a moment to think about it—for he was human enough to admit to himself that being turned down would sting. "I'll still consider myself in her debt."

His brother clapped him on the back. "You'll pass the interview just fine. Easy as cake."

That would have reassured him were not some doubt lurking in Mr. Mitchell's hooded face. Daniel had to tell himself that perhaps it was not from misgivings over his brother's optimism, but from longing for the object of his desire . . . smoldering on the Oriental chest.

✣ *Thirty-One* ✣

On Saturday morning, the twentieth of February, Sarah played draughts in the sitting room with her grandmother while Avis cleared away breakfast dishes and Marie worked her needlepoint.

"Are you quite sure you want to move there?" Sarah asked.

"I have a plan," Grandmother murmured, a bony finger pushing a red draughts piece onto an adjacent square. She trusted the leaps, which required picking up the pieces, to Sarah. "Hard to believe . . . before you arrived, I had played draughts only a handful of times in my life."

Marie let out a good-natured snort from her chair by the window. "That is because Madame's *odieuse* friends considered anything but *Quadrille* beneath their dignity."

Grandmother sent her a severe look. "We're not to speak ill of the dead, Marie."

"I do beg Madame's pardon," the lady's

maid said a little more humbly but with no hint of fear. "I did not think about Mrs. Fowler."

"Will you be wanting anything else, mum?" Avis said from the door, the trolley in front of her.

"No, thank you."

The door had barely time to settle behind Avis when it opened again, and Claire came through with the silver card tray. "You've visitors, mum. Vicar Sharp and that new curate."

Sarah carefully put the draughts table to the side and straightened the bow beneath her grandmother's high collar. Three minutes later the vicar and a tall young man he introduced as Ethan Knight occupied separate ends of the divan. Mr. Knight sat with hands spread upon the cushion on each side of him, as if poised to flee if necessary. *Shy*, Sarah thought, recalling a time when this room intimidated her as well. But he had offered a bow and "pleased to make your acquaintance" to Sarah and Grandmother, and even to Marie, who had grown quite protective of Grandmother and no longer slipped out when guests were present unless so ordered.

Sarah also thought him quite handsome. Chiseled into a sun-goldened face were a dignified Roman nose, full lips, and high cheekbones. Straight wheat-colored hair was combed back from a high forehead. These qualities she discovered in bits and pieces, for she found herself possessed of the same shyness. That was why she did not notice right away that the irises of his eyes were not the same color, but one was brown and the other blue.

"Mr. Knight's grandfather was of the cloth, too, may God rest his soul," Vicar Sharp was saying. "And Birmingham's finest pulpiteer, from what I've heard."

"Thank you, sir." The curate had a rich, resonate voice that was perfect for a man who would one day deliver sermons from behind a pulpit.

"And your father?" Grandmother asked carefully.

"He's an engineer, as are my two older brothers. Every Birmingham family is obligated to donate at least one member to the cause of railway construction."

"But what if no one in the family wishes to construct railways?" Marie asked, eyes wide. "How can they make you?"

"Well, you see . . ."

"Mr. Knight is teasing us, Marie." Grandmother turned again to the curate and said with a trace of wistfulness in her voice, "How proud your family must be of you."

The conversation turned to politics and the debate over Prime Minister Disraeli's push for Parliament to purchase shares in the Suez Canal. Mr. Knight's face began to assume a blank look, as if he found it difficult to maintain interest in political matters. *Or perhaps he's exhausted from traveling*, Sarah thought after daring another glance. And she could well understand how draining it was to orient oneself to a new environment.

———

That evening in their usual box at the Adelphi, she told Naomi and William about Mr. Knight's mismatched eyes while they waited for the start of the comedy *Waltz by Arditi*. "The condition is called *helerochroma iridis*," William said. "Only about one in a thousand people has it."

"What was he like?" Naomi asked.

"Rather quiet," Sarah replied. She had started to say *handsome*, but then they might mistakenly get the impression that she had some sort of silly schoolgirl infatuation for a young man she hardly knew.

The following day in church, she saw no sign of Mr. Knight from the pew she shared with Marie—the maid had stopped sitting in the gallery when Grandmother was no longer able to attend. Most servants would have enjoyed this elevated status, but Marie, who was not impressed with the upper classes, took it in stride. Sarah and Marie were moving down the wide aisle at the end of the service—their circumstances of birth separating them from the sea of people with whom they rubbed elbows—when Sarah spotted the curate in the vestibule with Vicar Sharp. When her turn at the door came, she offered her gloved right hand.

"It's good to see you again, Mr. Knight," she said a little shyly.

"Very good to see you, Miss . . ." His words faded, and his handsome face assumed the distracted expression of someone struggling to think in a hurry.

"Matthews," Vicar Sharp inclined his head closer to supply before Sarah could remind him.

"Do forgive me—Miss *Matthews*," he said warmly. She was about to reply that it was understandable that he would need some time to recall so many new names, but he had already released her hand, and his warm smile slid over to Marie and the others waiting behind her.

And so Sarah reminded herself, *He has so many new names to learn*.

On Monday morning, Daniel paused at the wrought-iron fence separating the service entrance of 14 Berkeley Square from the pavement and took three deep steadying breaths. *Father, help me through this*. The prayer calmed him enough to approach the steps, though he could still feel his hands trembling inside his gloves. A matronly looking woman wearing spectacles answered his knock, took his coat, gloves, and hat while asking about the city traffic and whether he was glad that the rain seemed to be gone for a while. Though she appeared only five or so years older than he, she reminded Daniel of his mother so much that he was put a little more at ease.

She ushered him upstairs and, after a soft knock on a door, led him into a parlor furnished with bold colors. He was introduced to Mrs. Blake, who did not remind him of his or anyone else's mother despite her white hair, but rather of a white-wigged judge holding court. Pale blue eyes appraised him with such intensity that he feared some of breakfast's marmalade lurked on his chin or that he had forgotten to fasten some vital part of his suit. The lady's maid, introduced to him as Marie Prewitt, was no less forgiving in her scrutiny. It was all Daniel could do to keep the tea in his cup while questions went on about his church background and education, even whether he indulged in smoking, drinking, or gambling.

"I do not," Daniel replied to the latter three questions.

"Have you ever patronized a brothel, Mr. Rayborn?"

I'm going to kill you, James, he thought. His "easy as cake" remark, surely meant to inspire confidence, had caught him completely off guard. "No, never."

"And you left King's College in 1861 to write textbooks?"

The question would have been so easy to affirm, because there was just enough truth in it to appease his conscience. But his mother's "half a truth is no truth at all" was so ingrained into him that he could do naught but reply, "I was dismissed because of my heavy drinking."

"But you said you did not drink." It was the lady's maid, Miss Prewitt, who spoke this time. Daniel turned his face to her.

"And I don't. Not for the past nine years."

Mrs. Blake, seemingly satisfied that they could ease up a bit, said in a more congenial voice, "May I ask what led you to ruin your lecturing career?"

"My wife's suicide."

There was a second of silence, and then, "Why did she do so?"

"She suffered a mental disorder, Mrs. Blake. Please don't ask me to explain. Surely Mr. Mitchell would not have sent me here if he had found out anything amiss."

"And you could only cope by drinking?" she asked softly.

Finally he could see evidence of the maternal feelings that had drawn her to his daughter. "I welcomed the numbness," he told her.

"I understand. I felt that way for years after my son and husband died. The pain of loss has very sharp edges, hasn't it?"

"It has. I'm very sorry about your husband and son."

"Thank you." She smiled, and all traces of the judge disappeared. "God sent an angel to comfort me, Mr. Rayborn. No doubt He has provided the same for you, or you wouldn't be sitting here today."

"That's so, Mrs. Blake." His parents, brother, neighbors, minister, and the good parishioners at King's College Chapel had kept him from a total slide into despair, even in the days when he was too inebriated to recollect their doing so. And now Sarah!

"The position is yours, if you wish. Mr. Mitchell has discussed wages with you, but he may not have thought to include lunches in the servants' hall."

Mr. Mitchell had only alluded to the wages and not provided a specific amount, but Daniel did not correct her. As long as he could pay Mr. Garrett, who had agreed to do the typing, that was all that mattered.

Mrs. Blake cocked a white eyebrow. "Your brother asked for time to consider the position and then turned it down. You aren't going to do that, are you?"

"I can start today," Daniel replied, his heart dancing in his chest.

"Today?" Mrs. Blake and even the maid chuckled. "Sarah would like that, but tomorrow will be soon enough. I'll send for her now, and you'll see why I drilled you so mercilessly, Mr. Rayborn."

Miss Prewitt rose to pull a bell cord that was answered almost immediately by a thin maid with auburn hair. She was dispatched to fetch Sarah, and when Daniel turned his face from the door, Mrs. Blake was staring at him with renewed scrutiny.

Uh-oh, he thought. Just because Sarah favored her mother physically did not mean he and she shared no family resemblance. James had even mentioned the eyes.

"Your tea, Mr. Rayborn. It's the best you'll find in London. Have you taken even one sip?"

Daniel looked down at the cup and saucer balanced upon his knee as if for the first time and thought it was a wonder that he hadn't spilled it upon himself. Out of politeness he took a sip of the lukewarm tea, which caused both women to smile. This

time he returned their smiles, and Miss Prewitt got up to take his cup and pour him
another.

"It's excellent tea," he said and took two
more sips before the door opened and a
fair-haired young woman came through it.

"Mr. Rayborn," she said, extending a
hand when they were introduced. It was
only then that Daniel realized he had somehow gotten to his feet.

"Miss Matthews." He clasped her hand
as if it were a fragile bird. She looked so
much like her mother, and yet there were
traces of *his* mother in her fine-featured
face. And James had rightly recognized the
green eyes.

You are so good to me, Father, he
breathed. He knew how the Biblical Jacob
must have felt at his first sight of Joseph,
after believing his son to be dead for so
long.

"Tomorrow?" his daughter was saying to
Mrs. Blake, who must have spoken when
he was in a stupor. The girl shrugged at
Daniel and smiled. "I suppose I can wait
one more day."

"Why don't you show Mr. Rayborn the library and the texts you've just com-

pleted?" Mrs. Blake suggested. "And then you may as well introduce him to everyone." To Daniel she said, "Have you time for that, Mr. Rayborn?"

It was like asking a schoolboy if he had time for a game of cricket.

———

On Friday, the twenty-sixth of February, Ethan Knight opened one eye and groaned at the quantity of sunlight slanting through the bedroom window. *Not again!* He threw back the bedclothes, his heart sinking with every "cuckoo" of the parlor clock, a farewell gift from his family's Prussian housekeeper, Mrs. Grundke. *Nine!*

Fifteen minutes later he was tying his cravat while hurrying down the staircase alongside the vicarage carriage house. The upstairs flat, his home for the past week, possibly would never be again after today. Once the Church booted him out, he would be pressured to join the Institution of Mechanical Engineers with his father and brothers. It was either that or the army.

School was no longer available as a refuge—his father had drawn the line after financing five years of minimal effort at Trinity College, Cambridge. That was when Ethan realized with a jolt that he was going to have to work at *something* for the rest of his life. The ministry seemed the easiest path, for hadn't his grandfather made it appear so? Deliver sermons in the pulpit, pay calls to the ailing, and count tithes.

If you haven't botched it all up! he thought on a sprint across the vicarage garden. He bounded up the steps two at a time, and before he could calm himself, he pounded on the door. Mrs. Lambert, the housekeeper, answered his knock. An accusing frown lengthened her narrow face.

"He's in his study, Mr. Knight," she said with a nod over her left shoulder.

Vicar Sharp answered Ethan's quieter knock with a "You may come in." The elderly man sat at his desk with pen in hand, open notebook, Bible, and a jar of ink before him. He continued writing for what seemed an hour but had to be less than a quarter of that time, for Ethan had yet to hear any part of Westminster chimes from the grandfather clock in the parlor next door. Finally Vicar Sharp held his pen over the blotter and looked up at him.

"You missed the morning reading, Mr. Knight."

"Do forgive me, Reverend! I was praying and completely lost track of time." Even as he spoke, his words sickened him. Just because the vicar seemed a bit naive, surely a man of his age and experience would not be so gullible as to believe the same excuse used on Tuesday. *You should have pleaded a headache*, Ethan chided himself. That one would even have the ring of truth, for there was a little stabbing pain behind his eyes from reading John Cleland's *Memoirs of a Woman of Pleasure* by lamplight into the wee hours. He winced inwardly as the aged eyes moved over his face and was on the verge of blurting out that he had overslept and promising it would never happen again when Vicar Sharp smiled.

"Your piety is to be commended, especially in one so young, Mr. Knight. And I myself am in the habit of beginning each day with prayer."

"Ah . . ." He had to clear his throat to cover his surprise. "Yes?"

"But I do not think our Lord meant for us to spend so much time on our knees that we neglect our duties."

He can't be serious, Ethan thought, feeling almost guilty at how easy this was. Vicar Sharp was obviously one of those rare souls who went beyond naiveté into innocence, so pure in heart that he believed only the best about everyone else. With eyes wide and a supreme effort to keep lips from twitching, Ethan asked, "Isn't prayer our most important duty, Reverend?"

"Without question, Mr. Knight."

The older man folded hands upon his open notebook, brow furrowed as if mindful of the gravity of giving the proper counsel. "But as Saint Paul wrote in the book of First Corinthians, 'Let everything be done decently and in order.' There are only a certain number of hours available in the day for making calls. In the evenings we have greater opportunity for lengthy prayer and studying Scripture without having to be mindful of the clock."

"Yes, sir." Ethan gave him a rueful smile. "I've still much to learn, haven't I?"

The vicar actually chuckled. "We all start out green, Mr. Knight. Do continue your morning prayers. But do aim for brevity as well."

"I will, sir. Thank you."

"Very good. And we'll get started, shall we? But wait . . . you've not had breakfast."

"I'm not hungry," Ethan lied. He had been granted a reprieve, but just enough of the morning's panic lingered to make him unwilling to cause any more delay. "May we go ahead and start?"

"Very good! Are you up to going out on your own today?"

"By myself?" He felt his Adam's apple push pass his cravat and wondered if the vicar heard the gulp that practically exploded in his eardrums.

"Lots of elderly people in Mayfair, Mr. Knight, and with winter weather still upon us, quite a few have taken ill. You'll do just fine—Mr. Mumford and I used to divide the duties often."

Bully for Mr. Mumford, Ethan thought.

Vicar Sharp wrote out three names with house numbers on a piece of stationery. "They all live on Maddox Street, so you won't be running all over the place. And if you allow a half hour per call, you'll be back in time for lunch."

Lunch, he thought with a bit more interest.

His first call was to a Mr. Fisher, a white-haired man confined to a luxurious but solitary bedroom. The phthisis that caused a whistle to be sent out with every breath did not prevent him from laboring to tell Ethan about being among the first to ride the Liverpool & Manchester railway when he was a boy. Ethan partially blamed himself, for he happened to mention he came from a family of railway engineers. His self-conscious attempt to break the silence backfired, for Mr. Fisher simply refused to give up.

"Twenty-five . . . miles an . . . hour!"

"Incredible," Ethan told him. "But perhaps you shouldn't be speaking like—"

"I . . . thought . . . we were . . . flying! But . . . this was back . . . in . . ."

"Eighteen-thirty, you already mentioned." *Twice, you mentioned.*

The elderly man nodded. "Eighteen . . . hundred . . . and . . . thirty."

His second visit was with a Mrs. Wright, suffering from dropsy. He stood as close to the bed as politeness allowed, averting his eyes from the grotesquely swollen feet propped upon pillows. "I'm in constant pain, Reverend," the woman told him, eyes watering. "But I'm trying to be strong."

"So sorry," he said and found himself moved enough by her suffering to take her hand. Almost. But he eased a step backward instead. *Surely the vicar wouldn't have sent me here if it were contagious . . . would he?* "I'll certainly pray for you. Do be strong."

"Thank you." She stared at him for a minute and closed her eyes. *Better let her sleep*, Ethan told himself and left the room.

His next call was to a Mrs. Stafford, who showed consideration by falling asleep before he actually rang the bell. All that was required of him was to assume a clergylike posture while listening to the account of the woman's palsy from her daughter-in-law, then promise to pray.

Out on the pavement of Maddox Street again, he took out his pocket watch and discovered he had almost an hour before time to return to the vicarage. *New Bond Street has shops*, he recalled, looking off to the west. A few coins rattled in his pocket—enough to buy something to hold him over until lunch. SIMMONS FINE BAKED GOODS beckoned from across the street soon after he turned the corner from Maddox and headed north. He bought a meat pie from a white-aproned man with dried pastry bits clinging to the hairs of his hand, wolfing half of it down by the time he crossed the street again. He was just about to head back for Maddox when movement at his left caught his eye. His own reflection stared back from the glass of a bow window. Narrowing his eyes, he took a step closer to peer past a display of open and closed parasols. An attractive woman stood behind the counter, reading.

Ethan stepped back a bit to read the gilt letters stenciled in upon the glass at chest level. W & J SANGSTER. His eyes then focused on a hand-printed pasteboard sign propped in the center of the display: *"Offering Every Variety of Sun Shades and Parasols, in Brocades, Glaces, Irish Lace, and China Crape for Fetes or the Promenade, From 7s.6d to 3 Guineas Each and Upwards."*

He realized with a start that the shopgirl was staring curiously at him. Ethan, fully aware of his own good looks, touched the brim of his hat and sent her the smile that had disarmed many a Birmingham lass. She looked for a second longer, then went back to her reading. His pride felt no injury, and in fact he took it as a sign of interest. Just as his arsenal included a boyish smile, many women used coyness in the same manner.

He debated using that same coyness and moving on—to give her several days to wonder if he would return. But he was so terribly lonely, and not for the company of the good vicar and his wife or aged parishioners with their ailments and stories.

A bell overhead tinkled as he walked through the doorway. The shop was tastefully appointed with subdued taupe fabric wallcovering, forest green carpet, and velvet upholstered chairs in muted floral patterns. And to his delight, it lacked patrons at the moment.

"How may I assist you, sir?" the shopgirl asked, neither smiling nor frowning.

She was dressed simply in a white blouse and blue bustled satin skirt, with a matching sash around her narrow waist. Without the glass between them, Ethan realized she was not beautiful. But beauty was overrated in his opinion, even boring. She possessed an interesting face instead, with lips a trifle too narrow and clear cheeks too angular. The eyes were nice, he discovered as he stepped closer to the counter. Dark brown flecked with golden lights like a topaz. So was her reddish-brown hair, flowing up into a chignon so precariously fastened that it appeared one tug of a hairpin could send it tumbling about her full bosom.

Though etiquette did not demand it, Ethan removed his hat. "I'm shopping for ideas for my mother's birthday," he said. After all, there were very few excuses for stepping inside a parasol shop, and this one served double-duty as another weapon in his arsenal. Most women adored men who were sentimental about their mothers—as long as they didn't overdo it.

"And when is her birthday?"

The voice, he noticed, was more polished than he would have expected from a shopgirl. While she maintained a posture of professional courtesy, there was some skepticism in her brown eyes, which suggested she knew exactly why he stood there with hat in hand. *She's older than you*, he told himself. He guessed twenty-six, twenty-seven. That only served to deepen his interest.

"Oh . . . November," he decided it prudent to confess, now that he realized she wasn't quite so young and naive. He allowed a touch of sheepish guilt into his smile, as if he had just toppled a vase by running through his mother's parlor. "I was actually curious about what you're reading."

Professional courtesy abandoned, she leaned elbows on the counter and leveled a bored stare at him. "Don't you mean . . . what I *was* reading?"

"Ouch!" He made an exaggerated wince. "Now I can see why this place isn't overrun with patrons."

"Most patrons are thinking about taking lunch now, if you please. I'll be closing up shop myself in half an—" She stopped, eyes widening. "Your eyes aren't the same color!"

"And *you're* the first to notice," he said with friendly sarcasm. He actually enjoyed his unique eye coloring for the attention it attracted, especially from women.

"I wasn't making sport."

The apology in her tone gave Ethan encouragement. He pressed on. "I took no offense. Now, what would a beautiful woman such as yourself be reading?"

She stared for a second or two longer, then shrugged and pushed an open book across the counter. *On Actors and the Art of Acting* by George H. Lewes.

"It's borrowed, so don't damage it," she warned when he picked it up.

"Wouldn't think of it. You know, that's incredible."

"What?"

"My very first thought when I looked at you through the glass was, 'She should be playing Ophelia instead of selling parasols.' "

Now she actually smirked at him, reaching for the book. "And you should be selling hair tonic on a street corner."

This time Ethan's wince was genuine. "All right, perhaps that didn't come to me straightaway . . . but I'm convinced you'd make a perfect Ophelia, or even Juliet. Why are you here instead of onstage?"

She made a little shrug, her expression softening to the point it almost seemed she would cry. "I've tried . . . studying plays, noticing how patrons speak, even writing their words down sometimes. I've been to at least a dozen casting readings. But I don't dare close up shop every time there's a reading or I'll get sacked."

"Hmm. I see what you mean." He was pleased to discover some stirrings of pity in his heart, proof that he was indeed cut out to be a man of the cloth. The bell jingled into his thoughts. Street noises accompanied a pair of well-dressed women through the doorway. When Ethan turned back to make a little farewell gesture, the shopgirl was already moving around the counter as if they had never spoken. He forced himself to nod politely at the two on his way out— after all, they could be parishioners at Saint George's.

Irritation burned in his chest all the way back to the vicarage, not so much at the patrons but that he had so little control over his time. Like the cuckoo in Mrs. Grundke's clock, he was forced to perform on the hour with others doing the winding.

It won't always be this way, he had to remind himself. As long as he stayed on Vicar Sharp's good side he would eventually be a vicar, with some poor desperate-to-please curate to pay calls for him. He would need only minimal time at study, for his parting gift from his parents was his sainted grand-

father's hand-scripted notebooks containing over forty years of sermons. Ethan felt
no guilt about it. Who was he to attempt to
improve upon what a better man than himself had labored so hard over?

"Did Mr. Fisher tell you about his first ride
on a train?" Vicar Sharp asked over a lunch
of boiled salmon, dressed cucumber, and
mashed potatoes.

Ethan smiled at his table companions,
which included, besides the vicar, Mrs.
Sharp, wearing her comically ill-fitting wig,
and her wigless sister Mrs. Greenoak, visiting for the day. "Fascinating story, wasn't
it!"

"Yes, fascinating." The vicar raised a
friendly eyebrow. "I feel I must warn you
that you'll probably hear it several more
times."

"Not at all," Ethan assured him. "If remembering gives him pleasure, who am I to
begrudge him a little time? I spent many a
boyhood hour sitting at my grandfather's
feet listening to stories of his ministry." Of
truth he was seven when his grandfather
passed away after suffering illness for two
years, and so his few memories of the man
did not go beyond pats on the head and an

occasional penny from his vest pocket. *Not your fault that he died*, he told himself when a little pang of guilt hit him for using a departed family member in a lie. *You would have sat at his feet had he lived longer.*

The women exchanged approving smiles, and Vicar Sharp even got a little misty eyed and expressed the wish that he had a grandson to whom he could pass down his own stories.

"I would love to hear them, sir," Ethan said, hoping that the vicar was not as prone to ramble at his stories as he had been in the pulpit on the previous Sunday. He realized then that he had forgotten to ask the shop assistant's name.

No matter, he thought while basking under the smiles of his lunch companions. *You'll know it soon enough.*

❧ *Thirty-Two* ❧

Bright green leaves were sprouting on Berkeley Square's plane trees by mid-March. As Mr. Rayborn explained, the species, *P. acerifolia,* was perfectly suited to cities because of a high tolerance to atmospheric impurities. "In other words, they're the only living things in London actually *fond* of the fog," he had quipped during a tutoring session.

Sarah liked him very much. Not only did he present facts but compelled her to think logically about them. In the library on Monday morning of the fifteenth, the first subject was British history and, in particular, Queen Anne's reign.

"Would you say that the peace of Utrecht 1713 was more beneficial to Britain or Spain?" he asked from his chair across from her at the oak table.

It took Sarah a full three minutes to compose a reply in her mind. That was another thing she liked about Mr. Rayborn. He had yet to show any sign of impatience, even when she struggled over Latin, which she had never come to appreciate in spite of William's assurance years ago.

"To Britain," she finally said. After three weeks of Mr. Rayborn's tutelage, she knew the next question would be 'Why?' so she went ahead and answered it. "The thirty years of peace allowed us to concentrate on commercial gains overseas, such as Hudson Bay for the fur trade. Also, with Austria taking over Spain's external dominions, there was no more threat of a French occupation of the southern Netherlands."

"And how would that have affected Britain?"

"We would have surely been drawn into another war . . . wouldn't we?"

"Most surely," he said, green eyes warm above his smile as if she had discovered something remarkable instead of simply answering a history question.

She wondered at the traces of wistfulness in his expression now and then, in spite of his good humor. Grandmother had told her of the suicide of his young wife, warning her to avoid speaking of any matter that might bring up any painful memories. But as sad as it was, the death had occurred years and years ago. Did he ever consider finding someone to marry again?

"Miss Matthews?"

Sarah blinked and hoped her expression had not betrayed her thoughts. "I beg your pardon?"

He smiled. "Shall we move on to calculus?"

At half-past eleven they stopped for lunch. They had fallen into a routine—while Sarah joined Grandmother and Marie in the parlor, Mr. Rayborn stayed in the library to pen notes into a notebook for the biology text he was writing. And when her lunch was over, Sarah worked on her daily composition assignment while Mr. Rayborn took his meal in the servants' hall.

Only today Grandmother had to be coaxed into finishing even a third of her stewed mullet, one of her favorite dishes, insisting that she would rather nap. "What if we add just a pinch of salt?" Marie asked. "What Doctor Raine does not know will not hurt him."

Sarah started to protest but then figured a little salt would be better than her grandmother taking in no nourishment. And of truth, she and Marie had had to sprinkle liberal amounts over their own dishes, for the mullet was uncharacteristically bland.

"No. I just want to sleep."

"I think we're finished," Sarah said to Avis when the coaxing proved futile. While Avis cleared the dishes, she and the lady's maid helped Grandmother upstairs.

"We should send for Doctor Raine," Marie said, hovering at Sarah's elbow while she tucked the covers around the frail shoulders.

"No," Grandmother said.

Sarah leaned down to smile at her, running fingers through the soft white hair. "It would reassure us if he had another look at you."

"I don't care to be prodded with those cold instruments today. I'm an old woman, and old women simply get tired."

Unsure of whether to plead with her or accept her wishes, Sarah turned helplessly to Marie. "What do you—?"

"Please," came from the pillow. Sarah turned again. Her grandmother gave both of them a weak smile. "I know that you care for me. But there's so little I can do anymore. At least allow me some say-so over my own person."

There was nothing Sarah could reply to that, and Marie nodded agreement—with one stipulation. "I will sit by your window with my needlepoint. You will not even know I am here."

"Very well," Grandmother sighed.

"I'll fetch it now," Sarah told the lady's maid. After hastening to the parlor and back, she remembered Mr. Rayborn in the library and hoped Avis had thought to tell him that he could go on downstairs. But when she reached the ground storey he was still in there, writing in his notebook.

"I'm sorry, Mr. Rayborn," she said. "We had to put Grandmother to bed, and I forgot all about your lunch."

"Has she taken ill?" he asked with concern on his face.

"Just tired, she says. Naomi will make sure there's some food left for you, but you should hurry before it gets cold."

It didn't even cross my mind to tell him." Avis glanced at the empty space between her and Claire. "Miss Matthews always does, but she and Marie put the missus to bed."

"Is Mrs. Blake all right?" Naomi asked.

"She said she just wanted to nap."

Pushing her chair from the foot of the table, Mrs. Bacon said, "I'd best go see about her. Do go ahead and pray, Mr. Duffy. I'll look in on Mr. Rayborn on the way."

Clinks of silver against china followed Mr. Duffy's "Amen." Presently Stanley, seated at Naomi's right, turned to her. "You know how fond I am of your cooking, Naomi, but the mullet's lacking a little something."

As she brought the fork up to her lips, Naomi tried to recall her steps after dishing out Mrs. Blake's portion. She frowned at the blandness. "Salt."

"That's easily enough mended," Claire said and reached for the saltcellar at her husband's end of the table. Susan took up the one at Mrs. Bacon's end, and both were put to use and then passed on.

"Now that's more like it," Stanley said, chewing. "Fish without salt just ain't natural."

"A gentleman would have kept his lip and allowed Naomi to discover it," Trudy teased.

Avis nodded owlishly. "Mr. Rayborn would have done so." Stanley winked at Naomi and glanced at the door. "Mr. Rayborn would say it was delicious if it was rotten."

"Stanley . . ." Claire warned.

"But he would," Mr. Duffy said, typically taking Stanley's side.

"You shouldn't be gossiping about the man like that when he's not here," Naomi said, though their words were probably true. Mr. Rayborn had yet to rise from the table without complimenting her and Trudy.

"It ain't gossip if it's the truth," Stanley told her.

"It's gossip if you have to look at the door first," Naomi countered.

Mr. Duffy slapped his knee. "She's got you there, Stanley."

"I say we try a little experiment," the groomsman said. "Take away the salt and see what he does."

"And what would that prove?" Claire asked.

"I'll wager he'll sit here and eat it without salt rather than call attention to himself by asking for some."

"That's silly," Avis said. "Besides, Mrs. Bacon will ask about the salt."

"Not if we go ahead and sprinkle some on hers," Trudy said with a conspiratorial light in her eyes.

Naomi couldn't believe her ears. Trudy, who could usually be counted on to take her side, encouraging one of Stanley's little pranks? The scullery maid answered Naomi's puzzled look with a shrug. "Would be fun to find out. It ain't like we'd be ruinin' his food."

Naomi was clearly outvoted, with even Claire looking interested. A cellar was passed to Susan, closest to Mrs. Bacon's end of the table. After the chambermaid carefully sprinkled salt over the house-keeper's plate, Stanley got up and whisked both cellars from the table. He was just walking back out from the kitchen when Mr. Rayborn came through the corridor door-way.

"Please pardon my tardiness," he said.

Stanley clapped him on the shoulder. "We've only started, my good man. But do hurry and dish up a plate. Naomi outdid herself on the stewed mullet."

All eyes followed the tutor from the sideboard as he brought his filled plate to the spot across from Naomi. Mr. Duffy, in an obvious attempt to break the suspicious watchful silence, cleared his throat. "And what did you teach our Miss Matthews this morning, Mr. Rayborn?"

"This morning?" Mr. Rayborn smiled to his left, his mullet-filled fork poised over his plate. "We began with British history, then calculus, Latin, and literature." He took in the forkful, chewed, and swallowed contentedly with not even the slightest change of expression.

"What's calculus?" Trudy asked when another silence threatened.

He was thoughtful before answering, as if trying to put it in terms that a scullery maid would understand. "It's a branch of mathematics—that is, numbers—usually having to do with how things change. For example, you would use it to figure out the speed of a falling body."

"Why?" Avis gaped at him in horror.

Mr. Duffy scratched his chin. "And they wouldn't be bodies until *after* they hit the ground, would they? Providing they fell from high enough to do a person injury."

With a patient smile the tutor replied, "Well, you see—"

"Even then, you can't be sure," Stanley cut in. "I fell out of an oak as a boy, and all it did was bruise me up a bit. Don't know how fast it was, but it seemed like forever. You know, like one of those dreams where everything moves slow?"

Claire nodded. "Except for whatever's chasing you in the dream, yes?"

"I wonder why it's always like that?" Susan asked. "It's as if your feet's stuck in treacle."

"I don't think Mr. Rayborn meant bodies the way we're thinking," Naomi said, resisting the impulse to slip into the kitchen for the salt-cellar.

Mr. Rayborn sent her a smile and addressed Avis again. "I should have explained myself, Miss Seaton. What I meant by 'body' is anything solid. A rock or piece of wood, for example."

Mrs. Bacon returned to tell them that Mrs. Blake apparently was just feeling the effect of age and rheumatism and not in need of Doctor Raine. "Delicious mullet, Naomi," she said after first taste. "But mine could use a wee bit more salt." Her bespectacled eyes scanned the table. "Where . . . ?"

"Allow me," Stanley said, hopping up from his chair and heading for the kitchen. The housekeeper gave Naomi a curious look but accepted without question the saltcellar when he returned and sprinkled a liberal amount with the tiny spoon.

"Anyone else?" she asked.

"Ah, none for me," Avis said, then moved her owlish eyes toward the tutor, who was chewing contentedly. "What about you, Mr. Rayborn?"

He shook his head. "It's perfect as is."

Naomi smiled to herself at the exchange of covert glances. While chairs were being pushed out at the end of the meal, he scraped up the last forkful and said after swallowing, "That was a wonderful meal. Thank you."

"What did I tell you?" Stanley sidled up to murmur to Naomi as the hall emptied. "I believe he's fond of you, Naomi."

"You'd best stop sampling the horses' mash, Stanley," Naomi replied, replacing the lid on the butter crock. "It's obviously fermented."

He chuckled. "We'll just see, won't we?"

That afternoon, she was on her way up to repin the straying curls that were maddeningly tickling her neck when she met Mr. Rayborn on the staircase between the first and second storeys. "Are you leaving now?" she asked, hand on the banister.

"I am," he replied, smiling.

"She's a good student, isn't she?"

"She's a joy to teach."

Naomi was glad he felt that way. While Mr. Colby had seemed conscientious and had surely taught Miss Matthews well, there was an impatience about him that made her wonder if he begrudged the routine and so much time spent indoors. "I can't tell you enough how this house changed for the better when she came here. We all love her dearly."

His expression grew even warmer. "Thank you, Miss Doyle."

It was a curious thing for him to say, with his having been employed only three weeks. And he had to have noticed puzzlement in her expression, for he shrugged a little self-consciously. "I'm thankful to be in the company of people who love children, Miss Doyle. Not everyone does."

"Well, it's their loss then, isn't it?"

"Yes, certainly."

Stanley's little prank in the servants' hall popped into Naomi's mind. "Did you notice *nothing* unusual about the mullet, Mr. Rayborn?"

"Are you wondering why I didn't salt it?"

It was the first time Naomi had detected mischievousness in his green eyes, and she was struck with how they looked somehow familiar, as if she had seen him sometime in the past. "Why, yes," she replied. "You didn't even seem to notice it was bland."

"I heard Mr. Russell outside the door when I stopped to make sure I wasn't barging in during prayer."

"So you were just pretending not to notice!"

"Well, not quite. On my way past the dumbwaiter, I had noticed a tray of used dishes inside and wondered if there might be a saltcellar. There was, and I poured a bit into my hand to add to my mullet at the sideboard."

Naomi pressed fingertips against her smile and imagined what fun it would be to tell Stanley how he had been outwitted. "I'm glad you weren't offended."

"Offended?" He shook his head, sentiment touching his smile.

"God has blessed me, Miss Doyle. It would be an affront to Him to allow myself to go about looking for petty little grudges. Besides, I grew up with a brother who was quite a prankster himself."

Later, as Naomi minced parsley, sweet marjoram, and basil for mock turtle soup, she thought about his statement about being blessed. Marie had told her about his wife's suicide and how he now lived alone. *How good that he still finds things for which to be thankful.*

"It's tender now," Trudy said from the stove, probing down into the pot with a long fork. "Should I turn off the fire?"

"Yes," Naomi agreed. "I'll tend to it when I've finished here. Go ahead and start a bread pudding for tomorrow."

Stanley's words came back to her. She shook her head as if the coachman were still murmuring them in her ear. Mr. Rayborn and she had never even shared a private conversation, save a little while ago on the stairs.

Yet she could not totally dismiss Stanley's speculation. Sometimes her eyes connected with the tutor's at the lunch table. Never was he forward, flirtatious, or bold; nor did he leer at her, yet there seemed in those green eyes an appreciation of her as a woman and not just a servant.

Perhaps she was only imagining it. *You're thirty-seven years old, Naomi*, she reminded herself on her way to the stove. Too old for such thoughts. And besides, picking the meat from a boiled calf's head for mock turtle soup did not lend itself to romantic daydreams.

———

"It's amazing that an artist can capture so much emotion with just a brush and paints."

William spoke in the hushed tone one uses in church, but he, Sarah, and Naomi were touring Parliament instead. The walls of the Peers' Corridor of the House of Lords displayed eight frescoes, the first depicting the parting of Lord and Lady William Russell just before Lord Russell's execution for treason.

"Amazing," Sarah echoed. Just last week she and Mr. Rayborn had discussed the attempted assassination of King Charles II when it came up in her history text. After exhausting all efforts at court on her husband's behalf, Lady Russell took their children to her husband for a blessing, then stayed with him to the last minute, never shedding a tear lest he should become unnerved. "Mr. Rayborn says there was very little evidence he was involved in the plot."

"I wasn't aware of that, Sarah," Naomi said. "But then, our little country school was doing well to teach us long division."

"He said that most of the evidence points to the Duke of Monmouth, the king's illegitimate son." She felt no discomfort using the hated word *illegitimate* to Naomi and William, for they would be the last people to equate it with her own situation. "Even though he was pardoned, he was excluded from the royal court for the rest of his life."

"We should ask Mr. Rayborn along now and then," William said with hands clasped behind his back as he moved on to the second painting, *The Departure of the Pilgrim Fathers*. "He could give us a lot more historical insight."

He turned to smile at Sarah. "That didn't sound the way I intended. You're doing a fine job of it."

"Thank you." Sarah moved with William toward *Speaker Lenthall Asserting the Privileges of the Commons*. Presently she wondered at the silence from behind and turned. Naomi still stared up at the tragic couple in the first fresco, her face wearing the same wistfulness that occasionally crept into Mr. Rayborn's expression.

"Naomi?"

"Such fierce devotion to each other," the cook murmured.

Naomi . . . lonely? It had never occurred to Sarah, at least not since William's return from Oxford. Contentment always had seemed such a part of her nature. But when she looked into the future, did she see herself spending most of her days in Mrs. Blake's kitchen? Did she long for courtship and a husband? Some women, like Marie and Trudy, did not seem to mind not courting, but then, they had no interest in novels. Surely someone who had spent so much time with the likes of the fictitious Messrs. Knightley, Darcy, and Rochester had some romantic yearnings.

Shame on you! Sarah told herself. *So wrapped up in yourself and your studies that you take one of the best people on earth for granted.*

Naomi snapped out of her reverie and turned to smile as if to negate Sarah's self-accusation. "Forgive me—I'm holding you back."

"Not at all, Aunt Naomi," William replied while yet ambling toward the fourth scene. Naomi and Sarah caught up with him, but when they reached the doorway leading into the Central Hall, Naomi paused.

"You know, I would like to look at the paintings a little longer."

"Let me stay with you," Sarah offered, but Naomi shook her head.

"I'll catch up. Now run along."

The vast octagonal hall contained statues of kings, stained-glass windows, and lofty arched doorways giving access to all parts of the building. Visitors with hushed voices stepped over beautiful encaustic tiles spelling out an appropriate *Except the Lord build the House, they labour in vain that build it*. "We may as well plan on staying until closing," William sighed, for ahead in the Commons' Corridor they could see still more frescoes.

"You shouldn't be so impatient with her," Sarah whispered.

He looked surprised. "I didn't intend to be. It's just that if we don't move quickly, we won't see it all before closing."

"Naomi would rather study a few things extensively than rush through a lot of them. When you were away it sometimes took us two or three trips to see all of the same place."

Pausing in front of the statue of George the First, he said, "Are you sorry I came back, Sarah?"

"Sorry?" The injury in his smoke-colored eyes made her feel oddly awkward, so she lightened the moment by plucking at his coat sleeve so that his arm shook. "You know better than that, silly."

His slow smile brought back the old William. "Very well. Let's go back and walk with her. And I'll try to notice more details."

"Just remember . . . quality is usually superior to quantity."

"Now you sound like a chemist."

"Heaven forbid!" She slowed her steps so that they would not reach Naomi too soon. When he had paced his steps accordingly, Sarah dropped her voice again almost to a whisper. "Do you think she's lonely?"

"Lonely?" He glanced toward the entrance to the Peers' Corridor. "We weren't away *that* long."

"I meant for a husband and children and all that."

"I do." His expression said that he had already given this a lot of thought. "But I can't see that changing any time in the near future. Not when she sees practically the same people every day."

Sarah happened to look ahead again. Naomi, just entering the Central Hall, smiled and lifted a hand. They would have to continue their conversation later. And perhaps it was best, Sarah thought, for the very embryo of an idea was forming in her mind.

❧ Thirty-Three ❧

"You won't mind waitin' if I'm not back here before you?" Stanley asked two weeks later on the Sunday following Easter.

"We do not mind." Marie stood with her back to the coach while she discreetly flounced the bustle of her maroon silk gown.

"Where's he going?" Sarah asked, watching him stride toward Saint George's.

Sending a smile in the same direction, Marie replied, "To the gallery."

"Stanley? In church?"

"As one ages, often there is more thought given to the condition of the soul. Stanley has been thinking of his for a while."

"I can't wait to tell Hester." Sarah linked her right arm through Marie's. "She'll be delighted."

"There are few things that do not delight Hester," Marie said, but with gruff affection.

They were halfway to the entrance when two young ladies approached. Sarah recognized Madeline Fowler from passing the family pew every Sunday, though they had never been introduced.

"May we have a word with you, Miss Matthews?"

"Yes, of course," Sarah replied, covering her astonishment with a smile.

Miss Fowler's smile dimpled the freckled cheeks beneath a set of wide brown eyes, dark curls, and pansy-colored satin bonnet. Her auburn-haired companion was not quite so attractive, for her slack jaw caused her lips to gap, something Mrs. Forsyth would have corrected had the girl spent but one day at Saint Matthew's.

"Oh . . . do forgive me." Miss Fowler rolled her eyes prettily. "May I introduce Miss Welsh, who has been my dearest friend ever since the most horrid year in finishing school that you can imagine!"

"I'm pleased to make your acquaintance," Sarah said but could not offer her hand for Marie's tightening grip upon her arm. "And this is Miss Prewitt."

The two murmured "how do you do's" and did not seem offended when Marie only nodded in reply. "Oh dear . . . we should hurry," Miss Fowler said after a glance at the worshipers filing through the church doors. "Miss Welsh and I are newly sworn members of the WCOS—"

"The Women's Charitable Organization Society," interrupted Miss Welsh, who allowed her jaw to resume its relaxed state afterward.

Miss Fowler nodded. "We're selling tickets for a benefit luncheon at the Grand Hotel on next Thursday. Whoever sells the most wins a pair of pearl earrings, and my papa agreed . . ." Her hands clasped together at her bosom for enraptured emphasis. ". . . *finally*, that if I so happen to win, I may have my ears pierced!"

"Mine were pierced last summer, so I'm giving my sales over to Miss Fowler," Miss Welsh said, as if assuming Sarah and Marie were wondering.

"They're a half-sovereign each," Miss Fowler said, then giggled. "The tickets, not the earrings."

Sarah realized that her smile had become stiff, and her head was bobbing like a wind-up toy. She stopped and relaxed her face. "I'm sorry, but I've only my tithe with me," she said, a little sickened at herself for being so grateful for the attention. The grip on her arm tightened even more, as if Marie feared she would end up offering the tithe from her reticule anyway. "But if you'll stop by the house, I'll purchase . . . four?"

It's for charity, she told herself to try to take out some of the sting of being used. At least charity would claim what was left after meals and pearl earrings were purchased.

"Thank you ever so much!" Miss Fowler said, beaming. "I'll send our footman, Taylor, over with the tickets tomorrow morning, if I may. Do tell Mrs. Blake I asked about her health." She did not wait for a reply but took her friend by the hand and pulled her toward a trio of older women walking nearby.

"But she did *not* ask about Madame's health," Marie grumbled as they continued walking. "Why did you do that? Surely you will not attend their horrid luncheon."

"No, of course not," Sarah said. "But I didn't have the heart to refuse."

"It takes no heart to refuse such people . . . just common sense."

"Would you like to have them? You and your sisters could—"

"Servants are not invited, Miss Matthews. You notice they did not ask me to purchase a ticket. And that does not break my heart. They should not be peddling anything at church."

A familiar presence was absent from the door. "I do hope the vicar is not sick," Marie said.

As much as Sarah shared that concern, she was relieved to have Marie's attention diverted from what had transpired outside. She felt sick enough about it. Once they had seated themselves, she twisted to smile up at the familiar faces in the gallery, who made her feel better just by being there. William and Mrs. Bacon waved, Naomi smiled, and Stanley continued to look sheepish.

Shortly afterward the worship service began. The very faintest murmurs rippled through the pews when Mr. Knight stepped up to the pulpit, only six weeks since his arrival in London. Marie leaned close to whisper, "Vicar must surely be ill. He would not allow a new curate to preach so soon."

"Perhaps he's only going to lead the Litany," Sarah whispered back, but later, after Morning Prayer and Litany, the curate gripped the sides of the pulpit, as if bracing himself for courage.

"Do pray for Reverend Sharp," he said, looking out over the congregation. "He is abed with a severe chest cold this morning, but I trust he will return to us next Sunday." An apologetic smile made his handsome face seem boyish. "I'm afraid you'll have to make do with me this morning. I feel like the knot one ties in a broken bootlace until he can get home to change it."

His manner was shockingly casual compared to Vicar Sharp's sober reverence, and another ripple passed through the nave. Yet when Sarah glanced about her, she saw several approving smiles, even chuckles smothered with hands. There were very few tight-lipped frowns—Marie's included.

"This morning I ask you to consider with me the words from the book of First Samuel . . . 'For man looketh on the outward appearance, but the Lord looketh on the heart.' "

In his rich resonating voice, he went on to tell the story of the beggar Lazarus from the book of Saint Luke who ate crumbs from the rich man's table and dying went on to Abraham's bosom.

"When we consider Lazarus, we should not be saddened by the account of the sores covering his body, but should instead rejoice at the treasure found beneath them. Treasure not of gold and silver and precious stones, but of wisdom and faith, of patience and endurance. For just as the surface of the ground may show only thorns and briars, yet, let a person dig deep enough, and abundant wealth is discovered. . . ."

Sarah became aware that Saint George's was as still as a tomb. No clearing of throats, no prayer books rustling, or even whispered maternal warnings to wiggling children. Even Marie's face had eased from disapproval to something akin to awe. Mr. Knight's eyes roved the congregation, never looking down, his fine voice sweeping through the nave with such emotion that Sarah's pounding heart seemed to match the rhythm of his words.

". . . are like that rich man, I fear, in that we do not see how great an evil sin is, and flatter ourselves, in particular, because we profess a better doctrine concerning God.

We resign ourselves to a careless slumber, pamper each one his own desires. We are not filled with pain at the necessity of our brothers; devotion is without fire and fervor, zeal for doctrine and discipline languishes. . . ."

During the closing prayer when Sarah could breathe deeply again, she added her own silent appeal, *Forgive me for being like the rich man, Father, and caring more about earthly things than those heavenly. I will spend more time in prayer and try to help my fellow man more.*

"Thank you for making me see how comfortable I was becoming," she gushed as Mr. Knight took her hand at the door.

He smiled and replied. "It was not I, but God who stirred your heart, my dear young lady."

She could still feel the warmth of his hand clasping hers as she walked back to the coach with Marie. They happened to cross paths with Miss Fowler, who looked the other way, as if their eyes had not met. Sarah told herself it didn't matter, that Lazarus would not have concerned himself over a personal snub, and took a sideways step to touch her arm.

"Have you any more tickets not committed?"

Now Miss Fowler became attentive. "Why, yes. Several."

"Send ten tomorrow, please."

"Why, thank you!" Miss Fowler exclaimed, and before moving on, she chirped, "Do have a pleasant day!"

Sarah was so intent upon pleasing God that she was able to withstand Marie's severe look when she returned to her side, telling her, "If only a shilling of each ticket helps someone in need, then it's money well spent."

Even Stanley seemed to have been moved. His eyes were reddened when he advanced toward the coach, and he made no jokes while assisting Sarah and Marie inside. During lunch Grandmother had Sarah repeat as much of the sermon as she could remember, which was quite a lot, since it made such an impact upon her.

"It was a remarkable sermon," William agreed later as Sarah sat with him in the garden while Grandmother napped. He had brought a tangled mass of twine from unpacking some laboratory equipment and was using his pocket knife to cut it into six-inch lengths to leave out for nest-building birds. In the branches of the crab apple tree, a small flock of rooks cawed raucously, as if chiding him to work faster. "Even more so when you consider it was probably his first ever."

"And I'd never thought about the Lazarus story that way," Sarah said. "Mr. Knight must study Scripture constantly. And such a dynamic voice . . . well, I scarcely dared breathe."

"Sarah! Mr. Doyle!"

They both turned toward the dovecote and waved at the brown head above the wall. "David or Rueben?" William whispered.

"David," Sarah whispered back. She could tell them apart, for Rueben's souvenir of their recent winter in Spain was a scar across his forehead from a topple from a horse. The twins were now eleven years old, their brother Ben, thirteen, and Mordie, accompanying his father on a trip to conduct banking business in Egypt, fourteen. "How do you do?" she called to the boy.

"Very well, thank you. But we need a fourth for tennis. I don't suppose you . . ."

"You know I can't on Sundays." Which

limited their play time, for the Rothschilds were not allowed sports on Saturdays.

"Mr. Doyle?" the boy said hopefully.

"Same here," William replied. "But I thank you for the invitation."

David frowned. "That leaves Nanny. She has to be begged, and then she's as slow as an old—"

"And if you don't come down from that wall, you'll be put to bed pitifully early tonight, Master David," came a female voice from behind. "Finally I can tell you apart, and you want to go gettin' a scar like your brother's."

The brown head disappeared, leaving Sarah and William smothering laughter. Presently William said, "Aunt Naomi and I are going to take a turn around the square once she has the soup in the kettle. Will you join us?"

"It sounds lovely, but I promised to read to Grandmother when she wakes."

"The newspaper?"

"We read that this morning. This time it's part of my homework assignment . . . Vision Three of *Piers Plowman*. Have you heard of it?"

William nodded, his eyes safely on the

knife in his hand. "It was required reading during my first term at Lincoln. Your Mr. Rayborn is certainly earning his wages, isn't he?"

Sarah picked a bit of twine from William's upper coat sleeve. "I forget he's being paid. He seems to enjoy teaching just as much as I enjoy learning."

"I'm sure he realizes that positive motivation is more effective than negative. The carrot as opposed to the stick."

"Yes." Mentally she searched for words to explain. "But it's not as if he's using some teaching technique by design. He seems genuinely proud of me whenever I put my mind to something difficult. Sometimes all that pushes me through Latin homework is the thought of how pleased he'll be that I persisted."

"I'm glad." He sent her another smile. "You deserve the best."

"Thank you," she said, smiling back. She was glad conversation had turned to her tutor, for her seed of an idea had bloomed fully in her mind over the past fortnight. "William . . ." Sarah looked over her shoulder to make certain of no advancing soft footsteps. "Does Naomi ever speak of Mr. Rayborn to you?"

"No," he said, cutting another length. "Well, she might have mentioned him when he first arrived here. But why should she?"

Before she could answer, he said, "Is that why you asked if I thought she was lonely?"

"I think he is too." Afraid that he would disagree before hearing her out, she rushed her words. "Think about it, William. Wouldn't it be lovely if they fell in love and married?"

He smiled and cut another length. "You've read too many novels, Sarah."

"I *knew* you would say as much," she said, clipping her words and tossing the bit of twine to the ground. "You just *mentioned* fearing you were too selfish. Well, isn't it selfish not to help two decent, lonely people find happiness when it's within your power to do so?"

"Now, now." He put aside the roll and knife. "I shouldn't have teased. And I was even tempted to introduce her to someone just a few weeks ago."

"You were? Who?"

"Someone who wasn't as eligible as I

first assumed. But regarding Mr. Rayborn
. . . they see each other at lunch every day.
Don't you think if a romance is meant to be,
it will blossom there?"

"You've eaten how many meals in the
hall, William? With Stanley and Mr. Duffy at
the same table?"

He chuckled and folded his arms. "Very
well. What is your plan?"

"Plan?"

"Well, you brought this up. You must
have a plan."

Sarah thought for a minute. "Remember
what you said when we toured Parliament?
About his joining us on Saturdays?"

"Vaguely. Shall we do that?"

"Yes, let's do. But I'm not sure if it's ethical to ask Grandmother to pay his way,
when we're only interested in matchmak-
ing."

"Then don't. If he can't afford to go with
us now and then, he has the option of turning us down. And it would surely indicate if
he wished to share Aunt Naomi's company."

"He'll want to. Who wouldn't?"

William raised an eyebrow. "Unless the
fact that she's a servant is a concern."

"I'm sure that won't matter to him in the least," Sarah insisted. "Mr. Rayborn's not a snob." Pressing her palms together, she found herself wishing tomorrow were Saturday. But then a practical matter occurred to her. "We should ask Naomi how she feels about it, William. Without giving away what we're up to. Just in case . . ."

"Just in case she doesn't like him." He finished what she was unable to say. "Good idea. You should do that, since he's your tutor. It would seem less suspicious for you to want him along."

She agreed, and standing, said she should go upstairs to see if her grandmother was awake. "The Zoological Gardens would be nice if weather allows, don't you think? And not too expensive."

"Fine." William got to his feet. But before Sarah could turn for the house, he gently touched her elbow. "Wait, Sarah."

"Yes?"

There was a degree of uncertainty in his expression. "You're positive Mr. Rayborn is a decent Christian man? You've known him less than two months."

I feel as if I've known him all my life, Sarah thought but knew it would not help her case to mention that. She was beginning to realize that men did not put so much stock into "feelings" as women did. So she said instead, "Mr. Mitchell investigated his background. And you know how protective he is of Grandmother."

A smile eased William's expression. "Very well, then. We'll see what happens."

Sarah spent the rest of the afternoon in the sitting room. After reading aloud from *Piers Plowman*, she played draughts with her grandmother. Halfway through the match she broached the subject of Mr. Rayborn.

"William and I were wondering . . . have you any objection to our inviting him along on Saturdays?" she asked. "That is, if Naomi doesn't mind. He's knowledgeable about so many things that we thought we could learn more about the places we visit."

"If you wish," Grandmother said, then shook her head and nodded to the draughts piece Sarah had picked up to move into the square she had indicated. "Not that one . . . move to *your* right."

Marie, turning the pages of a family photograph album passed from sister to sister, said, "Why do you not have Avis paint little numbers in the squares? It would make your game simpler."

Sarah and her grandmother looked at each other. "Why, that's a fine idea, Marie," Grandmother said but then made a pensive frown. "But then again, what if it damaged the wood? This table came from Egypt, you know. It's at least two hundred years old."

The maid shrugged over her album. "Then you must ask yourself if you receive more enjoyment from looking at it or playing with it."

After a thoughtful moment, Grandmother said, "I'll speak with Avis."

"Mr. Rayborn would pay his own way," Sarah said at length, almost disappointed that approval had been granted so easily.

"Nonsense. If it will enhance your education, that's for me to do. I'll tell him so tomorrow."

Sarah's pulse jumped. As wealthy as her grandmother was, she could not cause her to spend her money under false pretense. "Really, Grandmother . . . but we could just go to inexpensive places when Mr. Rayborn is—"

"Sarah, are we going to play draughts or

talk about Mr. Rayborn?" Grandmother snapped, but without rancor. "Why shouldn't he wish to be paid?"

"What Madame should be asking is why Miss Matthews and William would plan this without yet consulting Naomi," Marie said casually while turning a page in her album. "One would think they are playing Cupid."

"Cupid?" Grandmother leveled a shrewd look at her. "Are you and William match-making, Sarah?"

Protest rose at once to Sarah's lips but died, for it would not be the truth. She dropped her eyes to the fingers toying with the scroll design on her corner of the table. "They share a lot of the same interests," she said meekly. When she looked up again, there was a smile upon the aged face.

"Our own little *Emma*, Marie! What do you think about that?"

"This isn't the same," Sarah said in her own defense.

"I think it would be amusing to watch, Madame," Marie replied, as if Sarah had not spoken. "Mr. Rayborn seems a very decent man."

"Do ask Naomi today, Sarah," Grand-mother urged.

William won't like this. Not that Sarah in-tended to tell him. It dawned upon her, why the two women seemed so eager to partic-ipate in the scheme. They were house-bound, except for Marie's outings with her sisters and to church. A romantic drama occurring within their limited spheres would mean respite from the monotony of their routines. She could not fault them for that . . . especially knowing that their affection for Naomi would prevent them from ap-proving of someone not worthy of her.

"I'll ask her," Sarah replied, then felt compelled to warn, "But she may not agree."

"She will agree," Marie said smugly. "She may cook English, but I believe she has a touch of French in her soul."

———

At the sideboard after supper, Naomi was pleased to see the bottom of the tureen when she lifted the lid, for prawn soup did not store well overnight, and she hated to toss out good food. When she re-turned from carrying the tureen into the kitchen and putting on a kettle of water to boil, Miss Matthews was helping Trudy collect dishes from the table.

"How is Mrs. Blake?" Naomi asked.

"She's having a good day," Miss Matthews replied, returning her smile as she took up a saltcellar. "She asks if you'll make prawn soup again sometime this week."

"But of course. Anything to encourage her appetite."

They chatted of other things during trips back and forth to the kitchen: of how well Mr. Knight preached in church, and of Trudy's trip to Letchworth next week for a sister's wedding. "Hester's bringing Baby Milton along," the scullery maid said with flushed excitement in her face.

Naomi knew that Trudy missed having her cousin under the same roof. It was too bad that Hester and her husband could not afford servants, except for a charwoman twice a week, so that Trudy could at least be hired as their cook.

In the kitchen Trudy washed dishes while Naomi mixed dough for tomorrow morning's rolls. Miss Matthews, idly folding and refolding a dish towel into various triangles, asked how she felt about the Zoological Gardens for Saturday.

"That would be lovely," Naomi answered. "Providing this pleasant weather holds."

"What did you say, Naomi?" Trudy asked over the sound of running water.

Naomi could not blame her, excluded as she was from so many conversations, for listening in. Trading smiles with Miss Matthews, she said a little more loudly, "I said it would be lovely, but we'll have to watch the weather."

"Very nice. I like the monkeys."

Miss Matthews started folding the towel again. "Would you mind if we invited Mr. Rayborn along? With his writing a biology text, I thought he might give us some interesting information."

"That's for you to decide, dear." Naomi stirred the dough a little faster, ignoring a faint quickening of her heartbeat.

"But I wouldn't want to do this if you don't care for his company."

"Why wouldn't she care for his company?" Trudy said over the sound of sloshing water. "He's a nice fellow. Even ate unsalted mullet without complaining."

There was nothing Naomi could add to

this, so she simply replied, "His company is agreeable."

"Very good!" Miss Matthews said with more enthusiasm than even someone so fond of learning would show for something educational.

She's not trying to arrange something, is she? Naomi asked herself. She had become adept at discerning the girl's moods, but the green eyes over her smile were guileless.

Pushing out her chair, Miss Matthews hung the towel back on its hook and said she needed to finish some reading in her history text. "I'll ask Mr. Rayborn in the morning."

And he'll agree to it. The assurance surprised Naomi, even though its source was her own mind.

❧ *Thirty-Four* ❧

"In other words," Daniel said to his daughter in the library the following morning, "the organs or parts in different animals are *homologous* when they agree with one another morphologically in their fundamental structure. But that may have nothing to do with what functions they discharge. Do you understand?"

"I think so," she replied, brows drawn in concentration. "Such as a man's arm and the foreleg of a dog?"

"Very good. Would you add a bird's wing to those examples?"

"Ah . . . yes I would."

"Correct again. And are the three *analogous*?" He smiled to himself as she chewed her lip in thought. *Daniel . . . you are a happy man*. How remarkable, after so many years!

"They are not," she replied at length.

"Because . . . ?

"They perform wholly different functions. The arm for prehension, the dog's leg for terrestrial progression, and the wing is for flight."

The door opened and Miss Prewitt stuck her head inside. "Madame would speak to you in the sitting room, Mr. Rayborn."

"Of course." He pushed out his chair, as did his daughter. But the maid said to her, "Mr. Rayborn is to come alone, if you please."

Noticing the gravity on the face at the door—and now upon the younger one at the table—he prayed silently, *Father, please don't take this away from me.* "Why don't you finish reading that section?" he said, smiling to cover his concern.

Miss Prewitt walked ahead of him the short distance down the corridor and held open the next door. Mrs. Blake looked up from her armchair but did not greet him in the usual way or ask him to have a seat. "Mr. Rayborn, I would be much obliged if you would consider joining my granddaughter and Naomi Doyle and her nephew, William, for outings on Saturday afternoons," she said without preamble. "Your immense knowledge of history and such would serve to enhance Sarah's education."

Having feared something altogether different, Daniel needed a second for realization to sink in that he was being offered a *good* thing. That he would be spending more time away from his biology text was the only drawback, but he was still well on schedule and could make up the time by waking an hour earlier every morning. *And you can afford it*, he told himself.

He was opening his mouth to accept and thank her when Miss Prewitt cleared her throat. Mrs. Blake gave her a curious look; the maid lifted her eyebrows meaningfully.

"Oh." The elderly woman turned to him again. "I would naturally pay any expenses you incur."

"I would be delighted," he answered. "But as far as expenses, my wages are more than ad—"

"I do not ask people to pay for the privilege of paying me courtesies, Mr. Rayborn," she cut in. "Now, if you will resume Sarah's lesson, we will consider this matter concluded."

But he could not leave quite yet. "Thank you, Mrs. Blake." *For loving her so much, even while knowing she's not your son's daughter.*

She lifted a dismissive hand but smiled. "Sarah made a huge sacrifice . . . staying here without complaint while her heart longed to go to school. It is I who am grateful, Mr. Rayborn, that you provide the quality education she desires."

Back in the library, he explained, "I've been invited to join you on Saturdays. You don't mind, do you?" She shook her head and gave him a smile filled with such sweetness that he could have wept had he any less composure.

"I'm glad you're coming with us."

He was issued another invitation when he arrived home late that afternoon in the form of a note handed to him by his twice-weekly charwoman, Mrs. Chatham, who was just leaving. "Your brother stopped by a couple o' hours ago," she said.

Daniel thanked her and, after she was gone, opened and read: *Greetings, Stranger! Virginia and I insist you have supper with us. Take a hansom to 7 Bloomsbury Street.*

Only essential furnishings had been unpacked in the three-storey terrace house, situated around a communal garden with similar middle-class houses. "Mother says she's not sure which crate has our toys," twelve-year-old Catherine complained once she had warmed up to the uncle she had not seen in four years. "I miss my chess set." But three-year-old Jewel stood back a bit with polite reserve.

Sarah's cousins, Daniel thought. Wouldn't she be surprised when the time came to introduce them! Over supper James startled him by announcing he had accepted a lecturing position at King's College Junior School, connected closely with University of London's King's College.

"How can I explain?" he said. "I was in the Strand last week and on impulse found myself wandering the college grounds. Happened across my former English literature lecturer, Mr. Ripley . . . remember him?"

"Of course. I still see him at chapel."

"Well, we lunched together, and he urged me to look into an urgent vacancy at the Junior School." He shrugged. "Monday's my first day."

"And don't let his casualness deceive you—he's thrilled about it," said James's wife, Virginia, a comely gray-eyed woman with a plump figure and seemingly limitless energy.

His brother shrugged again but smiled. "With a classroom filled with boys, there is more possibility that at least *some* will be inspired to make something of themselves."

Catherine looked up from spearing a piece of rump steak to wrinkle her nose.

"You have something to say about that, daughter?" James asked, but with an affectionate light in his eyes.

She wrinkled her nose again. "Boys."

"Boys," little Jewel echoed, attempting to copy her sister's expression.

Daniel shared in the family laughter. He was relieved that neither James nor Virginia inquired about Sarah, clearly sharing his view that the girls were too young to know the unsettling details of the story. When Virginia excused herself to ready them for bed, Daniel and James took fresh cups of tea into the library, its bare shelves waiting for the uncrating of several boxes stacked in a corner.

"What's it like . . . seeing your daughter every day?" James asked.

Daniel smiled. "Sometimes I can scarcely

believe how this came about. And you know, as much as it pained me to hold off telling her the truth, I believe this is for the best. It's nice, becoming acquainted without the awkwardness of trying to reestablish the family relationship straightway. And soon I'll be spending even more time with her."

"Yes?"

"On Saturday afternoons." It was as he gave the account of Mrs. Blake's invitation that Daniel realized he had been so surprised that he allowed one bit of information to enter his ears without taking firm root in his mind. Miss Doyle would be along on the Saturday outings as well. He had never seen her out in the sunlight. Would her eyes be even more startlingly blue?

———

With Vicar Sharp still confined to his hearth, all the responsibility for paying calls fell upon Ethan. He actually didn't mind shouldering the whole load. "You'll forgive me for staying such a short while," he said regretfully in house after house, finishing up Tuesday's calls in less than three hours.

"But I do feel compelled to stay close to the vicar, should he happen to need me."

And he was delighted at having to put forth so little effort at conversation, for at almost every stop there was someone to praise him for such an insightful message on Sunday past. *Thank Grandfather*, he thought on his way to New Bond Street. But then, he felt himself due some credit for memorizing the sermon with so little notice. He would have to write his parents and tell them how he had proved himself his first time behind the pulpit. He didn't mind being in the ministry so much anymore. A fellow could find himself doing worse—such as the army or engineering.

"Good day t'you, Mr. Knight!" A coachman waiting outside a Bruton Street mansion tipped his top hat. "Fine sermon on Sunday!"

"Thank you!" Ethan replied, smiling. "And a good day to you as well."

It wasn't that he didn't believe in God. He had not succumbed to Darwinism at Cambridge, as was fashionable, nor had he ever joined any of the discussions around tables in smoke-filled pubs. Only a fool would look around himself and not realize such an intricately designed world would have to be the work of a Creator.

But he found the devoutness of his parents boring. That they did not find it so was proof that piety was more appropriate for those in their later years. He fully intended to take spiritual matters seriously when he emerged from youth to maturity, when he no longer felt such a pull toward life's sensory delights. Until then, it was enough that he showed respect to his parents and had never killed or stolen. That surely meant something to God, along with the fact that he could deliver a sermon with such conviction that even a servant would call out to him from the street.

Today, five female patrons were in the parasol shop, so he walked past GARLAND'S LTD., THE MODERN PHARMACY to a bookseller's and spent a half hour browsing the shelves for want of any other way to pass the time. He came across a small volume titled *The Autobiography of an Actress* and brought it over to the counter.

"Anna Cora Mowatt," said the shop's owner, an academic type who peered over square spectacles. "She was from the

States but made quite a mark on the stage here as well. You know she's buried here in London."

"She died, then?" Ethan asked before thinking, then grinned. "But then, one would hope that was the case."

The shop owner smiled as well. "Five years or so ago."

Ethan had discovered while just a boy that people were more agreeable when in good humor, so he decided to take advantage of the situation. "Say, you wouldn't mind knocking a shilling or two off the price, would you? A curate's wages allow for few luxuries."

The man didn't look as impressed as Ethan would have hoped, but he did say, "Twobob and it's yours."

This time his casual glance into W & J SANGSTER'S window happily revealed no patrons, just the shopgirl leaning idly against the counter.

"Shopping for your mother again?" she asked when Ethan entered.

"No, I wanted to see you." He walked up to the counter. "And I've brought you a gift."

"For me?" Wary eyes stared at the book in his hands. "Why would you do that?"

"Because I admire that you dare to have a dream for yourself," he replied, and it was at least partially true. He wasn't sure if she would appreciate hearing that he admired her buxom figure even more.

She took the book from him and turned it over in her hands. "I've heard of her." Looking up at him, she said, "I don't get many gifts."

"Indeed? Now, that surprises me." He found out her name was Myra Rose and that her family lived in the slums of Bedfordbury.

"I was lucky to get out. I've a flat up above the shop now. Barely room to turn around, but there's running water and a decent stove."

"All that will change when you're the toast of London's stage."

"Yes." But she sighed doubtfully.

Ethan tapped the book in her hand. "You mustn't give up. I'd wager Miss Mowatt didn't have an easy go of it in the beginning."

A smile curved her lips. "It's nice to have some encouragement."

She asked about him, and so he told her about his profession. There was no use deceiving her—he couldn't very well pretend to be wealthy and have her expecting him to bring a gift every time he came around. "But I don't intend to stay poor forever," he said. "Vicars do nicely for themselves. And judging by the reaction my first sermon received, that may be sooner than I had expected."

Before long she was revealing to him her real name, Alice Sewell. "But I changed it two years ago because it's so ordinary. Myra Rose is more romantic, don't you think?"

Ethan picked up her left hand from where it rested upon the counter and merely brushed his lips against it, so as not to appear too presumptuous. When she did not pull her hand away, he smiled at her. "Myra Rose is very romantic."

———

Saturday's weather turned out lovely enough for light wool wraps over Naomi's and Sarah's gowns. Colorful blooms in the flower beds at the upper end of Regent Park's Broad Walk gave evidence that April had firmly established itself. Roses also bloomed in the faces of youngsters reveling at the sight of forest creatures outside the pages of their picture books. Seated upon a bench facing the clock tower, Naomi sent up a silent prayer that Miss Matthews would keep her balance on the back of the camel that gave her two penny-worth of jolting ride around the tower.

"With the cord about her waist she's perfectly safe," Mr. Rayborn said, reading her thoughts.

Naomi turned to the man sharing the bench. "You're right, of course. We come here every summer, so this isn't her first time. She's even ridden the elephant. But perhaps you should reassure my nephew." William, who had decided himself too old to ride zoo animals a couple of years ago, stood just to the side of the queue and watched with his hands in his pockets.

Mr. Rayborn smiled. "He seems a very decent young man. You must be proud."

"Thank you. But he came to me that way when he was nine, so I can take little credit." She told him about bringing him home from Leicester. "I believe that's one reason he and Miss Matthews became so close, their both being orphans."

"That must be why he's so protective of her," Mr. Rayborn said with a look toward the two young people advancing arm in arm with faces flush with laughter.

"Yes," Naomi replied. "Like an older brother." She was also aware that William had feelings that went deeper. She prayed for both daily but could not go so far as to request that they marry sometime in the future, as much as she desired it. She had lived long enough to understand that God wanted what was best for William and Sarah even more than did she. In His infinite wisdom, He could have other, even better, plans. So she prayed with genuine sincerity, "Your will be done." And was human enough to add, "Just please don't let either of them get hurt."

"I thought my teeth would shake loose!" Sarah exclaimed when the two reached the bench.

Naomi stood to repin some of the flaxen locks shaken from under the girl's straw hat. "And as always, we won't mention this to your grandmother, will we?"

"I'll not even *think* about it while I'm in

the same room, or Marie will figure it out." She turned her head as far as Naomi would allow while still working on her hair. "Why don't you take a turn, Mr. Rayborn? We don't mind waiting."

"Actually, I did the last time I was here," he replied, returning her smile.

"Really? When was that?"

"Well, over twenty years ago. But once was quite enough."

"Unless you're Arabian," William said. "They'll be feeding the hippopotami soon. Shall we?"

Antony, the first hippopotamus to tread English soil, his mate, Adhela, and their daughter, Cleopatra, went about their business at the hippopotami house as if unaware of the press of people, some noisily expressing wonder or disgust when Antony opened his great mouth for a quartern loaf tossed from above.

"Antony was brought here as a calf in 1849," Naomi read on the bronze sign fastened to the wall. "So you must have seen him when you were last here, Mr. Rayborn."

"And Adhela as well," he replied. "In fact, we came here specifically to have a look at her. There was quite a stir about it in the newspapers, you know, Antony having a companion."

"I wonder what he thought when he first saw her?" Sarah said, standing next to Naomi with elbows resting upon the top of the wall.

"Well, he was captured in the Nile when only three days old, so he'd spent four years without even seeing another of his own species."

"No creature should have to be alone," Naomi murmured and, realizing what she had said, wished she could take back her words. She surely hoped Mr. Rayborn did not think her the type of woman to drop hints as a means of flirting.

But the smile he gave her showed no sign of having taken her words for anything more than what they were. "God knew best when He made them in pairs. He could have made all living creatures like amoebas."

"I wouldn't care to be here when old Antony decided to split in half," William said with a grimace.

As they moved on, Naomi could see why Miss Matthews wanted Mr. Rayborn along. His combined expertise in biology and history made for a much more interesting tour, such as his account in front of the sloth cage of how a South American explorer named Waterton was jeered in 1825 for describing an odd creature that slept upside down suspended from its limbs.

Two hours later they sipped lemonades at a table under a refreshment canopy several paces from the monkey house. Above simian and human background chatter, William leaned closer to Mr. Rayborn and said, "Forgive me if this is too personal a question, but how is it that someone with your interest in biology would only visit here once?"

Mr. Rayborn shook his head. "I gave that impression, didn't I? Actually, I've been here many, many times, since I was a boy."

"Hmm." William looked at him oddly. "Then why would you stop suddenly those twenty years ago?"

That's too personal a question, William! Naomi thought, willing him to turn her way and read the message her eyes were straining to send.

Mr. Rayborn did not seem to mind. Absently etching lines in the condensation outside his half-empty glass, he replied,

"When I last came here it was with someone who passed on just a few years later. I
suppose I've just been a coward about it."

"Your wife," Sarah murmured, her green
eyes filled with sympathy. And Naomi managed to capture the attention of those
same eyes with the "look" she had unsuccessfully attempted to send to William.

"Oh—I'm sorry," the girl stammered. "It's
just that Grandmother told me . . ." As if realizing she was heading in an even more in-
appropriate direction, she clamped her
mouth and just looked miserable.

"Please don't be," Mr. Rayborn said. He
smiled at her. "Yes, I was here with my wife.
I even coaxed her into riding the camel."

"Then she was happy."

"For a while . . . yes."

Then why did she kill herself? was the
unspoken question hanging in the air, and
Naomi feared Miss Matthews or William
would speak it. She was opening her
mouth to insist they continue their tour,
when he spoke first.

"You're wondering why a happily married
woman would do such a thing."

"*I* am," William admitted.

Mr. Rayborn nodded. "After our first year

of marriage, she began suffering from a form of mental delusion that I see now was with her all along. I was too young to understand how to help her fight it, which I profoundly regret."

"What was her name?" Sarah asked.

"Deborah."

In the awkward silence that followed, Naomi spoke up in a tone that invited no contradiction. "We've imposed upon Mr. Rayborn's obliging nature long enough. And we did come to look at animals, did we not?"

Mr. Rayborn did seem relieved and rose to pull out her chair, while William did the same for Miss Matthews. Later, as Mr. Rayborn and Naomi trailed behind the younger couple—they were always rushing ahead—Naomi apologized for the two. "You know how it is with young people."

"Of course," he replied. "But I do appreciate your coming to my rescue. It doesn't make for pleasant conversation."

But even after scolding her nephew for being so inquisitive, she could not help but ask, "Has this day been painful for you, Mr. Rayborn?"

He shook his head and regarded her with

the warmth she had seen in his eyes at times across the table. "Quite the opposite, Miss Doyle."

Now it was incumbent upon her to pretend she was unaware of the silent communication between them. But thirty-seven was a little old for coyness. So when he smiled and offered his arm, she smiled back and rested her gloved hand in the crook. And felt some regret that the aviary wasn't just a little farther away.

❧ Thirty-Five ❧

Vicar Sharp's cold settled in his chest and hung on tenaciously, which meant Ethan stepped up to the pulpit for two more Sundays. On the eleventh he preached "On Bearing Persecution," and on the eighteenth, "Sermon of the Plow." Both were more well received by the congregation than even he could have imagined.

His first call on the drizzling morning of Thursday, the twenty-second of April, was to 14 Berkeley Square. As he took the steps he recalled visiting here with Vicar Sharp during his first few days in London. The door swung open less than a minute after his ring. There stood Mrs. Blake's granddaughter, who attended St. George's with a maid. She was pretty, but too young, and her chaste lack of sophistication did not appeal to him.

"Mr. Knight!" she exclaimed. "I thought you were someone else."

"I'm sorry to have disappointed you," he teased to cover his blank memory of her name. *Something from the Bible?* All he could recall was that it wasn't Blake.

Her green eyes widened. "Oh, not at all. Grandmother will be so pleased. I've been quoting as much of your sermons as I can remember to her. After your Easter sermon, we both committed to spending more time in prayer."

"Splendid!" Ethan didn't mind accepting compliments, but he was beginning to wonder if she would have him stand at the entrance all morning. And so he smiled and held out his hat.

"Forgive me," she said, taking the hint. "Do come in."

When she hung the hat before offering to take his umbrella, he caught sight of the hand at her side. There were no fingers! Over the past weeks he had become an expert at hiding his repulsion at physical abnormalities, and so it took no effort to smile and thank her for offering to show him to Mrs. Blake.

"We've turned the library into a bedchamber," the young woman explained with a nod toward a door farther down the corridor. He walked on her right side, so he would not accidentally brush against the crippled hand. "The stairs were too much for her, and down here she can still walk out to the garden."

"How are her spirits?" he asked. He had heard the vicar ask that question of others, and people seemed to appreciate it.

Her voice lowered to a whisper. "She has good moments and bad."

"I'm so sorry."

The doorbell rang again, and she excused herself to answer it. A tall bearded man entered, hung his own hat, and put his umbrella in the stand. He was introduced to Ethan as Mr. Rayborn, the tutor. "He worships at King's College Chapel," the young woman said, as if she thought he might mistake him for one of his parishioners.

"I'm sure it's a fine church," Ethan said as the two shook hands. "Although you'd be hard pressed to find a finer pastor than our Reverend Sharp."

"It speaks well of you that you praise him so highly," Mr. Rayborn said, then turned again to the young woman. "Shall I go upstairs and arrange the lessons, Miss Matthews?"

Matthews! Ethan thought, then applying a trick Myra Rose had taught him—among others—for remembering the name of her patrons, said it over in his mind four more times. If only he could remember names as well as he memorized sermons.

"Yes, please," Miss Matthews replied. "I'll only be a minute."

While she watched Mr. Rayborn walk to the staircase, Ethan could not help but glance down at her left side again. *Why doesn't she wear some sort of glove?* Or at least keep it hidden from sight when visitors with queasy stomachs came to call.

"Thank you, Sarah," Dorothea said, and when she appeared tempted to linger just inside the sitting room door, added, "Now off to your lessons. And do have a seat, Mr. Knight. You remember Marie, don't you?"

"Yes, of course." Mr. Knight made a little bow to both before taking a chair.

That he did not mind extending such a courtesy to a servant was even more proof to Dorothea that Vicar Sharp had been assigned an outstanding young man.

If only Jeremy . . . tore painfully through her mind. She shook away the thought. Entertaining so much regret would only put her in her grave sooner. Doctor Raine had even said so. Every day she stayed alive was another day she could provide guidance for Sarah.

"May I send for tea, Mr. Knight?"

He gave a regretful shake of the head. "I can stay but a minute. I don't feel I should leave Vicar Sharp for too long."

Compassion and loyalty, Dorothea thought. "Marie and Sarah tell me that your sermons have been perfectly inspiring. How I wish I could have been there to hear them!"

"Perfectly inspiring." Marie's agreement came out muffled, for she was sawing at a needlepoint thread with her teeth. She finally let it loose to say, "They are the talk of Mayfair."

"You are too kind," he said modestly. "But I didn't come here to soak up compliments, dear lady. Do tell me how you're faring."

Dorothea had kept so much to herself, not wishing to worry Sarah. But the young man's distinctive mismatched eyes regarded her with such compassion that she began telling him of the humiliation of having to turn so much of her life over to others, and of how hard it was having to watch the library moved to the former breakfast room so that her bed and Marie's could be moved downstairs. "I had to get stern with my granddaughter, or her bed would have been in there as well."

Mr. Knight nodded. "I'm sure it's very difficult. But I'm sure you realize they only want what's best for you."

"That is what we tell her," Marie said. "Over and over . . ."

Dorothea sighed. "Yes, of course you're right, Mr. Knight. I thought I had finally reconciled myself to growing old, yet here I am complaining."

"There, there now. Sometimes it does us good to talk about our troubles." The young man twisted to glance at the chimneypiece clock, then gave her another regretful look as he got to his feet. "And I do wish I could stay longer, but with the vicar ailing . . ."

"But of course." She smiled up at him as he gently took her hand. "I do feel better now."

"I'm glad," he said. "I'll pray for you."

After the door closed behind him,

Dorothea turned to Marie. "You know . . . he would make someone a lovely husband."

Marie, closing an eye to rethread her needle, said, "You are too old for him, Madame."

Dorothea laughed and was glad that she could still do so. She grew contemplative again. "I should have had Sarah stay in here with us."

"And Miss Matthews is too young. Eighteen is still a child."

"I married at sixteen, Marie." *And Sarah is probably closer to nineteen*, Dorothea thought. Add to that a year for a proper courtship and betrothal, and she would be starting marriage at a mature twenty.

"Besides," Marie said at length, "Miss Matthews will marry William one day. You know they are fond of each other."

"Well, of course they are. They practically grew up together." And she was grateful to Naomi's nephew for being the brother that Sarah never had. He was as fine a young man as she had ever met, and certainly handsome enough to find a good wife, if he wouldn't divide every bit of his time between his work and time with Sarah and

Naomi. But Sarah had suffered enough socially for being the out-of-wedlock daughter of a servant. Were she to marry a
servant's nephew, a former servant himself,
the stigma would follow their children for
the rest of their lives. London was a city,
but with small-town ways.

It was a pity she could not mention this
to Sarah, for being reared with servants as
practically her only friends, she would not
fully understand. Dorothea had given up on
any of Mayfair society providing a decent
husband for Sarah while she still lived. It
would be after she passed on and it became known that the girl had inherited her
entire estate that younger sons without in-
heritances were sure to come around in
droves.

Unless she were already betrothed. What
better choice of a husband for an heiress
than a man to whom wealth meant little?
After all, if Mr. Knight were interested in
money, he certainly wouldn't have chosen
the ministry. The young man was earning
respect throughout the parish too.
Wouldn't those who turn their noses up at
her have to think twice?

"Madame."

Dorothea looked at the maid.

"Mr. Knight delivers a good sermon, yes." Marie's hands rested upon the needlework on her lap. "And he seems a kind man. But Miss Matthews hardly knows him. I hope you are not thinking of pushing them together."

"Naomi hardly knew Mr. Rayborn, and you were all for pushing them together."

"That is different. They are old enough to know their own minds."

At length and with a sigh, Dorothea replied, "Yes, of course. You're very right."

Marie seemed satisfied and returned to her needlework. Dorothea stared at the budding plane trees through the window and thought, *But if he ever shows interest in her* . . .

The only problem with acquiring a degree of fame in Mayfair, Ethan discovered, was that his comings and goings were also open to public scrutiny. There would surely be talk if he was seen too often stopping at a certain parasol shop. And so he made trips to New Bond Street when most of Mayfair was abed. Hours after he had visited Mrs. Blake and others, he shifted the hatbox to his left arm and rang the bell to Myra's flat. His heart thumped against his ribs while he waited in the hateful glow of the lamplight only six feet away, but seconds later he caught the sound of muffled footsteps. As soon as the door opened, he dashed into her sphere of candlelight.

In silence they climbed the stairs, for the chemist next door lived above his shop. Ethan closed the door of her flat and watched her replace the candle in its stand. She wore the silk Oriental wrapper he had brought her last week. "You're late," she whispered with a feigned look of injury, even while moving forward to fall into his arms. "I thought you'd fallen asleep!"

"Wait . . ." he said, laughing. "You'll crush your gift."

"Oh, let me see!" She took the box from him and brought it closer to the parlor lamp. Her flat was as tiny as she had described, with only a curtain separating her bed from a parlor crowded with a cast-off sofa the color of mustard, a lamp upon a scratched and nicked table that tottered dangerously when anyone walked past, and a rug worn bare in spots. Her eyes shone as she brought out the hat, white straw bound with scarlet velvet and trimmed with white marabou feathers, a scarlet bird, and an aigrette of spun glass. "Lovely!"

"I thought you could wear it to church," he said.

"Church!" She laughed, carrying the hat past the open curtain to the spotted oval wall mirror. On the chest of drawers beneath the mirror sat the velvet box containing the sterling silver bangle bracelet and earrings he had brought her just three evenings ago. Angling her chin to study her reflection, she said, "Wouldn't you find me a distraction?"

"A lovely distraction," he said, stepping up behind her to nuzzle her neck.

"It's beautiful." She ducked away from him and turned. "Seriously, Ethan, every Bond Street shopkeeper must admire your devotion to your mother. How are you able to afford . . . ?"

He took the hat from her head and replaced it in the box. "We should never look a gift horse in the mouth, Myra. Not while there are more pleasurable things to do."

On his way back to the vicarage some time later, he watched his shadows lengthen and disappear on the wet cobbled stones from gaslight to gaslight. Nagging at his mind was Myra's comment about shop-keepers. Vicar Sharp may be too trusting for his own good, but he was not stupid. If word got around that the new curate began a spending spree at the same time he was entrusted with recording the tithes, it would be a simple matter of the vicar asking parishioners if the amounts they gave matched the figures in the ledger.

His forehead clammed with sweat. Men were sent to prison for less, and ministry vestments were no protection against pros-ecution. If anything, a man of the cloth would be judged more harshly for taking from a church. He would have to cease for a while and not be so greedy next time. Mentally he brushed away the prick of guilt that accompanied the thought of *next time*. If he was doing the work of two men, shouldn't he be rewarded thus? Didn't the Bible say somewhere not to muzzle the ox who treads the grain?

❧ *Thirty-Six* ❧

Clad in a new Napoleon-blue poplin dress trimmed with black velvet bows, Sarah paced the hall after lunch the following Saturday. When William arrived in a black suit, burgundy silk cravat, and top hat, she presented him right away with a leather satchel.

"It's perfect!" he exclaimed, holding it out to admire it. "No more files spilling out. But you shouldn't have spent so much."

The subject of money embarrassed her because he worked so hard for his, and all she had to do was ask Grandmother should her allowance fall short. "I've been putting aside a little every week," she said, truthfully, then took his arm after he hung his hat. "And Naomi's waiting."

"Good." He gave her an apologetic look. "I'll go on down by myself. I need to talk with her, if I can get her away from Trudy for a second."

"Can it wait? Grandmother will be disappointed if we don't spend a little time with her before we leave."

"Of course," he said after only a second's hesitation. They paused in the hall before entering the kitchen so that William could admire the chocolate cake on the table. In the kitchen, Trudy was putting away the last of the dry dishes, and Naomi was removing her apron. Both planted kisses upon William's cheeks.

"Twenty-two years!" Trudy exclaimed, taking from her apron pocket a small pasteboard box. "It got a little wet."

"But the comb is perfectly dry," William said, taking out a tortoiseshell pocket comb that closed into its own case. He opened and snapped it shut, opened it again, and ran it through his hat-mussed hair. "Thank you, Trudy. I'll stay well-groomed on the job now."

From behind a cupboard Naomi brought out an umbrella with handle of polished wood, and he exclaimed over it, even started to open it until Trudy protested.

"Don't you know it's bad luck?"

"Of course," he replied and took it outside the service door. Sarah and Naomi traded smiles. Any other time William wouldn't have been able to resist teasing Trudy about putting luck above faith, but one tried to restrain from teasing someone who has just presented them with a gift.

When they stepped back inside the kitchen, Marie stood in the hall doorway, and after wishing William many happy returns, she said to Naomi, "You must come upstairs now if I am to help you with your hair."

A half hour later Mrs. Bacon ushered into the hall Mr. Rayborn, suited in black, like William, save the pearl gray cravat around his neck. Trudy pressed a dish of chocolate cake upon him, and Avis put a cup of punch in his free hand. "I would have brought a gift had I known," he whispered to Sarah, eyeing the unwrapped little gifts from the servants upon the table.

"He doesn't expect you to," Sarah assured him. The only information she had given her tutor yesterday was that he should come dressed for a matinee.

Naomi walked through the doorway in a bustled violet silk, her strawberry-blond ringlets cascading from behind a narrow brimmed straw hat trimmed with flowers and green leaves. Mr. Rayborn, in conversation with Avis and Mr. Duffy, looked in her direction. As both sets of eyes met, it seemed to Sarah that for a handful of seconds everyone else in the room had faded from their sights.

"Did you notice the way they looked at each other?" William murmured from her elbow.

She turned. "You don't mind, do you?"

He did not reply.

"Haven't we already talked about this? I've assured you he's a decent man."

William's expression did not soften. "I can't explain."

He's jealous, Sarah realized. As much as he claimed to want Naomi to have a husband, he was beginning to realize he would no longer be the center of her universe. She hated to think of her best friend acting like a small boy but told herself that he would grow used to the idea with time.

Later, Sarah and Naomi carried slices of cake up to the sitting room, William and Mr. Rayborn following. Under Grandmother's direction, Marie handed William an envelope. "Box tickets and cab fare and dinner at Gatti's," Grandmother said. "Be sure to try the lobster bisque."

"Thank you, Mrs. Blake," William said, smiling as he stooped to kiss her cheek.

"You're welcome. Have you time to tell us what happened this week?"

"But of course. That's why we left the party early."

Marie leaned forward attentively in her chair, and Grandmother's eyes widened as William related discovering a quantity of brick dust in Putnam's Pure Cocoa Powder, and even more shocking, poisonous chromate of lead in the green and yellow icings of a confectionery shop—*not* GUNTER'S, he assured them.

"Life would have been so dull if you had decided to become a doctor or banker," Grandmother said. Still smiling, she turned to Sarah and said casually, "You children will be sure to give Naomi and Mr. Rayborn the front seats. It is not seemly for young people to take the best places and force their elders to sit behind them."

Sarah cringed inside, embarrassed for Naomi and Mr. Rayborn. She sent Marie a mute appeal for help, but the maid was nodding enthusiastic agreement. "Respect for one's elders is a good thing."

The performance of *Nicholas Nickleby* at the Adelphi lived up to its praises in London's newspapers, William thought, though half his mind was on the two seated in front of him. Thankfully, they were more absorbed in the performance than he was, and he discerned no signs of flirting. Mr. Rayborn did offer his arm to Aunt Naomi for the half-block walk to Gatti's Restaurant, but he couldn't fault him for that because the pavement was crowded with theatre patrons. He himself had Sarah's hand in the crook of his arm to keep her from accidentally being bumped into the street. Not that he minded.

"What's the matter with you, William?" she said only loud enough to be heard over the street noises. "You're not still sulking, are you?"

Realizing the need to be a little less obvious, at least until he got to the truth, he frowned sheepishly. "Sorry. I suppose twenty-two is too old for that."

"Yes, it is. And Naomi's not going to stop spoiling you silly just because she's fond of someone else."

"Spoiling *me* silly?" He forgot his foul mood for a second and chuckled. "So says the Princess of Berkeley Square."

She protested, but laughingly so. Over supper, which included four lobster bisques, William forced himself to take part in discussing the performance. He even answered Mr. Rayborn's questions concerning his duties for the Commission.

Perhaps it's good that we didn't get to talk, William thought, giving his aunt a glance. The decent thing to do would be to speak with the man privately first. If he had learned anything from his job, it was that everything was not always as it seemed.

However, he could not imagine any explanation justifying what he had discovered.

"Please allow me." Mr. Rayborn withdrew a purse from his waistcoat pocket when the waiter brought the bill.

"There's more than enough in here," William said, riffling through the envelope. He certainly didn't want to be beholden to a man for whom he harbored misgivings. "Mrs. Blake is generous to a fault."

"My grandmother has so few pleasures left to her, Mr. Rayborn," Sarah said, seated adjacent to William's left. "She'll have me relate every minute of this evening and will consider it worth every penny."

Her face was filled with trust and affection as she spoke with the man. William clinched his teeth. At the touch on his sleeve he turned to Aunt Naomi, who gave him a questioning look. He gave her a blank one in return but forced himself to say, pleasantly, "But thank you for your kind offer, Mr. Rayborn."

The foursome strolled along the Victoria Embankment to look at the river afterward, but just for a little while, as fog was beginning to veil the city, and buildings were losing themselves in the dusky sky. This time William stuck to Mr. Rayborn's side and peppered him with questions about the textbook writing process so that the women had no choice but to walk just ahead of them.

He was relieved when Sarah and Aunt Naomi took the front-facing seat of the coach he hired, leaving the rear-facing one for Mr. Rayborn and himself. As the wheels began rolling he realized that wasn't a perfect situation either, for Mr. Rayborn and Aunt Naomi seated facing each other and could not help but stare at each other the whole way home.

"Has anyone any idea of the time?"

Sarah's voice pierced his gloom. William snapped out his watch, beating Mr. Rayborn to his. "Almost ten."

Aunt Naomi covered a little yawn with her gloved hand, and William remembered the time in the garden he teased her by provoking more yawns from her. He had wanted so desperately for her to find a husband in those days. A saying popped into his mind. *Be careful what you wish for.*

"I do hope Vicar has a stirring message tomorrow," she said sleepily.

"And *I* hope Mr. Knight preaches," Sarah said, then, "What I mean is, I hope Vicar is fully recovered, but allows . . . not that I don't care for Vicar Sharp's . . ."

William breathed a quiet sigh and looked at the lights through the window. Sarah was feeling some guilt over preferring Mr. Knight's sermons over Vicar Sharp's, and he was feeling some guilt for wishing Mr. Knight had been assigned to some other parish, for she did tend to go on about him at times. *Some birthday*, he thought.

"Good night," Aunt Naomi and Sarah said at Mrs. Blake's front door. The two men stood at the bottom of the steps and wished them the same.

"I'll see you at church," William added. When the door was closed, he turned to Mr. Rayborn. "You still live on Surrey Street?"

"Still?" the tutor asked.

"Haven't you mentioned your address before?" William said evasively.

"Perhaps so. I don't mind being last, by the way."

"I'm on Farringdon, actually a bit beyond." William gave the driver instructions and allowed Mr. Rayborn first into the coach. The man took the undesirable rear-facing seat. *My aunt's not here, so you can stop being such a gentleman*, he thought and felt guilty in spite of his misgivings.

When they started moving, William studied the dark outlines of his own hands and considered how to form his question. But Mr. Rayborn spoke first.

"I believe I've said something to offend you, Mr. Doyle."

"It's not anything you've said," William said, looking up. "But I've discovered something very troubling about you."

If there was surprise on the man's face, the dimness of the coach concealed it. "Are you referring to my dismissal from King's College for drinking, Mr. Doyle?"

"Actually, I didn't know about that one."

Mr. Rayborn smiled. "Then I suppose it's too late to say I was joking. . . ."

William almost smiled as well. It was difficult to maintain ill feelings toward someone who could bring humor to a confrontation. "Does Mr. Mitchell know?"

"He does. Mrs. Blake as well."

It was obvious he spoke the truth. But what William had learned was still worse than being sacked for drunkenness. "I paid a visit to Scotland Yard on Tuesday to instigate charges against a chemist who's been twice caught adding opium to infant's colic syrup. I asked the desk constable if he had any knowledge of a Daniel Rayborn or of his wife's suicide."

"Go on," Mr. Rayborn said with a faint edge to his voice.

"He did not, even after looking through his files. But he directed me to the *London Times*. Are you aware that they keep an expanding catalogue of every name that appears in their newspaper, as well as the dates when their articles appeared?" It was used when certain long-running stories required updating, William discovered, but he didn't think Mr. Rayborn would care to learn more about the process at the moment. "For sixpence per article, a clerk will bring out the corresponding newspapers from the archives. Today I spent my lunch break there."

Folding his arms, Mr. Rayborn said, "And so you read the details of my wife's suicide." Sadness dulled the edge in his voice.

He hasn't the right to any sympathy, William had to remind himself. He could go after the scoundrels who adulterated foods and medicines without flinching. Why did he feel almost as if *he* were the one who had done something less than honorable?

He cleared his throat. "Your own father-in-law said that you kept your wife a virtual prisoner because you were ashamed of your infant daughter . . . who had a crippled left hand."

William heard the sound of a long breath being released. Light from passing gas lamps painted Mr. Rayborn's face in alternate colors of sickly yellow and dark gray.

After a space of tense silence, the tutor said, "My father-in-law was bitter because I did indeed keep him away from my family.

And he is the one to blame for his daughter's death."

"The newspaper didn't say anything—"

"The articles were one-sided because I refused to talk with the reporter who hounded me at my wife's funeral. I did not wish our family tragedy to be played out like some stage melodrama. In retrospect, I can see that made me appear guilty."

"Why do you blame him for her death?"

The man sighed again. "From the day she was old enough to understand shame, she was accused of causing her mother's death in childbirth. I think, now, that she married me simply because I was the first to ask, and she desperately wished to escape him. But we were happy until she began carrying a child herself and started dwelling again on the horror of the past. And when the child was born physically less than perfect . . ."

"Her mental state worsened?"

Mr. Rayborn's face was an amber mask. "Obviously."

All of this had the ring of truth, yet the major issue still loomed large in William's mind. "Did Mr. Mitchell discover all of this when he investigated you?"

"No. Because I had admitted them to him beforehand."

"And does he know the rest?"

There was a silence, then, "What do you mean?"

"Your daughter's body was never discovered, was it?"

He did not reply, so William continued. "It struck me, after reading the articles, that Sarah more closely resembles you than Jeremy Blake's portraits. And the crippled left hand . . . ."

Finally Mr. Rayborn spoke. "Surely you've come across other coincidences during your lifetime, Mr. Doyle."

"There are too many here for comfort, Mr. Rayborn. The whole household knows of your wife's suicide, yet a daughter has never been mentioned, which means you did not share that information with Mrs. Blake. Why would you tell her about the wife but not the child? And the fact that Sarah came from an orphanage lends evidence to my theory."

That Mr. Rayborn did not ask him to explain his theory was proof enough for William. He spoke on. "I believe there was somehow a mixup at Saint Matthew's a long time ago, and you've recently discovered your daughter is an heiress. That's why you haven't told anyone who you are . . . because it's obvious Mrs. Blake will not live too much longer. If you wait, you'll be in control of a fortune."

That is, if you can convince Sarah not to tell anyone else, William added in his thoughts. But Mr. Rayborn did not know his own daughter well, for she would not keep money left to her under false pretense, no matter how much. He became aware of the cessation of movement.

The coach door opened, and the driver stuck his head through to say in an annoyed tone, "Sit here all you wish, gents, but it's going to cost you extra. I can't make a living if I ain't out looking for fares."

"Very well," William told him. "Give us another minute, please."

When the door closed again, Mr. Rayborn, his shadowed face as bleak as William had ever seen it, spoke. "You should come inside, Mr. Doyle. This may take a while."

William had worked long enough in his profession to understand that there were men who would kill for money, if not by assault, then by stealth, slowly, with poisons as their weapons. And some looked as decent as schoolmasters, so just because he did not feel threatened meant nothing. If his theory was right, Mr. Rayborn would have reason to wish him to disappear from the face of the earth.

As if reading his mind, the tutor nodded grimly and said, "Then look up Mr. Mitchell and tell him what you've discovered. Only please don't mention this to anyone before you speak to him—you can't imagine how important that is."

"We'll talk inside," William told him, reaching for the coach's door and hoping that his name would not soon occupy the D catalogue drawer in the archives of the *London Times*.

Two hours, four cups of tea, and a half tin of stale lemon biscuits later, William rose from the kitchen table almost totally convinced that Mr. Rayborn spoke the truth. But at the door he turned to say, "You understand that I'll still need to speak with Mr. Mitchell."

Mr. Rayborn nodded. "I would do the same if I were in your shoes."

❧ Thirty-Seven ❧

Sunday after breakfast Naomi stood in front of her mirror and studied the six-year-old gown of pale lavender gingham, which looked almost new again, since she had replaced the cotton lace, added a row of pearl buttons down the front, and gathered the overskirt back into a modest bustle. Satisfied that she did not look as if she had just waded through a rag barrel, she pinned the straw hat trimmed with silk violets over her thick chignon, fluffed the fringe over her forehead with her fingers, and took up her reticule to go downstairs.

She looked into the servants' hall, hoping that William had arrived early. Sure enough, he sat sideways in a chair, pillowing his head along the back in the crook of his arm. "William?"

He raised his head, blinked at her, and smiled. "Good morning, Aunt Naomi."

"Did you have trouble sleeping last night?"

"A little." Getting to his feet, he said, "You look very nice. New dress?"

So you've decided to be in a good mood this morning, Naomi thought. "Refurbished, but thank you for the compliment. Come with me, William."

"Where?"

"I don't want anyone walking in on us."

He pulled an anxious face. "What have I done?"

"Now, please." She led him through the kitchen and into the pantry. Naomi left the door open about eight inches to allow a little light, then turned to deliver in a low voice the speech she had composed while stirring buttered eggs this morning. "William, you must understand that just because I have some feelings for another person, it doesn't diminish the love I have for you."

His eyebrows lifted. "Then it's true."

"I beg your pardon?"

"You're in love with Mr. Rayborn."

"I didn't say 'love,'" she corrected hastily.

"Very well." William's expression was a

mixture of skepticism and amusement. "Is that why you brought me in here? You think I'm jealous of you and Mr. Rayborn?"

The conversation was beginning to remind Naomi of two locomotives passing each other on separate tracks. "But isn't that why you gave him those hard looks last night? And I can only imagine how you must have treated him after you dropped us off."

"Aunt Naomi," he said, then sighed. "I've *wanted* you to find someone for—"

"Sh-h-h!" She had to steady the swaying bottle of Lea & Perrins' Worcestershire Sauce on the shelf beside her after accidentally brushing it with her hand. "But if you weren't jealous . . ."

William's dark eyes became evasive. "I'll admit I may have misjudged him, Aunt Naomi. There is something I have to do first, just to be sure."

"What do you mean . . . *do*, William?"

"I can't explain just yet."

"But you will?"

"Yes." When her frown did not abate, William patted her shoulder. "I will, Aunt Naomi, I promise."

"Mr. Garrett, you are a godsend," Daniel mumbled at his desk while reading the perfectly typed chapter explaining correlation of growth. A knock sounded. Crossing the parlor he passed the side table where the Remington sat as lonely as a deserted ship amidst a stack of research books and papers. He was not surprised to see the figure on his doorstep. "Come in please, Mr. Doyle."

The young man stepped into the parlor. Hands in his coat pockets, he did not quite look into Daniel's eyes. "Mr. Mitchell and I spoke this morning. I worked through lunch to make up for the time."

"Then you must be ravenous." Daniel realized he was as well, though he had feasted on a fine Irish stew at Berkeley Square. "I've some bread and cheese in the kitchen . . ."

"No, thank you. I'll not stay long. I just want to apologize for doubting you."

"Mr. Doyle, my opinion of you has been raised tenfold because you cared enough about Sarah to investigate." He moved some books from the seat of an upholstered chair, motioned his guest into it, and pulled the chair out from his desk for himself. "There is no apology necessary."

"Thank you," Mr. Doyle said. "And you don't have to worry about my telling anyone."

"I appreciate . . ."

"Except for Aunt Naomi."

Daniel stared at him. "I beg your pardon?"

"Under the circumstances, she has to know. But you'll not have to worry—she's the soul of discretion. Why, for months she was the only person in the house aware that Mrs. Blake was looking for her granddaughter."

But Daniel's mind had latched on to only one phrase. "Under *what* circumstances, Mr. Doyle?"

"Surely you know, Mr. Rayborn."

"I'm afraid I don't."

The young man blew out a breath. "I was so certain . . ." He cleared his throat and shifted his dark eyes to stare at the rug. "Please forget I ever mentioned . . ."

But a warm ray of optimism had pierced Daniel's confusion. "Are you saying . . . she *likes* me?"

Another wince, and, "Can't you tell?"

Daniel had hoped he wasn't imagining the intimacy of spirit between himself and Miss Doyle. But she was so kind to everyone that he wasn't certain. "Has she said anything?"

Resembling more and more a small boy who has accidentally laughed aloud in church, Mr. Doyle muttered, "I've said too much already, Mr. Rayborn. Please stop asking."

"Very well." But Daniel had heard enough for a smile to curve his lips. *Marvelous!*

Even so, he considered trying to talk the young man out of telling her the secret. The more who knew, the greater the possibility of someone making a slip of the tongue. Yet another part of him argued that Miss Doyle wasn't just *anyone* and that even a fledgling courtship should be based upon honesty.

It was something he would surely toss to-and-fro mentally were he in a more somber frame of mind. But somberness was far from him, so he ended up insisting upon taking Mr. Doyle out for supper down the street instead.

———

On the morning of Tuesday, the twenty-seventh of April, Sarah and Mr. Rayborn discussed her composition on "The New Toryism in the Late Eighteenth Century" and were about to proceed to calculus when Sarah frowned at the papers on the table. "I don't understand."

Her tutor gave her a little smile. "What don't you understand, Miss Matthews?"

She sighed. "How could George IV try to divorce his wife right after Princess Charlotte was born? And then put them aside as if they were never his family?"

"He was an incredibly selfish man, Miss Matthews. And there was still tremendous pressure put on royalty to bear sons. The old 'Henry the eighth' disease."

"I still can't see how a man could not want to take part in even a daughter's life. Probably half the orphans in Saint Matthew's wouldn't be there if their fathers would have claimed them." She had to blink the salt from her eyes and look away from his kindly stare. *You haven't thought about him in months . . . why now?* He had put her out of *his* mind before she was even born. Why couldn't she do the same? Especially knowing how heartless he was to-

ward her mother and even her grandmother.

"Miss Matthews."

Turning her eyes again toward him, she
made a weak effort at a smile.

"Most fathers love their children," he said
gently. "With all their hearts."

She nodded, though unconvinced. "I'm
sorry, Mr. Rayborn. Studying King George
reminded me of my own father. He didn't
love me with even part of his heart."

"You have nothing for which to be sorry."

With difficulty she swallowed. The
thought flitted across her mind that one
day, when she was in a better mood, she
would ask Mr. Rayborn for a physical explanation of how lumps happened to well
up in the backs of throats during times of
distress. "I wouldn't even have noticed that
he was evil if he would have read stories to
me and patted my head once in a while."

"It was your father who lost the most,
Miss Matthews."

"I doubt that."

"Oh, but he did. And one day you'll understand just how much."

Mr. Rayborn had not even met Jeremy
Blake, other than seeing his portrait in the

sitting room. But he spoke with such conviction that Sarah found herself halfway believing him. It would be nice to understand one day.

"Thank you, Mr. Rayborn." She was able to smile with a little more sincerity. "We can move on to calculus now."

———

Two evenings later Sarah sat on the terrace under a half-moon with the servants, except for Marie, who was out with her sisters. Mild breezes scented of crab apple blossoms, hyacinths, damp grass, and even a trace of earthy, but not unpleasant, stable aromas bathed Sarah's face and swayed gently the crab apple limbs as they wafted through the propped-open French door. Mr. Duffy, coaxed by Claire into fetching his harmonica, played folk tunes and hymns by request.

"Play 'The Bonny Lighter Boy,' please," Susan asked. "My mum used to sing it on washdays."

"I'll play it if you'll sing it."

She ducked her head, grinning. "Oh, not by myself!"

"I'll wager Naomi knows it," Trudy said

with a nod toward the chair next to Sarah. "Do give us a song, both of you."

"Very well," Naomi said to silence everyone's pleading. And when the music started again, she sang in a voice as clear and unwavering as bell chords,

It's of a brisk young sailor lad, and he
*   apprentice bound,*
And she a merchant's daughter, with
*   fifty thousand pound,*
They loved each other dearly, in
*   sorrow and in joy:*
Let him go where he will, he's my love
*   still, he's my bonny lighter boy.*

Susan joined in, her high voice missing the occasional note, but the combination was pleasing to Sarah's ears.

Her father, he being near her, he heard
*   what she did say—*
He cried Unruly daughter! I'll send him
*   far away;*
On board a ship I'll have him pressed,
*   I'll rob you of your joy—*
Send him where you will, he's my love
*   still, he's my bonny lighter boy!*

"Very good!" The voice came from the doorway after the applause died down. Heads turned toward Marie, who came out to sit in the chair Stanley brought over for her.

"Did you have a pleasant evening?" Mrs. Bacon asked.

"Yes, thank you. We were invited to supper at the Savilles', who own the French bakery." When Sarah started to rise, she said, "I have just looked in on Mrs. Blake. She is sleeping peacefully."

And then Marie turned to Naomi. "You sing like someone who is in love."

"Marie . . ." Naomi said with rolled eyes, but no anger in her voice. "Do you French think of nothing else?"

"Why, no," was the immediate reply. "There is also food."

Even Naomi joined in the laughter that followed, and Sarah smiled and settled back in her chair to peer at the dark sky, while her ears took in the precious, familiar banter all about her. Wisps of clouds moved across the stars as rapidly as her days seemed to be passing. As much as she looked forward to growing older, she feared the changes that were certain to occur.

Some had already happened, such as Hester's leaving. Others were even now set in motion—with Grandmother growing weaker and weaker, how much longer would she live? She had long begun to suspect that rheumatism wasn't the only problem, however often Grandmother and Doctor Raine insisted that it was. Sarah's eyes filled, blurring the stars. How empty the house would seem without her maternal presence!

Mr. Knight's words from Sunday past came to her. *"Friendships sometimes waver and fail, family members pass on, but the divine Love will continue to flow unwearied and undiminished through our lives, and we may rest peacefully in His promise: I will never leave thee nor forsake thee."*

Her disquiet heart felt some consolation. If anyone should know about resting in God during times of change, it would be Mr. Knight, who had left home and family to come to London. Surely he felt the pangs of loneliness, yet had put serving God above his own comfort.

I will try harder to trust my future to your

loving hands, Father, she prayed silently, staring up as if she could catch a glimpse of His face between the stars.

And please comfort Mr. Knight if he's lonely.

"Are you all right, dear?" Naomi whispered.

Miss Matthews turned her face toward her and smiled. "I just wish nights like this would never end."

"Yes, I understand," Naomi said, smiling back.

But the night did have to end, at least the wakeful part, for duties and schooling would be waiting in the morning. Everyone bade each other good-night and began drifting through the terrace door. Naomi was heading in that direction when she heard softly from behind, "Naomi?"

She turned. "Stanley?"

He stood there with his hands in his pockets and apology in his shadowed face. "Will you stay for a bit?"

"Of course." She gently closed the door after the last person had entered the house. Then she and the groomsman returned to the circle of chairs and sat side by side. She wasn't certain if he was choosing his words or wanting her to ask what was the matter, so she decided to wait a bit and see.

He was leaning forward, elbows propped upon knees. Presently he blew out his cheeks. "I haven't got a proper night's sleep for weeks, Naomi."

"I'm sorry. Are you still thinking about Hester?"

"Hester?" He shook his head. "No sense to lettin' myself do that."

Naomi suspected she knew the reason for his lack of sleep. Still, she waited for him to speak again.

"It's those things I've done, Naomi," he said miserably after a little while. "It ain't even fittin' to tell you some of them."

"Stanley, do you remember Sunday's sermon? Mr. Knight quoted a fitting scripture . . . *'Where sin abounded, grace did much more abound.'* "

"I didn't know what 'abounded' meant," he admitted.

Naomi smiled. "I can see how that would be confusing, in that case. It means something like 'filled.' Meaning, the more sin there is in a person, the more forgiveness God is willing to give."

"It just seems too simple, Naomi. Just sayin' I'm sorry?"

"You're right. It's more than saying you're sorry. God knows the heart, remember? It was when I saw my sin through *His* eyes that I began to understand how much it grieved Him."

He sent her a sidelong smirk. "What did you do wrong, Naomi? Use margarine in the scones?"

"Nothing *that* evil," she quipped. "But, Stanley, it doesn't matter if my sins were fewer or greater than yours. God is holy and cannot allow a smidgen of it into heaven—just as I won't allow a smidgen of margarine in my kitchen."

"I just think I need to mend some fences first, Naomi. But I'm afraid to go about it."

"If you'll repent first and trust Jesus Christ to take control of your life, He'll help you go about it. I know it's difficult to believe, Stanley. That's why faith is such a stumbling block for so many people. It's based upon what He is willing to do for us if we'll trust Him. Not what grand things we can do for Him."

He wiped his eyes with the back of his hand and was silent for so long that Naomi finally felt compelled to speak.

"Stanley?"

When he turned again to her, he said, "I'm tired of feelin' so dirty inside. I'm going to do that, Naomi."

"I'm so glad."

"But I'd like to go on up to my room first. It's all right if I do this alone, ain't it?"

"Certainly." She nodded understanding. "But you'll not be alone, Stanley."

Thirty-Eight

One week later at breakfast, Vicar Sharp declared himself almost recovered enough to pay calls and said he would certainly be able to resume the pulpit. Ethan was relieved about the pulpit part, for Sunday was two days away, and he had not gotten around to selecting and memorizing a sermon. But he hated the thought of dividing the visits again. Once word got out that the vicar was out and about, Ethan would have no excuse for hurrying out of parlors and sickrooms before the doors had settled back upon their hinges.

His first visit of the day was to Mrs. Stafford, who was *not* considerate enough to be asleep this time and whose palsy, according to her daughter-in-law, had gotten so bad that she dared not hold a cup of tea. "Mr. Knight . . ." Mrs. Stafford greeted him with a wavering voice. She was propped upon pillows in a high bed with tied-back bed-curtains of gold damask. "How good of you to call."

He held the trembling hand she extended for an appropriate amount of time—never could he bring himself to brush his lips even lightly against the limb of any ailing person—and then released it to sit in the bedside chair. The daughter-in-law stuck her head through the doorway to offer tea, which Ethan declined. He had figured out that accepting refreshment of any kind meant he must add at least ten minutes to a visit.

"I won't be there to hear him," Mrs. Stafford said after Ethan announced that Vicar Sharp was almost fully recovered. "I'm no longer able."

"God understands, Mrs. Stafford."

Tears trembled upon her sparse lashes. "I can't even go downstairs anymore. I suppose I won't leave this floor until the joiner comes for my body."

Such talk horrified Ethan because of the macabre images it brought to mind. "Don't say that, Mrs. Stafford."

"Well, it's true."

An idea occurred to him, and he was rather proud of himself for it. After all, one of a minister's duties was to encourage. "You know . . . I called upon Mrs. Arthur Blake just last week. Are you acquainted with her?"

The woman gave him an odd look. "Yes."

"Her bed has been moved down to the ground floor so she can visit her garden occasionally and not have to use the staircase."

"Indeed?"

"Her granddaughter says it has made her much happier."

Mrs. Stafford's lips pulled into a spasmodic frown. "You know her mother was a scullery maid."

"Mrs. Blake?"

"The girl. And her father, Jeremy Blake, never even married the mother."

Ethan's mind was beginning to stray toward Myra Rose, so he could not have cared less. But he still had to pass five or so minutes before he could leave tactfully. "It's a shame when these things happen. But it's good that the girl goes to church." *Blast . . . what was her name again?*

"Hmph! Dorothea allows her to promenade all over Mayfair as if she's royalty." The wavering of Mrs. Stafford's voice intensified with the heat of her words. "What kind of moral example does it set for our grandchildren? That it doesn't matter if a girl is out-of-wedlock, as long as she stands to inherit a fortune? Shameful!"

The half of Ethan's brain that was idly listening nudged to attention the part that had been thinking about Myra. "My, my," he said, shaking his head. "I would have assumed some male relative . . ."

"She has none. And in her eyes, the sun rises and sets upon that girl. So what do *you* think?"

I think her name was Matthews, Ethan told himself. "Still, with her standing to inherit, she must have suitors calling."

"I doubt that. Reputation is everything here in Mayfair. And then there's that repulsive hand that she hasn't the decency to cover." Another frown tugged at her face. "Of course, when Dorothea passes on and word gets out that all that money was dumped into the girl's lap . . . no doubt there'll be callers in droves. But I can assure you they won't be the well-bred sort, with consideration for their family names."

Ethan made some commensurable "tsks." "Shameful, those kind of men."

"Dorothea was much more amusing company before she brought that girl there to live . . . even though she insisted on showing off her piano playing too much. *I* could have taken lessons too, but . . ."

The rest was lost to Ethan, who nonetheless nodded attentively while his mind was consumed with other things. As soon as propriety allowed, he bid Mrs. Stafford good-day and left for his next call. He thought about Miss Matthews more and more as the day progressed. *You can't be serious*, he chided himself between calls, yet his mind would return to the same subject.

Miss Matthews was not the only heiress in Mayfair, but Ethan was well aware that a curate, even a vicar, was not considered a suitable match for a daughter of the upper classes. No matter how often those daughters flirted with him on the church grounds.

But a girl on the outskirts of society, and flawed as she was, would surely be grateful to gain a husband of fine reputation. And assisting her in managing her estate would be so time-consuming that this husband would generously insist upon giving up his own vocation. What would it be like never to have to labor at anything tedious for the rest of his life? Not to listen to the aches and pains of parishioners or boring parlor chit-chat? Not to have to memorize sermons? To sleep as late as he wished? To have money without having to endure a lecture about thrift from his father or suffer the fear of getting his fingers caught in the tithes?

But the hand . . . he thought with a little shudder.

You would only have to endure the sight of it for a little while. She seemed extremely pliable. Soon after the wedding, he was sure he could charm her into wearing something over it. Myra was only a minor drawback, for he would never consider marrying her anyway. Women such as she did not tend to age well, and he had to think of his life twenty years from now. But it would be amusing to help Myra achieve her dreams—a nice flat in a discreet side street in the theatre district and a living that would allow her to quit selling parasols and start attending auditions. *And still leave plenty of time for her dear benefactor.*

The vicar was pottering in his garden late that afternoon. "You're in a jolly mood, aren't you?" the old man said, smiling as Ethan approached. "I could hear you whistling way back."

Ethan nodded and smiled back. "Peace of mind, sir."

"How nice to hear it. So many young men in the church these days don't seem to be completely certain of their calling."

"Oh, I'm certain," Ethan assured him.

———

On the Saturday afternoon of the eighth of May, Daniel suggested touring the Tower of London. Sarah, Miss Doyle, and William Doyle had been there as well, but they were agreeable toward the idea. To Daniel the Tower was not just viewing historical exhibits, but a journey back in time. Helping to perpetuate the illusion were the wardens or Beefeaters ambling the stony Green— each resembling a Knave of Hearts in a wide flat black hat and scarlet coat.

"You catch scraps of every tongue in this place, don't you?" Miss Doyle said in a soft voice so as not to offend anyone in earshot. Above, city sparrows quarreled and restless gray pigeons cooed as they fluttered from one stony nook to another.

Daniel smiled at her. "And Londoners, who can visit at any time, tend to put it off." He wondered again if her nephew had decided against revealing to her his identity, because he could see no difference in her expression today, nor had he all week at the lunch table.

Mr. Doyle ran fingers reverently over a shattered cannon. "Do you think someone growing up in the shadow of the Roman coliseum, for example, would think it as commonplace as we consider the stable?"

"You know . . . that may be so," Sarah said. She bent to pick up a cannonball with her good hand, propping it steady with her left. "People such as Mr. Swann and his daughters come from all over London to picnic at Berkeley Square, and often I pass right by without really *seeing* it."

"Here, may I have that?" Mr. Doyle stood and scooped the ball from her hand. "We wouldn't want it crushing your toes."

Protective without being overbearing, Daniel thought. *What a fine husband he would make for her*.

His eye caught a quick movement at his right. Miss Doyle was staring up at the White Tower, a hand raised beyond the brim of her yellow straw bonnet to aid in shielding her eyes from the bright sun. Twenty-one years ago he was drawn to a young woman's spirited effervescence, not understanding how a candle that burned too brightly could not burn forever. Now that he carried scars from that same flame, he appreciated the healing balm of a serene, unchanging nature. Was it so, William Doyle's hint that she felt some affection for him? And had she any inkling of how smitten he was with her?

Miss Doyle turned her face to look at him. Warmth sprang to Daniel's cheeks, something he could not recall happening since his drunken years—and then, for a different reason. "It's the oldest part of the fortress," he said lamely. "Built by William the Conqueror in the eleventh century."

Kindly she nodded, as if every British schoolchild did not already know that. But the quiet mirth in her blue eyes suggested that for all her maturity and poise, she was more than a little pleased to have caught him staring.

" 'A passage perillus maketh a port Pleasant. Authur Poole 1568,' " Naomi read aloud. It was not difficult to imagine the tedium that led captives to scratch names and estates, quaint aphorisms and despairing sentiments into the hard stone walls of the chief prison room of the Beauchamp Tower.

"It's good that he could think of heaven," she said to Mr. Rayborn, leaning a little closer to be heard above the dark-haired man translating some of the etchings into melodic rapid Italian for five others in his group.

"So did his brother, Edmund," Mr. Rayborn told her, and read: " 'That which is sown by God in tears, is reaped in Joy. E. Poole.' "

"I'm glad that they were together, at least," Naomi said. The Italian tourists moved on through one of the passageways, leaving her and Mr. Rayborn alone in the prison chamber. She went to the long window facing the White Tower and scanned the shadowy ground for any sign of William and Miss Matthews, who had declared themselves more interested in watching the soldiers' drills from the Waterloo barracks.

"Can you see them?" Mr. Rayborn stood beside her now.

"I can just make out her bonnet." She tapped the glass lightly with a gloved finger. "Through the branches there. But I don't see William."

"Surely he's not far away. Just in case of some insurrectionary soldier or a rabid pigeon."

Turning her face toward him, Naomi thought about how she liked the creases at the corners of his eyes, evidence that laughter had been a part of his life as well as tragedy. "A rabid pigeon, Mr. Rayborn?"

"Any warm-blooded creature can contract rabies, though it's extremely rare in birds." He gave her a self-effacing smile. "Forgive me."

"For what?"

"It was a silly thing to say."

"Silly?" She smiled back at him. "And here I stand grateful to have learned something new."

"You're very kind, Miss Doyle."

"Thank you." And ignoring the faint warning in her mind that their growing friendship could be irreconcilably damaged, she said, "And you are very noble, Mr. Rayborn."

"Noble?" The surprise in his expression faded into resignation. "When did he tell you?"

"Only an hour or so before you arrived." She had had to excuse herself to shed private tears for Mrs. Blake, though she had become aware by the amounts of food sent back to the kitchen that her mistress was losing interest in things that mattered to those with robust health. Like the Poole brothers, her sights were set on another place.

But she could not help but be delighted to learn that Sarah actually had a father, and a decent one who had loved her from the first.

"He said he had warned you," she explained, "so I assumed you would be wondering."

"I was," he admitted.

A fair-haired trio entered the room, two young men with the look of brothers, and a girl of about twelve. The young men exchanged polite nods with Naomi and Mr. Rayborn, while the girl read aloud from a guide book:

" 'The simple name JANE is always inspected with interest, being generally thought to be that of Lady Jane Grey, but if so, it could not possibly have been cut here by her own hand, though it may have been by that of her captive bridegroom.' "

Meanwhile Naomi and Mr. Rayborn pretended to study etchings on the wall again—or at least Naomi pretended and suspected Mr. Rayborn was doing the same. The trio did not linger but moved on when the girl whined, "The cells are too gloomy. And you *said* we could see the jewel room first."

When Mr. Rayborn turned to Naomi again, he wore a look of desperation. "I'm not attempting to defraud Mrs. Blake, Miss Doyle."

"Mr. Mitchell explained all of that to William, Mr. Rayborn."

"I owe her a debt for the kindness she's shown Sarah."

"Which you're paying, and then some," Naomi assured him. "It's remarkably selfless of you."

He stared at her in silence for a moment. "It's not so selfless. There have been some unexpected rewards."

"Well, yes. You still get to spend time with her."

"I treasure that time, Miss Doyle." The creases at his eyes deepened. "As well as the time I spend with you. Though it's not nearly enough to suit me."

As much as Naomi believed coyness more suited to the young, she understood that there were certain rituals to courtship that must be observed. And it was incumbent upon her at that moment to affect a degree of surprise. With a lift of brows she asked in a soft voice, "What are you saying, Mr. Rayborn?"

He gave her a little smile, as if he knew exactly what she was doing. "I'm saying that there is no place I would rather be this very moment than here with you."

Naomi returned his smile. "In prison?"

He moved closer to take both of her hands and lifted them to his chest. She could not recall any man, even the beau of her youth, regarding her with such warmth and affection. "It's somehow appropriate. You've totally captured my heart, Naomi Doyle."

Looking up at him, Naomi breathed a

quiet, contented sigh. "I like hearing that, Mr. Rayborn."

"Daniel?" he prompted in a hopeful tone.

"Daniel," she said, lifting her chin. His kiss was slow, thoughtful, and rendered her too lightheaded to be aware of anything but the two of them. Until they drew apart and the smattering of applause met her ears. She dropped his hands and turned to face a half-dozen smiles and exclamations of *congratulazioni!* and *benissimo!*

While Naomi covered her face with a hand, prompting laughter from the Italians, Daniel replied *grazie!* and took her by the arm to hurry them both through the opposite passageway. "We'll have something to tell our grandchildren!" he said, chuckling.

As they rejoined his daughter and her nephew on the Green and she could finally smile about it, she told herself that perhaps an appreciative audience was appropriate for a woman who waited thirty-seven years to be kissed and that indeed it would make a fine story to tell grandchildren. It would take that long for her cheeks to stop burning.

———

Vicar Sharp was back in the pulpit the next morning, looking a bit worn for the wear, but unwavering in his deliver of a sermon titled "The Three Spiritual Perfumes."

"It's so good to have you back, Vicar," Sarah told him at the door, feeling the hypocrite for her disappointment that Mr. Knight had not conducted the service.

But the curate appeared at her right elbow when she and Marie were halfway to the coach. "Miss Matthews . . . Miss Prewitt," he said, his mismatched eyes as affectionate as if he had bumped into two old friends. "You're both looking especially lovely today."

"Thank you," Sarah told him while Marie nodded and took the compliment as her due.

"How is dear Mrs. Blake?" he asked.

Sarah's smile faded. "About the same. I fear we'll not see any improvement at her age."

"She does miss coming to church," Marie said.

"Hmm." The curate grasped his clean-shaven chin between his thumb and forefinger. "You know, that gives me an idea. I don't know what you would think about this . . ."

"What is it?" Sarah asked.

"Well, the last time I stopped by, you mentioned repeating as much as you can recall of the sermons to her—and I'm sure you do a fine job, but truthfully, there is something comforting about having a representative of the Church perform that service."

Sarah wasn't quite certain what he was suggesting. "Are you offering to do that?"

"I haven't family responsibilities on Sunday afternoons like the vicar. I would come after you've had lunch, of course. And only if Mrs. Blake is willing."

"Yes, please do," Sarah said, clasping her left hand happily with her gloved right one. "Your last visit did her so much good."

"Shall I today, then?"

"Today?" It was too good to be true. She couldn't wait to tell Grandmother.

"Perhaps we should ask Madame first," Marie cautioned.

"But she'll be delighted," Sarah said. "You know how happy she is to have callers. An even better idea occurred to her. "Come early for lunch. It's the least we can do. Naomi usually has it ready about an hour after we get home."

She was just about to offer a ride in the coach but happened to glance past his left shoulder and wilted. A gaggle of young women, including Miss Fowler, were leveling scathing looks directly at her. *He shouldn't be speaking with you in public like this*, she told herself. She was used to the ostracism, but Mr. Knight had his reputation to consider. "Well, we should go now. . . ."

But he turned to look in the same direction. There was amusement in his face when he turned again to Sarah. "Forgive me for being so presumptuous, but if I rode over with you in your coach, Mrs. Blake and I would have time to chat before lunch. Just in case she's used to afternoon naps."

"That . . . would be nice, thank you."

"My pleasure." Then the curate did a bold thing. He positioned himself between Sarah and Marie and, crooking his elbows, offered arms to both. As they turned again toward the coach, Sarah could feel eyes burning into the back of her head, but she could not help but admire his lack of concern for local gossip.

Once he had traded greetings with Stanley and assisted her and Marie into the coach, Mr. Knight said from the open door with apology in his tone, "I should tell Mrs. Sharp not to expect me for lunch."

"That's very considerate of him, don't you think?" Sarah said to Marie, who was seated beside her so Mr. Knight could have a seat to himself. She had sensed a bit of aloofness coming from the maid, but then with Marie it was sometimes difficult to tell.

"I just wonder . . ." Marie's amber eyes peered past Sarah through the window. "There are others in Mayfair who cannot attend church. Why does he only offer this to Madame?"

"Because he's . . ." Sarah began before understanding what Marie was implying. Or at least she thought she did. Could Mr. Knight be trying to curry favor because of Grandmother's wealth?

She shamed herself for the thought. If Mr. Knight cared about money so much, he wouldn't have chosen the ministry. Did every act of kindness have to be viewed with suspicion? Besides, Grandmother wasn't the only wealthy person in Mayfair.

Mr. Knight stepped back into the coach

before Sarah could reason with Marie. "Again, I'm grateful for the lunch invitation. And Vicar Sharp, good soul that he is, will enjoy having a meal with just his family present for a change."

"You're most welcome, Mr. Knight," Sarah said as the wheels lurched into motion.

To her horror, Marie voiced the question again. "Do you offer this to all the ailing who cannot attend church, Mr. Knight?"

He looked at her for several long seconds. "No. I don't."

Marie folded her arms and waited for an explanation. Sarah clinched her teeth and lowered her eyes to stare at the toes of his boots.

"Mrs. Blake reminds me of my beloved grandmother, may God rest her soul."

Sarah's eyes shifted to his face again.

"She moved in with us when my grandfather died and was the person who most influenced me to become a minister." His distinctive mismatched eyes seemed to look into the distance while his lips curved into a smile. "That day the vicar and I first called . . . I was so struck with the resemblance. It seemed very much a sign from

God that just because I had left all that was familiar to me, it did not mean He wouldn't sprinkle little oases of remembrance across my path."

Sarah's eyes filled. When Marie spoke this time, her tone had lost its suspicion. "You miss her, Mr. Knight?"

He closed his eyes for a fraction. "More than I can say, Miss Prewitt. And more so now. Sometimes I can almost hear the sound of her piano softly playing."

"Why, Grandmother plays the piano too," Sarah said. "At least she did when she could use her hands."

"She did?" Mr. Knight shook his head with wonder. "Uncanny!"

❧ *Thirty-Nine* ❧

"What are they doing now, Marie?" Dorothea asked from her chair one week later.

Heaving an aggrieved sigh, Marie pushed herself to her feet and went to the window. "The same thing they were doing five minutes ago, Madame. Walking."

"Does it appear that they're getting along well?"

"I cannot see their faces well enough. But they are not spitting at each other."

"Marie!"

The maid turned an unrepentant face toward her. "Is it not past time for Madame's nap?"

"Later." Dorothea frowned at the light knocking at the sitting room door. "Now, who would that be during my nap time?"

She had only said it to irritate Marie, which was one of the few pleasures left to her. And it worked, for the maid grumbled in French all the way to the door. The only phrase that met Dorothea's ears distinctly was *C'est fou!* which she believed meant either "This is crazy!" or "This is cold!"

Stanley stepped meekly through the doorway. He had changed from livery clothes into clean work clothes and clutched his cloth cap in his hands.

"Might I have a word with you, mum?"

It was not like Stanley to present anything less than a jovial face to her. And Mrs. Bacon was the one to whom he brought any requests such as a raise in wages or something needed in the stable. Dorothea nodded. "Very well."

"Shall I leave?" Marie asked.

After a hesitation he shook his head. "Everyone's going to find out anyway."

"Then do come over here and have a seat where I can see you without straining my neck," Dorothea said.

"Oh . . . yes, mum," he said and scooted over to a chair as if he feared her neck would break off any second. Marie sat as well.

"You're not thinking of leaving us, are you?" Dorothea asked.

"I don't want to, mum. But . . ." He twisted the cap in his hands, his fringed blue eyes not quite meeting hers. "I'm goin' to be gettin' married very soon and wonder if I might bring my wife to live over the stables. And our son."

"Your . . . son?"

The twisting of his cap intensified. "He's seven months old. His name's Guy, after Penny's father."

"Penny is his mother?"

"Oh yes, mum. Penny Wallace. They live in Saint Giles."

"Saint Giles? The slums?"

He hung his head. "Penny lost her job as shopgirl in the draper's store on New Bond after she had the baby, so they moved in with her folks." Meeting her eyes again, his were beseeching. "She's handy with a needle and could take on mending to make up for the extra food we'd need, as there ain't a kitchen over the stables, but if mending ain't enough, you could cut my wages to make up for it. I already spoke with Naomi, and she said there's usually some leftover anyhow, so she wouldn't have to cook but a bit extra if you gave permission."

It was more than Dorothea had ever heard the groomsman speak at one time. She looked to Marie for help.

"I believe Stanley is desiring to put some wrongs to right," the maid said.

He nodded grimly. "Something I should have done a long time ago."

"Why are you doing it now?" Dorothea asked.

"It's what a Christian man's supposed to do. Take care of his family."

"And you're certain the child is yours?"

"Yes, mum." He blew out a long breath. "I acted shameful, tellin' Penny he weren't mine. But I always knew he was."

It all sounded achingly familiar to Dorothea, even though Jeremy had never gone so far as to own up to his paternity of the baby Mary Tomkin carried. "May I assume you do not love this Penny?"

The corners of his lips tugged downward, yet there was no distress in his voice. "That ain't the boy's fault, mum. As for love ... I'm just now learnin' that it ain't the same thing I thought it was for years. But I figure if I act decent and kindly toward her, we can give the boy and each other a good home. And maybe God will put a dose of true love for her in my heart one day."

Dorothea blinked the clouding from her

eyes. She could not go back and undo her act of turning out Mary Tomkin nor force her deceased son to own up to his responsibility. But here in her sitting room she was being offered an opportunity to build something upon past regrets. Stanley was not her natural kin, but as a child of God he was her brother. And his little son, an innocent who could benefit from the lessons she had learned.

"When will you marry, Stanley?"

"As soon as the vicar is willing. I want to get them out of Saint Giles as soon as I can. But if I have to look for another position . . ."

"You'll do no such thing," Dorothea ordered. "Go speak with the vicar first thing in the morning. Request a license, not the banns, so you'll not have to wait three weeks. Ask Mrs. Bacon for a couple of pounds from the household account for the fee if you need it."

Gratefulness flooded his expression. "I'll never forget this, mum. And I've enough. I wouldn't feel like a proper husband, startin' off marriage on someone else's two quid."

"Naomi wanted to try out some new ones, so I planted another row," Mr. Duffy said that same afternoon, pointing out seedlings of chervil, golden purslane, sweet marjoram, and borage—newcomers to the ever-expanding herbal neighborhood where angelica, sage, mint, fennel, tarragon, savory, burnet, hyssop, lemon thyme, pennyroyal, and sweet basil also resided.

"It all looks very nice, as usual," William said.

"Aye, very nice." Mr. Duffy bent to pull a blade of grass from the mound of savory and tossed it. "I don't mind tending flowers and fruit trees, but I've always leaned toward vegetables. Mayhap it's because Claire and I never had little ones. Nursin' a seed along until it's a shiny head of cauliflower or cabbage fills my heart with the same pride a papa must feel when his tot grows to be a decent fellow."

Were William in his pre-lunch mood, he would have teased good-naturedly that parents did not generally eat their children once they became decent fellows. But his mood had taken a turn for the worse when he discovered that Mr. Knight, who had lunched in the sitting room with Sarah, Mrs. Blake, and Marie for two Sundays in a row, was now escorting Sarah about the square.

"Right next to the radishes will be Egyptian turnips," Mr. Duffy went on. "Mr. Hammer, the Rothschilds' new gardener, gave me the seeds. He says they're the deepest bloodred—have you ever heard of such a thing?"

"I don't think I have," William said absently. It wasn't that he didn't like Mr. Knight. Who could dislike such a dedicated young man, whose brilliance in the pulpit was the talk of all of St. George's parishioners? And for a lowly curate to snub his nose at Mayfair's prudish society like that was nothing short of courageous. That was what made the discovery even worse. Had Sarah been accompanied by a scoundrel, anger could have burned up some of the melancholy within him.

After he had admired Mr. Duffy's brood of sprouts long enough for politeness' sake, and then a little longer for the sake of long-time friendship, he excused himself and started downstairs for the kitchen. His aunt, just putting the lid on a large kettle, turned to smile at him.

"Ah, there you are."

"Mr. Duffy was showing me the herb garden." He wondered how much of the flush upon her face had to do with the heat of the stove and how much with whatever happened between her and Mr. Rayborn yesterday. *At least one of us is happy*, he thought. And Aunt Naomi deserved happiness, if anyone did.

"Trudy will watch the soup," she said, reaching back to untie her apron. "Why don't we walk over and hear the bagpipers?" It had been discussed during lunch, the band from Glasgow assembling at Hyde Park at two. The Duffys, Avis, Susan, and Mrs. Bacon were planning to go, with Trudy declining out of dislike for bagpipes, and Stanley because, as he put it, he had some important things to attend. "Miss Matthews might care to come along. Was she out back with you?"

William shook his head. "She's walking the square with Mr. Knight."

"Really? I assumed he left after lunch." She tossed her apron into the soiled linen basket. "I suppose he may enjoy it as well."

"If you wish. I'm going to head for home."

"What's wrong, William?" she asked with fading smile.

"Nothing." He covered a make-believe yawn. "Just need to rest up a bit before tomorrow morning."

Her blue eyes studied his face. "It's Mr. Knight, isn't it? Surely you don't think he's initiating a courtship just because they're taking a walk?"

"Why wouldn't he?" William asked and thought, *Why wouldn't any man?* Sarah was so unique: pious and yet fun, compassionate without being maudlin, intelligent yet charmingly naive. He had discovered her inner beauty in the painstakingly even lines of her letters to Oxford, back while she was ungainly and as thin as a cat's elbow. But a person would have to be short-sighted not to notice her outer beauty now. And there was her grandmother's wealth, although William could at least appreciate that the curate was probably not interested in it.

His aunt stepped up to rest a hand upon his crossed forearm. "You love her, don't you?"

"I think I always have, Aunt Naomi."

"So you're going to go back to your flat and mope?"

"How could I ever compete with some-one like Mr. Knight? You've heard how she talks about him."

"I don't know that you have to compete, Will." She gave him a sympathetic smile. "This isn't a cricket match, with the trophy of her affection going to the one more skilled at wooing. Surely if she feels the same for you, and it's God's will . . ."

"It's the 'if's' that frighten me," he con-fessed.

"Could you be happy winning her heart by default? You wouldn't want to find your-self wondering one day if she chose you simply because no other suitors came call-ing. Worse yet, you wouldn't want to have *her* wondering it."

"No, I wouldn't care for that," he had to admit, though it would not be difficult to convince himself he would wish to marry Sarah under *any* circumstance. But hadn't he meant it when he prayed on the night of her birthday that God would send her a de-cent husband? He had even felt an un-canny assurance that the request would be granted. *If Mr. Knight is your choice for her,*

Father, please show me that clearly. And if it's so . . . please help me to be man enough to accept it.

"But does that mean I shouldn't tell her how I feel about her?" he asked.

"I think you should, William. And then give her some time. That way, if she ultimately chooses you, you'll know it's purely from love and not from pressure or the fear of hurting her dearest friend's feelings."

"I can do that," he said at length.

"Very good. In the meantime, shall we walk on to the park?"

"But what if we pass them in the square?"

"Yes, that's possible." She glanced toward a cupboard. "I've some flour sacks to cover our heads . . ."

"Flour sacks." In spite of the pain in his heart, William had to smile. "I don't suppose that'll be necessary."

"What an incredible turn of events!" Mr. Knight enthused as they turned southward in the square. A sweet little breeze ruffled the feathery limbs of the plane trees, and a number of crocuses and daffodils had pushed up their heads to flower. "From an orphanage to a mansion at age thirteen."

"I'm grateful there were people in both locations who cared about me." Sarah was also grateful that he did not ask how she happened to be in the orphanage in the first place. He likely knew anyway, but unpleasant stories did not become less so with the telling. Her right hand rested in the crook of his arm, which he had offered before they crossed the street. At first she wasn't certain if it was proper for her to take it, as they were not chaperoned and she hardly knew him, but then she reminded herself that Mr. Knight was not the sort of man to engage in any impropriety.

"You know, Miss Matthews," he continued after sending a smile toward the couple and two small children sharing a picnic lunch on a quilt, "it's quite remarkable that I should make your acquaintance. I've never felt the liberty to mention this to anyone before now . . . but one of my burning passions has been to institute a home for orphaned boys one day."

Sarah's stopped walking, causing Mr. Knight to do the same.

"Is something wrong?" he asked. Before

she could reply, he hastened to say,
"Please understand . . . it's not that I
haven't compassion for girls in that situation. But in Birmingham there seemed to be
so many more boys out on the streets."

"I think it's wonderful," Sarah replied.
She had almost said *you're wonderful* but
caught herself.

"Thank you for understanding, Miss
Matthews. There's always that drive to do
more, but . . ."

"You have to follow what God puts in
your heart, Mr. Knight." She was humbled
that he would confide such a lofty aspira-
tion to *her* and amazed that she could
speak with him so forthrightly. "Mrs.
Forsyth and her husband were led to care
for girls. I'm sure they had to trust that
there were others led to do the same for
boys."

"Yes, indeed."

He smiled with such warmth that Sarah
pretended a sudden interest in a painted-
lady butterfly flitting past. They strolled a
bit farther in silence, nearing tables that
GUNTER'S CONFECTIONERY had set up
on the square. A number of the young upper-class fashionable set sent curious and

even indignant looks in their direction. Sarah attempted to veer away from them but could not, for Mr. Knight's steps remained constant.

"Would you care for an ice, Miss Matthews?"

"No, thank you."

"They're only jealous of your beauty," he said in a low voice.

She couldn't help but give him a bitter little smile. "I don't think that's what they're whispering about."

"Then you haven't looked in the mirror lately, Miss Matthews."

Again she had to look away from embarrassment, though it was nice having him say it. When they had passed the tables and she could breathe easily again, he asked about her studies, and she found herself confiding how frustrated she had been at the thought of missing college before her grandmother hired Mr. Rayborn.

"You're happy with that arrangement?" he asked.

"Oh, quite! I'm learning so much more than I ever thought I could."

Mr. Knight said in a wistful voice, "I do envy you, Miss Matthews. As much fulfillment as my vocation brings, I do wish I could attend the occasional Cambridge lecture again. But I have made a habit of reading thought-provoking material before retiring, no matter how weary I am from visiting the sick and studying Scripture."

"How admirable. What are you reading now?"

"Now?" Turning his face to her again, he raised an eyebrow. "Why, nothing. I'm walking with you."

Sarah smiled. "No, at night."

He patted the hand resting in the crook of his elbow. "Forgive me, I couldn't resist. I'm actually digging into *Essay Concerning Human Understanding* by George Camden."

Don't you mean John Locke? Sarah thought but had not the heart to correct him on that nor the fact that Camden's given name was William and not George. A mind so filled with responsibility toward others would, of course, experience memory lapses now and then. Why, it was a wonder that he had the time to walk with her now.

They were nearing the area across from her grandmother's house again. Sarah hap-

pened to glance off to her left and noticed
Naomi and William on the pavement across
the street, heading in the direction of the
park. The longing to accompany them
lasted only until she reminded herself of
how honored she was to be escorted by
someone as wise and esteemed and compassionate as Mr. Knight. But she did wave
with her free left hand.

"Who are they?" Mr. Knight asked as the
two returned the wave.

"Our cook, Naomi, and her nephew,
William. My two dearest—"

Sarah noticed he was looking at the
hand she still held out in front of her. There
was no mistaking the pain in his eyes,
though he was quick to shift his attention
back toward Naomi and William.

"It doesn't hurt," she assured him as she
lowered it to her side.

"I beg your pardon?"

"My hand. I hardly even think about it.
And it seldom hinders me from doing anything . . . though I'd be a poor juggler."

He smiled and patted her other hand
again. "I'm so glad, Miss Matthews. Not
only for the absence of pain, but that you
have such a healthy outlook about it. It

would grieve me to think of your having to suffer."

"Thank you for saying that." She didn't know how else to reply to such compliments, which she would have almost considered flattery coming from the lips of someone less sincere than Mr. Knight.

She sent a fleeting glance over her shoulder at Naomi and William. Their heads were together, their attention upon whatever it was they were discussing. She wondered what it was, but then Mr. Knight gave her that warm smile again and began telling her how much he enjoyed chatting over sermons with "dear Mrs. Blake," and how fortunate she was to have such a loving grandmother who reminded him so much of his own.

And she thought how incredible it was that she, Sarah Matthews, conceived in the most wretched of circumstances, born out of wedlock and put out in a pail like refuse, should happen to be walking in Berkeley Square on the arm of an esteemed man of God.

❧ *Forty* ❧

On Tuesday, the eighteenth of May, Daniel watched his daughter stare reverently at the flyleaf of *Voyage au centre de la terre*, or "Journey to the Center of the Earth."

"However did you get Mr. Verne to sign it?" she asked at the library table.

"William Blackwood and Sons—my publishers—are distributing this English version." He glanced at a set of shelves to his right. "I've noticed three of his other books . . ."

"I adore them! And William's been haunting booksellers waiting for this one. I can't wait to show him." Hesitancy entered the green eyes above her smile. "But you don't want to give it away, do you?"

"Working for a publisher means I've more books than time to read," he replied with a little smile. "Shall we move on to Latin?"

He had to downplay the gesture, as well as the pains he had taken to obtain the autographed book, because propriety did not allow a tutor to present a gift to a young female student. But he could not allow the day to pass without some sort of acknowledgment, even though Naomi had informed him that Sarah believed herself to be born in January of 1857 instead of nineteen years ago today. Neither could Naomi ignore the occasion, he discovered, for the main dish at lunch was chestnut-stuffed pullets.

"It's her favorite dish next to oysters, but those aren't in season," she explained as they sat on a wooden bench between two trees in a shady spot carpeted with patches of wild violets. They had established the habit of visiting in the garden after lessons were over for the day *and* before Naomi had to complete supper preparations and Daniel's walk over to the omnibus stop at Piccadilly. Ofttimes Mr. Duffy, Stanley, or even Mrs. Blake and Marie would join them. Which was why today Daniel suggested the square.

"It was very thoughtful of you, Naomi," he said, their clasped hands resting on the bench between them. "One day we'll tell Sarah the significance of both gestures."

And then Daniel hoped to make the day even more meaningful. "Do you remember my saying in the tower we would have something to tell our grandchildren?"

"I remember," she said softly while staring out toward the passing carriage.

"It would be nice if they were the same children, don't you think?"

She turned her face to him. "Are you asking me to marry you, Daniel?"

"I love you, Naomi. I can't imagine life without you."

"Doesn't it concern you that we're not equals?"

"Not equals?" That such a thing would even enter her mind pained him. But with a little smile he teased, "Don't be cruel, Naomi. I would try my best to be worthy of you."

His effort to coax away her misgivings failed, for she frowned and said softly, "Do be serious, Daniel. Could you bear what your family and friends might think?"

"I would be a most wretched man if I allowed the opinions of others to guide my life." Daniel lifted her hand to his lips and kissed it. "Besides, I can't imagine anyone in my acquaintance not loving you as I do. Please say yes, Naomi."

When her frank stare did not alter, he winced. "Or even 'perhaps'?"

This finally brought a smile to her lips, and there seemed no lessening of affection in her bottle-blue eyes. But when she did speak, her tone was quietly solemn. "I'm thirty-seven years old, Daniel. And this is my first proposal."

Fearing blurting out the wrong thing at such a crucial time, he could only give her a puzzled stare. And then understanding happened upon him from nowhere, or perhaps from God growing impatient with his thickheadedness. Pushing aside the satchel at his feet, Daniel slipped down on one knee and took up both her hands. They smiled at each other.

"Naomi Doyle . . . will you make me the happiest man in England by consenting to be my wife?"

"I will, Daniel," she replied and leaned slightly forward. He kissed her, long and tenderly, and thought his heart would burst from happiness.

"I can hardly wait until we can tell Sarah she's gaining a wonderful mother," he said when they sat side by side again. Realizing then the full meaning of that statement, he added, "Not that I wish Mrs. Blake would hurry and . . ."

It wasn't necessary to finish, for Naomi squeezed his hand. "I understand, Daniel. And I'll be so pleased to call her 'daughter.' "

Daniel leaned to kiss the tip of her pert little nose. "That'll soften the blow of learning who her father is."

"As if!" she said lightly. "She may need a little time to sort out everything she believes about herself, but she'll be pleased. And so will William to have you for an uncle. He's been reminding me of your good qualities ever since you and he had that talk."

"Intelligent man." With a contented smile, Daniel wondered if Job had felt half so blessed upon learning he was to have a family again. And realizing that Naomi would need to return to the kitchen soon, he hastened on to practicalities.

"Is early October too soon for you?" The Biology text would be completed by mid-September, meaning a substantial advance royalty. There was also the money set aside from his tutoring wages, after paying Mr. Garrett. She deserved the very nicest honeymoon he could provide. "We could travel to Florence or Paris . . . anywhere you'd care to go."

"October is fine, Daniel." A second later uncertainty passed over her face. "But . . . will you be disappointed if we have to delay the trip? If Mrs. Blake is still with us by then, I wouldn't want her to have to get used to another cook. It's difficult enough to coax her to eat."

"Of course." And he would want to be here for Sarah, should Mrs. Blake pass on during that time. But his pride felt some injury that she would still work in someone else's kitchen. "I was looking forward to providing for you," he confessed.

"And you will, in due time," she reasoned. "Besides, you'll still be tutoring Sarah. We could come in and leave together, and you'll still be able to flirt with me over lunch."

Daniel had to smile. "Have I been that obvious?"

"Just ask Stanley." The idea was made far more palatable by her assurance that Mrs. Bacon would work out a schedule convenient for them, including having Trudy and one of the others taking over breakfasts and cleaning up after supper.

"Practical as well as beautiful," Daniel said, raising her hand to his lips. "I like that in a wife."

"Yes?" She returned his smile, a light in her blue eyes. "She's not too practical to turn down Paris when the proper time comes."

Naomi was not surprised at Mrs. Blake's reaction to the news. "Marvelous!" she exclaimed, crooked hands clasped together against her chest.

But she was stunned by Marie's. The maid rose from her sitting room chair, caught her up in a suffocating embrace, and wept upon her shoulder. "I am so happy for you!"

When she was finished with Naomi, who was beginning to shed tears herself, Marie caught Daniel up in a quicker, though no less emotional, embrace. "She will make you a wonderful wife!"

Miss Matthews came forward to embrace her and then Daniel. But even as she smiled and extended best wishes, in her green eyes lurked the lost-look from her first days at Berkeley Square.

Naomi realized why. Turning again to Mrs. Blake, she said, "We would like to continue on here, Madam, if you've no objections."

"I'm grateful for that . . . both of you," the elderly woman replied.

And Miss Matthews visibly relaxed, relief flooding her expression. "William will be delighted. We rather hoped you two would . . . well, you know."

"Indeed?" Naomi said dryly, recalling the times she and William had managed to veer off to themselves during their Saturday outings.

Covering another smile with her hand, the girl said, "Were we that obvious?"

"Oh, not as obvious as others." Naomi did not look at Mrs. Blake and Marie, but a second later their guilty chuckles told all. Daniel joined in, then his daughter and Naomi were laughing as well.

"Now, that was a tonic," Mrs. Blake said, wiping her eyes when the laughter was spent.

A more sobered Marie said, "When will you tell William?"

Naomi's smile faded. She would not see him until Saturday. She didn't want to send such news by wire or messenger. But she hated the thought of him being the last to know.

"I'm heading over there now," Daniel replied as if they had already discussed it. After they made the rounds to announce their engagement to every servant, Naomi accompanied him out to the porch.

"What will you do if he hasn't made it home yet?" she asked. "Don't worry." He hefted his satchel. "I'll find a café and work on my text."

"That's so good of you."

"Good of me?" The creases came to the corners of his green eyes. "I want to tell the world, Naomi." After kissing her cheek, he bounded down the steps and turned to wave. "I just may shout it from the street corners!"

Smiling her way down the service steps, Naomi sent up a silent prayer for William. He would be happy for them, of course. But she hoped the fact that she was able to find love would not cause him remorse over his own uncertain situation. She had to remind herself, as did William, of the promise in Scripture that all things work together for good for those who love God. Grace, no less abundant than when it was poured over Noah, would be available for her nephew no matter what lay in store for the future.

———

At half past seven, William closed the door, tossed his satchel to a chair, and lit his parlor lamp. His eye caught the rectangle of white on the floor that had been kicked aside a bit when he entered. He picked up the sheet of paper, torn from a notebook, and read the uniform script:

Dear Mr. Doyle,
  Will you join me for supper . . .

"I'm on my way, Mr. Rayborn," William said, putting out the lamp. On the bottom landing he took the sandwich wrapped in brown paper from his pocket and fed it to the landlord's yellow tabby. "Now, don't be telling Mr. Ruebenstein I fed you ham," he warned in a low voice. He walked to Ludgate Circus and entered Webley's, a café amply filled with patrons because the food was cheap and generously portioned to make up for the limited menu choices. William stopped there only once a week or so, preferring to bring sandwiches or meat pies home for his supper. If one had to dine alone, it was better to do so in the privacy of one's flat with a newspaper or book for company rather than surrounded by others wrapped up in socializing. He spotted the tutor at a table for two at the window.

"Mr. Doyle," Mr. Rayborn said, pushing out his chair. "I'm glad you could make it."

"This is a pleasant surprise," William said as they shook hands. He nodded toward the window, through which busy street traffic on the dimming Circus was still visible. "You must have been waiting a while to get the best spot."

Mr. Rayborn began clearing notebook and papers from the table. "You know, I didn't even notice the place had filled. You know how absorbing work can be."

"I do indeed." When they were settled in facing chairs, William asked, "Will you finish by year's end?"

"I plan to finish well before then, God willing."

The proprietor's daughter, a dark-haired

girl of perhaps fourteen, brought William a cup of tea and refilled Mr. Rayborn's empty one. William ordered beef-barley soup, and when Mr. Rayborn, who ordered fried sole, suggested he might care for something a little more substantial, William shook his head. "All those years at Berkeley Square— my stomach still craves soup most evenings."

"I understand."

As he unfolded his linen napkin, William could no longer contain his curiosity. He hoped they were well enough acquainted by now for him to be honest. "I do appreciate your invitation, Mr. Rayborn, for the company as well as the supper. But with your being willing to wait here so long, I can't help but wonder if there's a special occasion."

Gaslights outside the window were beginning to hiss, but the light in Mr. Rayborn's eyes came from another source. "You're very astute, Mr. Doyle."

By the time the meal was finished, they were addressing each other as Daniel and William.

"You aren't going to insist I address you as 'Uncle Daniel,' are you?" William said as they walked out onto the pavement and toward a hansom stand. He was delighted with the news and had told the tutor so several times over supper.

Daniel feigned disappointment. "Why not? It has a nice ring to it."

Smiling, they clasped hands and wished each other good-night.

Thank you, Father, William prayed while washing his face an hour later. Aunt Naomi deserved someone who would appreciate her and treat her accordingly. He had no doubt that Daniel would do so. And Sarah deserved a real mother for the first time in her life.

We'll be cousins . . . sort of, he realized. What had Aunt Naomi said so many years ago? *Queen Victoria married her cousin and they were very happy*.

"I wonder if *he* tormented himself over *her* too," he muttered to the dripping reflection in his washstand mirror.

———

It was not often that William saw the inside of Dr. Arthur Hassall's office in the building on Whitehall that housed the Commission. Dr. Hassall was something of a

legend in those halls, having written the series of exposé articles that led Parliament
to pass the Adulteration of Food, Drink,
and Drugs Act of 1872. But it was with an
unassuming smile that the man pushed out
his chair to shake William's hand on Friday
morning.

"I wish to commend you for your dili-
gence in that dairy investigation, Mr.
Doyle," the doctor, bearded and mildly
stoop-shouldered, said when they were
seated on either side of a desk cluttered
with papers and books. "My youngest
grandson is very fond of cheese, so I take
personal offense when someone has the
cheek to color it with chromate of lead."

"Thank you, sir," William replied, and because having Dr. Hassall notice his work
filled him with so much awe that there was
no room left for thought faculties, he
added, "I'm fond of cheese myself."

Kindly, Dr. Hassall nodded. "I wonder if
you would consider being assigned to
Manchester for six months, Mr. Doyle? The
Commission is founding a branch there
and requires someone to assist in inter-
viewing chemists and providing training for
investigative work."

It was an honor to be asked, considering his youth. And the premise of helping to start a new work was exciting. But all William could think about was how good it had felt to step onto the platform of Paddington Station just five months ago, finished with five years of semiexistence between Oxford and London.

"I realize this allows very little time for preparations," Dr. Hassall said, misinterpreting William's inability to reply. "But the Commission will pay the rent on your flat while you're gone, so it's basically a matter of packing clothing and personal necessities." Smiling, he added, "I'm leaving out the best part. While the fact that you haven't a family to consider—children to uproot from schools and such—helped to sway us in your direction, we would not select someone with any less dedication and expertise. I say 'offer' because this is considered a promotion, with an appropriate raise in wages. We really need you there."

"I'm flattered, sir," William told him. Overwhelmed was more appropriate. But six months? Yet he could understand the difficulty such an assignment would pose to those with wives and children.

"You have some questions, Mr. Doyle?"

"I just wonder if I can expect six-day work weeks there as well." He hastened to add, "I've never been afraid of hard work, Dr. Hassall. But even though I've no wife or children, I've loved ones here, and Manchester is too far for Sunday visits. I've also an important wedding to attend in October."

The older man shook his head regretfully. "I won't deceive you. The workload would be even more intense than here. But as for the wedding, I can guarantee you two or three days off."

William asked for time to think about it, which was granted. As they shook hands again, Dr. Hassall said, "Why don't we meet again Monday morning?"

The remainder of the day was devoted to conducting laboratory tests and recording the results, so he had sparse time to attempt to gaze mentally down both forks in the road. It was in the evening as he tidied his flat that he had opportunity to wonder how such an absence would affect his relationship with Sarah.

Aunt Naomi had advised professing his love and then allowing her some time, he reminded himself while sweeping the rug that had surely been old even when the tenement building was constructed. His thoughts strayed in an unwelcome direction toward the curate who had walked so confidently with her in the square on Sunday. Sarah was obviously enjoying Mr. Knight's company.

But she enjoyed *his* company as well. They had had that bond for years now. Did that mean she loved him? Or was he like a pair of old slippers to her; worn and comfortable and a trifle taken for granted? Was Dr. Hassall's offer an answer to his prayer for direction, an opportunity to give Sarah time and distance to study what was in her own heart? Could it be simple coincidence that Aunt Naomi became engaged just two days ago, thereby freeing him of the worry that she would be lonely? He scarcely knew how to pray that night except to ask for a wisdom greater than his twenty-two years.

It was as he stood at his washstand mirror the next morning pressing a towel against a razor nick in his chin that he realized what he had to do. He would tell Sarah how he felt for her, as Aunt Naomi advised. If she confessed the same for him and asked him not to go, he would stay. If he sensed any uncertainty, he would accept the assignment. He quashed the worrisome thought that by leaving he would give Mr. Knight more room for courting. As Aunt Naomi had said, he was not engaged in a cricket match.

———

"Did Madame enjoy the visit?" Marie asked on Friday afternoon, spreading her needlepoint canvas on her lap while Vicar Sharp's retreating steps still drifted through the open window.

"Very much," Dorothea replied. "You didn't mind my sending you away, did you? There are some things best kept between one's clergy and one's self."

The maid waved a hand. "Not at all, Madame. I was telling Naomi the places in Paris she must visit on her honeymoon."

Dorothea smiled and thought how nice it was to be warmed by the glow of even someone else's love. And she smiled at her own cleverness in making her case to the vicar. *"The young man labored like a Trojan when you were ill . . . sermons, visits, morning readings. Don't you think he de-*

serves a bit of gaiety now and again, so he doesn't become discouraged?"

She was certain that Sarah and Naomi and the men wouldn't object. It wasn't as though it would be *every* Saturday, for the vicar declared he could not usually spare him in the hours preceding Sunday's services. Mr. Knight was as personable as a man could be, almost a saint, and everyone certainly adored him. And to silence that little nagging doubt over her actions, Dorothea reminded herself that as the one financing the excursions, she had the authority to make a decision without calling for a referendum.

Now that she had made her peace with God, Dorothea could only believe that Ethan Knight had been divinely appointed to Mayfair so that she would have assurance that Sarah would be well looked after when she was gone.

The girl came through the doorway with a book under her arm. She wore her corn silk hair tied with a blue ribbon to match her frock, and for a second Dorothea was reminded of the waif who stood in her parlor and insisted in a wavering little voice that she did not have lice.

"I was about to start the book Mr. Rayborn gave me and wondered if you'd care for me to read it aloud," Sarah said, patting the top of Dorothea's head as if she were but a small child. "What do you think?"

Dorothea told her it would be nice, but then, the girl could offer to read the dictionary to her and she would agree just to hear her voice. Marie crimped her nose and began putting her needlework back into its basket. "I will take this upstairs. Just ring for—"

"Mr. Verne is a Frenchman, Marie," the girl said, and Dorothea caught the wink she sent her way.

"Well . . . I suppose I could sit for a little while," the maid said with affected gruffness.

As Sarah took her place beside her on the divan and almost reverently turned past the first few blank pages, Dorothea considered giving her the news. But then, Marie would probably voice something negative about her not consulting the others before issuing the invitation, and Sarah could become confused. *Why tell her at all?* Dorothea asked herself. If there was one thing Sarah enjoyed, it was a surprise.

Forty-One

The thermometer on the gardening shed read an unseasonably high fifty-five degrees on Saturday morning, the blue sky cloudless. "Wouldn't the park be lovely this afternoon?" Sarah hinted to Naomi after helping Trudy clear breakfast dishes from the hall. "I've yet to sail William's boat."

Naomi, rubbing potatoes with lard for baking, nodded. "It would be nice just to sit out in the sun."

"Then it's only a matter of talking the men into it."

"What did you just say, Miss?" Trudy said above the sound of running water.

Sarah smiled at Naomi and repeated herself a little more loudly. "I said it's only a matter of talking the men into it."

"I expect you could talk them into visitin' the dustyard."

"No good. We tried," Naomi quipped.

As Trudy's laughter mingled with the

sound of sloshing dishes, Sarah watched Naomi, who seemed to have blossomed almost overnight. Or perhaps it was that her own perception had changed. In addition to seeing her as a friend and her grandmother's cook, she could see a woman serenely aware that she is adored by a man. How simple their love seemed, with none of the befuddlement that plagued her own mind over exactly which feelings were supposed to be in her heart and for whom.

"You're staying on because of Grandmother, aren't you?" Sarah said low enough for only one set of ears.

"Yes," Naomi replied just as softly. "And because of you."

That confirmed Sarah's suspicions that the cook knew what she had known for a while. "Thank you, Naomi." She swallowed. "For how long?"

She meant for how long *afterward* but couldn't bring herself to add that part.

"Until you no longer need me."

Sarah had to smile. "Then you'll be here forever."

"You won't need me for *that* long." Naomi returned her smile as a slender hand reached for another potato. "But I'll always be nearby."

"Always?"

"Yes."

The simple word reassured Sarah as much as if someone else had taken an oath. Remembering her promise to read to Grandmother and Marie before lunch, she got to her feet, touched Naomi's shoulder, and was at the door when the scullery maid's voice stopped her.

"Miss Matthews?"

"Yes, Trudy?" Sarah said, turning.

Elbows deep in suds, Trudy gave her a sweet sidelong smile. "I'll be here too."

After lunch Sarah changed into a shell-pink organdy gown with cuffed *Marie Antoinette* sleeves and a straw hat lined with pink faille. She walked downstairs to wait, for Naomi had just gone up to change, and neither of the men had arrived. Under her arm she held the box containing William's boat and thought about how pleased he would be that she hadn't forgotten about it.

When she entered the sitting room, Grandmother sent her a smile and nodded toward the chair from which Mr. Knight was rising.

"Come in, Sarah!" she said. "Help me convince Mr. Knight that you'll be delighted to have him along."

The curate, handsome in a camel-colored tweed suit, set his cup and saucer on the tea table and advanced to take her hand. "I was telling Mrs. Blake it was most wicked of her to spring this upon you, Miss Matthews."

"Nonsense!" Grandmother declared, while Marie silently concentrated on sewing a button on the gown in her lap.

Mr. Knight brushed his lips against Sarah's hand. Smiling as if they shared a secret joke, he lowered his voice and said, "I can always plead a headache and leave. I don't wish to become a pest, just because I so enjoy your company."

"Please don't." Sarah returned his smile and dipped into a little curtsey. "You're most welcome to join us." She meant it, too, telling herself that her initial stab of disappointment was due to Grandmother's not giving fair notice. After all, she would have certainly worn one of her newer dresses had she known. Given his disregard for his own reputation by keeping company with her, she owed it to him to look as nice as possible.

———

William whistled "My Man John" all the way from Piccadilly to Berkeley Square, though he disliked the song because an organ-grinder near the omnibus stop in Ludgate Circus played it incessantly. He had awakened with an unexplainable confidence that today was going to be perfect, and the weather helped to carry that notion. Too pleasant for a stuffy museum or art gallery or even the theatre. He wondered if Sarah would mind spending the afternoon at the park, perhaps sailing the toy boat. He was certain Aunt Naomi and Daniel would be happy just to sit on a bench and cast doe eyes at each other.

I'll give to you this cushion of pins
And that's the way our love begins,
If you will be my bride, my joy,
If you will be my joy . . .

He caught the suspicious looks from two dowagers heading in the opposite direction and realized he was softly singing. On wicked impulse he tipped his hat and was pleasantly surprised when they broke into smiles. Avis answered his ring at number 14, and with her owlish eyes wide, she told him of the rat Mr. Duffy cornered in the gardening shed last night. Then she nodded toward the sitting room. "Naomi's still upstairs, and Mr. Rayborn ain't here yet. But Sarah's in there, and Mr. Knight."

Daniel glanced at the door. "Mr. Knight?"

"He's going with you today. I heard Mrs. Blake say it when I brought in tea." She sighed dreamily. "My fiancé, Edwin, ain't nearly so handsome, and I expect he couldn't preach a sermon to save his skin—but he's a good fellow, mind you. That's why I set my cap to marry him when my brother—"

The sitting room door opened. Sarah came out and closed it behind her. Her smile was strained, as if she wasn't quite certain if she should be wearing one. "William," she whispered with an apologetic side glance at Avis. "Please come with me."

Thankfully, Avis took the hint and did not attempt to continue her story. William followed Sarah into the dining room and stepped aside when she motioned her intent to close the door.

"I was hoping that was you out there," she said. "Avis told you about Mr. Knight?"

"She did," William answered. Though he would not allow the disappointment in his chest to rise to his face, he could not help but ask, "You invited him?"

"Grandmother. Only she didn't warn me." Her words started tumbling out faster. "You've said yourself what a fine person he is. And he's so lonely without his family. He has a clever wit. Why, with you and Mr. Knight and Mr. Rayborn, we'll have sore sides from laughing." Then almost as an afterthought she added, "We'll sail the boat. It's in the sitting room."

William could not help but smile at her discomfort, but not in a mocking way. She was so young. And clearly confused. His presence only added to that. As much as he longed to pressure her to decide right away whether or not she loved him, he had to consider if she would second-guess herself for years in the future.

"I checked the vinegar bottle to make sure it hadn't—" she began, but William raised a finger to her lips.

"I can't stay, Sarah."

"But—"

He smiled again, surprised at how easy it was when his heart was so heavy. "I have to pack, make some arrangements to go away for a while. But I need to speak with Aunt Naomi first. So if you see her before I—"

Now it was she who interrupted. "But where are you going, William?"

As succinctly as possible he explained, and when tears sprang to her eyes, he assured her, "I'll be back for the wedding, so it isn't as if I'll spend the whole time away."

"But still . . ." Her lip trembled. "I thought we'd finished saying good-bye."

"So did I." He shrugged. "I didn't foresee this."

"This isn't because of Mr. Knight, is it?" she asked. "Grandmother asked the vicar to invite him, or I'm certain he wouldn't agree to accompany—"

Again his finger touched her lips. "No. Not because of Mr. Knight." *But because you don't know how you feel about Mr. Knight.* "And because your grandmother will have someone looking for you any minute, I need to tell you something, Sarah."

"Yes?" she said in a small voice. "I love you, Sarah. With all my heart."

"I love you too, William."

It was music to his ears. He smiled and took up her hand. But it was not the proper time to ask if she meant it as love shared by a brother and sister or the kind that led to a lifetime commitment. He would always wonder if her disappointment over his leaving had colored her emotions.

"You'll write to me?" This time he had no hesitancy about asking.

"I'm afraid it's my fault," Naomi said to Daniel as they sat on a bench and watched the young couple stroll on the bank of the Serpentine. "I advised William to tell her how he feels and then give her some time instead of trying to outdo Mr. Knight in a courting contest."

"That was wise counsel, Naomi. Sarah's not going to forget about him."

His words gave her some comfort, for indeed she did not forget him when he was at Oxford. But then, Mr. Knight was not in the picture in those days. Yet as much as Naomi loved William, how could she fault the young curate for recognizing those qualities in Sarah that caused everyone at 14 Berkeley Square to adore her? What if God was orchestrating circumstances as part of a divine plan to draw the girl and Mr. Knight together?

I don't even know what I'm supposed to think, Father, she prayed silently while Daniel held her hand. *I have to turn all of this over to you. Please give me the faith not to keep taking it back again.*

"Why don't we put you on a hansom so you can spend the rest of the day with William?" Daniel said. "I'll chaperone Sarah and Mr. Knight myself and then join you both with supper in a little while."

Naomi gave a quiet sigh of relief and wondered why such a plan had not occurred to her. Whether or not God intended for the young couple strolling in the distance to be together did not negate her obligation to her nephew, or even her longing to spend some more time with him.

"It's dear of you to think of it," she said as they rose from the bench.

"Would you like me to rent a boat?" Mr. Knight offered.

Sarah looked at him, aware that she had

not spoken for several minutes. Laughter rippled over the water of the Serpentine from boats occupied by family groups or courting couples. A handful of children, under the watchful eyes of nursemaids or parents, held strings attached to toy boats that bobbed in the shallow water near the bank. She had not the heart to bring William's boat. It didn't seem right to launch it the first time without him.

"Forgive me . . . I'm not very good company," she said.

He smiled sympathetically. "Why don't you tell me what's wrong? Sometimes it helps to talk."

Salt stung Sarah's eyes. She blinked and hoped she would not start weeping. She needed to talk, to give some release for the melancholy filling her chest. "William's going away for six months."

"Miss Doyle's nephew, you mean."

"He's been offered an assignment with the Hassall Commission . . ." she began, and catching his blank look, she realized she had not the energy to explain. "Anyway, I've not had time to get used to the idea. We barely had time to say 'goodbye.' "

The curate nodded. "And you're very close, aren't you?"

"Yes, since we were children. At least *I* was a child."

At the sound of footsteps from behind, Sarah and Mr. Knight turned. Mr. Rayborn and Naomi were approaching, her hand resting in the crook of his arm.

"I'm going to slip away for a minute and help Miss Doyle find a hansom," Mr. Rayborn said.

"You're going to see William?" Sarah asked Naomi.

"Yes." She was smiling, but lurking in her blue eyes was the same loss Sarah was feeling. "He'll need some help packing."

"Why don't you all go?"

It was Mr. Knight who spoke. Everyone looked at him.

"Good soul that Mrs. Blake is, I realize she rather sprang me upon you," he said with a self-effacing smile. "I'm sure it would mean a lot to Mr. Doyle to have all of you with him, as well as give you more time for farewells."

Ethan stepped back a bit from the hansom at Hyde Park corner when the driver snapped his reins. He smiled and returned Miss Matthews' wave, and when the cab was well on its way toward Piccadilly, he started looking about for a hired coach. It wouldn't do to walk several blocks out in the open when the vicar assumed him still in the company of Miss Matthews and her friends, and a hansom wasn't private enough. He found one and ducked inside after giving the driver the address.

He smiled at his own cleverness. He had no worries about giving Miss Matthews opportunity to be with Mr. Doyle, even if there was any sort of romantic feeling on either side. In the first place, they had known each other for years, as she said. What was one more time, especially with her tutor and cook present?

The beauty of his "sacrifice" of his afternoon plans was that he raised Miss Matthews' esteem of him more by his absence than by offering sympathetic little platitudes on the banks of the Serpentine. Even the tutor and cook had thanked him, and he was certain that their opinions meant much to her.

Meanwhile, he was free to spend the rest of the afternoon and evening with Myra, who would be closing shop soon. Tapping his thumb on his crossed knee to match the *clip-clop* of the horses, he smiled and thought how relieved he was that courting was even easier than he anticipated. Especially with Mrs. Blake doing most of the work—God bless her sweet feeble self.

When guilt threatened to come out of the mental box he had shoved it into, he reminded himself that he would make Miss Matthews a fine, attentive husband. Just because he had some secret indulgences did not mean he intended to be any less than a gentleman, and he despised any man who would abuse his wife.

She'll never know I married her for money, he vowed to himself, and the guilt subsided again.

———

At nine o'clock, William walked Aunt Naomi, Sarah, and Mr. Rayborn downstairs, and when the cab he hailed pulled to a stop, he embraced Aunt Naomi. "I love you," he said and almost changed his mind about leaving when she began wiping her cheeks with a handkerchief.

He embraced Sarah next, quickly, but

could not say the words he had voiced in the dining room earlier, or anything else. And so he patted her back and then helped her into the cab next to his aunt.

He shook hands with Mr. Rayborn. "Thank you for taking care of them," he said.

Mr. Rayborn wrapped an arm around his shoulder. "And we'll thank you to take good care of yourself, William."

"I will," William promised. He watched the hackney until it was swallowed up by fog and darkness. He was thankful Aunt Naomi understood that he would not be at Saint George's tomorrow. There were other churches even closer—perhaps he would even worship at King's Chapel with Mr. Rayborn. He had already said his farewells once at 14 Berkeley Square and did not have the heart to go through them again. And hopefully by Monday afternoon he would be on a train heading northwest.

Please make the time pass quickly, Father, he prayed on the way back to his flat.

❧ *Forty-Two* ❧

Six weeks later on Thursday, the first of July, Grandmother closed her eyes to breathe in the fragrance of white, yellow, and purple irises that had been delivered from the vicarage garden.

"They're not too overpowering, are they?" Sarah asked, pushing the Wedgwood vase out of danger of getting knocked off a chest of drawers in the former library. "I can move them to the other side."

"And have Marie pretend they're hers? It's bad enough that I allow her to frolic all over London with those sisters. You'll have a wretched time keeping her in line when I'm—"

"Grandmother . . ."

"And I do wish you would stop shushing me every time I speak about passing on."

"Yes. Forgive me." She had actually protested without thinking, for she had not yet reconciled herself to the inevitable. But Ethan, with his vast experience at comforting the dying, had helped her to understand that it was good for Grandmother to make requests concerning how life should go on afterward. In soft jest, Sarah said, "I'll rule Marie with an iron rod."

"Hmph! Just make sure she's not ruling *you* with one." Grandmother nodded toward the note in Sarah's hand. "What did he write this time?"

Sarah read the lines aloud:

" 'Dearest Mrs. Blake,
    In reply to King Solomon's famous
    query of Proverbs thirty-one . . .
    Ethan Knight has found two!
              With fondest regards,
              Ethan' "

"Proverbs thirty-one." A smile eased some of the pain in Grandmother's expression. "*Who can find a virtuous woman?* Isn't he a dear?"

"Yes, he is," Sarah replied, smiling back. No one in Mayfair would disagree with that. A hand went up to the little gold cross on the chain about her neck. An identical one was draped over a picture of Jeremy on Grandmother's bedside table. It was not proper etiquette for an unmarried man to give jewelry to an unmarried woman, but Grandmother had allowed Sarah to accept hers, since he was a servant of the Church who had presented both gifts as reminders that he prayed for them daily. He was constantly doing thoughtful things like that, causing Sarah sometimes to worry that Ethan would take Grandmother's passing even harder than she would, for it would be like losing his own beloved grandmother a second time.

She leaned to refasten a button on the yoke of the elderly woman's gown. Sometime in June Grandmother had decreed herself weary of black bombazine cloth, and that she would spend her remaining weeks garbed as comfortably as possible. Penny Russell, whose skill with a needle was all that Stanley had boasted it to be, stitched her several simple calico gowns with pleated yokes, suitable for the sitting room and yet comfortable enough for napping without changing into nightgowns.

The white of Grandmother's hair and pillows caused her to look a little more fragile in the afternoon sunlight slanting in from the garden window. At times Sarah thought she resembled an angel, sweet-faced and ethereal.

Her grandmother pulled a hand from beneath the covers. Carefully Sarah took it.

"It is such a comfort to me," Grandmother said, smiling up at her, "that Ethan cares so deeply for you. I have fretted so often over who would care for you when I'm gone."

Sarah kissed her fingers and wondered whether or not to believe the complete innocence in her expression. Surely Ethan wouldn't have told Grandmother that she had asked for more time to consider his proposal. But he often did stop by on his way to pay other morning calls when she was at lessons. Sometimes it seemed that the two were aligned against her, or rather, in favor of Ethan's place in her future.

If only William had not left! With the two in the same vicinity, she would clearly know whom she loved the most. She could not bring her inner struggle to Naomi, simply because of her kinship with William. Marie was too outspoken and would scold Grandmother for pressuring her. Hester was for putting off any decision until William returned, but Grandmother's longing to see her wed before she passed on was a difficult tide against which to row.

"The flowers are beautiful," she told Ethan in the sitting room when he stopped by about an hour later. They sat alone on the divan with the sitting room door propped open for the sake of propriety. "But I'm afraid Grandmother's napping, so she can't thank you."

"I'm just glad she's able to sleep," he said with a little smile. He rested his head sideways against a back cushion, his eyes a little glazed from having sat up most of the night with an ailing widow on the other side of the square.

"You're so good to her. And why don't you be good to yourself and go back to your apartment for some sleep? Vicar Sharp would understand."

"Because I enjoy your feeling pity for me."

She feigned an exasperated sigh. And because she was finding it easier and easier to confide in him, said, "I think you remind her of what she wished her son could have been, if that makes any sense."

"It makes perfect sense." His half-closed eyes filled with understanding. "You're speaking of your father."

"I've entertained horribly wicked thoughts lately of the satisfaction it would give me to toss his portraits in the fireplace when Grandmother is gone."

"And you think that would take away the pain of being abandoned?"

"I'm not sure, Ethan. But I confess I do get some comfort from picturing the flames licking the canvases. I suppose I've inherited more of his character than I imagined."

"That's not so," he said, his hand covering her left one on the upholstery between them. Immediately he lifted his again.

You can't hurt it, she would have reminded him had Jeremy Blake's intrusion into her thoughts not sobered her mood.

Ethan was now so accustomed to extending sympathy to those with real sufferings that he still did not quite understand that she was no more fragile than any other healthy young woman. "In fact," he went on, "you're the best person I've ever known. I understand now why God sent me so far from home and family, when I certainly railed against it in my prayers. His reply was a very discernible 'wait and see what I have for you' . . . just as He said to Abraham."

"It's kind of you to say that, Ethan." If God would make such a promise to Ethan, who walked so closely with Him, was that her answer?

He got to his feet and held out his hand to assist her to hers. "But you asked me to give you some time, and here I am going back on my word. Do forgive me, Sarah."

Sarah smiled up at him, her right hand still clasped in his. "Of course, Ethan. And thank you for understanding."

"You would bring out the best in any man, Sarah. I do love you so."

She held her breath and even automatically raised her chin. But mercifully he only touched her cheek and smiled when she, lightheaded, could only blink at him.

He left then, saying he had more calls to make. Sarah went upstairs to transcribe some Latin phrases but found herself thinking how much harder it was to construe the feelings of her own heart. *Won't you show me just as clearly, Father, as you did Ethan and Abraham?*

"Mrs. Bacon is going out to the shops in a little while," Naomi said in the sitting room the following morning. "I just wonder if you have any cravings for any particular soup for supper." It was so difficult to encourage her mistress's appetite that Naomi sometimes found herself at a loss as to what to prepare. Thankfully, even if Mrs. Bacon planned no shopping trip, one of the maids was always happy for a stroll to market.

Mrs. Blake lifted a hand from the chair arm. "Whatever you wish to prepare, Naomi."

"Madame is fond of peas," Marie said when Naomi sent her a helpless look.

"Well, yes," Mrs. Blake said, brow furrowed beneath her white top-knot. "Are they in season, Naomi? Because I don't care so much for the dried."

Naomi smiled. "They are, Madam. Green pea soup it is."

"With butter? It makes me miss the salt a little less."

"I'll be sure to remind Trudy."

"That's right. It's Saturday." Mrs. Blake smiled. "Where are you and Mr. Rayborn taking my granddaughter today?"

"Saint Paul's, Madam," Naomi replied, returning her smile.

"Hmm. I wonder if Vicar Sharp would allow Mr. Knight to accompany you? He really doesn't see much of London, you know, and it's a shame with it being an important church—"

Naomi seldom interrupted her mistress, and she felt sympathy for her constant pain. But she could no longer hold her tongue. "Mrs. Blake, I admire Mr. Knight as much as you do. And if God wills him to court Miss Matthews, I will have to accept that. But I do not think He requires me to participate in the courtship . . . nor should you. Not when my nephew cares so deeply about her."

"William? But he's not even here."

"His heart is here, Madam." Naomi pressed lips together and stared back at the pale blue eyes that regarded her with such consternation. She would not budge even if it cost her her job. Daniel would marry her tomorrow if she needed a place to go, or she would simply move into William's empty flat.

It was Marie who eased the tension from the air by saying, "It is a reasonable thing that Naomi says, Madame. Besides, too much familiarity takes the mystery from a young woman in a man's eyes."

"It's quite remarkable that they found each other," Dorothea said to Ethan at the lunch table Sunday, after telling him of Mr. Rayborn's sad past and how Naomi seemed to "glow" these days.

She glanced at Sarah, who pushed her roast lamb and vegetables about on her plate, her head obviously in the clouds. If only she could see that she had the same opportunity for happiness as Naomi, instead of torturing herself with indecision! What did she expect? An answer to be written in those same clouds? *I just want you to be cherished and protected, dear Sarah. And who would do that better than a man of God—especially one to whom family meant so much? I can't rest until I'm certain of your future. And I'm growing so tired.*

Sarah wrote on the following day,

Dear William,
Grandmother and Marie were delighted with your account of the investigation of that horrible butcher. Marie said that in France he would be ground

into sausage with the cat meat, so perhaps it is a good thing that he is in Manchester and out of the reach of Marie and her sisters.

Mr. Rayborn and Naomi brought me with them to tour Saint Paul's on Saturday. It is so kind of them to insist on having me along. But our little threesome seems so incomplete without you!

Penny Russell is sewing Naomi's wedding gown from twelve yards of moiré silk. And because I can see you scratching your head, I will explain only that it is very fine silk and will complement the Brussels lace to good advantage. Stanley and Penny's son, Guy, is a sweet baby. He loves to lie on a quilt in the garden and watch Mr. Duffy work. Only he has been fretful for the past two days. Doctor Raine had a look at him today and said it was probably another tooth breaking through.

My lessons are still progressing. Mr. Rayborn is encouraging me to try my hand at writing some short fiction, as I am so fond of novels. Years ago Trudy expressed a wish to read a story of a scullery maid who becomes Queen of England, so that was my first endeavor. The workmanship was lacking in areas, but Trudy loved it and had me bring it down to the hall and read it to the others during supper on Friday past.

She wrote on, sharing such things as tennis matches with the Rothschild boys, Avis's news that her fiancé, Edwin, would be home for good in February, and any other little tidbits that would bring a bit of home to him. But as close as she was to William, as free as she had always felt to pour out her heart to him, there was one matter that she had not even the boldness to assign to ink and paper, but could only ask in her mind:

I must bring up your declaration of affection that last time we were alone together. The reason I make mention of it is that the disquiet in my heart is almost more than I can bear. Mr. Knight has proposed marriage twice, and I must admit to some deep feelings for him. He is thoughtful and kind and treats Grandmother with so much compassion that it sometimes brings tears to my eyes. Truly, he has made these ebbing days of hers far more bearable.

There is only one obstacle to my accepting his proposal, dearest William, and it is in the form of a chemist who resides in Manchester. How can I pledge to "forsake all others" when you also occupy no small space in my heart? Please help me to understand if the love I have for you is what Naomi feels for Mr. Rayborn or if it's the love of a sister toward a caring and wonderful brother.

Oh no, Ethan thought when Myra opened the door late that same Monday evening, for the candle she carried emphasized the pout in her expression. In silence they climbed the steps, she sulking and he wishing he had gone on to bed. Between courting Sarah Matthews, tending his church duties, and seeing Myra, he was beginning to feel like an old man and could not recall when he had last enjoyed a decent night's sleep.

"What is it?" he asked in a flat tone after softly closing the door behind them. He only inquired out of a futile hope that she would not raise the same subject they had fought about on Thursday evening.

But his hopes were dashed when her bottom lip started trembling. "You're ashamed to be seen in public with me, aren't you?"

He sighed heavily. "We'll go to the burlesque one night." He smiled as his face was covered with kisses and reassured himself with the thought that if the neighborhood surrounding the Rainbow Palace was half as seedy as she described it, there would not be a Saint George's parishioner for miles. "Now, you can show your gratitude by pouring me a drink."

————

Sarah raised her head from her pillow. *A cat*, she thought, for sometimes strays from the mews climbed the garden wall. But the sound was eerily not quite the same. When her ears caught adult voices, she got out of bed and went to the open window. She could hear Mrs. Bacon's voice coming from one of the four figures beyond the terrace. Five, she realized, for the little one in Stanley's arms was the source of the sound that woke her from sleep. She threw her wrapper over her nightgown and raked her slippers from beneath the bed.

"The croup," Mrs. Bacon, ashen-faced, said when Sarah found the group in the kitchen. Baby Guy's cry had a horrible fluid sound that made Sarah want to clear her own throat. Penny hovered at Stanley's elbow, patting Guy's fuzzy head, her own light brown hair in disarray as tears ran down her splotched face.

"Should we fetch Doctor Raine?" Sarah asked with knees trembling. She could still picture the grief on the faces of the Rothschild boys five years ago.

Claire, running hot water into the sink, said, "Roger's saddling up now."

"Make it as hot as he can stand it," Mrs. Bacon was saying to Claire. "You'll have to test it with your elbow."

Naomi and Trudy came into the room, also in wrappers over their gowns. "What can we do to help, Mrs. Bacon?" Naomi asked, for it took no time to comprehend the situation.

"He's going to need calomel and tartar emetic," the housekeeper replied. "We shouldn't wait to make sure Doctor Raine isn't off delivering a baby."

"I'll go." Stanley handed his weeping son over to Naomi, for Penny was leaning against a cupboard with hands covering her face.

———

"I *have* to get some sleep," Ethan argued, laughingly so, as he tried to edge out of the door to Myra's flat. But when he turned away from her on the landing, she wrapped both arms around his shoulders from behind and hitched up her knees on either side as if he were a pack animal.

"Carry me, if you're so strong."

"Myra . . . they'll hear us next door," he whispered over his shoulder.

"Sh-h-h," she said and belched a waft of gin. "Carry me."

He had no choice and made it down the stairs, though he was himself unsteady on his feet. "Now, go upstairs," he whispered, depositing her on a step near the bottom. Still she clung to him, kissing the back of his neck and following him through the doorway leading to New Bond Street. With something between a laugh and a growl, he turned to kiss her, almost tempted to heed her pleadings and go back upstairs.

"You're a Delilah, you know," he said when the kiss was over and he was unwinding her arms from around him.

"What's a Delilah?" she giggled.

It was then that he heard a snort and looked to his right. A horse, bridled but not saddled, stood outside the chemist's shop next door. Ethan blinked, trying to understand why a faint light glowed in the shop's bow window when everyone should be asleep. *Someone got sick*, pierced his foggy mind. He saw no persons but knew it would be a matter of minutes before whoever was in the shop came out again. He held Myra at arm's length and growled, "Go inside now."

She gaped at him but obeyed. He closed the door behind her, winced at the sound of muffled stumbling on the steps, and glanced at the window again. Still no one. Almost weak with relief, he ambled to the vicarage in the shadows and smiled to himself several minutes later at the faint sound of hoofbeats.

No one complained about having only porridge and tea for breakfast the next morning. There was relief in each set of bleary eyes about the servants' table, for when Stanley popped in to bring back his and Penny's breakfast to the stable, he reported that little Guy was sleeping peacefully next to his mother, his coughs not so chest rattling. By Wednesday he had even better news, for the child was taking in milk again and rarely coughed at all.

After supper that evening Stanley came again to the kitchen and asked Naomi if they might speak in private.

"I'll finish cleaning up," Trudy offered. Naomi and Stanley went out to the terrace and then to the dovecote bench, for the groomsman worried that some of his words might carry through some of the open windows.

"What is it, Stanley?" Naomi asked.

"It's that Mr. Knight," he replied, his tone as somber as if he were delivering the news of the death of a friend. He glanced over his shoulder and lowered his voice. "I've got some information, and I don't know what to do with it."

"Yes?"

"I was at the chemist's, waitin' for Mr. Garland to mix the medicines the night little Guy was the sickest and couldn't recollect if I'd tethered Dudley or not. It wouldn't do to have him wander off, so I went to the window to look. I saw Mr. Knight with Myra Rose, and not in a proper way."

"Myra Rose?"

"She's works in the parasol shop." Quickly he added, "I ain't even talked to her in a year, Naomi."

She understood his meaning about that last part and allowed it to pass, as it was water under the bridge. "Stanley, are you certain? You were in such a frantic state."

The coachman nodded. "Naomi, that's what's tormentin' me. If I was still a wagering man, I'd put my last shilling on it bein' him. I saw him only from the side before backing away from the window, but the gaslight was bright." He shook his head.

"Just don't know what to do about it. If I'm wrong, I don't want to go stirring trouble against a good man. But if I'm right . . . poor Miss Matthews."

"Yes." *And poor Mrs. Blake and Vicar Sharp and everyone else who trusts him.* That included Stanley, still so young in his faith. "Stanley," she felt compelled to say. "Mr. Knight's still just a man, you know."

"Beg pardon?"

"If it turns out that it was him . . . well, people are going to fail you, even sometimes those in the church."

Giving her a weary little smile, the groomsman said, "Are you thinking I'll lose faith?"

"Well . . ."

He patted her shoulder. "You're a good woman to worry about old Stanley, Naomi. I'm sad about Mr. Knight, but it weren't him who took away that rotten spot in my soul. And it ain't him who's makin' our little Guy get well."

"You're a good father, Stanley."

"Got a lot to make up for," he said with a shrug. "But it suits me better than I ever would have thought." After a second, he said, "Don't you think Miss Matthews ought to know?"

"She'll need to know," Naomi agreed. But she wasn't quite certain what she was to do with this information. "Would you mind keeping this to yourself for now?"

His nod was decisive. "You can be sure of that."

_____

"So William was right again," Sarah said at the library table early the next afternoon.

Daniel smiled at her. "You've discussed Mr. de Boisbaudran?"

"Elements. He once assured me that not all had been discovered. I suppose he's delighted to have another to stare at through his microscope."

"Well, it would have to be a spectroscope . . . at least until gallium is able to be isolated in the metallic state." He closed the July issue of *Popular Science Review*. "I suppose that concludes our lessons today. Unless you've any questions?"

"None having to do with gallium, I'm afraid," she said with a slight roll of her eyes.

He chuckled and they walked together

downstairs as Sarah related how she and Marie had finally convinced Mrs. Blake to use a cane. They parted company on the terrace. For a minute Daniel watched her walk out toward the stable to see about the Russell infant, then he chatted with Mr. Duffy, busy thinning onions in the kitchen garden. Naomi came up the cellar staircase presently. At the top she gave him a grave look. "Let's sit in the square, shall we?"

On the same bench where Daniel had proposed marriage, Naomi told him of a conversation with Stanley last night. "He's certain of what he saw. But admits he was frantic over his baby that night and could have been mistaken. I don't know what to think."

Daniel could understand that. He had not quite known what to think about Mr. Knight for weeks. It was obvious that everyone in the household respected and even liked him. He had shown admirable generosity by encouraging Sarah to bid farewell to William before he left and was nothing but personable during the couple of brief encounters Daniel had had with him afterward. But he suspected Mr. Knight was the source of the anxiety that passed across his daughter's face now and again, and he wasn't certain if that was a good thing.

"What should we do?" Naomi asked.

"I'm going to have to speak with him," he replied. "Today."

———

"Dress-up dolls are popular with the girls," said the shopgirl at HINDE'S POPULAR SHILLING TOYS on Old Bond Street. From a shelf she took a curly-haired doll adorned in a frilly dress. "You can buy a trunk of clothes to go with this one. When is your niece's birthday?"

"Oh, January," Ethan replied, leaning against the counter. He liked her full lips and the way her eyes became slits when she smiled, which was often. Her dark hair wasn't as thick as Myra's nor her figure as womanly, but her heavy perfume told him she wanted to be noticed, and she had casually allowed her hand to brush against his on the counter twice already.

"January!" She pretended annoyance, but the full lips still curved upward. "Do you even *have* a niece?"

"Well . . . I may one day."

Lightly she slapped his hand on the counter but giggled.

Ethan smiled back. "Do you like working here?"

She shrugged. "It's a job. Better than a butcher's shop."

"Hmm." He glanced around. "And I suppose you get to stay above?"

His hopes fell when she shook her head. "Mr. Hinde and his wife. I live in the Hays Mews with my brother. He's a coachman."

"Ah. Well, too bad."

"Ain't it?" Again her hand brushed against his. "He's such a mean old thing. Plays cards every Tuesday night with his friends and leaves me all alone . . . for hours and hours."

This time Ethan remembered to ask her name and on the way back to the vicarage walked with his hands in his pockets, singing softly the song it brought to mind:

O Sally, my dear, but I wish I could
　　woo you,
O Sally, my dear, but I wish I could
　　woo you.
She laughed and replied,
And would wooing undo you?

"Good evening, Mr. Knight."

He started at the sight of the man sitting on the stairs. Mr. Rayborn, he recognized. Hand up to his chest, Ethan said, "You gave me a fright, sir."

"Sorry. I should have given warning." The tutor got to his feet and glanced at the door at the top of the stairs. "May we speak inside?"

"As you wish," Ethan said, mind racing to figure out what the man could possibly want. "I'll be expected in the vicarage for supper in an hour."

"It won't take that long."

———

"You'll have to forgive the crampness of my parlor," Mr. Knight said, lighting a lamp. He motioned Daniel into one of two wooden-framed armchairs upholstered in dark green velvet. "But I seldom sit in here, so it suits me. After all, Saint Paul could be content in a prison cell."

Daniel nodded. He knew he should be more sociable, because Mr. Knight had not yet been given opportunity to explain himself and could very well be innocent. But the gravity of the situation had settled into his face, and a smile would be a mere pretentious stretching of his lips. The young man was regarding him with worry in his eyes despite his pleasantries, so Daniel decided to spare them both the suspense and get right to the matter.

"Mr. Knight, I have to ask if you're seeing a shop assistant by the name of Myra Rose." He left out Stanley's part in it, as Naomi requested. It seemed best to protect a new believer from a possible confrontation with a minister. Besides, he didn't want to give away too much information at the onset.

The curate blinked. "I beg your pardon?"

Daniel repeated himself.

The incredulity in the young face surged into indignation. "You had best explain yourself, Mr. Rayborn."

"There is nothing to explain, Mr. Knight. Are you involved romantically with her?"

"Absolutely not," the man seethed. "I take issue with you for even asking."

He was convincing, and Daniel wanted so to believe him. But with Sarah's future possibly at stake, he could ill afford to walk away with any doubt. "Mr. Knight, I would be overjoyed to learn that I'm wrong about this. So you'll understand why tomorrow I'll be asking shopkeepers in that vicinity if they've noticed your spending a lot of time . . ."

"Ask all you wish, Mr. Rayborn." Mr. Knight rose from his chair. "Then I'll thank you to come back here and beg forgiveness."

"I hope that's what I have to do," Daniel told him, getting to his feet. "I do apologize for ruining your day, Mr. Knight."

"It's *your* day that will be ruined, Mr. Rayborn. You'll see."

Daniel turned for the door, leaving the young man glaring at him from the center of the room. But when he was halfway down the staircase, the door opened. Daniel stopped and turned.

"Wait," the young man said.

Ethan had to think, almost impossible with Mr. Rayborn standing in his parlor staring at the indecision in his face. *When did he see us?* If he could figure out exactly how much the man knew, he would work up a proper explanation. The light in the chemist shop's window flitted across his mind, but just as quickly he reasoned it away. Mr. Rayborn took omnibuses to and from Berkeley Square. And anyway, he would not be in Mayfair that late at night.

Still, how did he know Myra's name? And when no ready solution presented itself, he sighed. "How much do you want?"

The tutor raised an eyebrow, his green eyes knowing. Ethan curled his hands at his sides until the nails bit into his palms. "I'm very well respected here, Mr. Rayborn. People trust me, even ask me to comfort their dying. And I know all about your past. If I were to suggest that I was simply giving Christian counsel to a shopgirl one day and you stumbled by reeking of spirits, whose story would you think more credible?"

"Probably yours," the tutor said. "Then why did you ask how much I wanted?"

"Because even though I'm innocent, if you go about raising questions, people will naturally assume the worst. Ten pounds to stay away from the shops and forget about all of this."

"Not enough."

"Twenty-five." Ethan glared at him. "And I pegged you for a scoundrel the first time we met."

"It takes one to know one, Mr. Knight. And I would prefer fifty."

Clinching his fists again, Ethan thought about how he would like to wipe that maddening little smile off the man's face. But he was backed against a wall at the moment. "Very well. But you'll have to wait until Monday."

"Dipping into the tithes, eh?"

"That's none of your business." An idea occurred to him, so clever that he had to force himself not to smile. "Prove yourself a patient man, and you'll get ten times that. Just as soon as I've married Miss Matthews."

"Five hundred pounds?"

Mr. Rayborn seemed to consider this, while Ethan held his breath. But at length the man shook his head. "I'd rather not. I have a feeling once you've married her, you'll not be so concerned about your pristine reputation."

He left after Ethan reluctantly agreed to meet him at the statue of Archilles in Hyde Park on Monday afternoon. It was with heroic effort that Ethan participated in conversation at the vicar's table ten minutes later. Forkfuls of boiled brisket of beef, carrots, potatoes, and suet dumplings went down his throat like they were made of pasteboard, tasting all the same. He could only force down a bite of the black-currant pudding and was about to plead a headache and ask to be excused when the vicar looked up from spooning cream liberally on his own dessert.

"Have you stopped by the Blake house lately, Mr. Knight?"

"Not since Sunday," Ethan replied.

"I'm just wondering how the Russell infant is."

"Russell?"

"The groomsman . . . Stanley Russell. I happened upon Doctor Raine this afternoon, and he said the child might have died a couple of nights ago had Mr. Russell not gone out for medicine."

———

"You see, it'd be like takin' a stroll of about seven thousand steps," Mr. Duffy said to Trudy over bowls of chicken soup, trying to explain the 2,310-yard length of most rowing races in the Henley Regatta currently taking place at Henley-on-

Thames near Oxford. "Providing you had big feet such as mine, that is."

" *And* provided you could walk on water," Stanley added. Next to him Penny divided her attention between the conversation and little Guy, who sat upon a rug near the bare hearth and droolingly chewed on the tail of a toy wooden horse.

"I don't like boats," Avis said with a shudder. "Was in one that tipped over when I was a girl. I don't even like to look at 'em."

"Then it's good you're marryin' a soldier and not a sailor," Susan told her with eyes wide.

"Ain't it, though?" Avis agreed. "I've said to Edwin many a time—"

"Pardon me . . ."

Naomi turned toward the corridor doorway at the sound of the familiar voice. She was not surprised to see Daniel. *You knew I would be wondering*.

"Miss Prewitt let me in," he explained.

"Will you join us, Mr. Rayborn?" Mrs. Bacon asked while Naomi rose from her chair.

"No, thank you. I can stay but a minute and would like to speak with Naomi, if I may."

Three minutes later Naomi sat with him outside on the darkened steps to the service entrance. She was glad she had insisted on bringing out a bowl of soup, for he took in five spoonfuls before sighing contentedly and thanking her. "Stanley was right, Naomi."

"Oh dear. Mr. Knight admitted it?"

"Never. But he agreed to pay me fifty pounds not to say anything to anybody else."

With sinking heart she listened to his account of their meeting. In spite of her prayers for God's will, she had not been able to surrender a tiny hope that William would be the one to win Sarah's heart. But she still did not want to believe that Mr. Knight could have feet of clay.

"But what if it's so, his wanting to guard himself against false rumors?" she asked.

He shook his head. "Innocent people fight against lies, Naomi. They don't pay to have them silenced. And they especially don't steal money with which to do it."

"What will you do?"

"I'll meet him as agreed and bring the money to Vicar Sharp right away."

"Shouldn't you involve the police?"

"That will be the vicar's decision. I would imagine he would want to look at his tithe records. My major concern is keeping Mr. Knight away from Sarah."

"Should we tell her beforehand? He'll be here Sunday, you know."

"I thought about that on the way over. It's important that he isn't frightened away from meeting me the next day. He's a clever fellow and would sense any change in her attitude. Besides, I won't have proof until we meet."

"She'll take this hard," Naomi said.

He nodded agreement. "Better for her to be disappointed now than for the rest of her life."

❧ *Forty-Four* ❧

"A curate?" Disdain mingled with disbelief in Myra's angular face. "I don't even go to church. Why would I wish to keep company with some milksop preacher?"

Across the counter from her, Ethan nodded. He was careful not to act too familiar, as he still could not afford to present a suspicious picture to anyone passing by. "And who were you with Monday evening, Miss Rose?"

She lifted her chin, as haughty as a dowager. "My beau's name is Robert. He's a carpenter, and we plan to marry next year. And that's all you're getting, sir, because my personal life is none of your affair."

Ethan smiled. "I knew you could act."

On his way to the mews behind Berkeley Street, he thanked whatever fate caused the vicar to mention the Russell infant last night, for it had set his thoughts down the path leading to a solution to his predicament. Well worth the sleepless hours it took to explore it from every possible angle. His steps were light now upon the pavement in spite of the fog in his head.

In his inebriated condition Monday evening, the horse had looked like any other. But he knew now that Stanley Russell had been in the chemist's shop. And since Ethan never saw *him*, that meant that Stanley never looked him fully in the face. Hence, the beau named Robert. After all, a man worried about his child would not be in total command of his senses.

As to Mr. Rayborn's threat to query shopkeepers . . . Ethan had realized some time in the wee hours that no shopkeeper would be offering information to a stranger about someone who was always an agreeable customer. And what would anyone have to say? He seldom ever went inside W & J SANGSTER in the daytime. As to being seen in the vicinity, he couldn't be expected to circle *around* the street of shops in the course of paying calls to the sick.

All Mr. Rayborn had against him was a panicked groomsman's dubious recollection. And he had proved himself to be a blackmailer, a far more serious offense in

the eyes of the law than courting a shopgirl.
Not that Ethan intended to turn Mr. Rayborn in. The sooner this blew over the better, and he could ill afford too many
questions about his own activities. But he
would certainly see that the man paid for
his threats and had no more opportunity to
influence Sarah against him.

*And then you're due a long nap, young
man*, he told himself, covering a yawn. The
headache excuse would come in handy after all.

He looked through the wide doors of the
coachroom of the stable behind the Blake
house. The groomsman was squatted to
grease a wheel axis of the coach. Ethan
cleared his throat. "Good morning, Mr.
Russell."

Stanley Russell stood. His hands were
black and shining, as was the rag he held.
"Mr. Knight."

"You'll understand if I don't offer to shake
hands," Ethan jested, stepping on inside.
"But I just learned your little son had some
trouble Monday night and wanted to see
how he's faring."

"Ah . . . he's almost recovered." The
man's shirtsleeves were rolled up. He

passed a bare arm across his sweating forehead. "Thank you for asking."

"I'm so relieved. But now I have to scold you."

The groomsman blinked. "Sir?"

Folding his arms, Ethan said, "Neither Vicar Sharp nor I would have minded getting out of our beds that night to come here and pray."

"Ah . . . thank you, sir." Uncertainty was as thick on his face as the grease on his hands.

"Well, what's past is past. At least the little fellow's well. But it must have given you quite a fright."

The groomsman's eyes shone. "I thought he'd die, Mr. Knight. I love the boy."

"But of course you do." Stepping closer, Ethan risked a little grease to squeeze the man's shoulder. "Any man who'd ride bareback to save his child is a hero in my book. But do remember what I said if you ever need us again, Mr. Russell. We're not only servants of God, but servants to our congregation as well."

"It seems the French paid a heavier price for the war than we did," Sarah said to her tutor in the library. "What with their own revolution following on its heels."

Mr. Rayborn nodded. "Quite so. Trade actually *increased* between Britain and the new country. Our industrial and trading expansion marched hand in hand with the American expansion westward."

"I beg your pardon?"

They both looked to the door where Mrs. Bacon stood wearing an apologetic expression. "Mrs. Blake would like to speak with you, Mr. Rayborn."

"Now?" Sarah asked.

"That's what she said, Miss Matthews."

As Mr. Rayborn pushed out his chair, Sarah noticed an odd resignation on his face. "Do you know what this is about, Mr. Rayborn?"

"I may. But why don't you go ahead and read the Coleridge ballad?"

"You're not leaving, are you?" she said when he picked up his satchel from where it leaned against a table leg.

The green eyes were still sober, but he smiled. "Everything will be all right, Miss Matthews. Sooner or later, you'll understand. Please remember that."

"Understand what?" But he gave her a

nod and turned for the door, where the housekeeper waited self-consciously as if to escort him. Or was it to see that she didn't come along?

After staring at the empty doorway for a full minute, Sarah pushed out her chair. Mrs. Bacon stood in the corridor near the landing. "Oh, but Mrs. Blake wishes to see him alone, Miss Matthews."

Sarah could still hear her tutor's footsteps on the stairs. "I'll tell her you warned me," she said, passing her on by. The door to the sitting room was just clicking shut when she reached the ground floor landing. She hastened over to open it again. Mr. Rayborn, halfway between the door and a chair near Grandmother's, turned toward her. Grandmother and Marie looked at her from their chairs, and Ethan from the divan.

"Mrs. Bacon gave me your message," Sarah said before anyone could speak. "But I would like to know what is going on."

Ethan shook his head and got to his feet. "I'm sorry, Sarah, but this is not an appropriate subject for a young lady."

"She is eighteen, Madame," Marie said. "Madame cannot shield her forever."

Still looking at Sarah, Grandmother nodded. "Very well."

While Mr. Rayborn went on to the chair to Grandmother's left, Ethan hurried over to take Sarah by the arm. "Come, Sarah, sit with me."

"What is this about?" she asked, allowing herself to be guided across the room.

"It concerns Mr. Rayborn," Grandmother said. "Avis is wiring Mr. Mitchell, but I will have some answers right away."

Mr. Rayborn nodded. "Very well, Mrs. Blake."

While Ethan held her right hand, Sarah sat in mute bewilderment. The anger in Grandmother's expression caused her to appear less frail and more like the woman who had so intimidated Sarah in the parlor five years ago.

"Mr. Knight here has brought us an incredible story, Mr. Rayborn." Grandmother's stare was unwavering. "Drunkenness? Attempted blackmail?"

"Grandmother—"

"The only reason I didn't go to the police," Ethan interrupted, squeezing Sarah's hand, "is that you and Sarah have suffered enough from local gossips. But I couldn't bear the thought of this man spending one more day under your roof."

"What have you to say for yourself, Mr. Rayborn?" Marie demanded, as if she herself were the lady of the house.

"I would ask Mr. Knight why he agreed to pay me fifty pounds, if I were you," Mr. Rayborn replied, crossing one knee over the other. He did not seem frightened of the accusations slung his way.

And he had practically admitted being a blackmailer. But it couldn't be so! Sarah *knew* him, and Naomi loved him. Heart pounding against her ribs, Sarah said, "Will someone please *tell* me what's going on? Why on earth would Mr. Rayborn blackmail you, Ethan?"

"I'm afraid that part isn't fit for tender ears." Ethan gave her a regretful frown. "Mrs. Blake, I do implore you to send Sarah from the room."

"Mr. Knight says that Mr. Rayborn went to his apartment in a drunken state last night," Marie said with an impatient roll of the eyes. "He threatened to spread rumor that Mr. Knight has a paramour if he does not pay fifty pounds. You do know what a paramour is, yes?"

"Yes," Sarah replied. *Since I was nine years old*. "But why would—"

"And to think that I trusted you with my granddaughter!" Grandmother said to Mr. Rayborn, her chalk white cheeks flush with color. "And poor Naomi!"

"Perhaps we should wait and allow Mr. Mitchell to handle this, Madame." Marie got up to stand beside Grandmother's chair. "It is not good that you overtax yourself."

"I'm fine, Marie. And you have not explained your actions, Mr. Rayborn. Gossip or no, you are in grave danger of being turned over to the police."

"Very well, Mrs. Blake." He was staring back at her with a curious tenderness in his expression. Then he reached down for the satchel at his feet. "I didn't want it to come to this. But I'm positive you'll agree that Sarah's well-being is more important than any of our wishes or notions."

"You will address her as 'Miss Matthews' . . . especially now. And what do you mean by wishes and notions?"

He took a flat wooden box from his satchel and stood. But it was Sarah he approached. "I had a feeling I should keep this at hand this week."

"That's close enough, Mr. Rayborn," Ethan said, squeezing Sarah's hand so hard that it hurt.

Mr. Rayborn glanced at him but kept coming. Sarah pulled her hand from Ethan's. As she reached up for the box, her eyes met her tutor's. His seemed to be saying, *Everything will be all right*, as he had assured her upstairs. But how?

"What have you there, Mr. Rayborn?" Grandmother demanded while Sarah raised the lid.

"Her past, Mrs. Blake."

A tintype in a silver frame lay on top of some yellowed newspaper clippings. Sarah picked it up and recognized a younger Mr. Rayborn, even without the beard. The woman beside him stared up at her, seeming so familiar that Sarah's breath caught. "My past?" she asked as Ethan leaned closer.

"She's your mother. Her name is Deborah. That was taken on our wedding day."

Sarah looked up at him again. "But that can't be."

"Please read the clippings."

"Mr. Rayborn . . ." Grandmother began.

The voices around Sarah faded as she read the first clipping, then the next. She looked at the portrait again. She then remembered the disquiet she had experienced on London Bridge and the face of the older girl who told her how she was brought to Saint Matthew's in the arms of a drunk man. Mr. Rayborn, in his chair again, was watching her. Sarah asked, "You're suggesting the child your wife jumped with is me?"

"You were that child."

"Impossible," Marie said, shaking her head. "She is Madame's grandchild."

Mr. Rayborn turned to her. "Mrs. Blake is aware that she isn't. And Mr. Mitchell will confirm my story."

"But Jeremy Blake was my father," Sarah said. "Isn't that right, Grandmother?" She looked to the elderly woman for confirmation, but something disturbingly like fear was in the blue eyes staring back at her.

"Grandmother?"

The door opened, and Mr. Mitchell strode into the room smelling heavily of pipe tobacco. He stopped just outside the circle of chairs to give Mr. Rayborn a questioning look. Receiving a nod for a reply, Mr. Mitchell pulled a straight-back chair over to Grandmother's side. "I believe I have some explaining to do."

"You may begin by telling me who this man is," Grandmother said.

Mr. Mitchell blew out his cheeks. "He's Sarah's father, Mrs. Blake."

Time seemed to freeze in that moment, and it was as though every person in the room dared not breathe. When Ethan broke the silence it was to insist, "That doesn't *prove* he's not a blackmailer. Why didn't he tell anyone who he was?"

"At the time it seemed the best thing to do," Mr. Rayborn told him, not unkindly.

"What you mean to say is . . . you've been waiting for Mrs. Blake to die so you can leach money from Sarah. It's only to save your own skin now that you identify yourself."

Mr. Mitchell turned to stare curiously at Ethan. "I've not made your acquaintance, young man, and I'm not sure what's going on here. But I assure you Mr. Rayborn's character is above reproach."

Ethan's eyes threatened to bulge from their sockets. "I'll have you know I'm a minister of the Church, sir. So if you wish to discuss *character* . . ."

"It was you," came a voice from the doorway.

All eyes went to Stanley, who stood with bare arms folded and chin thrust forward. "You tried to make me second-guess myself, Mr. Knight. But that was you with Myra Rose. I never told anybody I rode bareback that night, not even my wife."

"Then it's true?" Marie said. Shrugging Ethan's hand from her arm, Sarah got to her feet, set the box on the cushion, and went over to kneel at her grandmother's knees. As she laid her head upon the lap quilt, she felt trembling fingers stroking her hair.

Dorothea watched the blurred figure get up from the divan and move to the door. She blinked and Ethan Knight came into focus. *I remind you so much of your grandmother* . . .

"Nothing has been proved here!" he wheeled around to growl. Stanley stepped aside, and the curate stalked out of the room. All faces but Sarah's turned to Dorothea, all expressions wary.

"Shall I send for Doctor Raine, Madame?" Marie asked.

Dorothea stroked the girl's corn silk hair again. She felt physically drained, but some stronger part of her mind pressed onward. "No. What I would like is for everyone to sit down and explain."

Stanley moved an ottoman over for Sarah before telling his part and returning to the stable. Between Mr. Mitchell and Mr. Rayborn, Dorothea heard the rest, beginning with the reason James Rayborn turned down the tutoring position and ending with why a tutor would question his student's suitor about his nocturnal activities.

With a heart filled to aching, Dorothea looked at Sarah seated on the ottoman at her knees. "I should have told you the day I discovered you weren't Jeremy's daughter. But I didn't want to stop being your grandmother."

"You'll always be my grandmother," said the girl. Still, wonder filled her face every time she glanced at Mr. Rayborn.

I almost ruined your life. Dorothea's eyes felt the sting of tears again. "I wanted so badly to know that you would be cared for when I'm gone."

"She will be, Mrs. Blake."

It was Mr. Rayborn who had spoken, and he gave her a smile so genuine that Ethan's doting looks of affection now seemed like play-acting. "And I have wanted to tell you for a long time how much in awe I am of your selflessness."

"Selflessness." The word was painful to speak, for in Dorothea's recollection of her long life, she had been anything but that. "I failed my son, Mr. Rayborn."

"You learned from your mistakes, Mrs. Blake. You continued to love a child you knew was no relation."

"Madame even gave up her friends for Miss Matthews," Marie said, then crimped her nose. "Such as they were."

Mr. Mitchell nodded. "And there are over eighty orphaned girls playing in the sun in Hampstead today because of you."

You are loved, Dorothea told herself, pressing her lips together to keep from weeping. Even more wondrous, she was beginning to understand that it was the love she *gave away without expecting anything in return* that now brought her the most happiness and would live on when her aching limbs no longer hobbled her little part of the world. Saint Matthew's girls would warm themselves by coal fires every winter, Stanley Russell's little son would climb the crab apple tree and grow into a sturdy young man, and her servants would have tidy pensions to provide for them when they grew old.

And Sarah will have a real mother and father. Dorothea basked in the warmth of her smile. Perhaps she would even marry dear William one day. But that was between Sarah, William, and God, she told herself. Old women had no business meddling in young people's affairs of the heart. She would tell Marie to remind her of that, should she forget.

———

"You'll remember that pounded spices keep their best flavors for only a month." Naomi stood with Trudy at the spice cupboard while the leg of mutton and potatoes roasted. "That's why it's best not to buy more than you think you'll be able to use during that time."

Trudy nodded, her spaniel eyes wide. "I'm used to you tellin' me all this, Naomi.

How will I remember when you're gone for good?"

Recalling her own fears when she took over the kitchen, Naomi gave her an understanding smile. "You'll have much more confidence in yourself by then." Mrs. Bacon would soon be hiring a scullery maid to take Trudy's place while she learned the more complicated details of culinary art. "And just think—no more washing dishes."

"No more dishes," Trudy said and sighed wistfully. "Do you recall tellin' me I'd be a cook in a fine house one day? I never thought that dream would come true."

"I do recall." Naomi thought how nice it was that both of their dreams were being fulfilled. Her own tidy kitchen and the liberty to cook whatever pleased her husband and herself! Or *not* to cook once in a while, when the pages of a novel refused to loosen their grip.

She heard footsteps and glanced over her shoulder. Daniel and Sarah stood near the worktable. Sarah's eyes were reddened, her face splotched.

"Miss   Matthews . . . what's   wrong?" Trudy asked.

Naomi looked at the smiles on both

faces and knew. Just to be sure, she asked Daniel, "You told her?"

"I did."

Naomi moved a step toward the two and held out both arms. A fraction of a second later Sarah was in them.

"Will someone tell me what's wrong?" Trudy asked.

While Daniel explained in a quiet voice to the scullery maid, Naomi stroked Sarah's hair and listened to her murmur, "Do you remember that night my first week here when you came to my room and told me not to worry about something I'd overheard in a shop?"

"Yes," Naomi replied thickly. She could recall it very well, for the thought that accompanied her out of the girl's room that evening was *How wonderful it must be to have a daughter!*

❧ *Forty-Five* ❧

The next morning Sarah and her father stood at the brick wall separating the Victoria Embankment from the Thames while Stanley waited with the coach several feet away. Noisy gulls dipped and soared upon a relentless eastern wind. Stretched out from bank to bank before them was the multiarched Waterloo Bridge where Deborah Rayborn had sought to drown out her tormenting thoughts.

A line from one of Edmund Spenser's poems came to Sarah. *Sweet Thames, run softly, til I end my song.*

"What was she like?" she asked in the moving coach when the bridge was no longer visible through the window.

Memory softened her father's smile. "She was kind and funny and energetic. Always wanted to go somewhere, see people. I understand now why she feared the quiet."

Sarah had no recollection of Deborah

Rayborn and had probably never even felt her embrace until that fateful night. Still, a knot rose in her throat as she asked, "Would she have loved me if I had been perfect?"

His green eyes were frank upon her. "You *were* perfect."

"I mean . . . if my hand had not been like it is," she said, though touched by his pride in her.

"We'll never know," he said at length. "But I suspect her illness would have come out in some other form eventually."

"Is my mother's father still living?" She would never consider him her grandfather.

"I don't think so."

"But we have other family."

"You've already met your uncle James."

"Who has a wife and two young girls."

"Your aunt Virginia and cousins, Catherine and Jewel."

"When may I meet them?"

"We'll go tomorrow evening so they can meet Naomi at the same time."

Sarah hugged her folded arms to herself and wondered at the whole incredible turn of events of the past two days. After taking a much needed rest yesterday afternoon,

Grandmother sat with Father, Naomi, and Sarah to discuss plans for the future while Marie left—and seeming reluctant to do so for a change—to be with her sisters. It was decided that the present routine would be altered only a little for now. Grandmother still intended to leave Sarah her estate. Father would still come back and forth from his home to give lessons, and Naomi would move in with him after the wedding. Perhaps that would change after Grandmother's passing—after being without a father and mother for so long, Sarah hoped that he and Naomi would consider coming to live under the same roof as her. But for now Grandmother's comfort was the supreme concern.

"Are you terribly hurt over Mr. Knight?" her father asked as the coach crept up Piccadilly, clogged with traffic. It was the first time he'd mentioned Ethan since the scene in the sitting room yesterday morning, and his tone was hesitant, as if he wasn't certain if he had the right to ask. It would take some time, Sarah realized, for both of them to feel completely at ease in their newly reestablished roles as parent and child.

Sarah had to think before finally replying,

"I miss very much the person I *thought* he was. So does Grandmother. But I don't suppose that person ever existed."

He nodded understanding. "Pity."

"Do you think he even believed his own sermons?"

"In his head, he probably did. As to the heart? Hopefully one day. He's still very young."

"What will happen to him?" As disappointed as she was in him, she could not help but hope he would not go to prison.

"That's up to Vicar Sharp and the church hierarchy. For now I suspect the tithe ledgers are being examined. If they show evidence of fraud, they'll have to decide whether to turn him over to the authorities or to impose Church discipline."

Concern was still heavy upon his face, and after a space of silence, he said, "I hope this experience—and what you knew about Jeremy Blake—doesn't cause you to mistrust all men, Sarah. There are still many who are decent."

"I know that, Father." She wished she could summon the words to add how proud she was of him for possessing that same decency of which he spoke.

"I'm glad." His expression eased. "William Doyle, for example. Now, there's a decent young man."

Sarah nodded. "Very decent."

"Genuine through and through." He cleared his throat. "If you happen to write to him any time soon, do pay my regards."

"I plan to write him this very evening, as a matter of fact."

"Very good," he said in a trying-to-sound-casual tone. "You exchange letters often, do you?"

"Very often," she replied, amused at his obvious attempts to advise her without appearing to meddle.

"You must be quite fond of him."

So much so, she realized, that the thought of how close she had come to choosing another over him gave her chills.

Her father smiled, and she smiled back. They sat wrapped in a silence that grew more companionable as the plane trees of Berkeley Square moved past the window.

Back in the library a short while later, they were discussing poets of the Romantic Movement when another question occurred to Sarah. She supposed there would be many more in the coming days. "How old am I?"

"You were nineteen just two months ago," he replied, closing a copy of Wordsworth's *Lyrical Ballads*. "You were born on the eighteenth of May."

"Wasn't that the day you gave me Jules Verne?"

"And the reason Naomi prepared pullets for lunch."

"Very thoughtful of both of you." Musing aloud, she said, "How odd it will be . . . to have a complete set of parents after all these years."

Her father raised an eyebrow. "You don't mind, do you?"

"Mind?" Sarah smiled. "I can't imagine anyone being more blessed than I am. Naomi and you . . . two of my favorite people in the world . . ."

The relief that washed across his face, as if all the while he had feared otherwise, filled Sarah's heart so that little room was left for awkwardness. She reached across the table to touch his hand. "I love you, Father."

His green eyes filled as he pushed out his chair. "Oh, Sarah . . ."

An instant later she was standing in his embrace, hearing him say thickly, "I thank God every day for bringing you back to me."

The security from resting her head upon a paternal shoulder brought a lump to Sarah's throat. Yet there was a familiarity about it that puzzled her, until she recalled the dark times when another Father had wrapped unseen arms of grace and comfort around her. Mrs. Forsyth's words drifted back to her from so many years ago. *Remember, Sarah, you have someone who is a Father to the fatherless.*

That evening she wrote a long letter to William, pouring out everything that had happened over the past two days.

I have to get used to thinking of myself as nineteen now. But at least I'm pleased to have back that year I lost when I came to Berkeley Square.

"Nineteen to twenty-eight, if you please," Grandmother told Sarah in the sitting room exactly four weeks later.

Sarah moved the round black draughts piece, thinking how much easier the game was now with Avis's neatly painted numbers. Marie, still working the needlepoint of Jesus in the Garden, continued a conversation she began a few minutes earlier by saying, "It was so much fun to watch. We have decided we will try it ourselves next week."

"And you'll be needing your own cane when you get home," Grandmother cautioned. "You're not so young anymore, Marie."

"All the more reason to try it," Marie insisted.

The "it" of which she spoke was the talk of London, since the opening of the world's first roller skating rink just days ago. "Would your sisters mind if I came along?" Sarah asked. "I could ask Father to shorten the lessons next Thursday."

"We will be happy to have you with us, Miss Rayborn."

"Yes, they'll be happy to have someone young enough to catch them as they fall," Grandmother warned, but teasingly so. "I do wish you would pay attention to the game, Sarah."

"Oh . . ." Sarah gave her an apologetic smile, then focused her attention on the seven red pieces remaining on the checkered table. She had no choice but to move one diagonally to a border square, where it risked becoming trapped by one of Grandmother's two kings. "I could really use a crown," she murmured, then started when she realized Marie stood at her side.

"What—?"

"Sh-h-h."

Sarah looked at Grandmother. The elderly woman rested the side of her head against the chair wing with eyes half-closed. Marie gently held her wrist for several seconds.

"She's gone?" Sarah asked, feeling the sting of tears.

"Yes." After closing Grandmother's eyelids, Marie leaned down to kiss the wrinkled forehead. Her amber eyes glistened when she turned to Sarah. "Madame's last sight was of you, and now she looks upon Jesus. It is the way she would have wanted to go."

———

Saint George's pews were filled on Wednesday morning. Whatever opinions were held about the widow who chose an out-of-wedlock crippled child over the good opinion of Mayfair, she had been a fixture in the church as long as health allowed and given due respect with her passing. Even Mrs. Gill attended, her blinking eyes mournful and her cheeks wet as she pressed one against Sarah's.

Blake Shipping employees, given the day off, brought their families. Mrs. Forsyth and the Rothschilds, Hester and Addison Smith, Marie's sisters, James and Virginia Rayborn, Doctor Raine, and Mr. Mitchell were some of the more familiar faces. Each face, even those not so familiar, gave Sarah some measure of comfort. Not that her grief could be divided and parceled, but it helped to be reminded that Grandmother mattered to so many.

While Vicar Sharp conducted the service, Sarah sat on the first pew with her father, Naomi, Marie, and William, who had arrived late the night before. Behind sat the rest of the servants, along with little Guy Russell, asleep on his father's shoulder. The women in the two rows wore black gowns, and the men were in black suits and had black crepe bands around the hats they wore in the churchyard, where Mrs. Blake's body was laid to rest between her husband's and son's.

"I still find it remarkable that she wanted

me to believe she was my grandmother, even after learning the truth," Sarah said to William that afternoon as they sat on the dovecote bench. The last mourner had left, and the house and garden were permeated again by natural quiet instead of a subdued bustle.

"You were a blessing to her," William said. It was their first time to speak privately since May, and it would not last long, for Father and Naomi would be seeing him off at King's Cross Station in two hours.

"And she to me." Her face felt the prickling sensation of threatening tears, so she drew in a deep breath to make it go away. "She tried to get me to think ahead about this time, but I usually made light of it and changed the subject. Now I see that I should have made some plans, for I'm not quite sure what I should do."

He nodded. "May I make a suggestion?"

"Of course," she said. But an unsettling dread came over her, for his smoke-colored eyes were filled with affection, just as when he professed his love in the dining room. *Please not now, William. My heart is too filled with missing her.*

"You have the liberty of not having to

make any radical changes at the moment. Don't think about the future just yet. There is time enough for that later."

Yes, later. "I'll do that, William."

They sat without speaking for a little while, then she asked, "Are you hungry?"

"Starving. And you?"

"The same." She felt guilty to admit it. "I've not had a bite since supper. Marie and Naomi tried to coax me, but it didn't seem right to sit down for a meal today."

"Not right to eat?" Getting to his feet, William held out his hand for Sarah's and helped her to hers. "And what would Mrs. Blake say about that?"

"She would order me to eat." Sarah didn't even have to think about that one. They walked toward the terrace holding hands. "You'll still be back in October for the wedding?"

"I'm hoping for good."

"A month early?"

A hopeful smile dimpled his cheeks as he held open the door for her. "The laboratory's ready, and the two chemists we hired are already making investigative calls. It would be nice not to have to leave again."

Very nice, Sarah thought.

———

A letter arrived from Birmingham a fort-night later, addressed to "Miss Blake."

It grieves me to learn of Mrs. Blake's passing, Ethan wrote, . . . *and that I shall have to wait until heaven to beg her forgive-ness. But I do beg yours and will be writing to ask the same of your father.*

He wrote that he would soon be leaving for the Rajasthan Desert, one hundred and fifty miles southeast of Delhi. Four years of service in a leper mission as opposed to at least ten years in prison, had the Bishop so minded to press criminal charges. Ethan counted himself fortunate.

. . . as a matter of fact, I am strangely ea-ger to begin this task. I can see that I am a shallow soul, Miss Blake. Without the dis-traction of temporal pleasures, I have the hope of learning to walk intimately with the God who, wonder of wonders, has forgiven me.

"Do you think he's sincere?" Sarah asked her father, who had received his own letter that same day.

With a smile he replied, "That he would write at all is a good sign."

❧ *Forty-Six* ❧

June 18, 1876

"My stomach's growling like a bear, Naomi."

Naomi closed the oven door and turned to smile at her husband of eight months, who stood in the doorway with a page in hand. "There's that leftover sandwich."

"I'll wait," he said after a thoughtful hesitation. "My appetite's demanding quail." Stepping into the room, he put an arm gently around her shoulders and pulled her close to kiss her forehead. Daniel caught the scent of Pears soap, in spite of the aroma of *Les Cailles aux Feuilles de Vignes*—the supper she was preparing of quail wrapped in fine leaves and bacon, roasted in a bed of chopped mixed vegetables.

"You're not overtaxing yourself, are you?" he murmured into her hair.

"I'm not." Automatically she lifted a hand to the side of her faintly protruding stomach and felt the flutter of movement. Since the first twinges of morning discomfort, not a week had gone by that Daniel didn't suggest hiring a cook. But Naomi couldn't see the sense in adding that extra expense as long as she was able to move about easily. And cooking for two—sometimes three or four—was easy, her menu usually plain English fare. This evening, however, was a special occasion. It was time to share with Sarah and William the existence of the secret that had nestled inside her for five months.

"Have you a minute?"

"Yes. Where are you now?" she asked, for often he asked her to listen to freshly written passages of his book. They had arrived home from their three-week honeymoon in Paris back in early November to find three messages slid under the front door, urging Daniel to call upon William Blackwood and Sons at his earliest convenience. The result was a contract and healthy advance royalty for *A History of the Tower of London*.

"I'm still in the Armory. So much of it is fascinating."

Their kitchen table, made of fine mellow oak, was only ten paces away. Naomi liked the idea of having meals in the kitchen rather than having to transport the food to another room. She settled into the chair he pulled out, folded her hands on the table-top, and waited for him to walk around to the other side. For a reason even he wasn't able to explain, he could not read to her anything he had written without pacing just a little. Brow dented with concentration, he began.

" 'The suits of armor worn by Queen Mary's warriors invariably remind us of that worn by Don Quixote's Sancho Panza, in which he could but wag his head and hands like a turtle. They were so massive that sometimes the wearer fainted merely from the weight of his armor, and once down he could not remount until hoisted up by his attendant. We cannot wonder but that the unfortunate knight had only to be unhorsed to be at the mercy of an enemy.' "

He stopped pacing and lowered the page.

"Most interesting, Daniel," Naomi told him, wondering how the horses felt about all that weight.

"It has nothing to do with the history of the tower per se, but surely the reader will appreciate learning little details having to do with the exhibits."

"But of course. And so you're offering a raised pie."

"A raised pie?" Her husband smiled and took the seat opposite hers, lying the pages of inked script upon the tablecloth. Every fifty pages accumulated were sent to Mr. Garrett to be typed. "And how is that, Naomi?"

"Because you're telling the story in layers. For example, the crust can represent the facts having to do with the Tower's construction; the forcemeat, the details surrounding the exhibits; and the mushrooms, the stories of those incarcerated through the years." She angled her head in thought. "Hmmm. I'm not sure I know what the gravy represents."

"Well, I do."

"Yes?"

"Definitely that first kiss we shared up there. That's why I'm so fond of the place."

Naomi straightened and smoothed her apron. "Well, you'll not be putting that into print," she said with feigned primness. "We can't have folks assuming the author's wife was once a loose woman."

"You were pretty loose," he teased. "Kissing in front of all those Italians."

"Oh, and the lobster bisque is heavenly," Sarah said, moving to the edge of her seat as Stanley opened the coach door.

"Thank you, Miss Rayborn." Penny Russell, wide-eyed, had never dined in a restaurant, and supper at Gatti's tonight was to be Stanley's birthday gift to her. Claire and Mrs. Bacon were minding little Guy back at Berkeley Square so the couple could enjoy an evening out together.

"What time shall I call again for you, Miss Rayborn?" Stanley asked after assisting her to the pavement. Instead of livery clothes he wore his Sunday black suit.

"I'll share William's cab on the way home. You'll want to stroll the Embankment after your meal."

She traded farewells with the two and walked the few steps to the door of her father and Naomi's house, hearing behind her the coach door close and the creak of springs and harness. Her knock was answered right away by William, clad in his gray wool suit with a finely woven burgundy silk cravat at his neck. He ushered her inside and kissed her hand.

"Good evening, Sarah. How lovely you look."

"Thank you." Returning his smile, she brushed a fold of her silk gown of sage green and cream-colored stripes. She was still not quite used to seeing herself in colors again. "Father said it was a special occasion, so I thought I should dress up—as did you, I see."

From the kitchen came the muffled sounds of china and silver being laid upon cloth. It pleased Sarah that her father was consistent about helping Naomi set the table and clean up after meals. She didn't think men, even the most considerate ones, noticed to do such things as that. Lowering her voice, Sarah said, "But he wouldn't say what this was about. Have you any idea?"

"I asked Aunt Naomi," he whispered after a glance back to the doorway. "She only gave me that dreamy look she's been wearing lately. But yes, I've an idea."

"What is—" Reading his eyes, Sarah raised her fingers to her cheek. Down her glove slid the gold bracelet Father and Naomi had purchased in Paris and saved for her twentieth birthday last month. "You don't think."

"What else could it be?"

"Well, hello there, Sarah." Sarah's father stood in the kitchen doorway with a water pitcher in one hand. "Have you been here long?"

"I just now arrived." Avoiding William's knowing eyes, she moved past him to kiss the bearded cheek Father leaned down toward her. "Good evening, Naomi," she said when he stood to make room for her to enter the kitchen.

"Sarah." Her stepmother set a dish of cucumber vinaigrette upon the already lavishly set table and came around to embrace her. "How lovely you are!"

"And you as well, Naomi," Sarah said, wondering if the roses in her stepmother's cheeks were from oven heat or if William's observation was correct. She would have imagined herself to be ecstatic at such news. So why was melancholy beginning to seep into her chest?

They passed the mealtime with light conversation, Father telling of the progress of the Tower book, William sharing one of the incidents from his job that used to delight Grandmother so. Naomi was her usual serene self, content mostly to listen.

It's true, Sarah thought, glancing again at her stepmother's secret little smile. The inexplicable melancholy welled within her, belaboring her breathing. *You would adore a sister or a brother*, she told herself. Why, the little dear would sleep upstairs in the same nursery that was once hers before the waters of the Thames swept away all there was to that life. William gave her a questioning look from across the table, so she sent him a smile that did not lighten her heart.

"Sarah." Naomi's bottle blue eyes were affectionate upon her. "Your father tells me that you're a natural at Greek."

"I do enjoy it," Sarah replied, the heaviness easing a little. "Has he told you we've begun reading the book of Luke?"

"He has."

"I was surprised you wanted to study another language," William said while dishing out another serving of quail so tender that a knife wasn't necessary.

"I surprised myself," she admitted. "But there's something special about learning the words of Jesus and the words the disciples actually spoke."

The dessert was a delight—a tall-stemmed tazza dish of strawberries accompanied by wedges of Cheshire cheese. When the course was finished, Father dabbed his lips with his napkin and laid it upon the cloth. "What a fine meal, Naomi."

William and Sarah echoed the compliment, and Naomi thanked them with no false modesty. Then she gave Father a little nod.

"We have something to tell you," he said, eyes bright about his smile.

Sarah could not help but glance at William, who winked. To her horror, she felt the sting of tears. She blinked them away, but more came spilling onto her cheeks.

It was Naomi who spoke first. "Sarah?"

"Forgive . . . me," she said through her tightened throat. "I'm so . . . overjoyed."

There was stunned silence for a fraction of a second, then scraping sounds as chairs were pushed out. Sarah allowed William to put an arm around her and lead her like a child into the parlor, where she was helped to the divan between him and Naomi. Father pulled a chair close. Feeling wretched for having ruined what should have been a joyous moment for everyone, she covered her face with her hands and wept.

"Please tell us what's wrong, Sarah." Her father's voice was anxious.

"Wait, Daniel," Naomi said.

Sarah's right hand was nudged away from her face as a handkerchief was pressed into it. She wiped her face and blew her nose. On her left, William patted her arm awkwardly. When she found her voice, Sarah told them, "I don't know what came over me."

"Are you feeling ill, dear?" Naomi asked.

"No, not ill." But understanding struck her like a lightning bolt. It wasn't resentment of an innocent little baby that was the source of her angst. She was still in mourning. No longer for Grandmother, God rest her soul, but for the loved ones who were gradually building lives apart from hers. Father and Naomi were so leery of taking advantage of her sudden wealth that they could not see past it to her need for them. They declined her invitation to move to Berkeley Square nor would they accept any money from her. Why, Father no longer allowed her to pay for the tutoring sessions when surely he and Naomi needed the income.

Even William was more formal since his return from Manchester. She had thought it was because she was in mourning, but nine months had gone by since Grandmother's passing, and still some invisible wall stood between them. Were there not occasional unguarded sparks of adoration in his smoke-colored eyes, she would wonder if she had dreamed his profession of love in Grandmother's dining room almost a year ago.

"Sarah?" Softly Father spoke, leaning closer.

"Please forgive me, Father . . . Naomi," Sarah said, clutching the wadded handkerchief. "I'm truly happy for you. I loved visiting the babies at Saint Matthew's—and Stanley and Penny's little Guy has been so much fun."

A maternal hand rested upon her shoulder. "How did you know?" Naomi asked.

"Aren't you?"

"Why, yes."

"Wonderful!" William declared in a subdued tone, as if not wishing to cause another eruption of tears.

"Why did that make you sad?" Father's green eyes were gentle. "Were you afraid we would love you less?"

Sarah shook her head. She was very well aware of their love for her. How could she articulate that there still lived the penniless waif beneath the trappings of her wealth?

She was searching for words when William said, "I believe Sarah fears she lost you both when she inherited Mrs. Blake's money." He gave her an uncertain look. "Is that it, Sarah?"

"But that's simply not so," Naomi said. "We love you more than ever."

"I realize that, Naomi." Sarah swallowed, the back of her throat aching. "But I haven't felt so alone since those first days at Berkeley Square. I had hoped so much that we would all be together when Grandmother . . ."

"Daughter, we can't allow you to support us," her father said, firmly but gently.

"But there are rooms just sitting empty. And you could continue writing your books for spending money, if you wished."

William was studying her thoughtfully. "You know, I never realized the importance of family until mine was suddenly taken away." He looked past Sarah to give Naomi a grateful smile. "God has blessed Sarah in an incredible way, Aunt Naomi, Daniel. I know your intentions are noble, not wishing to take advantage of her fortune. But isn't that a bit selfish?"

"It's selfish that we are trying *not* to be, William," Father corrected.

"By robbing her of one of life's greatest joys? She has always had a giving heart. Didn't Christ himself say that it is more blessed to give than to receive?" Again William looked at his aunt. "Should I assume that because you contributed a good sum of money toward my livelihood and education that I was a burden whom you begrudged?"

"Never, William." Emotion filled Naomi's quiet voice. "Not for one day."

———

"Incredible!" Sarah hugged herself in the hired coach two hours later, then seized William's arm and leaned her head upon his shoulder. "I can never thank you enough!"

"It is I who must thank you," he said. "I've always wanted Aunt Naomi to have an easier life."

"She'll not have to lift a finger!"

He smiled but shifted away a bit. A fraction of an inch, but just the movement itself was profound in that it represented the gradual distancing of himself from her since his return from Manchester.

"Sorry," Sarah said, pulling her arm from his and sliding closer to the window. The euphoria that had soared her spirits only seconds ago evaporated, and the plunge back to earth was devastating. She stared at passing gaslights to keep from weeping.

"Sarah." He touched her sleeve.

"I'm fine, William," she said, eyes moving from one light to another.

Strained silence filled the coach, sharpening the sounds of hoofbeats and iron-rimmed wheels against cobbled stones. It was after they turned onto Piccadilly that William broke the silence.

"You've already had one man court you for your wealth."

"More than one," Sarah said dully. Lord Holt of the diving bell incident had attempted to pay two condolence visits— both times she sent his calling card back downstairs with apologies. The same for a young Mr. Wardell, whom she had never met, but whose family name she spotted in *The Times* having to do with a brokerage firm on the verge of financial ruin.

"You have?"

The surprise in his voice was gratifying to Sarah, balm for the wound he inflicted by shifting away. She turned to face him and could read his expression in the dim light. *Why did you never tell me?* he was thinking. *We used to tell each other everything.*

Because you can't freely confide in a person who holds part of himself back was her unspoken response.

"They don't matter" was what she said, and it was just as much truth. "None of those men took time away from their studies to write to an awkward little girl with an uncertain future."

It was time to say everything she had held in for months. She could not bear the thought of wondering one more day how things stood between them. Memory softening her voice, she asked, "What happened to the young man who declared his love in my grandmother's dining room?"

Their eyes locked, his dark ones filled with evidence of inner struggle. Sarah held her breath, did not allow herself even to blink.

Then he glanced away. "I was too brash, Sarah. It hadn't fully sunk in that you would control such a vast fortune. And that my wages would barely pay what you spend on hats."

She allowed the unfairness of his remark to pass. Protesting that she had not purchased a hat since her mourning bonnets would stray from the point. "Did you listen to anything you said to Father and Naomi tonight?"

"That's different, Sarah. A man is supposed to provide for his family."

"And so my father is less of a man for allowing me to help him provide for his wife?"

"No, I didn't—" He closed his mouth, lifted his hands helplessly, and dropped them.

"I didn't earn a farthing of that money, William," she pressed. "It was given to me.

It's something I happen to own, but it doesn't define who I am."

Another silence followed, then the cessation of movement. Sarah looked out the window at the illuminated sitting room window of No. 14 Berkeley Square. She could hear William's unsteady breathing beside her. Any minute the cabby would open the door, and the moment would be gone. And so she gathered courage from wherever she could think to look—heavenward with a quick silent prayer to God and then into her own memory, picturing herself as the nightgown-clad girl standing in the parlor while aged hands played the piano.

"If you believe I could ever love you any less because our incomes are not equal, then you never really knew me, did you, William?" she said, bold enough to speak, but not enough to turn and witness his reaction.

"I knew you," he said at length, his voice thick.

Sarah watched her faint reflection in the glass. "You helped raise me."

"Yes." A wave of memory carried William back to the first time she touched his heart.

It was pity he had felt that day for the waifish girl so alone on the dovecote bench. How could he have imagined that pity would metamorphose into love so overwhelming that he could no more imagine life without her than life without air and water?

And why was he allowing such a temporal thing as money to stand between them? *Pride,* he realized at once. The knowledge stung. Such a petty emotion! Instead of rejoicing that the person he loved most could have a comfortable life, he sulked because he was not the one to provide it for her.

Yet was it possible that she still managed to love him, foolish man that he was? Not only as a friend and brother, but as completely as he loved her?

"Sarah?"

She turned to face him.

"You . . . love me?" He had to ask to be sure, with reverence and wonder in his voice.

"I have always loved you, William," she answered quietly.

They stared, then smiled at each other. And then the door swung open. Only it was

Marie who thrust the upper part of her dressing gown-clad body into the coach.

"Miss Rayborn . . . Mr. Doyle!" Her face was a frowning mask beneath the curling papers. "It is not proper for you to sit out here unchaperoned like this. Why, you are not even engaged!"

William covered Sarah's left hand upon the seat beside him. "If you'll give us but three minutes, Marie, I'll try to remedy that situation."

The maid looked at Sarah, who nodded.

"Very well," Marie huffed, though with unmistakably less ire. "And you may have five minutes, Mr. Doyle. Not one second more."

The door slammed shut, rocking the coach a bit. Sarah turned to him again, her face so filled with trust and affection that a lump welled in William's throat. He pressed her formless hand against his chest. "Will you forgive my foolish pride and marry me, Sarah?"

With her gloved right hand, Sarah brushed a tear from his cheek. "Yes, William."

"I'll do everything within my power to be a good husband to you."

"I know that, William." She was as sure of it as she was that the sun would rise in the morning. Returning his smile, she said, "And I'll strive to be a good wife."

He caught her up into his arms and kissed her. And she kissed him back, her head feeling lighter and lighter until banging upon the coach door drew them apart.

"We'll tell Aunt Naomi and your father tomorrow?" he asked, touching her chin.

"Tomorrow," she agreed.

On the pavement Sarah stood next to Marie to watch the coach fade into the night. The lady's maid turned to her. "He asked you to marry him?"

"He did, Marie. And I accepted."

"That makes me so happy!" Marie said, catching her up into an embrace. Over her head, Sarah heard a muttered, "And it is about time!"

As she was helped from her gown into her nightgown up in her room, Sarah could not recall climbing the staircase. *I must have floated*, she thought. Later, settling into the nest of bedclothes and comfortably flat pillow, she talked to her Father, thanking Him for all that had happened today. And then she respectfully asked a favor. *Will you please tell Naaman's servant girl that she was a blessing to more than one household?*